The Lodging House

The Lodging House

Khairy Shalaby

Translated by Farouk Abdel Wahab

The American University in Cairo Press
Cairo New York

First published in 2006 by
The American University in Cairo Press
113 Sharia Kasr el Aini, Cairo, Egypt
420 Fifth Avenue, New York, NY 10018
www.aucpress.com

First paperback edition 2008

Dar el Kutub No. 14765/08
ISBN 978 977 416 239 8

Dar el Kutub Cataloging-in-Publication Data

Shalaby, Khairy
The Lodging House / Khairy Shalaby; translated by Farouk Abdel Wahab.—Cairo: The American University in Cairo Press, 2008
p. cm.
ISBN 977 416 239 0
1. Arabic fiction I. Abdel Wahab, Farouk (trans.) II. Title
892.73

1 2 3 4 5 6 7 8 14 13 12 11 10 09 08

Designed by Fatiha Bouzidi/AUC Press Design Center
Printed in Egypt

Wikalat Atiya

I never thought I could be brought down so low that I would accept living in Wikalat Atiya. Nor did I imagine that I would become such a rotten bum that I would come to know a place in the city of Damanhour called Wikalat Atiya. It was a place someone like me would not dream of under any circumstances; my feet could not take me to such a far-off place, which the sons of the city themselves might not even know, even those who traveled through it from one end to the other, and who knew every rat hole in it, had I not—as it became clear to me—broken the world's record for bumming and homelessness.

I am supposed to be a student at the Public Teachers' Institute; I mean that's what I was over two years ago. I was on the verge of becoming a teacher after a year, since my talent was obvious in pedagogical studies and in lesson planning, including the modern methodologies, though I was plagued by a math teacher who was despicable and disgusting and a bastard. He was not happy that sons of detestable peasants from villages and hamlets, more like barefoot riffraff than anything else, could excel in education over the true sons of schools, originally from elite backgrounds and good, wealthy folks; and so he would screw with me in every exam, provoking me with dirty looks, writing me up every time I sat up in my seat or coughed or turned around to ask one of my classmates for a ruler or compass or an eraser, things that I don't think I ever bought once throughout all my school days. This pissed him off, and it made him even more bitter that I never bought a book he required or a quad-lined notebook which, he urged, was necessary. So the son of a bitch saw fit to prevent anyone from helping me one bit; he even kicked out a classmate who snuck me a compass. When he cussed me out, I began to aim looks of suppressed hatred at him, such that I enraged him terribly, and he took away my blank answer sheet, and then, like the swaggering, pompous ass he was, kicked me out. I froze as if nailed in place, shaking with fury; my eyes must have been like flaming arrows, since he bared his teeth and said, "Why are you looking at me like that, boy?"

Still I persisted in my gaze, I don't know why or what I could have done. He kicked me, his kicks forcing me toward the classroom door, and I was down flat on my face, I who had not so long ago fancied myself a venerable, respectable teacher. I lost it but quickly pulled myself back together. Like a wild, rabid dog I threw myself at the gut of Wael Effendi the math teacher with all my might. I snapped at the flesh of his face with my teeth, and I bashed in his nose and teeth with my forehead, I kneed him in the groin and stomped on his shins, until he fell down to the ground, and I kneeled over him holding his collar and burying my fingers in the flesh of his neck. The whole exam hall sprang to life. I felt like an entire city was raining blows on my body, trying in vain to extract him from me. The clamor grew and cheating flared up and tons of crib notes and cheat sheets began piling up, and the dean came running in panic, and more than one policeman came, and the billy club slammed down on my back, my rear end, and my head. But every blow I received, I returned to Wael Effendi by raising his head then smashing it on the ground as if I wanted to shake out his brain. Then when it appeared to me that he'd given up the ghost and all his limbs had collapsed and he turned yellow and the light in his eyes had gone out completely, I went limp, and I responded to the hands that lifted me from him. When I stood up I started stomping on his stomach, on his groin, on his face, until I left him in a shredded heap, stained with blood, my blood and his.

They took him to the hospital in critical condition; they handed me over to the city police in pitiful condition, accompanied by the dean's curses and his description of my family and all my kind as despicable hooligans, and he cursed Taha Hussein as the one who destroyed education and polluted it with lowlifes like me. I knew that he would say this, but I didn't give a damn; for I was certain that I had quenched my thirst for revenge and avenged my wounded pride, and many of my classmates were looking at me with a great deal of sorrow tinged with something like admiration; and besides, I felt that I hadn't finished the piss that I must yet piss in Wael Effendi's mouth, but I would still go to jail and my future would be ruined at his hands, and that I would undoubtedly kill him the moment I was free again.

The court took pity on me, giving me a six-month suspended sentence and expelling me from the Institute. A year after that I went to school one day, on the pretext of getting my transcripts, intending to stick a knife in the heart of Wael Effendi, and I was surprised to find that he had been disfigured by the loss of an eye where apparently, in my madness, I had gouged it out, and the marks my teeth had dug in all over his face were still there, and he walked to class a broken man, having given up his arrogance and swagger and lowered his perpetually bellowing voice with his lisping, fancy tongue. As for the distinctive elegance of his dress, it had faded completely. I noticed my grip on the knife handle loosening in my pocket and I was overcome with a kind of pity for the both of us. He had seen me out of the corner of his good eye but he didn't recognize me since my appearance had changed drastically, for my hair had grown long and was visibly messed up and my beard had grown, and my clothes were wrinkled and dirt had accumulated on my face and my hands and my clothes, so much so that most of my classmates did not recognize me as they passed by me in the schoolyard or the secretary's office. Actually I liked that, as I hadn't wanted them to remember me, and I only wanted to get my papers and put them in the pocket of my gallabiya to use as identity papers when necessary.

That incident meant that I would never return to my village at all, and that I would make the city streets my home. I spent all day and all night wandering the streets and alleys and neighborhoods, from Susi Street to Mudiriya Street to Iflaqa Bridge to Shubra to Abu al-Rish to Nadi Street. I spent some time at the public library reading stories and novels and poetry, looking for a better world to shelter me for a few hours, after which I turned back to the asphalt streets of Damanhour, stingy by their very nature, dry in character, and inhospitable to strangers. I cut across Susi Street from al-Sagha Street after I had smelled enough of the ful midammis wafting upward from al-Asi's restaurant, the most famous ful-maker in all of Egypt, for they say that he presented King Farouk with a pot of his ful, and when the king had a dish of it for breakfast, he gave him the rank of bey via urgent cable, the title by which he was now called by the dozens, no, hundreds of visitors who came to his restaurant every day, from all over the country, for a dish of his famous ful.

When I turned off Susi Street and onto Suq Street, I was greeted by the fruits of Fakharani in a complete garden of awesome and appetizing scents, so it pleased me to plunge into the bazaar, to mix in my nose the smells of apples, dates, guava, and lemon with the smells of fish and meats and gargir and dung from the horses drawing wagons. The crowded street, paved with broad, flat stones and crisscrossed with little canyons of dirty water, spat me out onto the main street which was the height of cleanliness, running from the railroad station to Iflaqa Bridge on Mahmudiya Canal. By that time the smell of frying ta'miya had intoxicated me and I was convinced that I had eaten my fill, even though my insides were completely empty. When the dark night came all sensations gave way to stifling cold or fear or loss. I knew sleep inside the drain pipes and under the trees on the rural thoroughfares and near the twenty-four-hour bakeries and on the sidewalks close to the low-class coffeeshops, yet I hadn't fallen so low as to know the place called Wikalat Atiya.

The Square

Vagrants stick to each other like sticky fluid on a downward slope. That's how it was with Mahrous and me; we stuck to each other. The first time I saw him was on the back road leading into town; he was sitting in front of a pile of radishes and gargir spread out on a sack, calling to the customers in mawwals that extolled the virtues of his radishes and gargir with a fervor and vitality surpassing that of Abu Nawas for his wine; the green eyes were in his radishes, and as for the gargir, it was a lover's eyelashes, it was the tassels on the draperies in her boudoir, and it was the tattoo engraved on his very heart in the name of the prophet Muhammad, peace be upon him. I was enthralled by the sweetness of his vocabulary and how it contained sincere and captivating sentiments; I stood next to him for a long time, and he never repeated the same mawwal, he just went from one into the next; thus there was no doubt that his radishes and gargir were symbols of many beautiful things to him. When he noticed that I'd enjoyed listening to him while standing there, he sang so glowingly that he really gave me true joy; I nodded my head with admiration, then left.

A few days later, I was walking aimlessly down Khawalqa Street just before sunset when a bicycle stopped in front of me suddenly and a handsome boy with rugged good looks got right up in my face, opened his mouth wide and shouted with enthusiasm and affection, "How are you?" I instantly recognized him and said, "Hello, hello, how are you and how are your radishes and gargir?" He said with uncanny craftiness, "What's the matter? Did you lose something?" Then he said, inclining his head toward the rear seat of the bicycle, "Ride on the back seat!" I feigned surprise that he had been so bold, "Why? And how?" He ignored my snub, "I'll treat you to a glass of tea at the Bakers' Coffeeshop. It's nearby. You obviously liked the mawwals. I'll let you hear all the mawwals you want!" I got on behind him. We ended up in old Damanhour next to the railroad station, where the tracks appeared heading for the lower depths and where—as our history teacher told us—this raised street was built on top of the ruins of the ancient Egyptian city, which was called Demi-en-Hor—city of the god Horus, son of Isis and Osiris, who was supposed to avenge his father against his uncle Seth, the god of evil, but for some reason or other—if memory serves—he could not, or maybe he was unsuccessful. I had forgotten history, as I had forgotten all subjects since I had been summarily thrown out on my ass and found myself up a creek without a paddle and certainly no canoe.

The new city passed further into the distance behind us. We passed by the remains of an ancient ruin, and scattered stones like those of a pyramid, and other structures with pitched roofs, spread out over large areas—they must have been cotton gins or factories. An inner voice told me to come here the following morning and ask for a job with my elementary school diploma. At an alley sprouting from the surrounding expanse, the bicycle stopped and Mahrous propped it up, saying, "Just a minute, I'll return the bike to the rental shop."

I stood waiting for him for several minutes, then he pulled me by the arm toward a well-built hut with wooden and tin-plate walls; it appeared to be a coffeeshop and a hashish den, and—wonder of wonders—Mahrous was so well known there that the tea came in a clean pot without our even ordering a clean one. Mahrous got up and disappeared for a few minutes, then returned smiling, a man following at his heels carrying a goza.

It was the first time I'd ever smoked hashish; I was weak with hunger, and I fainted after a few puffs and felt nauseous. And yet I enjoyed the mawwals that Mahrous sang in an astonishing torrent as if he had an infinite repertoire. It was past midnight when out of the blue Mahrous really floored me when he said, "Oh, by the way. I once saw you late at night sleeping under a tree. And a second time I saw you sleeping on the sidewalk of a coffeeshop in Shubra, Damanhour. Where do you think you'll sleep tonight?"

I didn't answer; I sat, all sight gone from my eyes and all speech gone from my tongue, finding no answer for him. Finally I found myself saying, "I sleep at a hotel for ten piasters."

"Per month?"

"Per night."

"You must be rich! Are you a government official? Are you a notable?"

I laughed. He said, "Come sleep at our place for a piaster a night."

"Where?" I asked happily.

He said, "At Wikalat Atiya. You can pay two piasters to sleep in a room, or pay a piaster and sleep in the courtyard. Sleep is sleep. And it's safe."

"Where is this Wikalat Atiya?"

"Let's go!"

And I got up without hesitation.

The power lines extended into the distance along the paved road that reflected the lit lamps. To our right the fields were like an endless, grayish-green sea. To our left were some ancient buildings like red bricks stacked one on top of another and held together by fraternal warmth and patient companionship and resistance to time, but the color of the brick had faded and turned gray near the top, and detestable old age had caught up with them. It was clearly a wasteland, the wind loudly hissing through it. After walking for about a quarter of an hour the fields disappeared, replaced by a tall mountain that extended as far as the eye could see. At its foot small buildings began to appear, and loomed larger as we approached. Then, lo and behold, we were in the heart of a small, dainty city, which still felt rural.

Soon I realized that the distance to it might be short—might be very short indeed—if I approached it from the direction of the Salah al-Din neighborhood that connects the outskirts of the city to its center via many shortcuts across tiny perpendicular alleys, indicating that Damanhour was founded more than once throughout history, or perhaps it was a group of suburbs that multiplied over time and intertwined in an amazing, magical way.

We came to a square courtyard like a wide-open public square surrounded by buildings on all sides. Facing us was a very ancient building, maintaining some of its old dignity, wrapped in decrepitude like the richest of men now brought down to nothing. The walls of square stone and rectangular windows with wooden mashrabiyas were obscured by decay and darkness, and the stones of the walls seemed, as a result of the humidity, like a piece of harisa that would crumble at the merest touch. It had a large gate with two tower-like circular jambs, the same type of architecture that I had often seen in history books of Wikalat al-Ghouri and old mosques and pharaonic temples.

"There, there's Wikalat Atiya," said Mahrous as he slipped under my arm toward the gate. Just then I remembered a massive tradition of images and memories that people passed down in our villages adjacent to the city of Damanhour about Wikalat Atiya. Actually, it was more famous than any other landmark in Damanhour, especially among us country folk. In fact, Wikalat Atiya, in the minds of some of the villagers, meant the city of Damanhour, even though Damanhour did not mean Wikalat Atiya. And yet it has a reputation as a dump and a refuge of the downtrodden and a place of ill repute. Any seasoned murderer who ran away from his crime was immediately sought in Wikalat Atiya; when any peasant woman had fallen pregnant and gotten away before being slaughtered by the family knife or the wagging tongues of the villagers, the family's secret envoys would immediately go to Wikalat Atiya, for perhaps the girl had fallen into the hands of one of the rogues who dwelled there. On the other hand, the wikala was invested in their minds with an air of enchantment and great fun and pleasant nights, and thus word spread that most of the women dancers and beautiful singers and instrumentalists and wedding impresarios were alumnae of Wikalat Atiya in the olden days. This is what I'd heard and what I kept in mind before I became a student at one of the schools in the city of Damanhour. When Mahrous informed me that we could spend the night at a wikala for a piaster, I never imagined he meant that famous wikala; perhaps because its mythical presence inside me made impossible any connection between me and it or the edge of its abyss; then amazingly I had found myself deliberately driven to it as if I were seeking something new, about which I knew nothing at all, but as soon as I saw it with my own two eyes it sucked me in instantly as a reality standing on its own, demanding attention. The old myth awoke to meld with reality. It seemed to me the wikala in its present condition was much smaller than it appeared in the myth; perhaps less magical; yet I felt a strong urge to dive into it headfirst. The very myth that was supposed to repulse me and make me hate it was the same myth that now propelled me toward it, enticing me to enter. That same myth transplanted me into the wikala, with all the power of magic, and all my willingness and desire to see and uncover and experience.

The gate was blocked by a door, which, it seemed to me, would need at least ten men to push it open. Mahrous lifted the large copper knocker hanging on the door, and knocked softly several times. Then he nodded toward an adjacent building quite a distance away which resembled the wikala in its style, only it was a bit newer and taller and larger, full of windows and some sort of rectangular balconies, and gates, and at every window and gate stood a stone statue of a proud horse's head. Mahrous said, "The Royal Stable. It's now a market for livestock that's held every Tuesday. This place is filled with God's creatures of every shape and size. It's the one day when I sell bundles of barsim and bales of green hay along with radishes and green onions and leeks. God bestows His favor on me and I sell everything out and I have one hell of a dinner."

Then he pointed toward a distant three-story building that architecturally resembled the wikala, only more modern, with a small coffeeshop below it, like a caféteria, that stayed open until morning; and he whispered in a trembling voice, "And as for this! Pardon the expression—the whorehouse! Imagine, this was the king's resthouse? Can you believe it? The old owner of the wikala clearly remembers those days when King Fu'ad had property here. They were the property of his brother-in-law, the brother of his wife whose name was Shukaar Hanim. Did King Fu'ad have a wife named Shukaar Hanim? Didn't they teach all of you this in school? My friend, the old man says amazing things and absolutely swears that he would divorce his own wife if he was lying when he says that he saw her himself! Oh! I remember! This brother of King Fu'ad's wife was named Muhi al-Din Sharaf al-Din Seif al-Din, or something like that. I'll trick the old man into telling the story once while you're there. He says this brother-in-law of the king's shot the king in his neck, making a hole in it, and the doctors hurriedly patched up the hole with a plug of silver that would whistle if he laughed or cried out! And King Fu'ad ordered that his brother-in-law be sent to a mental asylum abroad. Is this possible? Why didn't he kill him? Anyway, he swiped his brother-in-law's property here and gambled away half its worth and left this respectable home to a slave girl that he had. And finally, his son King Farouk came and spent the rest of the estate on women! Can you believe it? He would boil two hundred baby pigeons in a pot, reducing them to a stock and drink it before meals, then get up and go fuck his brains out! Where did he get enough pigeon cotes? The idiots make a living off the crazy ones. The home has now become a brothel with a license from the government. On market day it also gets crowded and to do one you have to cough up twenty piasters, but on normal days all you have to cough up is ten. The girls in there are soooo damn sexy, but the money is soooo damn hard to come by!"

He knocked on the door again, a bit harder this time. To my surprise, the door was thrown back like a leaf in a gust of wind. From behind the closed half there appeared a dim light coming from a lantern. There was a large hand with fingers like snakes reaching to turn up the light. The light filled the vast expanse of the gateway entrance; there was a man stretched out on a concrete bench attached to the wall, at least three meters in length, covered with a bunch of tattered sacks patched up with surplus army blankets. His appearance left no doubt that his body had not known water throughout his entire life and he never got any water in whatever he ate or drank, so that his skin was so rough it seemed like the trunk of an acacia tree burned by a blazing sun. His fingernails and toenails were long like fearsome talons, and his face like a black clay pot, the hairs of his beard sticking out like barbed wire. Out of his face peered eyes like those of an old camel, with red sparks flying out of them, and a mouth wide as a toilet bowl without a single tooth, and a nose like a roasted corncob.

Mahrous said, "Good evening, Amm Shawadfi!"

He shouted at us with a voice like rolling thunder, except it was dry, "Hello Mahrous, my boy! What have we here?"

Mahrous said, pointing at me, "One of my relatives! Comes from good folks, and an elementary school graduate. He's spending the night with us, it's no big deal. He is thinking about staying for good—depending on his circumstances."

The rolling thunder spoke as if he had not heard a word of what was said, "Outside or inside?"

"Outside tonight. And God will provide for tomorrow." Mahrous said, handing him two piasters.

The two piasters disappeared beneath a firm pillow the color of earth. The rolling thunder said as he pushed the door closed with a cudgel and locked it, "You know the way." And thus we entered the courtyard of the wikala.

The courtyard was very wide and circular, with no ceiling, just the sky directly above, and piled up on its ground were hundreds of bodies like corpses left behind by a fierce war from many centuries ago, grown rigid in place and turned an earthen hue, in no particular order, the head of one on the feet of another, and other feet on each others' necks and bellies. Others were joined as if they were one body, and though the courtyard was wide they all left the central clearing and piled up before the primitive arcades, nestling together.

The wikala consisted of just two floors, despite the height of its walls, of small interlocking rooms; a spiral stairway with corroded steps clinging to each upper room from the outside, leading to the uppermost room. In front of each room was an area of at least two meters covered by a pitched wooden roof atop wooden columns in the shape of arcades. Most of the rooms on the two floors were open, soft light peeping out of some of them, with subdued voices and noises like arguments, like love, like joking, like sighing, like sex, all resounding in the wide courtyard. Odors weighed heavily on the nose all at once: rot, sweat, burning alcohol, smoke from a coffee roaster, sardines and smoked herring, dung, and urine, but from time to time the wind carried a fleeting whiff of perfume that hit the nose with a heavy, offensive stink. I felt dejection and disgust and shame; I almost puked my guts out; I was sure I had fallen into the noose and tonight I would be easy prey for all of these vagrants and vagabonds and thieves and beggars. Mahrous seemed to sense me trembling and my throat drying up, for he pointed to piles of bodies as if to set my mind at ease, "Do you think they're all men? Among them are many women who greet you on the street with children, asking you for help, for God's sake! The children don't stay here. Amm Shawadfi has ordered this. It is the purveyor of children who stays here in one of these rooms. And they get the children back from him every morning. They settle their account with him at the end of the day and each takes her commission and the children go to a place known only to the purveyor. In the morning they come back by themselves, each one eating a piece of bread with ta'miya in it for breakfast. Your Amm Shawadfi is a good man! He rules this wikala with an iron fist. Nobody can open their mouth. Whatever he wants is done. Were it not for him, things here would go to hell in a handbasket and the police would shut the wikala down and condemn it. If you lose a single piaster here, he will search everyone and, come hell or high water, the stolen item will turn up, but the problem is that he will take half of it as a reward!"

"You say this is Wikalat Atiya. So who's this Shawadfi?"

"Shawadfi leased it from Atiya around ten years ago and Atiya could not kick Shawadfi out and he lost everything. Then he fell ill and the hundred sixty piasters that Shawadfi paid him in rent for the wikala was not enough medicine for even two days. And Atiya could not sell it because he had also rented it from the waqf in the olden days. I will show him to you; he comes often, leaning on his cane, to drink tea with Amm Shawadfi."

Mahrous chose a place in the middle and headed for it as, behind him, I forced myself to follow him, wading through bundles and sacks and large baskets and cages and crutches. There were also black barrels that had eyes glinting within them and hands rolling cigarettes. With his foot Mahrous pushed a stretched-out body, its limbs splayed out away from each other, saying with a coarseness that had more friendliness in it than it did rudeness, "Move, you son of a bitch!" The youth sat up right away without saying a word, and there was enough space for us and then some. Mahrous took off his gallabiya and his undershirt. He bundled up his gallabiya and gave it to me, saying, "Off my back!"

My eyes began to grow accustomed to the dark speckled with flecks of pale yellow. I stared at the sky for a long time; then the rooms of the wikala began to appear around me in gray, and all of a sudden the moon came out. It seemed that Mahrous was sound asleep and snoring faintly through his nose, but he turned and brought his head closer to me, whispering, "You'll love it! If you were a really smart man, you'd reserve yourself a room for thirty piasters, pay on the first of the month, and still owe thirty piasters, but each night you'd pay a piaster as you enter the gate. You'd take a key, which is worth the entire world, and put it in your pocket and lock the room on your clothes and your money. Sixty piasters per month and take a key, hell, that's nothing! I wish *I* could, but the hashish doesn't leave me with thirty piasters, ever. It is my only vice and joy and I can't give it up. I can't get to sleep if I don't smoke two pipes at the end of the night, as you have seen. And the day I save ten piasters after my hashish I will buy a ticket to our village of al-Toud to see my mother and come back. Radishes are not sold in our village and there is no hashish there so why would I stay at my mother's side?"

Then suddenly he quit speaking and snored even louder. The sounds became clearer, and everything became clearer. I was certain that in more than one room people were gambling, and the smacks of the cards were loud. And in more than one room people were getting drunk and yelling at each other combatively. And in more than one room a woman announced her rapture clearly and provocatively, without restraint or shame. The drunk voices were muffled under a veil of deceptive silence. I thought I was just imagining it, for even though at the peak of exhaustion, whenever my back touched the ground, sexual delight crept into my limbs. I could hear the intermittent wanton cries flaring up from time to time from one room or another, followed by total silence for a while.

All the lights were put out in every room, one after another; there was a noise lasting several minutes caused by footsteps coming down the stairs and passing here and there; they were followed by doors opening and closing and the sound of rattling, brittle bones, then it didn't take long for silence to come back once more accompanied by a gray sheet interwoven with rays of the moon, rising like a banana on a silver platter. Everything tempted you to listen carefully and reflect and contemplate, but I was like somebody who stumbled suddenly upon a precious find in the street and hid it to delay its rediscovery until the time to take pleasure in inspecting it came, and at the same time hid it to support a thread of secret hope and to drive pessimism and fear from its contents. I found myself succumbing to a deep sleep, the likes of which I had never known before in my whole life, not even in a cozy bed. Then I found myself strolling in a serene mood, unafflicted by fear, in a jungle thick with trees, with no beginning and no end, just a mass of cumulus clouds. I dove in it and lo and behold it was richly verdant, threads of pale gray light creeping out of it; and the wolves and foxes and dogs and lions and tigers were sleeping beneath the tree trunks, yawning in boredom, paying no attention to my intoxicated, foolish footsteps, which frequently touched some of their paws and fur and trampled their bellies; yet no more than a roar or a gentle lunge was made in jest, making my hair stand on end. It seemed as though I knew all these beasts personally and they likewise knew me well and between us was an ancient friendship that was perhaps the bond of searching for a morsel during the day and for shelter at the end of the night; I imagined that some of them were about to invite me with a sidelong glance, almost leaving the bones which they were busy tearing to pieces to say to me: Here, have a lick or two for yourself. I was about to do so, for the smell of the broth of the hot marrow bones and the calves' feet was intoxicating, coming from someplace or other, redolent with the smell of browning onions that I heard sizzling. I continued passing from damp, bright clouds to dark, wetter clouds until empty space suddenly stretched out before me, stripped of everything. The sun was inclining its red head on the shoulders of the clouds, red blood showing clearly above it, and I began to feel the heat of the air little by little, then I began to drip with sweat, and my clothes clung to my body, and there were playful movements, perhaps the hooves of some of the jungle beasts walking behind me. They started scratching my back and jumping on my face, and the earth touched my lips, and I tried to rise, and I opened my eyes . . . and to my surprise I was sleeping alone in the heart of the courtyard, and Shawadfi's rough, burly hand shook me forcefully awake. When my eyelids freed themselves, with difficulty, from the sticky discharge caked between them, I saw his face, like the face of a mythical animal, smiling and saying in a friendly tone, "Hey, uh . . . ! Have you not slept in years? What's with all this sleeping, my good man? Don't you have work to do?"

I quickly sat up, and rubbed my eyes. He motioned with his arm, which resembled a thick acacia tree branch, toward a wet spot at the edge of the courtyard near the gate. He said, "Go wash your face with a handful or two of water."

I looked closely where he was pointing, and I noticed a water pump in a small cement basin. I quickly stood up and staggered over to the pump. I took the pump handle, I moved it upward then downward several times and the mouth of the pump issued a hiss and a blast of air. I remembered that I had to prime the pump by putting some water from the basin in its mouth in order to get the water flowing up from deep inside the earth. I let go of the pump handle and cupped my hands and scooped water from the basin—it was cool, soothing, and seductive—and I splashed my face with my cupped hands then dried them off with an earth-colored handkerchief that was always rolled up in my side pants pocket, the smell of sweat in it more repulsive than the smell of a putrid waterhole. I got ready to leave the wikala.

The Gate

As I turned sideways to squeeze through the gate, I saw Shawadfi sitting cross-legged on the concrete bench; in front of him was a brazier of fire kindled with corn cobs, on top of which was a black tin pot with a wire handle twisted firmly around it. Shawadfi held it and started gently shaking the pot and the penetrating smell of tea rose to my nostrils.

"Have a good day, Amm Shawadfi."

"Sit down and have a sip of tea."

"Thank you, and God bless you."

"I said, sit down!"

He said that with decisiveness and simplicity and generosity, and pointed to the edge of the bench, so I sat down watching the forenoon held back in the heart of the large courtyard and keeping it away from the early morning which was being pressed through the open, cold gate that opened out to the gray emptiness. I was suddenly caught off guard by the smell of the hot broth and the cows' feet and the limes. Shawadfi licked his lips as he said, "This monkey woman cooks cows' feet from before dawn when my mouth had totally dried up. I don't know what it is she adds to the soup to give it that intoxicating smell. If she didn't send me a bowl for lunch, I would make her life miserable all night!"

Then he opened his mouth up wide and grinned broadly, and went about pouring tea in the glass on top of the sugar, then poured it back into the pot to pour again in a small tin mug with a handle. Strong, reddish-black tea. He set the cup before me, "Drink while it's hot." With sheer joy I took the first sip. I couldn't restrain my desire; I kept sipping loudly until I had finished the mug and returned it to him to fill for himself. He took a small sip then set the mug down and took out a grimy pouch and withdrew from it a stack of rolling papers. He blew into the stack, lifted the edge of a paper, grasped it, tore out the paper and put a quantity of tobacco, which I discerned was from re-packed cigarette butts, onto it. He rolled a cigarette, put it between his lips, and leaned his head over the brazier, letting it touch the burning cobs as he puffed on it with tremendous pleasure, as the smell of the roasted tobacco arose around my nose. He took another sip, followed by a deeper drag, and said, "Shall I expect you tonight?"

"God willing!"

"In the courtyard or in a room?"

"Depends on my circumstances. God will provide."

"Would you like to pay some earnest money?"

"I'll pay when I come."

"Come whether you have money or not."

"God will provide."

"You say you have an elementary degree?"

"And I was on the verge of graduating as a teacher, if only I hadn't been expelled from the Institute for excessive absence."

He leveled a terrifying look at my eyes from his own wide, red eyes with no eyelashes and no whites, "No doubt you're a rotten, God-awful, filthy kid! Your family deprived themselves of fruit and good meals to send you to schools in the city and you fool around here? You dare to say for excessive absence? Why the absence at all, by the devil? Where did you go?"

I regretted what I'd said, especially since he'd touched a sore spot by saying that my family had deprived themselves on my behalf and this was quite true. He used my father's very words. I started looking for another excuse, but he didn't give me a chance.

"Now you're an official vagrant! Begging your pardon. So what do you do now? How do you live? Do you have a job?"

"I'm looking for one."

"You're looking?"

Then he gave me another glass of twice-boiled tea: "This is the ultimate sign that you're a good-for-nothing, no offense. You don't look for work, you find it. You create it out of thin air. Jobs are a dime a dozen, but people like you don't see it because you, sir, are looking. Man, go to the Barakat cotton ginnery or the Dawood cotton ginnery or the Qaffas cotton ginnery. In Damanhour there are so many cotton ginneries that thousands like you wouldn't be enough for them. Go to a bakery, to a coffeeshop, to a factory, to a merchant shop. Work as a peddler. Or do you want an office and a newspaper and a cup of coffee and a cigarette? The whole lot of you are idiotic! The government has spoiled you all and filled you with false pride. They raise effendis for us with newspapers and cups of coffee who live off the backs of the poor. Here in this wikala I have young fellows who earn money out of thin air. They play with gold. No diploma and no nothing. Only a boy with his eyes wide open, a boy with real smarts, will come to any good in this world. Listen, my friend, now that you have left the school, forget about the schools and schooling and let's get to the point. Do you smoke? Of course, it's clear on your lips and on your fingers. Have yourself a few drags on this."

I took a puff and it was like the teeth of a plow tearing up my chest. The rotten smell of cigarette butts made me gag, and I started coughing violently, but I took another drag, and I returned the cigarette to him, getting up, "I have an appointment with a good man who will find work for me."

"Sit for five more minutes, we might need you."

And he gave me a glass of the weakest and sweetest thrice-boiled tea. No sooner had I finished the last sip of it than we were joined by two people, a man and a woman. The man was tall like a lamppost with a head like the head of a hoopoe, his face smooth and innocent like the face of a small bird, toothless, and white complexioned like a foreigner whom fate had worn down and rolled in the dirt and mud. He wore a gallabiya covered on all sides with patches that looked like magic pockets. As for the woman, she was somewhat plump, of medium stature, fat on all sides, with a prominent and bloated chest, as if two small children were enfolded between her breasts. Her head was elongated and pointed like a watermelon and wrapped in a dingy scarf stained with oil and dirt beneath which appeared black hair rough and braided; her eyes were swollen and narrow as though their eyelids had been sewn with a tailor's needle after he had folded them inward in a wide fold like that of a pants leg; it seemed as though she were beaten on her eyes constantly and violently. Her cheeks hung loosely, and next to the man she seemed to be his mother's age, even though she couldn't be more than fifty, whereas he was nowhere near that old. They were smiling with a great deal of joy and bashfulness and a great deal of naiveté.

Beaming, Shawadfi called out, "Welcome to the bridegroom! And welcome to the bride! You came just in time! Hey! Are you sold out, with God's permission?"

The man sat down in front of us on the ground: "Thank God anyhow!"

The woman waddled toward me and sank down at my side on the bench, panting. She set her hands on her knees, looking at me in curiosity from between her narrow, slanted eyes: "How are you, young fellow? You look like a fine young man."

Shawadfi bellowed at her, "Knock it off! Let's get to the point—are you old friends?"

The woman smiled with feigned bashfulness. She put her hand into her side pocket, then took it out clutching a handful of money. She started counting the shillings and ten-piaster coins and the hexagonal silver two-piaster pieces and the pierced silver piasters and red copper and the half milliemes and the red milliemes. She counted around sixty piasters and presented them to Shawadfi, who was watching her count attentively.

Shawadfi collected the money and slipped it into his pocket, saying, "This is the rent for the room. What's more important is that I have the fee we agreed upon, where is it? The both of you cannot live here unless you're properly married!"

The woman looked at him out of the corners of her eyes, as if she wanted to prove to me and to him that she was experienced in the matters of flirtation and coyness and feminine seduction. Actually in this glance there had appeared a great deal of the whorishness with which she was blessed. Then she wiggled her eyebrows with amazing speed, and she flicked out the tip of her tongue and moved it along her lips in a telltale motion. Shawadfi stabbed a pointed look at her eyes as if he was stabbing his sword into her stomach and said spitefully, "Behave, woman! I'm through! I no longer have any use of my knees! I was done in by whores like you a long time ago. It's the young men's turn."

"I swear by this night that we don't have any more. This is all that we made throughout the past week for all of our sweat. Forgive us the five piasters and God will bless you! For the sake of this honorable guest!"

"You don't have any business with the guest."

Then he grabbed the piasters and began flipping through them, and selected a half millieme and gave it to the distressed man, "Buy us a sheet of paper. Broad and ruled. From any store."

The man got up, took the half millieme and left. Shawadfi slipped the piasters into his pocket and looked for the pouch of tobacco until he found it under his hip, opened it, rolled a cigarette, tossed it down next to him, and rolled another one and gave it to me: "Smoke!" then rolled a third for himself and lit it from the remaining embers, then lit mine. The man came back with the ruled paper and gave it to Shawadfi, who gave him the cigarette: "We want to marry this woman to this man."

I didn't understand; I looked back and forth between them in confusion: "What did you say?"

He waved his hand as though annoyed with my stupidity: "We want to write a marriage contract. What? Don't you understand?"

"But this is the job of the marriage registrar! Are you an official registrar?"

He lashed me with a harsh look: "This is a modern invention. Legal marriage is the agreement of the two sides to marry."

The cigarette burned me and I threw it away in vexation: "But this is against the law, Amm Shawadfi!"

He snorted as if gurgling sarcastically, "Law? What kind of law are you talking about? The law is for dimwits! Just do what I tell you, I guarantee. I'll even pay you to do it. Here's a whole piaster in exchange for you writing the contract."

He threw a pierced silver piaster in my lap. I pushed it aside nervously: "I don't understand this kind of thing, Amm Shawadfi, I'll pass on it."

He clutched my arm with two fingers like a pair of pliers: "I'll dictate and you'll write. Don't be a blockhead, or I will be angry with you. I sincerely advise you not to be a smart-ass with me. Try to win me over to your side. Come on now, write!"

I adjusted the sheet of paper on a board: "Write what?"

He sat up straight, raising his right knee to support his arm on top of it, and began dictating to me: "I affirm and avow that I am Abd al-Fadil Bayyumi al-Toudi from the village of al-Toud, Behaira, and I reside in Wikalat Atiya at the end of Old Shubra, Damanhour, and my occupation is hanuti, that is, I wash the dead—I have wed, that is, married, Sabiha al-Birshoumi Hasanayn, occupation daiya, that is, midwife, who also resides in Wikalat Atiya; our marriage is in accordance with Islamic law and the sunna of the Prophet, a dowry known only to each of us, and a dowry balance in the amount of five pounds that I am obligated to pay to the last milieme if we are to divorce on fair terms. Did you write that? Then, start a new line: I affirm and avow that I am Sabiha al-Birshoumi Hasnayn and I work as a daiya, that is, midwife, and I reside in Wikalat Atiya at the end of Old Shubra, Damanhour, I have agreed to this matrimony in accordance with Islamic law and the sunna of the Prophet and I have taken possession of the agreed-upon dowry and I have become his rightful property and he can do with me whatsoever he wills within the limits of the law. The first party, Abd al-Fadil, pledges to provide for me and fulfill my needs for shelter and clothing and food and other . . . put 'other' in parentheses because it means the well-known marital duties—and the second party, Sabiha al-Barshoumi Hasnayn, pledges to be an obedient wife. And the two parties pledge to live in harmony. Did you write that? Excellent, excellent! Give me your finger, man, and give me your finger, woman . . . write in the middle of the line: in confirmation thereof, and below it Abd al-Fadil Bayyumi al-Toudi and opposite it at the end of the line Sabiha al-Barshoumi Hasanayn."

Then he took the paper from my hand and held the finger of the man and moistened it with his saliva and passed the point of the indelible pencil over it until he stained it, and pressed it on the paper, and it left a clear fingerprint. He did likewise with the finger of the woman. Then he asked that a copy of the same words be written on the other half of the contract and I did, and he put the same fingerprints on it then returned the two copies to me.

"Write here: 'Written on day such-and-such.'" I wrote the date, and he took the paper and pencil and with a trembling hand he drew the letters of his name, then he gave me the paper again: "Write that you are a witness to the contract."

"No! Let me out of this, I beg you!"

His eyes nearly burned right through my own eyes: "And you call yourself a man! If you don't sign, you're a sissy. No offense. I will not respect you from now on. Come on! Be a man and witness with me. You are no better than me."

So I took the pencil and scribbled something illegible. He began scrutinizing it: "I swear, it's better than the signature of the chief justice of the court! Bravo! Now, I'll take the piaster from you as a down payment for spending the night. You will naturally be spending the night here so I owe you a piaster. If you want to spend the night in a room bring another piaster or you can sleep like yesterday in the same place. Now you can go along your merry way, may God help you find your way."

The woman said, "Go, and may God guide your steps."

The man said, "Good to make your acquaintance, God willing."

As for Shawadfi, he divided the sheet in half and gave half to Abd al-Fadil, the other to Sabiha, but each of them returned their paper to him, asking that he keep them with him so that they might not lose them. Then he said to them, "Your room is immediately after the monkey-woman's room. Now get the hell out of my face! I want to hear your sounds of delight now, woman! And if this old man fails you, call me and I will live up to your expectations even if I have to disinfect you with lemon juice first."

The woman snorted: "How dare you! I swear by the Prophet, the most honorable of God's creation, there are none cleaner than me in all the land that is watered by the Nile!"

When I left through the gate for the world outside, the heat had risen and the asphalt of the road burned my feet with fire, and I burst out in laughter that shook my entire body, but the words of Shawadfi concerning work echoed in my brain and seemed very logical indeed.

My Cousin's Alley

Susi Street is one of the most important commercial streets in Damanhour and one of its most crowded and lively. I can walk it up and down and to and fro all day long without anyone noticing me. It is very intimate; I am captivated by its intense crowds and the smells of the fruits and foods and the new fabrics, and the sight of the well-dressed peasants coming from the nearby villages shopping or attending the court sessions in their unending cases or presenting themselves to the doctors and hospitals of the city, and eating ta'miya which is considered, for them, a delicacy they savor with great delight.

This street and I go way back. On the street directly behind it there is the al-Houfi Bookstore which loans secondhand books to read in exchange for five milliemes, and just steps away from it—on the street where al-Asi's shop, specializing in ful midammis, is found—lives Wadida, my uncle's daughter, who is married to Hagg Mas'oud al-Qabbani, who works as a bursar in the Administration building. He is of medium height, heavyset, wide-mouthed, noticeably thick-lipped in a way that sometimes provokes laughter and disgust. He wears a striped cotton vest and over it a wool gallabiya with long, wide sleeves, summer and winter, and a tall fez on his fat head, perpetually thrown back to reveal his broad, fat forehead. He walks with his chest puffed out and arms swinging in the manner of cotton merchants and pashas. If he turns around, his fat neck appears from behind to have a slab of dead meat like a weasel stretched over it crosswise; it is said that it is a skin disease and that he has paid a lot of money for doctors and for home remedies, yet he has not succeeded in alleviating it. He is from a large and somewhat wealthy family; however, the bursar business was the first step to true riches for him, and he bought many feddans of cultivable land in the village, land tilled by his many nephews; and he acquired many herds of cattle and lambs, and helped those in need of money, which they repay with twenty-five and sometimes fifty percent interest at harvest time, and he bought water pumps to get water to dry places, and engines for plowing and machines for seed scattering and haymaking, and he built a mansion in the village for taking vacations; and he bought a house on this street right smack in the heart of the capital of Behaira, made up of five floors, each floor consisting of one apartment with three rooms; he lived in it with his eleven children, seven boys and four girls: Hawwas, the eldest, is in his last year of law school; Badi‘ is in his last year of engineering school; Maguid is in business school; and Karam is at the Teacher's Institute; they consider him to have gone astray by his entering the Teacher's Institute, which none entered but the riffraff and barefoot rabble, and they often taunt him for his failure to go the university route leading to law practice and medicine and engineering and high, important offices. Safwat is in senior year of high school; Sharif is in preparatory school; Mimi is in elementary. As for the girls, they are the older: Tahani is married to her cousin in the village who is almost her father's age; Badriya, of whom it is said that she was born on a full moon night, hence her name; and Yusriya and Shukriya are spinsters and have reached menopause, and they were not helped by their father's wealth because they are the spitting image of him with thick lips and globular foreheads and inflated bellies and disproportionate bodies, except for Badriya who inherited her mother's body and her father's face. Each of the children has their own room with comfortable, clean furniture. There is a room for out-of-town guests on the roof, with coops for chickens, ducks, and geese.

I have heard of this cousin of mine, Wadida, since my early childhood when her life story had been told over and over again in our old parlor with its bare wooden benches, even though—so they say—it used to be replete with fancy upholstered chairs before hard times caught up with my father, the government employee pensioned off many years earlier. My father was not very bright at farming either; he began selling his inherited land one carat after another to provide for his many children from four marriages. My father would light up whenever mention was made of my cousin Wadida, and he would say, his old face gleaming with hope, "God willing, you will complete your studies in Damanhour and live with your cousin free of charge and stay under her patronage and the patronage of her children."

These children of hers would visit our parlor in the village on some holidays; they were effendis and beys and hanims grumbling about the dust from the floor of the parlor and the roughness of its benches and about my father's black tea and about the sight of the stained earthenware jars and their always-broken mouths. Despite this, we celebrated their coming. Our parlor would be crowded with people greeting one another and checking out their fancy clothes and muffling shy laughter at the sight of the men's genitals visibly rolled up in the pants; besides their hips were parted, each buttock on a side, to say nothing of the choking ties hanging from their necks; as for the fragrant perfumes, they would fill our entire alley with delight and joy. My mother and all my relatives were hoping that I would turn out like my cousin's son Hawwas or any of his brothers. And I too hoped for this, until I obtained an elementary diploma from the village school which awarded this degree for the first time in its history, and our honorable teacher presented our application to the Teachers' Institute in Damanhour, and we underwent a medical examination, which made my acceptance conditional upon obtaining prescription glasses; and when, after great effort he came up with the price of the glasses, my father gave me the money, saying, "Go to Hawwas, your cousin's son, tell him your grandfather so-and-so says hello and tells you to come with me to the doctor for an eye exam and to the eyeglass store to make glasses. And if the money's not enough, let him pay the difference."

I put on my striped, new, cheap cotton gallabiya, saved since the last holiday for an occasion such as this, and black shoes and white socks, and I traveled to Damanhour with my cousin's address. To my surprise I found myself before a woman like a dolphin, with a very small head and a very long neck, and a body pointed with massive flesh, her neck twisting when she spoke and her small head swaying like the head of a snake; narrow-eyed and with a plump, wrinkled face, in her eyes a look frozen into something like disgust and displeasure, or maybe even loathing. She looked at me from head to toe and started wagging her finger disparagingly and said with bitter sarcasm, "What's this! You don't have a better gallabiya than this? Or even shoes cleaner than these shitkickers? Does my uncle intend to disgrace me here in front of the neighbors? What will they say? My family are nothing but beggars and paupers!"

Tears began to well up in my eyes and evaporate, forming a dense fog heralding thunder and lightning. Her children had withdrawn into corners on beds and chairs and got busy reading while stealing glances at me from time to time with disapproval tinged with confusion and awkwardness. I remained standing before my cousin holding the handful of money stuck in the corner of a bandanna after I gave her my father's letter. Finally she threw the letter down next to her and pointed to her son Hawwas saying in disgust, "Get up and go with him!"

The tone of her voice said that this is a price we have to pay and we'll leave the rest to God. Hawwas was short and broad of face and shoulders. His face was wiped clean of features; his lips were much less thick than his father's and brothers'. His eyes were covered with apathy like a layer of chaff over putrid water, and when he spoke the apathy was broken and a burning evil flame shot out. There was a small defect in his tongue which his urban dialect made sound somewhat beautiful in his unrestrained, but not entirely clear, voice, when he mixed the 's' with the 'th' and at other times the 'th' with 'z.' From his hiding place behind a small desk, on top of which was a lamp pouring out light in the midst of bright daylight, he said, "And why didn't your father come?"

I said, fighting back burning tears, "He's tired these days." He looked away from me and bent over the desk lost in thought.

My cousin turned her glance to a distant corner: "Would you go with him, Badi'?"

Badi' was reclining on the bed holding an illustrated magazine. Even though he was the second son among the males, he always seemed to be the oldest, a composure in his orderly features that he inherited from our family, and normal, unblemished tongue and elocution, and a clearness in his wide eyes that looked exactly like the eyes of my father, and his tall, thin stature like his uncle Mahmoud, my cousin, who lives in a part of our house in the village, and his fair, ruddy complexion like our complexion; in addition, he got the nickname 'Chief Engineer' three years earlier and he will indeed become one in just a few months. He took the magazine away from his face, and in the utmost earnestness he said, "I wish! You know, ma'am, that I'm going to have my teeth cleaned!"

Hawwas said with a great deal of annoyance apologetically, "Your father should have come in view of the many possibilities that may arise!"

Here Hagg Mas'oud appeared descending an inner stairway near the balcony, wearing a house gallabiya of poplin with a collar and cuffs, and on his head a skullcap of the same cloth. He began mumbling in a voice betraying his good nature, and lisping with his tongue that was even more defective than his son Hawwas's, and he kept wiping his thick lips with the back of his hand, yet he did not succeed in stopping the flow of dribble spraying from between them. I figured that he was saying to his son Hawwas, "Son, how could his father come when he is such an old man? Have you forgotten that he is over seventy years old? And that he is in pain? And has so many children? Get up, son, God will bless you for it! Don't let the young man down!"

Hawwas breathed nervously, and angrily put down the papers in front of him, then got up and disappeared through a secret door concealed by decorative paper. All of that went on as I stood in my place not budging, without anyone saying to me, "have a seat," and the world before my eyes had become a black sheet, spread out and rippling. Finally Hawwas came out wearing a full suit with a necktie, and shoes shining like a mirror, just like his exquisitely coiffed hair, and the handkerchief matching the color of the necktie arranged like the three pyramids in the pocket of his jacket on his chest. He pointed to me in mock affection: "Let's go, buddy!" I extended my hand to him with the bundle of money, and he pushed it away: "Keep it with you!" I put it in my pocket, and proceeded behind him like a lowly servant. At the moment I started down the stairs behind him with loud, clomping steps, I realized the distance between him and me was too far, and that I would not be like him, not ever, even if all the heavens themselves were on my side. The entire age to come would not be enough to catch up with his heels. Then I hated him, and I said to myself that it does me no honor to be like him.

Here I am stopping in front of the juice shop on the corner of their street from one of the alleys connected to it. Millions of times I caught myself redhanded carried away with thoughts inciting me to go ahead and do it and leave it all in God's hands: that I would visit them trying for a loan of a whole pound or fifty piasters from my cousin, or even a quarter pound, or at least she would feed me a rich meal with meat and vegetables and rice; and it might help that I had not visited them for many long years; let me claim to them, for example, that I am coming from the village bringing them greetings from their uncle Mahmoud and their aunt Nagiya, stay with them an hour or so for perhaps they had changed during these years and compassion had entered their hearts. And millions of times I was overcome by the same spectacle in its entirety as if I experienced it for the first time: the optician had given us an appointment five days from now to get the glasses, which extended to a week since I was a stranger and traveling; the optician's name was 'Ads, and he was Jewish, and he was originally a watchmaker, and his shop was directly in front of the Administration Building among a row of upscale shops with display windows chock full of everything exciting and exotic. And this was not out of the ordinary, for most optometrists at that time were originally watchmakers, and the lenses and frames were displayed between the watches. Hawwas picked out a frame for me that he liked, an exact replica of Ghandi's glasses. I was forced to spend this week as a guest of my cousin. The only bed with enough room for me was the bed of the boy Sharif because he was a tiny boy. It was a bed with posts and a mosquito net enveloping it on all sides, with two mattresses and two pillows and a sheet and a bedspread and a comforter encased in a cotton covering. I compared that with the mat on the floor of the large room in our home, on the bench next to the bread oven; and I recalled our evening gatherings in the barn listening with genuine belief to the flights of fancy of the boy Ganoum who would assure us that lice-infestation is something natural in the human body, like worms in the mish which are forever there, and that King Farouk himself, without a doubt, had in his body lice and fleas. When I slid into the smooth bed under the cool, beautiful comforter and the smell of perfumed soap reached my nose, I reckoned that the world was deeper and subtler than I had imagined; then I flew off on the wings of sleep to great distances during which I would wake up to the shaking of the boy Sharif as he threw himself on the ground shouting with intense rage and buried hatred: "It's impossible! It can't be!" When I awoke near dawn to the call for help, I noticed that he was not sleeping next to me. The following night he left me the bed to myself. And on one morning they surrounded me with insinuations and innuendos and muffled laughter loudly expressed, and many words from which I understood that I farted all night and filled the room with the smell of sewers, not to mention the smell of the rotten socks on my feet, and the fleas that I brought with me from the mat in the village and how now they would have to turn the whole house inside out in the sun. On the morning of the last day Hagg Mas'oud led me to 'Ads's shop, so I picked up the glasses and he checked them with me on the eye chart in the shop and made sure that I could see the smallest letters with them. Then he led me to this juice shop, where he bought me a glass of sugarcane juice to drink and it tasted so good that I wished for another at that moment, as if I was drinking the water of life that I had heard of in tales and proverbs. Then we walked to Mudiriya Street, where he shook hands with me with a hand as thick as a leather slipper, saying with his speech impediment, "Goodbye, *sh*onny! *Sh*ay hello to your father!"

And he left me and went off toward Mudiriya Street with quick steps. As he was about to disappear I remembered that what I had left over from the glasses was around four and a half piasters, but I needed seven more piasters to get back to our village. I was thinking about running after him to explain this to him, but I could not do it, so I walked toward the station following the recommendation of Ads not to take off the glasses ever until I got used to them; the ground below my feet seemed like something grooved and bulging, yet everything was well lit, and the streets seemed to have new depths which I had not seen before. I booked a ticket to the city of Disuq, and from Disuq I booked a ticket to the town of Sanhour. My plan was to sneak past the conductor in the two remaining stations, but I did not succeed, and he insisted upon collaring me; however, the miracle of the glasses had their effect instantly, as a kindly man looked closely at my appearance and said, "He seems like the son of good folks! Let him go, sir, and here's your money!" So the conductor let me get off at Bekatoush station to walk eight kilometers to our village.

Except I felt now that I had a goal in walking on Susi Street, other than wasting time and getting full from the free smell of food.

Soon I could see it. Here I was circling around it; it was the shop of Muhammad Abu Sinn, middle-class fabric merchant, neither rich nor poor; it was enough that his shop was on Susi Street, on the front, and his shelves were full of clothing of all kinds and colors but they were not overstocked and they did not indicate back storerooms or great capital. However, the store continued to do a good business, especially with the peasant customers who came from the villages and nearby hamlets; since they found a person in the shop who looked like one of them, they understood him with ease and simplicity and credibility, and therefore they felt at ease with him, and his words to them were straight and simple. He had a cheerful and likable personality, a narrow forehead and eyes, a small nose and big nostrils, a wide mouth, always showing yellow teeth, each tooth separated by wide gaps, as if each tooth was smiling by itself right down the line. There were two dimples upon his cheeks, and the purity and goodness and innocence of his face won you over as if he was one of your relatives, because of that intimate familiarity about him. All his customers trusted that his prices were lower than the market price by two piasters and maybe ten piasters per meter; besides, his fabric's quality was guaranteed. As for the measurement per meter, his hand was liberal: before he cut he went beyond the point of measurement by five inches. He had made this shop from his unceasing sweat and his toil over twenty years, since he was a peddler with a pushcart. That was Muhammad Abu Sinn, a member of the Muslim Brotherhood Society, the prayer mark like a sparrow on his brow. He never had the experience of prison even though most of his close lifelong friends had spent half their lives in prison. The reason was that he was very clever; he stayed away from the demonstrations and direct political action, he stuck to acts of worship and religious obligations and duties, volunteering to preach calmness in a voice free of innuendo or political incitement, with highly charming words that had sunk in his head from very accomplished speakers, who would corner us in the Society headquarters in Nadi Street and divide us into boy scout groups and drama clubs and the National Guard and the Popular Resistance. It was he who led me to this society in an extremely nice and intimate manner. For even though I utterly despised Hagg Mas'oud and my cousin and her children, willfully and resolutely, and to a degree almost reaching the point of wrath and enmity, I used their kinship to my advantage. In their name I was able to get around in this area freely and with total safety without being subjected to what strangers were subjected to in a city like this; it was enough for one of the local boys to know that I was a first cousin of the Hagga Wadida, then he would leave me sitting at his café for a long time with a drink and, sometimes even without my ordering anything; perhaps something would be ordered for me as a way of greeting, or the store owner made me feel welcome and let me amuse him in between customers, or he greeted me warmly if he met me on another street, or he protected me from sudden hostility.

The home of Muhammad Abu Sinn was directly opposite the home of Hagg Mas'oud; and deep affection was reciprocated among the women across the balconies and houses, and fancy words such as "oh Auntie" and "oh Abay" and "oh Anisa" filled the mornings and late afternoons with melodious women's voices in urban accents heavily tinged with an unmistakable peasant accent. It was my good luck that Muhammad Abu Sinn saw me on the balcony several times. He wished me a good morning once and I bid him good evening twice as he drank late afternoon coffee on the balcony before going down to the shop after a lovely siesta; then I went by him in the shop with Hawwas more than once during the making of the eyeglasses because it was on our way. Then I began to pass by him after I started school and I lived with three of my fellow village boys in a room near Iflaqa Bridge, on the other bank of Mahmudiya Canal where the Institute headquarters were, in a house rented from one of the boatmen, and Abu Sinn would greet me warmly and introduce me to his customers and guests with great honor, embarrassing me. He had noticed that I loved reading and I carried novels and collections of poetry and books on literature and cultural magazines; and he began to discuss them with me in a way that shocked me, a fact which confirmed for me that he had read all of those books and magazines and had an opinion of them; he even took to providing me with books I had heard of but never seen. Even stories by Ihsan Abd al-Quddous and Yusuf al-Seba'i, whom the preachers in the mosques attacked, were in his library and he loaned me the ones I wanted, on condition that I brought them back clean. It was he who drew my attention to a monthly series called *al-Kitab al-Dhahabi*, specializing in publishing stories and novels of prominent authors, and to the series *Hilal Books* which he had in its entirety. He also drew my attention to the political side in the writings of al-Aqqad; and he supplied me with all of his works and the works of Taha Hussein and al-Mazeni and Mustafa Sadeq al-Raf'i and Haykal and Ahmed Hassan al-Ziyat and Ahmed Zaki Abu Shadi and al-Manfalouti and Muhammad Farid Abu Hadid and the plays of Ahmed Shawqi. The best of all was that he told me news that blew me away: he informed me that in Damanhour there was a society for authors and its headquarters were the Messiri Coffeeshop and its president Abd al-Mu'ti al-Messeri, the owner of the coffeeshop; and he acquainted me with some of this coffee man cum author's marvelous books, and the books of the Damanhouri authors like Amin Yusef Ghurab and Muhammad Abd al-Halim Abdullah and Ahmed Muharram and Ali al-Jarim. And it was he who advised me in the end to forget Abd al-Quddous and al-Seba'i and the like, and instead to read carefully an unknown author called Naguib Mahfouz who depicted life as it truly was. How beautiful it was that he invited me to visit the Messiri Coffeeshop just a few steps away from his store, where we sat at a nearby table and began sipping tea, and watched the authors as they brought the tables together and conversed, and some of them read and the rest listened intently; and al-Messiri followed the whole thing as he followed the flood of drink tokens on his platform from the hand of the waiter who was his nephew at the same time. That night Muhammad Abu Sinn confessed to me that he gave up education after elementary school and discovered reading at an early age, and his voracity for reading grew by virtue of his association with great intellectuals in the Muslim Brotherhood.

Muhammad Abu Sinn was very kind to me, and insisted on giving me dinner or lunch, and gave me some piasters as a kind of long-term loan. However, since I was expelled from the Institute, I had not seen him; embarrassment of failure prevented me from stopping by to see him. My poor appearance and weak condition came between me and the door of his store, so I found myself circling around behind the store so he would not see me, although I really hoped that he would see me, provided that it seemed to be mere coincidence. So what's with me today, as for many days past, I felt that I was scheming so that he would see me without my seeming to intend that?

The Brothers' Street

Even though I was quite a way away from Abu Sinn's store, directly behind it but from the alley winding around it, his associate (and doppelganger) found me. Suddenly there was a voice shouting my name, calling, "Hey you—yeah, you!" Because I remembered the voice instantly, I picked up the pace. The voice called out to me again, closer this time, so I doubled my speed, trying to melt into the crowd in my cousin's wide alley, which connected to the large Mudiriya Street, where the Administration Building before me seemed to stretch out facing the alley like a great mural so that approaching it from the alley was like coming into an entrance hall in its house. However, I was surprised at who stood before me clutching my arm: "You don't want to answer, you despicable scoundrel?"

I raised my head as if I was surprised; my eyes met a brown face split like a half sandwich of ful, or ta'miya. Everything in his face was split or chipped, the nose and the cheeks and the chin and the forehead, as if every one of these features was chipped before it was built, even though circular shadows rippled beneath the skin tanned by the sun and above it, even his long black beard, which was tapered like a provocative pyramid. He was wearing a suit over a light cotton T-shirt and placing a bundle of rolled-up newspapers under his arm, putting his left hand in his pants pocket while his right hand clutched my arm. I was afraid at first but I was soon laughing as I greeted him warmly.

It was Abdullah Abu Hantour, Muhammad Abu Sinn's best friend. A very important figure in the Muslim Brotherhood branch, and among the fiercest speakers on any occasion that he wished without appearing parasitical or out of place. He went to jail more than once during the days of Ibrahim Abd al-Hadi, prime minister in the times of the monarchy, and participated in the popular resistance in Isma'iliya, Port Said, and Suez.

He worked as an Arabic language instruction inspector in the Ministry of Education. Universally dreaded by all the Arabic language teachers in the school district, because, despite his inherently good spirit and unceasing generosity, he did not accept compromise in matters of teaching regardless of reason or circumstance, and did not accept mediation, and he likewise detested stupid, dim-witted students and he cursed their teachers before their fathers. The worst curse he had at the height of his anger was "May your eyes be blinded!" or "God forgive whoever taught you!"

Ever since he found out that I was a student at the Teacher's Institute, he had treated me with the respect due to a teacher and always addressed me as ustaz. He never denied me access to his valuable books. And I, in his presence, felt I was a noble, intelligent, respectable, and successful person; I felt afraid that this image of me, in his view, would be tarnished for one reason or another.

"Hello! Welcome!" "Very well, thank you." We had resumed walking and were two steps away from the long, shiny Administration Building, its solid walls white and dignified and its awe-inspiring long windows adorned with canary-colored ledges, their jambs daubed with burnt brown, and the windows with protruding friezes of marble. As for the main gate in the center of the wall, it was raised from the ground by marble steps, and its appearance was awesome, making one wish to ascend the stairs and enter. There were all kinds of people, including effendis with fezzes and sheikhs with turbans and peasants with skullcaps, ascending the stairs or descending in dignity and aplomb. It was as if we were watching them in a movie, since this image seemed from afar like a background blocking the alley, distancing itself whenever we drew nearer to it, only to reveal, after a little while, the corner of Mudiriya Street directly in front of it. All we needed to do was to take a sharp right on Mudiriya Street, to pass by the large al-Maliya coffeeshop adorned with mirrors on all the walls, and tables with clean tablecloths, and waiters with white wings like angels, and the smell of distilled water and tea and coffee and cinnamon and shisha tobacco perfuming the street with an incomparable blend of aromas. At the end of the coffeeshop sidewalk there were only two steps to the sharp right also on Susi Street to find ourselves in front of Muhammad Abu Sinn's fabric store.

Abdullah Abu Hantour was not easy; he turned me sharply to the right and we found ourselves right in the middle of the coffeeshop inside. He chose a table next to a balcony overlooking Mudiriya Street; he pointed a chair out to me and I sat down, in a great deal of embarrassment, on the chair pressed up next to the wall, and I cast a glance into the mirror facing me. I began to watch the people coming toward me on the street when actually they were coming from behind me. Abdullah clapped and the waiter came and he asked if he would be so kind as to bring us a pot of tea and a shisha. It was as if the order had been waiting for our arrival. Stirring sugar into the tea, looking into my eyes with a penetrating gaze that would not be satisfied with anything other than the absolute truth without beating around the bush, Abdullah said, "So! What happened to you? How come you're so down and out?"

The way I looked was totally uncouth: the shoulders of my shirt had grown dirty from sleeping on the ground and my collar was eaten away at the edges; my pants were bulging at the knees, frayed at the edges, and the cuffs were also eaten away; as for my shoes, their tops had become rolled up and filled with wrinkles and pimples and their soles had been completely worn out. As for my own face, it closely resembled my shoes. I found myself breaking down; a river of tears flowed out from under the lenses of my glasses whose frame was welded visibly above the nose.

Abdullah tossed his handkerchief to me over the table in a quick, decisive movement, and the muscles of his face had contracted in intense sternness as if to shout at me: Don't be a crybaby. I wiped away my tears immediately, then held them back by force.

Obviously I told him the story from beginning to end; he appeared to be extremely sad; his anxiety mounted so much that he started taking drags from the shisha then puffing them out in vexation. He remained silent for several long minutes. He stood up and took a ten-piaster note out of his pocket and tossed it down on the serving tray and pulled me by the arm and left, with my arm firmly planted under his. We went beyond Susi Street, and I was somewhat relieved; however, he turned us off of Souq Street onto Khairi Street, then back to Souq Street again. We passed by the Tawfiqiya Press. Memories both agonizing and delightful coming out of this press with the smell of paper and ink, mixed with the smell of fish stink and sewage, took me by surprise: this press had printed a booklet for me bearing a story that I had written entitled *The Smooth Cheek* whose price I collected in printed receipts from my colleagues and my teachers in the Institute, then I distributed it to them; it was more like a Ramadan imsakiya, which listed the schedule for the beginning and breaking of the fast every day during the month, but I loved it profoundly; my name was printed above it in a large black font like the great authors, except that I would beging to feel my heart sink whenever I remembered it now, since my family and all the folks of my village chalked it up alongside loose city women as one of the main things that had corrupted me and turned me into a lowly depraved boy. I remembered that it did not please Abdullah Effendi Abu Hantour, even though he encouraged me to print it by paying me a whole pound in exchange for a blank receipt that had no information, just as all my teachers in the Institute did. When he read it in a quarter of an hour as we sat in Muhammad Abu Sinn's shop he scolded me harshly because I had not shown it to him before printing it, and he pinched my ears for the brilliant rhetorical paragraphs I had lifted from al-Manfalouti and Muhammad Abd al-Halim Abdullah and

Amin Yusuf Ghurab and Yusuf al-Seba'i, then I stuck them all together in the text: whenever I wanted to describe the beloved with the smooth cheek I borrowed a whole paragraph of what one of those writers had said to describe a different beloved. But integrity demanded that I not do something like that; and if it was necessary, I had to put these paragraphs between quotation marks and put a note in the margin to say that it was taken from such-and-such a book on such-and-such a page of such-and-such an edition; that's if it was even possible for that to happen in stories and novels. In addition to this pinching lesson, he did not like anything in the story except my enthusiasm which he thought went too far and gave me the audacity to print and publish without thinking.

Abdullah stopped us at a big store selling fish and fasikh, filled with barrels and tables and customers. In a corner far away from him sat a man with a square face, pale like a candle with a long beard, a prayer-mark on his brow like a big date. Abdullah signaled me to stay standing where I was, then crossed the shop. The square-faced man stood up with great respect; Abdullah leaned to his ear and became absorbed in whispered speech; I noticed that the man stole fleeting glances at me full of shyness and spontaneity; I moved away from the door, keeping my back to the door. After a long time Abdullah came out, put his arm in mine, and off we went. We entered al-Khairi Street, where we headed toward the nearby alleys, where Abdullah stopped at shops and stores, then he disappeared for a moment and returned to take us to al-Sa'a Square. The square was truly beautiful; the walls of Mu'ati schools and the Municipal Cinema, and behind it the Municipal Library, which resembled all the official buildings in all the capitals saying "I am a government building"; and the Students' Café with glass walls and the long entrance hall like a banquet hall and the wide sidewalk raised above the ground, filled always and endlessly with patrons, most of whom were students and teachers and some employees and businessmen, young men with muscular bodies and girls with blue aprons and white caps and ornamental bags covering full bosoms, their pleasant bustle creating a friendly atmosphere and a delight to the eyes, the sounds of the backgammon pieces and the dice, and the shuffling cards and the sound of the bubbling shishas and the high-pitched laughter of women; and the cups and teapots and the trays gleamed brilliantly, and the floor as well, and the tablecloths, and the glass of the walls, so much so that the coffeeshop in the night looked like a swimming pool with bright neon lights demarcating its walls. Before it al-Nadi Street, the pride of the city with its cleanliness and its expansive, verdant garden, and the government officials' club, and the Delta train, which goes through a part of the street coming from nearby villages going to other villages or adjacent suburbs, letting out its whistle like the cry of a mother bereaved of her child, its cars looking empty except for some peasants, effendis, students, and livestock on their way to the market or to the slaughterhouse.

Abdullah would stop at some stores, think about going in, then leave at the last moment, until I was surprised by him heading for the company that specialized in selling goods made in Egypt. He pulled me inside to stand a few moments in some corners and at some counters, and he bought me a pair of pants of beautiful blue waterproof fabric, and another pair of gray woolen trousers; and two shirts with wide collars, and two sets of underclothes and two gallabiyas for sleeping, and shoes without laces, and two pairs of socks, and two handkerchiefs. He measured all of it on my body with perfection and accuracy with regard to color and taste and material. Then he paid a large sum which startled me and plunged me into oceans of embarrassment and sweat while secretly I felt delight and joy. He carried something and I carried several things; then he hailed a horse-drawn carriage, pushed me into it, then got in next to me shouting to the driver, "Salah al-Din, Usta!" The driver tightened the reins; I bounced along with the clopping of the horses' hooves on the street asphalt, then on the wide cobblestones unevenly arranged like intertwining islands between the ruts of wastewater and drainage in the alleys of Salah al-Din neighborhood. We got off in front of an ancient three-story house with identical balconies on each floor. He went in ahead of me; we climbed the worn, winding marble stairway. On the third floor we stopped before a double door facing another door. He knocked on a door, then turned around and stood in front of the opposite door, which opened after a short while and from within which appeared a small child who quickly left us and darted off inside. The traditional sofas were facing us, upholstered in velvet fabric. On the opposite side was a set of gilded salon chairs, and on the ground an expensive bright colored rug. On the wall facing us was a picture of Sheikh Hassan al-Banna, with his kind and gentle face, and his short fez and short, well-groomed beard as if it had been merely painted on with a brush by a steady-handed painter. On the side wall was a picture of the Colonel Gamal Abdel Nasser completely absorbed in a game of chess. On the facing wall was a very ancient picture of a very old man wearing a wool cloak and skullcap of crushed wool like a Maghribi fez; his features betrayed his Maghribi origins, and I guessed that he was the grandfather of Abdullah Abu Hantour.

He closed the door and placed the things on the sofa, then asked permission and entered; he lifted the curtain to reveal an open corridor. I sat down; on the oval-shaped marble table I saw a large number of magazines: *al-Da'wa*, *Minbar al-Islam*, *al-Risala*, and *al-Thaqafa*, and some Islamic school plays written by Sheikh Abdel Rahman al-Banna, and a large copy of the Qur'an with commentary by al-Jalalayn, and the *Mukhtar al-Sihah* dictionary; and directly behind me a large, wide bookcase with closed glass doors through which rows of precious bound books with their titles written on their spines in gold leaf were visible. I had no sooner started flipping through a few issues of *al-Risala* when the curtain was thrown back and Abdullah Effendi appeared wearing a fine cotton *gallabiya* and a skullcap; he said, "Come on." I got up and followed behind him down the long passageway. We passed by an open kitchen from which appeared rows of cooking pots and plates and a refrigerator and a gas stove and oven, and the aromas of heated ghee and mouth-watering grilled meat.

At the next door we stopped; it was the bathroom. He motioned me to enter, then made a circular movement with his hand around his head and chest and body. I went in, I saw the shower and the loofah and the perfumed bar of soap above it, and the big towel hanging on a hook behind the door, which Abdullah closed from outside until the latch clicked into place. I took off all my clothes, turned on the shower, and began scrubbing my body with the loofah and soap in a torrent of rapture under a downpour of rain and a splashing noise, which mixed with the sound of the radio in the next room in which I could make out the voice of Mahmoud Sharif in the program *Qisam* as he sang enchantingly about good times and happiness with his family and children. No sooner had I turned off the shower and the splashing noise stopped than the sound of the radio suddenly got louder with the sound of the earthy nay with the burning sighs immediately followed by the voice of Rafi'a al-Shal moaning *I wonder where you are, Marzouq*. Then soon after that came to me the image of my mother as she squatted on the doorstep of our house in the village crying as she heard this same sentence directly after this nay, as if she too had a missing Marzouq she was consumed by desire to meet.

I heard footsteps on the other side of the door, and someone clearing their throat, and the sound of light tapping. I wrapped the towel around myself, I opened the door a crack, I grabbed the underwear and the white gallabiya, and the smell of the new fabric was intoxicating. Then I came out of the bathroom a completely new man, such that Abdullah Effendi looked at me and nodded his head in satisfaction as he led me toward the room with the radio, which was occupied by a dining table and chairs and its glass china cabinets chock-full of china dishes and glasses and cups and silverware. The food dishes were set out on the table like a full banquet from which rose steam and spicy, delicious aromas. He sat down opposite me, offering me a small folded napkin and I put it under my elbow. He said "In the name of God, most gracious, most merciful," then began eating; and I did likewise: we had rice and green beans and mulukhiya with meat; and panfried chicken and salads and pickles, and bananas and pears and guavas, and dishes of pudding.

In the sitting room he lit a cigarette for himself and another for me then he said, "Why don't you get up and try on these clothes?"

I put on a shirt with the light blue pants, and socks, then the new shoes. I found myself wrapped in the beautiful perfumed smell as if I was on the first day of the Eid getting ready to receive a gift of cash from my father and to go out to run around in the streets where I would ride on swings and buy cotton candy and cones with hidden prizes and sugarcane and harisa. Abdullah Effendi disappeared, then all of a sudden he came in wearing street clothes different from those he had had on when I met him. He was holding an old, beat up suitcase but which had working locks and a handle. He leaned it on the sofa and opened it, and I saw my own old clothes within it. He said as he pointed to them with his beard, "You can throw them away anywhere or donate them to the poor."

Then he unfolded that day's newspaper on top of them and carefully placed the rest of my new clothes inside; then he closed the locks and gave it to me. I took it and felt, in spite of its shabby appearance that I had become a true, genuine effendi. He led me and closed the door behind him and went out and I followed him.

Another horse-drawn carriage dropped us off at the beginning of Susi Street, where we turned directly into Muhammad Abu Sinn's shop. He was sitting as usual behind the counter next to the door, leaving the selling up to two young men who were my age but who were highly trained, both of them healthy and strong, holding the roll of fabric in their left hands, and bouncing it like a ball to loosen its folds before proceeding to measure it with the yardstick, which was only two marks dug lightly into the wood of the counter itself. They displayed great patience, which they learned from their master Abu Sinn. Each walked with the customers, especially the peasant women who came to pick up bridal trousseaus; it didn't bother the two young men to climb the ladder, showing great skill and agility, dozens of times to pull out some cloth from between blocks packed tightly together, then come down and separate the rolls on the counter, holding them by the edge and rubbing them with the tips of their fingers meaningfully to prove to the customer that the fabric was good and would not wrinkle, that it was well-woven and would not wear out. A customer might turn his face away at that moment and request that purple fabric which was near the ceiling; and in that case—without any hesitation—one of the young men would climb up and bring it and another one like it for him; yet the husband or the mother-in-law might refuse it before touching it, pointing to another roll in a faraway corner and he would take out the portable wooden ladder and head upward on it into that faraway corner to bring the fabric. What mattered was that the customer be satisfied with the merchandise; as for haggling over the prices, this was usually settled as soon as Abu Sinn intervened, giving the last word, so that the customer would leave completely satisfied with his purchase.

Muhammad Abu Sinn got up quickly, embracing me with a great acclaim: "Oh, oh, oh . . . oh my God! You old bum! Would this do—is this any way to behave toward your friends? Where've you been? We were talking about you yesterday. Abdullah Effendi is the one who remembered you and it is he who found you, it's a miracle!"

I lifted the flap in the countertop and passed through it to the inside. As for Abdullah Effendi he sat on the counter and dangled his legs in childlike glee, then slid inside and got off the counter. At that moment the tea vendor carrying the serving tray with the glasses and the large steaming teapot on it came by; he poured the small glasses of tea for us. The tea was better than coffeehouse tea, with a wonderful fresh homemade flavor.

Within several short sips, and with extraordinary eloquence, Abdullah Effendi summarized my problem in its entirety, then—as if it never happened—he concluded by saying, "What's important now is to find him work to support himself, perhaps he can change his career, or whatever God chooses to do with him."

At that point the eyes of Muhammad Abu Sinn had traveled to a far-off unknown land, they appeared so heavy with suffering that I felt that my own father had not grieved like this for me. Then he heaved a heartfelt sigh, and extracted his voice from a rusty sheath, "And Hagg Mas'oud? Where does he stand? Does he know what has happened?"

I bowed my head searching for an appropriate response; but Abdullah Effendi jumped in with an intelligence for which I thanked him, "Which Hagg Mas'oud, good friend? Leave it up to God! You know the whole story. Hagg Mas'oud can disown his very flesh and blood. Have you forgotten how he bought this house he lives in? How can you forget this horrific tragedy when you are his neighbor and you saw it with your own eyes when you were a child?"

Then he turned to me, certain that I perhaps did not know a thing about the story of this house which the husband of my cousin owned in the most important and affluent location in this large commercial city: "This house was inherited by a poor man whom God chose not to bless with children. He was addicted to gambling and he was indebted to the government for an advance from the bank for which the house was collateral. He lost the money in an unsuccessful risky business deal. The government foreclosed on the house. And that ape of a hagg was the one entrusted with collecting since he lived in the same house. He played a game in which his bid was successful at an auction and he bought the entire house for the price of one of its rooms. Immediately afterward the man died and it was said that the ape of a hagg had slipped him slow poison in cups of booze. God knows, but that ape of a hagg, no offense, is not a real man."

The intense embarrassment was clearly visibly on Muhammad Abu Sinn's face, after he raised his hand a number of times to silence Abdullah Effendi pointing with his chin toward me indicating that this bad-mouthing insulted me because this ape of a hagg was ultimately the husband of my cousin who was like a sister to me. Except Abdullah Effendi was embittered toward this man, not only because he was a dishonest thief hiding in hagg's clothing, but also, and especially, because he "has no loyalty to any of his relatives." And he added in disgust, "Look how he treats a poor boy like this! Isn't he like the brother of his wife? Look how he despises him and gets disgusted with him. If Hagg

Mas'oud had one drop of blood he would have given him any room on the roof to live in."

I remembered that I must have told them a little of how I was treated on the day I came to get prescription glasses and how they received me grudgingly, just as I told them many stories about my old father and his past full of riches and politics and the Wafd party, and how he was fired from his job as soon as the Wafd cabinet lost power. Yes, surely I had said that without knowing it, then I forgot I said it; and this must have been the reason for their sympathy for me. Abdullah Effendi said decisively, "Now our task is to find him a job in a hurry."

Muhammad Abu Sinn, sighing deeply in thought, said, "My shop cannot support three, but I will talk to my uncle Amin Saqr to take him on at his large shops, under the supervision of my brother. My uncle is a good man. My younger brother Mahmoud works for him at the buttons counter. The large shops sell all kinds of haberdashery. The buttons department alone needs many of a particular type. They need a salesman who is gentle, calm, with good breath, well-mannered, and silver-tongued because most of the customers at this counter are women. I think that you would fit in at that counter and I'll tell my brother Mahmoud to take you with him. But for now, where do you live? How do you spend the night, and where?"

Abdullah Effendi signaled to him with his lips trying to clear things up a little bit for him, saying, "He is totally penniless. God has been generous to the Brothers so we have brought him new clothes. One hopes that we could find additional blessings for putting him up—this is your task."

Abu Sinn asked me, "Have you left the room where you lived with your colleagues?"

"Long ago."

"So where have you been staying?"

"At the Firdous Hotel behind the station."

They both wrinkled their noses in disgust, and Abu Sinn said, "Couldn't you find anyplace else? It's a hotbed of vagrants, thieves, swindlers, crooks, and homosexuals. And lice, fleas, and bedbugs! It's at least a hundred years old and they haven't changed the furniture since it opened. The good villagers know bedbugs intimately because of their long familiarity. Whoever stays there, no one respects him. The government is constantly raiding it and rounding up all the tenants."

I felt a tremor of fear; if these words were spoken about a licensed hotel with a fancy name, what would be said about Wikalat Atiya? And what would he say if he knew that, deep down inside, I felt a liking for Wikalat Atiya? If the Firdous Hotel, which operates with an official license and charges ten piasters a night for the lowliest bed, and requires that a guest have an I.D. card and precise documentation, has a reputation like this, then Wikalat Atiya does not represent a lower standard.

Suddenly Muhammad Abu Sinn said, "How about supper?"

I looked around and found that night had surrounded us a long time ago, and that we had spent a good long time talking, three-fourths of which escaped me at the very least. Abdullah Effendi said, "We ate lunch at my place but God's not against supper. Especially your supper which is like a work of art!"

"Baked, paper-wrapped beef is the recipe that never fails."

He motioned to the boy Handouqa on the opposite counter, and he sprang across the counter like an acrobat then disappeared down Susi Street. And after around a quarter of an hour he came back carrying a large bag with meat, onions, lemons, tomatoes, garlic, and gargir in it. He chopped them all into small pieces and put them on top of each other in a rectangle and wrapped it in paper, then wrapped it again in a slice of thick butcher's paper, then took it to the public bakery where he shoved it into the middle of the oven and left it for an hour; then he returned carrying it on a pile of hot pita loaves. Atop a pile of newspapers the wrapping was opened, producing a symphony of ingenious aromas wafting, creating feelings of longing, delight and appreciation for the good life. Let's let all of Susi Street with all its shop owners and customers share the banquet with us, I thought, it would certainly be enough for all of us and then some; but oh how roomy stomachs are; we dove into the food and we made a huge dent in it in several minutes. A tea seller passed and a seller of T-shirts and men's underwear who sold from a push cart next to Abu Sinn's shop, and the boy from the juice shop, who as soon as he saw us as he made his rounds, saw visions of four bottles of Spatis that could be ordered, and he stayed until he had eaten his share too. And the boy who greased the hinges of the storefront shutters came and found some grease and crumbs of the meat and fragments of onion and tomatoes and gargir and the rest of the pita bread, and he ate with gusto, and he did not forget in between every bite to utter prayers for our well being and the good fortune of the house, then he gathered the papers and remnants and kept them with him to toss them in a garbage can suspended on a lamp-post in the main street; and he volunteered to wipe the counter with his shirtsleeve. Muhammad Abu Sinn was pleased with him and ordered him another bottle of Spatis so that we would not have harmed him by taking prayers for less than what he had given us; and besides that, he gave him the usual tip for greasing the storefront shutter.

After this rich dinner we went toward the Abu al-Rish neighborhood, but we had not gotten far when we stopped before a building lit from outside by a sign saying: The Princes's Hotel. We went in. A man with a long beard and a distinct prayer mark on his forehead as large as a fig was holding prayer beads in his hand. Muhammad Abu Sinn approached him, putting his hand on my shoulder: "How are you, Hagg Salah? This man is special to us. Let him stay here for a few days. Look after him. Choose for him a bed in a single room befitting his person. Here—this should cover him for a whole week. After that he'll settle the account with you on a day to day basis, or maybe month to month."

Hagg Salah said, "In the name of God, most compassionate, most merciful," and "there is no power and no strength save in God," then opened the long, thick guestbook smeared with dirt and sweat. He requested my information. I dictated it to him.

"Do you have anything to deposit?"

"I have my suitcase with my clothes."

"Keep it with you, the place is safe. What I meant was, do you have anything valuable, like a lot of money or gold boullion or anything like that which someone would be tempted to steal, in order to put it for you here in the safe deposit box and give it back when you want?"

"Thank you Hagg Salah, I don't have anything."

He called, "You there." A black young man with a sense of humor and gaps in his teeth rushed to us. Hagg Salah said as he took from a board behind his head on the wall a key with a piece of brass with an engraved number upon it, "Take the ustaz to number forty-five!"

The room was cozy; in it was a beautiful bed with brass posts, a long wardrobe with a double-door, a small wooden table, and a bamboo chair. The table was covered with an old newspaper, an ashtray, and a glass of water. Abu Sinn pushed me in, putting his hand firmly in mine when, to my surprise, a whole pound ended up in my hand; I got goosebumps all over my body from delight and gratitude, then I put it in my pocket. He said, "Let me see you often. Give me half a month to arrange the job with my uncle. Good night!"

I left them at the door of the hotel. I went back to the room. I remembered that I had been craving a cigarette all day; I returned to the street to buy two Hollywood cigarettes. When I went out I felt how pleasurable it is for a man to walk at night on city streets certain that he had shelter to which he could return whenever he wished.

"You've Eaten Our Bread, Elaishy"

I visited Muhammad Abu Sinn at his shop regularly in the evening. I would stay with him until the nightly gatherings began at the home of Sayyed Elaishy, a friend of his. Sayyed was a third-year student at law school and a prominent member of the Muslim Brotherhood, where he was quite active at the local branch and very popular with the young men who took part in numerous artistic, sporting, and boy-scouting activities. He loved to travel, especially to faraway places such as al-Wadi al-Gadid, Fayoum, Safaga, and Hurghada to get acquainted with the young men, our many "brothers." He believed firmly that a new friend was like a new book that you read and learned from, not to mention the strength in numbers that you acquired when your family of acquaintances and friends grew larger. He was a very nice man, sturdily built with staid, solid features. He had a big head and face, clean-shaven with short-cropped hair like other respectable city-dwelling effendis. His round, red face looked like the sun just before sunset. He was always smiling, always on the verge of emitting a sharp, joyous laugh that reverberated like the sound of a pestle hitting a mortar. He displayed great poise and his polite way of speaking hinted at shyness. He was modest in the way he dressed and the way he chose colors, reserved in the way he walked and looked, as was befitting someone about to become a future district attorney or illustrious lawyer within a few months. His father was an old, established grain merchant who had inherited his business from his father and grandfathers. The business was so well established that the elders of the Salah al-Din neighborhood said that the store that Hagg Salim al-Elaishy operated was the very same that a long line of grandfathers had operated for centuries. All that had changed, they insisted, were fresh coats of paint and the addition of a few modern chairs. Even the old wooden bench next to the door was said to be as old as the store itself. They said that from Mamluk times up to the Second World War throngs of the poor and hungry had gathered in front of the door of the store, shouting in disapproval, "You've eaten our bread, Elaishy!"

That was because the original Grandpa Elaishy was a tax collector for the sultan in charge of the whole province: he collected an agreed-upon amount of crops from the peasants. What happened was that he delivered the crops from his own granaries, then he himself dealt with the peasants. The sultan supplied guards and policeman who helped him collect, sometimes by force, or occasionally by land confiscation. And even though that system had been abandoned as time went by, Elaishy III, IV, or V, each in his own era, had been well-versed in politics, economics, and agricultural crops and hoarded the crops for long periods of time to sell at many times their actual value in times of shortage, especially during wars and droughts. So, whenever there was a shortage in bread, people immediately thought of Elaishy whose name had become synonymous with such crises and they gathered in front of the ancient store, shouting angrily, "You've eaten our bread, Elaishy!"

It was Sayyed Elaishy himself who told such stories, jovially making fun of his family of grain merchants who had come to own half the real estate in both the old and new Salah al-Din neighborhoods and agricultural land in Kom Hamada, Itay al-Barud, and other places. Most of their land had consisted of vineyards and orchards producing guavas, mangoes, pears, and bananas, tended and guarded by new generations of Elaishys who married and settled near those orchards. Elaishy's gifts to his friends and colleagues were bushels of grapes, mangoes, oranges, tangerines, and all kinds of dates. And even though there were always tons of food at all the Elaishy households, Sayyed loved to have supper nightly at the famous and clean Khat'an Restaurant where he was shown great respect and consideration befitting his family's position. Dishes of kabab, vegetables with lamb shanks, rabbit, and cracked wheat-stuffed pigeon would be served four nights a week when he invited his favorite group of friends, which included Abu Sinn and Abu Hantour. There was also an old lawyer named Mahmoud Abu Tor, a young lawyer named Suleiman Balba', a high-school English teacher named Salah al-Askari, and a student in the Faculty of Arts named Umar al-Laqani. These men, however, I knew only by name and occupation and I met them only, for the most part, at these gatherings with Sayyed Elaishy. Abu Sinn would close his shop at about ten in the evening or quit at nine or so, leaving his nephew in charge. The latter, Fikri Fayid, an intelligent and polite high school student who resembled his uncle in most respects, would come after school to help his uncle and, in his absence, sat at the cash register in his place.

Abdullah Effendi Hantour, Muhammad Abu Sinn, and I would go to a café in Khairy Street where friends gathered and from there we all went to Khat'an Restaurant for dinner or, on the other three nights of the week, at the place of either Suleiman Balba' or Umar al-Laqani. On such occasions the quality of the supper would be quite inferior to what we got at Khat'an's. Sometimes it would be pitifully improvised, especially at Laqani's place since his mother was in poor health and he himself was not married, for the time being, in protest against the rampant permissiveness among Egyptian girls, brought about by the July Revolution in the name of women's liberation and all the decadence auguring the Day of Judgment. After supper we would all go to Elaishy's house on Salah al-Din Street in his father's Buick, which he used only at night and in which we could all fit comfortably. After that Elaishy would hurry to the store to fetch his father, who would be done for the day and waiting for his son with the door left ajar.

Their home was quite awesome, built on a huge lot that occupied two street corners. It had four floors with wide, round balconies that had friezes and a colorful iron railing. The rooms were big and the staircase had very wide and long genuine marble stairs. We would go upstairs, all the way to the roof whose floor had big, colored tiles. All around in a circle stood potted plants resting on metal holders like those supporting huge water-cooling jars. As for the thick, round wall, it contained rectangular brick-lined black-soil flower beds with roses and aromatic flowers. Facing us, in a big corner of the wall was a beautiful staircase shaded by hyacinths, grape vines, and rows of jasmine. That was the special room, originally meant for a laundry room but Sayyed had taken it since he finished primary school and made it his personal study where he read and received his friends. It was a true gem, big enough for a whole apartment. As soon as you entered, you would be surprised to see a huge library, all the walls lined with carved wooden bookcases, filled with dozens of large and small books, magazines, and newspapers. There were copper, bronze, and marble statues and precious rugs and French-style chairs and Egyptian-style sofas. There was a small banister connected with what looked like a door to the right of the entrance. Upon closer inspection you'd find a very elegant and clean staircase leading down to the apartment where Sayyed's mother and his siblings lived, opposite the other apartment where his father's older wife lived. Sayyed's paternal uncles and their married sons lived on the other floors. Sayyed would often leave us to go down that staircase and return a short while later carrying tea or coffee or orange juice or lemonade and chilled and delicious plates of out-of-season fruits. Then the evening would begin with a reading in one of al-Aqqad's *Genius* series or Taha Hussein's *al-Fitna al-Kubra* or one of Khalid Muhammad Khalid's works. Each of us would read until he got tired and another would begin. After every few pages, voices would rise all at once in a somewhat unstructured conversation, which would soon subside when the person reading resumed, asking that discussion be postponed until the end of the chapter at least.

Recently I began to see Sayyed Elaishy in a new light: I was surprised at how I hadn't thought of him since my painful homelessness began. I thought I should probably talk to him now about my personal circumstances; maybe he would find me a job in one of their well-established, prosperous stores or at least put in a word for me with one of the big merchants in the city who had stores chock-full of merchandise and workers. The city of Damanhour was full of huge, very well-stocked stores such as those of Mahmoud al-Khawalqa whose housewares stores were filled with all the needs of kitchens and bridal trousseaus, so much so that a visitor would need a whole day and night just to stop at all the counters and corners. Then there were the stores of Messiri, which sold underwear, cotton garments, and bedding and bath goods produced by his own factories and which also exported the stuff overseas. Ghurab's haberdashery stores had signs that said they had at least a hundred-thousand items for sale. Each of those merchants led a wondrous life and one of the most amazing things about that was that all the people of Damanhour saw it and almost touched it and were affected by it for the better or worse, and yet they didn't believe it if someone told them about it. No one believed it, for instance, if someone were to tell him that the housewares merchant or his peers had his own butcher shop whose primary duty was to supply his house with meat that was guaranteed fresh; as for selling to others, that was just icing on the cake. Nor would they believe it if they were told that some of those merchants had apartments, not only in Alexandria but in London, Paris, Frankfurt, and Switzerland as well. Or that they had stores on the side selling vegetables, fruits, and poultry that suffered no shortage because they were provisioned by these merchants' own farms and orchards in Behaira's fertile countryside. These wealthy people had no problems with the tax department since everyone was quite well fed. So, it would be beautiful and wonderful if Sayyed Elaishy, who was a "brother in God" as he often said, could get me a job with one of those moguls as a bookkeeper or sales clerk. It would be even more beautiful and wonderful if he were moved by my psychological and housing conditions and allowed me to live or just to spend the night temporarily in this fantastic clean room.

Thus I had made up my mind to find an appropriate moment to talk to him about my situation. But it occurred to me: if that were possible for Sayyed Elaishy, why hadn't it occurred to Muhammad Abu Sinn when he was thinking how to help me? I was afraid that if I talked to Elaishy about myself that Abu Sinn might get angry. So I decided to postpone it until Abu Sinn had told me that he had given up on his uncle's stores finding me a job. On the night that I was convinced I should give Elaishy an idea about my situation just to pave the way for an outright request, something I hadn't expected at all took place. We had been treated by him to a supper of grilled pigeon at Khat'an and had eaten so much we could hardly move. We had no desire to read especially since the night before we had finished reading Ali Abd al-Raziq's *al-Islam wa usul al-khum* in a rare and smuggled edition and had not settled yet on which new book to start reading. We sat on the cushions on the rug smoking voraciously and drinking strong tea. It was then that Umar al-Laqani suddenly told Sayyed Elaishy, "Brother Abd al-Hamid Mehaina asked about you by telephone twice at the branch and he was persistent."

Sayyed Elaishy wrinkled his nose and waved his arm in disgust which made Umar al-Laqani add, "I almost brought him here with me."

Sayyed Elaishy sat up suddenly and pointed his finger in a serious threatening gesture: "Don't you dare! Unless you wish to lose me!"

Al-Laqani's face turned as red as a ripe watermelon from embarrassment and surprise.

"Why? He is a poor, struggling young man with a heart of gold. He truly and undoubtedly loves you. Besides, he is polite and devoted to his religious obligations, to the Qur'an and to the feelings of his friends. And, as far as I know, you love him."

Sayyed Elaishy knit his brow and twisted his neck in a bored gesture of dismissal. Then, feigning calm, he said, "I know all that and it's true. Otherwise I wouldn't have helped him. You know I've spent hundreds of pounds on him and I'm ready to go on spending hundreds more. I'm willing to pay his tuition and expenses at al-Azhar until he graduates. I'm also willing to buy him and his family clothes from the zakat money that my father sets aside every year, which is plentiful, thank God. But I am not willing to sit with him or give him a chance to be my friend and sit with me like an equal. He comes from a very low background and his father is from one of those nomadic gypsy tribes. Besides, he's envious and I hate envious people. If you get friendly with him, he will stop looking up to you and when that happens he will grow bolder and make fun of you and that which might have begun in charity will become almost an obligation on your part. I know this kind of person. My father's store is a huge place that gives me ample opportunity to watch them and observe their character traits. But, in any case, let's forget about him now. We want to clear our heads to read Aqqad's book on Iblis!" Laqani fell awkwardly silent as if he had been insulted. Strangely enough, neither Abu Hantour nor Abu Sinn made any comment or tried to argue with him even though both were visibly displeased. After a short while Abu Hantour stretched his long neck with his chipped face, which under the lights coming from the corners of the room, looked like a group of intertwined triangles. In a profoundly sly and roundabout way as if telling a jovial joke, he said, "Who needs Iblis tonight? We need to send him away rather than to summon him!"

Abu Sinn grinned, showing his big teeth which revealed a smile simultaneously intelligent and dumb. He dropped his jaw in a significant gesture as if afraid of the consequences of Abu Hantour's barb. It was at that point that I realized the futility of any hope as far as Elaishy was concerned. I also became certain that if he found out that I had rearranged the math teacher's face and pounced on him, resulting in my dismissal from the institute and my becoming a bum, and if he also found out that

I came from a poor, destitute family to begin with, he would hold me in great contempt and maybe would tell his friends not to bring me along when they visited. Something inside me told me to deliberately show him excessive contempt, to stop going to his place on my own and to act indifferent if I came upon him by chance. I also decided to stop going to the Muslim Brotherhood branch completely for I was not yet a member. Besides, I was no longer dazzled by their sermons as I kept reading, with them or on my own, even though I loved many of them dearly and had great respect for them.

And I did stop going to the branch of which I was not fond to begin with but especially after I discovered the National Guard headquarters at the garden of the government employee club, which had many soccer and other ball fields, boxing and wrestling rings, tracks for running, hurdle jumping, shot-putting and military drills, and the like. The main attraction for me, however, was the drama club whose membership comprised the cream of Damanhour high school students and university students who studied in Alexandria and who commuted by train. It also comprised another group of students who had failed to graduate like myself and Wael Abu al-Nasr, who hadn't finished high school but was a good oud, saxophone, and accordion player and who adored acting in view of his good looks and attractive physique. He had thick, well-coiffed hair that parted in the middle and slightly covered his forehead. He was indeed a good actor, what else could he be with his looks and his fancy shiny patent leather shoes? He had achieved considerable fame in Damanhouri society from popular stages to the employee club to large school parties to official celebrations organized by the governorate or the Liberation Organization on national occasions such as Evacuation Day, celebrating the departure of British troops, or July Revolution anniversaries. He even took part in weddings celebrated on the Municipal Cinema stage or on platforms set up in the street, performing his own skits together with his own troupe made up of available amateurs. In some of the skits he performed monologues that he wrote, or those written by Damanhouri poets and songwriters such as Hamid al-Atmas, Hamdi al-Ni'na'i, or Abd al-Muttilib Mungi. The monologues were accompanied by short, very well-presented theatrical pieces that consisted of jokes and anecdotes about popular types familiar to all strata of Damanhouri society. He also played the leading role in the play *Noble Honor* which he wrote and directed for the National Guard theatrical troupe. In that play he played a college student who was so incensed by the British occupation that he volunteered to fight in the city of Ismailia, declaiming Ahmed Shawqi's verses:

True honor cannot be protected against harm
Unless blood is shed for it;
Only blood covered hands can open freedom's red door.

Wael had taken a liking to me after he was convinced that I was a true theater afficionado and after I had given him some artistic observations on the structure of his play and the acting troupe. So he made me an understudy for the role of the pasha in case our friend Ma'mun Farid Ghanim, who went to the Faculty of Arts at Alexandria University was unable to take part. I memorized the lines and played the role during the nighttime rehearsals when our friend couldn't attend. That made me so happy that I walked the streets of the city at the end of the night feeling that I was somebody, at least for a few hours, after which everything collapsed on the threshold of sleep.

Remembering that I had stopped going to the rehearsals for some time gave me a deep feeling of delight as if I had discovered some freedom inside the prison of the night. I immediately started looking in my memory for the real reason I had stopped going to rehearsals for quite a few nights. I realized that my shabby clothes and wretched appearance had made me ashamed of going to the club or even passing in front of it. So, when I found myself dressed in the still new clothes, I enthusiastically headed for the club in a semi-military step by which I had always tried to emulate the way city effendis walked. In the end, however, I arrived after nine o'clock at night since I usually first dropped in on Muhammad Abu Sinn's shop to drink tea in the hope of finding out something about the job he was trying to get me at one of his uncle's stores. After a while, however, I got tired of that futile daily routine, so I began to go only once every few days. My prepaid stay at the hotel had elapsed but I continued to live there at Abu Sinn's expense. That lasted for many months. One morning, the man with the long beard at the hotel very politely told me to take my suitcase with me. I understood at once that I shouldn't return to the hotel without money in my hand. I felt quite dispirited. My new clothes were going to become dirty again from homelessness and aimlessness in the dirty night and the wet and dusty sidewalks.

Badriya

I had no money at all. The suitcase seemed like a heavy burden, a serious problem. I couldn't just go on carrying it everywhere forever. I had to get rid of it somewhere safe. God inspired me to pass in front of the store of my friend, Hamdi al-Zawawi, who sold cigarettes, shisha tobacco, and some candy. I used to stop by his store and stand there with him for hours talking about nothing in particular. If a long time passed and only a few customers came by, I would sit on the counter with my legs dangling over the entrance with a cup of tea in my hand, with Hamdi al-Zawawi next to me on the inside of the store leaning his elbows on the counter. He would draw my attention to the bodies of women passing by, which he considered works of art from God the Creator. It was at noon and the sun was tarrying above his store, setting it on fire and he had lowered the canvas awning and stood behind the counter, bent and busily squeezing a lime on a plate of ful whose aroma cried out: "Long live al-Asi ful!"

I turned and my stretched shadow extended, covering the plate of ful, the two loaves of bread, the two onions, and the salad and pickle plate. Hamdi straightened up, his eyes popping in surprise. He had not seen me in a very long time. He bent, stretching his arms across the counter, his right eye with a light pellicle squinting. He extended his long thin nose that looked like a flattened pencil and his thin eyebrows heavy with black shadows and his fine mouth under the yoke of a thick mustache that had been carefully and visibly trimmed by tweezers and thread. I bent over the counter and embraced him and we kissed on the cheeks. Then I placed the suitcase on the counter in such a way that he understood that I had been carrying it in the streets for months. Then I jumped and sat directly next to the ful plate. Hamdi craned his long, pointed neck toward the street shouting: "Fahmi!" whereupon a ten-year-old boy who looked like a small man in a full formal suit, including a necktie, and who carried himself with equally fitting decorum, appeared. That was Fahmi al-Nazir, son of Hamdi al-Zawawi's sister from the goldsmith whose shop was directly next to Hamdi's store. Fahmi was a primary school student, a member of the National Guard drama club who played the role of the pasha's eloquent son with amazing ability. He shook hands with me warmly, like a man, considering that we were colleagues in the same troupe and acted together like peers in many scenes. His uncle shouted, "A plate of ful and four loaves, quick!" He disappeared right away only to reappear immediately, gesturing with his arms elegantly indicating that our order was already on its way. And indeed, as soon as we finished the first plate, a young man in a white apron with 'al-Asi' knitted in red lettering across the chest next to a drawing of a ful pot out of which peered the elegant hand of a ladle, came in, placed the tray with its precious plates in front of us, then left.

What an appetite! Hamdi al-Zawawi had quietly withdrawn and lit the alcohol burner under the counter and placed the teapot on top of it and soon the aromatic scent of the tea filled up the place as I continued to wipe the plate with the last morsels of bread with great pleasure. When I held the small frothy glass teacup, my mouth was chewing that last morsel of ful. With utmost pleasure I took my first sip of tea which washed down the last of the ful as Hamdi al-Zawawi handed me a fresh Hollywood cigarette and pushed the empty plates aside and leaned his elbows on the counter next to me as usual. He began to draw on the cigarette as his cheeks receded into his mouth and his lips wrinkled as if he were

French-kissing a houri, with infinite lust. As he exhaled thick puffs of smoke he said, "What kind of friend do you call yourself? Where've you been? Is this any way to treat your friends?"

I nudged him with the tips of my fingers in his frizzy hair, "Life is a disgusting, trifling affair. Isn't that what we've always agreed upon?"

As usual he didn't ask me about any details despite his willingness to listen endlessly. And because I was certain of his absolute confidence in me and everything I said, and felt that he wouldn't hesitate to empty his cash register into my pocket if I asked for a loan or any other thing, I always refrained from trying to borrow money from him. He always looked so kind that I imagined, I don't know why, that he was the wretched victim of a con game that robbed him of the store that provided him with his livelihood, while he stood there, puzzled and meek and helpless, always on the verge of tears. His well-off family often taunted him as the only failure in the family because of his goodness and naïveté. His brothers counted among their number a lawyer, a doctor, a police officer, a teacher, a school principal, and a garment factory owner. He, on the other hand, barely finished primary school and for years was a source of shame to his mother and father until his well-off mother helped him by renting this store and filling it with merchandise, leaving him on his own to sink or swim in the river of life. He struggled to stand on his two feet and had it not been for living rent-free he would have had an even harder life. Hamdi decided to hold off marriage until he was totally independent.

Hamdi always looked pitiable, especially as he got ready for the cigarette delivery tricycle, as he awkwardly tried to put together the price of the merchandise, even though only a short while earlier he had given a whole pound for some charitable cause or another. If he hadn't done so he would have easily paid off the invoice. Hamdi was the only one who would lend me whatever I wanted without hesitation or asking about the details, and yet I found myself completely unwilling to borrow from him, contenting myself with the cigarettes that he showered upon me and the tea that he treated me to whenever I stopped by his store.

There was a humming noise filling the city sky, providing a thick background for the sounds of cars and car horns and vendors' calls in the vegetable and fish markets and Susi Street directly behind us. The sound gradually drew nearer and more distinct as the music of bagpipes, drums, bugles, and brass instruments played on. It was the police band which soon appeared, its sound drowning all the sounds on the street. Behind it there appeared columns of very tall men wearing khaki uniforms with red belts and sashes. Behind the band marched long lines of policemen to the delightful sound of the drums. Some women on balconies greeted the procession with resounding shrill joyful ululations which prompted Hamdi al-Zawawi to proclaim in a voice hoarse with desire, "Boy, oh boy! That's the real thing! The real police! Let the police force show off as much as they like. The ululation police are much more potent!"

Like everyone else we went to stand by the door to watch the police parade, which was organized by the security department almost every week. In addition to the different branches of police—the traffic cops, the public security corps, the fire brigade, the public utilities squad, and the markets police—there were also school children carrying banners with the names of their schools or institutes and their own music bands wearing boy scout uniforms with green sashes, neckpieces, and khaki shirts and shorts. Somewhat dejectedly I remembered that I could've been among them had I not, through my misbehavior, been kicked out of the paradise of effendis and become a homeless imposter.

The rear of the small, pint-sized parade was now receding with its clamor when I paid farewell to Hamdi al-Zawawi, asking him to keep my suitcase until I collected it, sooner or later, depending on circumstances. No sooner did I step out than he called me back and shook a pack of Hollywood cigarettes that was in his hand and, looking inside it he found six cigarettes. He threw it to me and I caught it and, without a word of thanks, I hurried off, as if I had a pressing appointment in one government office or another. I began to walk aimlessly on Sagha Street, thinking of heading for Wikalat Atiya. But how could I go there without money? My mind became foggy so I walked around with no particular destination, looking at the shop windows as if I were planning to rob or invade them.

There passed by me a figure tapping the asphalt rhythmically with heavy heels: tuck, tuck, tuck, tuck. I watched the body from the back. It seemed somewhat familiar: that solid straight back with two clearly delineated cheeks, from the broad shoulders to the narrow waist and the large, round, dome-like behind. An edifice oozing femininity and lust; a giant that only the god of sex himself could satisfy. Two well-turned legs with calves as white and rich as genuine marble. Two succulent heels on sandals displaying their captive crimson blood. Quite a spectacle, especially given that the dress she had on was so tight it clearly revealed all the hidden contours of her body, and so translucent you could see the straps of her pink shift that matched the color of her body and from which there appeared little swatches of skin between the shoulders and the arms, and the neck covered by thick, shining black hair held in place on the forehead by a red ribbon resting on the back in the form of a broom. Everyone who walked behind her hastened his steps until he caught up with her and then whispered something in her ear as she dashed like an arrow, totally indifferent even though she seemed happy and delighted with the commotion she had created on the street. But no sooner did the man catching up with her see her face than he retreated, turning his face away. Perhaps he would utter a shocked cry of disbelief or unashamedly mutter something like, "I take refuge in God!" or "God Almighty! I am not objecting to Your will!" That was because there was a huge difference between her face and her back. Yet there were always boors who harassed her. When that happened, she would stop for a moment, staring at him in mad anger and sharp rebuke or a fearless, deterrent slap on the face or she would call the police.

I, in turn, hastened my steps after her, as if I were not aware of her. She had stopped and was muttering angry words in a low, threatening voice at some young men standing on the street corner. I went a few steps beyond her then turned, as if spontaneously, to face her directly. What embarrassment! It was Badriya al-Qabbani, my cousin's daughter who was about forty, still unmarried because of her huge lips. For even though she had such a beautiful and radiant face, full of vitality and appeal, her huge and unnatural lips were so shocking that one wished she'd have surgery to reduce the two pouches of fat. You'd imagine that if you kissed her your whole head would disappear between those lips that looked like the trunk of an elephant or the mouth of a sack tied with a sturdy rope.

"What's wrong, Badriya? What happened?" I asked her.

Blood rushed to her face and her wide eyes grew so wide that I felt myself drowning in her black eyes. "Hello! How are you?" she said in genuine warm welcome and shook my hand affectionately. I felt my thin hand disappear in the grip of a soft and tender hand, topped by a wristful of gold bracelets. "It's nothing. Just some good-for-nothing boys standing on street corners."

The boys had withdrawn to a far corner, pretending to be preoccupied in great shame and embarrassment.

"Don't mind them! Can I be of service?" I said.

"Thanks," she said and resumed walking, gesturing me to walk with her. I did and after a while she said, "How are you? We haven't seen you in quite a long time. How's the Institute? Tell me, what's the story that my brother Karam tells us about the Institute? Is it true that you wanted to kill the math teacher and that they kicked you out?"

I felt as if the earth were swaying under my feet and I said, "Yes, it is true."

She looked at me in disbelief: "How? Why? How could you? Since when did we have murderous killers in our family? I can't believe you did that!"

I told her the real story briefly. She looked genuinely moved: "It's a pity! You've ruined your future for nothing! What are you going to do now? By God, this is so sad!"

"I will go to Alexandria to work at the Banna watch factories. As you know, he's one of my father's closest friends, before he became rich, from the days that he was poor and destitute in our village."

Her lower lip dropped to reveal straight beautiful teeth. She said, "Does Banna remember the days he was poor? How are you going to meet him? Do you have a connection?"

I hadn't thought about the prospect at all before. It must have been lying dormant deep inside me and only now made its spontaneous appearance. I found myself saying what I thought of doing, "I have a letter from my father and one from Banna's uncle from the village. I'll send them from the factory gate and wait for permission to enter."

"God be with you."

I was surprised to see that we were in front of their house. I stopped as she kept walking. She came back two steps toward me.

"Why did you stop?"

"I'll leave you in God's care."

She looked at me in protest, unlike her family's coldness: "That's not done. Come on in."

She put her hand on my shoulder and gently prodded me to cross the door to the staircase directly. My heart danced fast in my chest, filling me with feelings of fear, delight, elation, and anxiety.

The house was uncharacteristically still like a tomb. The staircase was clean, recently washed. The door of the first floor was closed and so were the second and the third. At the fourth floor Badriya stopped on the landing while I stopped a few stairs below, leaning on the banister, my nose almost diving between the two large, strong buttocks and the smell of an overpowering feminine perfume almost intoxicating me. She opened her bag and took out the key, opened the door and entered. I followed. On this floor Badriya, Yusriya, and Shukriya slept in an apartment that had four bedrooms and a square parlor furnished with Asyut-style bamboo chairs. From the parlor a narrow spiral staircase descended to the third floor, also made up of four rooms where Hagg Mas'oud and Hagga Wadida slept and a parlor from which a staircase descended to the second floor where Mimi, Sharif, Safwat, and Karam slept. As for the first floor above the ground floor that two furniture stores occupied, the three oldest sons, Hawwas, Badi‘, and Maguid slept and there also the family received its guests.

I sat in the parlor on one of the chairs while Badriya disappeared in her room. After a short while she came out wearing a sleeveless translucent silk gown, having gathered her hair in a single, hat-like plait. Then she fixed me with her eyes: "Shall I get you a gallabiya?"

Without waiting for an answer she disappeared down the spiral staircase. The stairs squeaked as I kept looking around in astonishment: where had everybody gone? The house was now totally empty, except for her and me. The wooden stairs began to squeak again as Badriya reappeared carrying one of her brother Karam's gallabiyas. Karam was the same age but somewhat bigger than me. She threw the gallabiya merrily toward me making sure it was spread over me. Then she let out a resounding laugh as she watched me trying to free my head from it and said, "There you are. Take off your clothes and come help me in the kitchen."

Then she headed for the kitchen which was only two steps away. I undid my belt and let the pants drop to my feet, then freed my feet and took off my shirt and folded it and my pants and put on the gallabiya and walked in my bare feet.

"You are here all by yourself, Badriya. Where did everybody go?"

"They all went to the village to attend the wedding of Samir, son of my sister Tahani. They left me here to watch the house because the Hagg has many enemies and everyone covets what we have. I'll catch up with them in a week after the Hagg settles his accounts with people over there for the crops and comes back with my sister Shukriya. Then I will go. Shall I make you tea? Or would you like some soda? We'll have lunch together shortly."

The ful was still sitting in my stomach so I said, "I'll have some soda."

She motioned with her chin to the refrigerator while she washed some dishes in the kitchen sink. It was the first time for me to open a refrigerator and see the inside. There were layers of colored lights and shelves and corners and drawers filled with meat and fish and chicken and fruits and bottles of water and soda. I looked at the contents with pleasure then took a soda bottle and closed the refrigerator door. I saw the bottle opener hanging on a rope on a nail on the wall. I opened the bottle and began to drink the sharp liquid with great relish. Badriya was now moving quite freely before me and as she bent to open a cabinet, the collar of her gown would recede, revealing her unrestrained bulging breasts and the gap between them. As her backside kept me hemmed in as I stood, sweat poured all over me. She threw me a bunch of onions and said, "Peel these onions. I will fix some pigeons stuffed with genuine Saidi green wheat for lunch. I bet you haven't tasted pigeons in a long time!"

"I had some at Khat'an's restaurant a few days ago."

"You ate some thin sparrows. You'll eat real pigeons now. Khat'an doesn't use genuine Saidi green wheat stuffing and Khat'an is not Badriya. Badriya's cooking is unparalleled in Damanhour or the whole land of Egypt! Whoever hasn't married me is unlucky because he is deprived of the tastiest food in his life!"

"That's my good fortune, Badriya." As I began to peel the onions my tears flowed while Badriya kept laughing at the way I looked. I was trying to banish a naughty thought that had taken hold of my imagination and which made me persist in watching Badriya's body as it twisted under the silk gown like a perch weaving about in the midst of the waves, her thin waist almost totally absent. It was as if her upper body with its jutting chest and broad shoulders was connected to her lower half with its strong, prominent buttocks by hidden gravity, as if what held the two parts together were a mere outline depicting in front a slender belly flowing down like a svelte cone. Under the translucent gown the panties looked like a small patch, more like the fig leaf that covered our mother Eve's nakedness. Despite my strong desire to banish the naughty thoughts and my attempt to avert my eyes from that splendid body, focusing only on that shine hidden in the midst of her features, reminding me of her mother's figure and shine, which must be part of the blood code whose mysterious shine I could see in all the faces of my family members no matter how different from the others each of them looked—despite that, in reality I desired her. The lips caused some aversion toward her and I didn't really know whether I truly desired her or felt the fire of repression and deprivation raging inside me, burning my ears.

I hurried to wash and dry my hands and eyes, then went out to the parlor and noticed a big Philips radio placed on a table next to the kitchen door. I turned it on with pleasurable anticipation. The voice of Abdel Halim Hafiz singing in a calm tone suffused with sadness: *They were not fair to it! They were not fair to the unsuspecting heart! They promised it!* Badriya shouted elatedly from the kitchen: "Turn it up a little!" and her voice almost drowned out Abdel Halim's turned-up volume as she very efficiently accompanied him. Her voice was much more tender and more sensitive to the fine ornamental melodies of the music. I caught a glimpse of the opposite room. Obviously it was Shukriya's room for there was her framed picture on the nightstand next to the bed and some of her clothes and slips hanging from a clothes tree beside the bed which was modern in style, piled with cozy decorative bedding. I entered the room trembling with pleasure. I stretched out on the bed, rolling in something that was forbidden to me, as if I were rolling over Shukriya's body to crush her arrogance. She was the youngest and prettiest of the sisters. I caught myself pressing myself against the bed. I was overcome by a mysterious feeling of pleasure and aggression. So I got up and began to hold the slips and clothes, sniffing and pressing them against my face and lips, then returning them to their place. Then I moved to the next room, Yusriya's, which was arranged in the same way, except in a more orderly and modest way. I stretched out on the bed, rolling and burying my face into the pillows. Next I moved to Badriya's room. It was the biggest and overlooked the light shaft and the back street with two windows that captured the sun and the moon in two corners and kept their lights for a long time. The bed was of shining brass with ribbed posters and covered with a rose-colored mosquito net, open like a tent entrance. I went in and began to roll on the bed, thinking that if the Hagg or the Hagga or any of the brothers was here I wouldn't have been able to enter the house, let alone roll so freely in the girls' rooms. I trembled a little but took great pleasure in rolling as if, with great pleasure also, I was making fun of the Hagg and the Hagga and all their arrogant, boorish sons. I was puzzled as I wondered: how did Badriya dare to invite me to enter her home when she undoubtedly knew her family's feelings of aversion toward me? What if one of them were to drop in on us now? It would undoubtedly mean perdition both for me and Badriya. She must have been absolutely certain that they would be gone for a long time. But how did she act in defiance of her family's sentiments and invite me in so simply and move before me so freely, almost naked? Admittedly, in a sort of archaic family convention, I was almost like her maternal uncle since her mother was my first cousin but she would not have behaved with me the way she did had anyone from her family been here. I remembered that in the week I had spent here before I wasn't allowed to go to the fourth floor in particular. The girls went down to the third floor for lunch at the big dining table that was part of their mother's furniture and had been placed in the parlor of the house before it all became their property. And when they did come down they were dressed conservatively and modestly and did not laugh gaily. So, I wondered, what has made Badriya so liberal with me? Could the whole family have changed in my absence and developed tender feelings? Or, was Badriya different from all of them?

Then my heart began to beat fast as I suddenly remembered many disquieting bits of news in my family circle during my childhood and early youth about Badriya in particular. We heard many times that she had been admitted to the psychiatric hospital in Alexandria for a month or longer. We also heard several times that the girl was not normal, that she had a slight condition. Some of the men in my family attributed that to a psychological problem that affected the girl because she hadn't married and no one had proposed to her despite her father's wealth and which she might inherit. Saad, my cousin who was older than my father yet he addressed him reverently as 'uncle,' commented on that by saying that no one wanted anything to do with Hagg Mas'oud and that the girl, even if she were a beauty queen, even if she had no lips at all, would not be married because no one wanted to deal with her materialistic animal of a father. He cited as evidence of that that all the girls had missed the train of marriage, that if they had not found a cousin to marry, like their sister Tahani, they would never get married at all. Even their own cousins did not think of them as potential wives. After a long silence, my father commented saying that all Hagg Mas'oud's daughters were so unfeeling that it was unlikely that they would suffer psychological problems. Besides, he added, you shouldn't forget that mental problems were common in the Qabbani family because of marriage among relatives. "Have you forgotten that the Hagg's own mother, his father's own cousin, died in the Abbasiya mental hospital? Have you forgotten Umm al-Izz, the idiot woman who hung out with the dervishes, wearing Sufi garb? She's the Hagg's first cousin. And why go far? The Hagg himself loses it for the slightest of reasons and doesn't see things around him and gets out of touch with everything. He once shot a rolled mat propped against the wall that his uncle's women had forgotten. He was coming back at the end of the night after watering the land. The bullet pierced the wall and hit the head of a poor bull in the animal shed. He was so out of it that he refused to pay his uncle half the price of the bull as the family elders decreed. And he went as far as to accuse his uncle of many outrageous things, claiming that he had been lying in ambush to kill him and that he had wrapped himself in the mat!"

The sound of female slippers approaching with Badriya's voice: "Where's he gone?" She entered the room and looked around. Then she saw me stretched out behind the mosquito net. She smiled involuntarily and shouted in a tone that I wasn't sure whether she disapproved or was tempting me to go on, "Well, well! Don't you dare go to sleep. Lunch'll be ready in a few minutes."

She hesitated for a while as if thinking of what she would do next, then headed for the dresser's mirror and began to look at her face and touch her hair with the comb. I could see myself in bed, facing her in the mirror. I could see her whole back and her whole face and I couldn't control myself. I felt as if ants were going through my veins, then I began to expand little by little until the gallabiya rode over my legs. I felt great embarrassment and I pushed myself hard between the legs but I felt myself rising with greater strength. At that moment our eyes met for a fleeting moment and she smiled knowingly, then said as if trying to overcome an inner feeling of regret, "Please tell me the truth and swear on it, so and so: am I ugly? Do I have any real defect? Tell me without any embarrassment."

I noticed that she was trying to shrink her lips in a spontaneous manner. I jumped, sitting up, then got off the bed and walked toward her, standing behind her back, placing my chin on her shoulder next to her head. Just like that. And said, "There's no doubt that you are beautiful and anyone who denies that is either blind or has no taste for women!"

I expected her to slap me or to push me and teach me a lesson in manners, but she fixed me with a surprised glance indicating that she was pleased by what I said. She even leaned her cheek on my head, whispering in a breaking voice, "Are you just being nice to me, you devil you?"

I brought myself closer to her back by standing up straight. "I am telling you the truth. This agrees with my personal taste!"

She smiled and passed her cheek over my head: "You and my father agree on this. He tells me the same thing so as not to hurt my feelings. He always feels guilty toward me; saying his own big lips are the reason I am not married. Are my lips so repulsive? I feel that from the way the people look at me and what they say when they see my face. Even girls seem to be repulsed by my face."

I pressed against her back until I completely disappeared between the buttocks. I reached with my arms embracing her chest and holding a breast in each hand. I began to press them gently as I shook with confused, passionate desire. Then I said in a hoarse voice, “Show me those lips that I might test them.”

I stood on tip toe until my lips got close to her lips then I bent her a little and she gave way like a bamboo and I started kissing her lips hard. To my surprise they disappeared under my lips and turned very hot. Then she collapsed. I discovered to my surprise that I had pulled her toward the bed, lay her down, and took off her gown when, amazingly, she looked like a live painting by one of the great masters with fatally seductive features. I became insane with desire and I got lost in a dream without beginning or end. I don’t know how many hours passed but I could see through the intoxicated vertigo the faces of Hagg Mas‘oud, Hagga Wadida, Hawwas, Badi‘, Karam, Tahani, Yusriya, and Shukriya, only serving to increase my fervor and ardor and absolute pleasure. It was as if I were kneading them all under my razor-sharp sword, which doubled my pleasure and made it more profound as well as providing me with total relief and joy. As for her, she was a totally different woman, a ball of fire that burned and cracked and made dozens of sounds and hissed in a way that cost me the rest of my reason. However she suddenly snapped into consciousness shouting, “The food’s on the stove! It must be burned by now!” I let go of her and she dashed into the kitchen and I dashed behind her. She turned off the stove and then, naked, like a panther she went into the bathroom and I followed her under the rain and we exchanged body rubs with the loofah. Then she dried my body with the towel as if I were her child.

I ate the most delicious food of my life. I was certain that once you forgot what those lips looked like, you got a one-of-a-kind woman. We drank soda and ate chilled fruits then got up for another round during which we were more crazy, stronger, and longer. After that I was fast asleep. During my sleep I found myself doing the same thing with Hagga Wadida herself in front of the Hagg and all their sons who were all acquiescent in humiliation. When I opened my eyes the moon was visiting the room. Badriya was sitting in front of the mirror, combing her hair. I sat up and Badriya said, “By the way, you can spend the night here. In that case you should go downstairs to sleep in the boys’ room.”

“Why?”

“To guard against surprises. Maybe someone will drop in on us, in which case you will be in the right place.” Then she fixed me with an enchanting glance and asked, “Supper?”

“Sure.”

She prepared the little metal kitchen table on which she spread some loaves and different kinds of cheese and honey and yogurt and boiled eggs. As we ate I told her, “There’s a question that’s puzzling me.”

“I know it.”

“So what’s the answer?”

“It’s the owner of the house, may God have mercy on him. He raped me in the stairwell when he was drunk. I was a young girl. Afterward he offered to marry me but my father didn’t accept. My cousins came and held him prisoner in a faraway place and threatened to kill him. In the end he agreed to transfer the title of this house to me as a price for his mistake on condition that they didn’t turn him in or create a scandal. After the transfer they put poison in a liquor bottle and he died so the matter would stay a secret. That was twenty years ago. Back then I was stupid and I had problems with my nerves. But tell me: where do you sleep?”

I told her that I had rented a room the day before in the Iflaqa neighborhood and that I needed some money to buy some furniture. She said, “Don’t worry. Furnish it for the time being until we find you an apartment in a respectable neighborhood so I can come and visit.”

“What do you say we get married?”

She laughed merrily: “We’ll think about it from different angles!”

After supper we went back to the room without giving the matter much thought. We woke up the following day before noon, then the third and fourth and fifth day, in the same blind, relentless, mad way. On the morning of the sixth day before noon I was descending the stairs by myself, carrying on my shoulder a package containing a blanket, a comforter, and a pillow from the family's surplus that she gave me. I had three whole pounds in my pocket and a scrap of paper with their telephone number so I could call her when I wanted to, pretending to be Muhsin, the hairdresser.

On the street I stood for a while and stopped a horse-drawn carriage. I passed by Hamdi al-Zawawi and retrieved the suitcase and told the driver to go to Wikalat Atiya. I was surprised, and pleased, that he didn't know where it was and hadn't heard of it. I felt proud directing him to go right or left. From time to time he looked at me over his shoulder with surprise and skepticism.

A Room with a Mastaba

The sound of the horse's hooves on the street asphalt and the clanking of the carriage wheels intoxicated me and made me feel pampered and spoiled. I automatically felt my body swaying with the movement of the wheels, not only because the motion made me sway but because, as a child, I used to see the overseers of the large estates and the sons and daughters of the big farm owners in our village swaying in ecstasy with the movement of the horse-drawn buggies in the village streets. I remembered the women's hair dancing down their faces with excitement and pleasure.

The carriage was not going fast now as the streets were filled with passersby and vendors and vehicles. My eyes were on the street and deep down I wished some of those who had seen me in wretched circumstances would see me now; perhaps they would realize that I hadn't always been miserable. But unfortunately no one saw me even though I'd asked the carriage driver to pull the top all the way back so I could present myself in my full regalia, reclining with a lit cigarette in my mouth, and the blanket and comforter and pillow package placed under my feet. Gradually traffic grew lighter and the crowds thinned out. I realized that the carriage was going through the street parallel to the railway station, entering the quiet neighborhood deep in the heart of the old city. It looked like a newly established part of town with low-income housing forming a long street extending to the edges of distant agricultural land forming at the horizon a strip where green and ashen colors met. The driver was now going through that street to lengthen the distance—an old trick since people took horse-drawn carriages nowadays essentially for joy rides. So the driver felt he had to show the passengers many places in hopes of getting a large tip. Yet the driver stopped at a corner and asked permission to buy some fodder for the horse. So I figured out that he had taken that route for that purpose specifically since I had stopped giving him directions. I began to observe the street and was struck by the sight of a woman who looked exactly like our village, sitting on the sidewalk wearing a gray cotton gallabiya and on her shoulders a black shawl covering her head, neck, and chest. She could be the mother of several respectable men with an oval face that had fine features even though it was covered with wrinkles and furrows. Her toothless mouth was closed and looked like a small women's purse, but her eyes were strikingly wide and radiant as she looked to the right and left as if furtively suspecting something mysterious. Before her was a large palm-frond crate on which she had placed a flat wooden board with raised edges, heaped with crude candy like halva sticks with sesame seeds, banana candy, taffy, and round sesame hard candy. Perhaps she was the same woman who sat at the entrance of our village, selling candy to children coming from the fields and accepting anything in payment: some corn on the cob, a handful of wheat, a bunch of clover or green grass for the rabbits or some bread and cheese. I was truly astonished to see such a woman in the city and I wondered whether she was selling her wares for payment in kind or cash. I guessed, however, that she was selling her stuff for cash because next to her was an upturned palm-frond basket. Our eyes met several times and I thought she somehow knew me. As a child I used to love to sneak out of our house during siesta time and cross our roof to that of my uncle's house and stuff my pockets with ears of corn that had been spread on the roof to be dried by the sun and made ready for the mill or millstone. Then I would make my way to the edges of the fields at the entrance of the village or perhaps come across more than one woman from whom I would buy some candy to eat on the way to the other one. I almost got off the carriage to talk to this woman. Actually I craved one of those banana candy sticks that used to melt in my mouth right away. But the driver returned and the carriage shook hard as he jumped on to it to take his place. He tugged at the reins and the horse sped away. As we approached the wikala, I was able, from where I sat in the carriage, to discover details that I hadn't noticed before, such as the old, two-story house immediately behind the wikala, separated from it only by a narrow alley on the other side of which a line of dilapidated houses stretched, getting smaller and leading to huts made of bamboo, mud, and palm fronds.

The gate of the wikala was ajar and with a slight shove it opened. I was met with two eagle eyes that had sparks of anger in them. No sooner did I step forward toward Shawadfi who was reclining on the mastaba than he fixed me with a sharp glance that showed not the slightest recognition of my person. I said, "Peace be upon you," and from where he was reclining he pointed at the gate in a sharp, harsh tone saying, "Get out of here at once!" I froze where I stood carrying the package containing the blanket, the comforter, and the pillow, now shaking in terror. The man I was seeing now was not the same Shawadfi with whom I had drunk tea and smoked cigarette-butt sabaris in a very friendly manner. He was not the man for whom I had written the marriage contract for two of his wikala's crazy tenants. The man I was now standing before was a real monster who, if I did not obey at once, might pounce on me and gobble me up. I felt totally disheartened as I turned around to leave in slow humiliation but I was surprised to see his features relax a little, as if he had remembered me and felt sorry for the way he had received me. Then he smiled and said, "Go out, then knock on the door first, then I'll tell you to come in or not to come in."

I did that in an exaggerated, theatrical fashion and he sat up and shook my hand with genuine warmth. He made room for me next to him and leaned toward me in genuine affection: "Shall I make you some tea?"

I thanked him and offered him a Belmont cigarette from a pack I had. He looked at the pack in delight then made a gesture with his fingers as if saying: "Hey, we've come a long way!" Then he took a cigarette and quickly lit it and mine too and pulled the brazier and broke up some blackened corncobs and blew on the embers until he uncovered the flame, then added some new corncobs and the fire took. Then he held the earthenware water jar in his right hand and the rusted tin mug in his left and poured some water in it, then shook it and tossed the water with the dregs in the damp gate entrance and poured new water in the mug and placed it in the middle of the quietly burning embers. Then he stretched his legs across the mastaba and his knee and joints made a thick cracking sound.

"Where've you been all this time?"

"I was in the village."

"And how's the family? Well, I hope, praise the Lord?"

"They say hello."

"Hello to them and to you."

He began to look at me—my clothes and my clean, just-bathed appearance. His glances rested on my suitcase and the package placed on top of it below the mastaba. He raised his arm, opening his big palm ending with long fingers that looked like thick iron nails. The expression on his face almost said, "What elegance!" but his mouth said something that added to the unsaid phrase, "Now you can be a tool!"

I was taken aback as I sat on the mastaba; all my muscles contracted upon hearing this sentence, odious in our village. For the word 'tool' was used to refer to homosexuals and was spread by students studying in the city, imitating city-dwellers. It was one of the bad habits that our village learned from contact with the obscene city. But Shawadfi's face did not betray any such intent. He even immediately added, "If Sayyed Zanati saw you now he'd ask you to join his team!"

He bent to follow the boiling tea, holding the wire handle of the mug and shaking it to brew the tea, as he added, "By the way, I hope you were not offended when I yelled at you. You took me by surprise as you came in and made me a nervous wreck. I thought you were one of them, our dear friends the secret police, who bless us and everybody else all the time with their presence! I thought you were a detective or someone from the vice squad who had come to amuse himself by getting on my nerves until I end up giving him a bribe that equals the fear he puts in my heart. But who do they think they are dealing with? I treat them the way you've seen, and when he reveals his identity to me, I pull the wool over his eyes; I make him feel that I am his slave and that he's my master, but gently. I frighten him before he frightens me! He must realize that I am tough while he's still at the gate. And when I give him something, I appear as someone who has done him a favor since, in the end, I can rearrange his face!"

Shawadfi took great pleasure in pouring the tea. I said, sarcastically, "Amm Shawadfi, does it make sense that an officer will come to you carrying a package like this and a suitcase like this?"

He fixed me with his eyes as he were driving two burning nails into my eyes, then he let out a resounding thunderous snort, "They come in women's clothes with all kinds of makeup, blowing bubble gum! Are you an idiot?"

He offered me a cup of tea and picked up his tobacco pouch to roll a cigarette, so I offered my pack and he reached with his fingers then hesitated and said, waving his hand: "No, sir. This tobacco here is too refined for me; it just doesn't do it for me. This coarse tobacco does the job better."

He began to roll his cigarette slowly: "Have you decided to stay with us, God willing?"

"Yes."

"So, you'd like a room with lock and key?"

"That'd be great."

"What do you think of this room?"

He pointed to a room next to the gate: "It's yours. It seems you're a good man, for it's been waiting for you. It is the only one with a mastaba like this one here. I rented it to an effendi like yourself and a good man too, but I don't know what he does exactly. He would come and spend a week or ten days at most then disappear for many months, keeping the key in his pocket and paying the rent for a long time, sometimes for one or two months in advance. When he stayed away for a long time, the mailman would come to my door with a money order that he had sent from wherever he was and I would run to the post office and cash it. This time, however, he's been gone for a long time. It's been almost a year since I got any letters from him. I feel that that boy has done something bad and been caught by the government and put in jail. I am willing to bet anything that I am right about him. Listen to me, my friend: if a person is not frank and truthful about everything, then he is a sly lowlife. You know? I have no fear of frank liars—those who know that you know that they are liars. They lie honestly, without any shame. These people I don't give a damn about. I give them my ass, not to play with but to fill their noble noses with my farts and good perfume. The ones I fear are those who pretend to be frank and put on masks of truthfulness. These I figure out right away and read like an open book. The mask will undoubtedly press against the face and will give them pain and it will show. He will try to relieve the muscles of his face from the pressure of the mask, if only for a short while. Thereupon such a person will be found out and I will greet him saying: come and sit yourself on the lap of your hungry, horny, and tired brother. Woe to him when I lay my hands on him! There are guys who lie innocently and in good humor to get on and these usually are not malicious and cause no harm. But this friend of ours, the one who rented this room, I liked him and held him in high esteem but at the same time I felt there were things he was holding back from me. He's never talked to me about himself or anything else for that matter except for general things. And if I asked him about himself, his job or family or village, how he was doing, he would be quite evasive and say things that could be understood this way or that. The latest he said was that he was an inspector with the city. Would you believe that? What kind of inspector would come and live here? True, his clothes are always washed and ironed. He is well-spoken and polite, but in the end, ultimately and deep down, he is miserable. Anyway, I gave up on his coming back, so I opened the lock and gathered his junk which was an old suitcase and some magazines and newspapers and paper that had addresses and telephone numbers and names of towns and some old clothes and worn out shoes and a threadbare comforter and a frayed mat. I stuffed all of it in a sack and threw it in a storeroom until our friend shows up. The room has a window overlooking the street and it has a wide base that can accommodate this suitcase and rows of books. If you open its upper part and leave the door of the room ajar you will have such a cross-breeze and the breeze will be like that on the beach of Alexandria. Now, how many months did you want to pay for?"

I was surprised by the question. I thought about it for a little while then blurted out, "Two or three months."

"Okay, give me the money."

I gave him a pound and eighty piasters. I took it out with my eyes closed, like someone closing his eyes and holding his nose as he drinks a bitter medicine. I was afraid to hesitate or to go back on my word because it was a huge sum that would make quite a serious dent in my finances, but I soon calmed down since I received shelter for three whole months during which I'd be spared the daily anguish of finding a place to stay, after it had been a great wish to greet the evening one day without fear, anxiety, or depression. The night in Damanhour was beautiful and pleasant and yet I didn't like it because it provided me no cover. I've always longed to sit at night at al-Messiri Café to listen to the discussions of men of letters without worries or to stay up with Mahmoud Ne'ine', the haberdasher who composed interviews and original songs that he called 'modern,' or spend evenings at the Government Employees Club with the theatrical troupe or go on a walk along Mahmudiya Canal on the paved street, passing by the vocational training and the agriculture schools up to the village of Sharnoub, talking about art and literature. I've longed to do all of that without worrying about the night with every step. Now, and only now, I'd be able to do that for three months for a hundred eighty piasters. As for food, that was manageable, for I had acquired a tremendous ability to withstand hunger for days on end. Besides, more than one friend or even others who were not friends could give you lunch or supper more than once but there wasn't a single friend who could give you shelter in his home for one night.

As he pulled a small key from under his big pillow, Shawadfi said, "May it be the beginning of a good friendship, God willing! I've taken a liking to you since you are straightforward and don't beat around the bush. And so long as you remain like that you will have me on your side, always. As for work, don't worry. May God enable us to help you with that."

I remembered his word which had offended me and I said with a trembling smile, "What did you mean when you said that now I can be a 'tool'? You said that a few minutes ago but you didn't explain."

He laughed gruffly in a subdued voice: "A 'tool' means work. You'll understand it when you've lived here for some time. Don't be in a hurry, you'll see and understand many things. I have here a cinema and movies that you haven't seen in any regular cinema. But I didn't mean to offend you in any sense that might occur to you. I know that that word for you, in the countryside, has a special meaning, but I didn't mean it and I only realized it when I saw your face when you heard it. Now, go put your things in the room and inspect it and rest a little."

I went up to the room and opened its crude padlock passed through the staple of a hasp that seemed to have been nailed and removed dozens of times using bent nails. I decided to reattach it or maybe change it and the padlock itself at an opportune time. The door gave way and went in and opened the upper jamb of the window overlooking the shiny, asphalt covered street that was as wide as a square. A beautiful light poured in, bathing the room in the color of the sky, which was the only thing I could see. The mastaba was very beautiful, extending the length of the whole wall. A person reclining on it could lean his elbows on the base of the window to read or watch the courtyard of the wikala. The room was indeed beautiful and its floor was straight and flat. I saw on the base of the window some leftover folded newspapers. I opened them and found them to be several issues of the *al-Ahram* newspaper in which the presidential decree dissolving political parties was published. The front pages were yellowed with age but the middle pages were still white and new. I spread them out to cover the length and width of the mastaba, which could accommodate two people. I spread the blanket folded lengthwise and placed the pillow next to the wall and it reached the edge of the window base. I folded the comforter four times and placed it at the end of the mastaba, then made a mental note to buy a needle and thread to mend the few holes through which the cotton showed. I placed the suitcase on the window base, then cast a final exploratory glance around the room and I noticed the presence of many bent nails driven into the wall to serve as pegs on which to hang clothes. I was overjoyed at the discovery and with great relish I got up and left, pulling the door behind me. I secured the staple to the hasp and pressed the padlock until it snapped shut and I pulled hard on it to test it and found it to be solidly shut. So I opened it again and entered the room as an idea occurred to me that I acted on at once: I took the remaining money after wrapping it in a piece of paper and stuffed it in the bottom of the suitcase. I kept ten piasters with me for necessary food expenses. Then I went out and closed the padlock and went out to the streets of the city, free and in a good mood as if getting to know Damanhour for the first time.

Shawadfi

I would sit with Shawadfi at my favorite perch every afternoon, watching the sun as it beat a retreat from the courtyard of the wikala, leaving the rooms encircling the courtyard bathed in gray as if they were remnants of medieval ruins in which life still surprisingly breathed. Suddenly I saw her entering through the gate, the same woman I'd seen one day selling candy on the sidewalk. There she was carrying the palm-frond crate filled with subdued chickens that let out faint clucking sounds that gave them away, for the crate was wrapped in a rag and on top of it the basket was also full.

"Evening, Shawadfi," she said.

"How's the chicken?"

She stopped and was about to sit down and show her merchandise but she just said, "Beautiful, thank God. But you never buy any."

She headed for a room exactly opposite mine on the other side. So, she was living here! Something about her face was very familiar to me. I could've sworn she was the same woman who sat at the entrance of my village and all villages, with the same baby-like features that called me as a child to buy from her. And there she was now calling me to talk with her, expecting her to ask me how my family was. But she reached behind her back across her shoulder and pulled a strand of thread braided with remnants of tufts of her own diminishing red hair. There was a key tied to the thread of a tassel. She held it with two fingers and with a trained move she plunged it in the bottom of the padlock and moved it and the tip of the padlock jerked upward. She twisted it and freed it from the hasp and with her knee she pushed the door and bent down a little so she could enter. Then she sat down and put the crate on the floor and the chicken cackled and clucked in confused panic.

At that point I saw on the stairs of the room exactly opposite the wikala gate, a man of medium height, with a red face like a European man in disguise, like a prince with a round face and full cheeks in the middle of which was a mustache with pointed sides so high they almost touched the eyelids. His eyes were small but looked like two precious jewels that shone in a way that dazzled the eyes and mesmerized them in such a way that they sought release after a short while out of sheer terror and perhaps confusion brought about by the penetrating eyes that knew no shyness or fear. He had a broad chest and muscular shoulders and pectoral muscles that moved like masses of rock under the skin of his chest and his biceps appeared through the wide sleeves of his peasant-style gallabiya of cream-colored silk worn only by village headmen and rich folks. He had on a pair of house slippers of soft leather. He looked like a real dandy and smelled of perfumed soap.

He went down the stairs in childlike delight with the grace of a ballet dancer, noiselessly. As he came close you could see that he was in his mid-thirties, maybe younger. With a very polite gesture he raised his hand with a casual greeting in the manner of dandies as he strutted toward the woman's room where the chickens were. He had pulled back his white cotton skullcap revealing thick coarse hair. In my confusion I returned his casual greeting with a full "And upon you peace and God's mercy and His blessings." From behind his broad, sturdy back, he greeted me again with a gesture of his hand, his legs appearing under the translucent gallabiya and in the light of the sun looked like two branches of acacia that had been well-clipped even though tufts of hair on them seemed to have escaped the clippers. He said in an elongated tone meant to mimic city-dwellers and at the same time to make fun of her, “Good evening, Etaita!”

“Come, Master Sayyed. You’re in luck today. We have young Indian chicks!”

She held one of them under the wings to show how plump its thighs and breasts were.

“You’ll find a bunch of soft eggs in her belly!”

He waved his hand with many gold rings on the fingers: “Go ahead. Pick seven.”

Then on his way out: “Follow me, bringing one at a time.”

He squatted in the courtyard and took out of his pocket a switchblade which he opened quickly, and as the sharp blade shone, Etaita brought a chicken, holding it at a slaughtering angle, bringing its neck close to him. He extended the fingers of his left hand and held the neck in a display of genuine supplication: “In the name of God. God is great. May God grant you fortitude to endure your tribulation. May God make your death better than your life.”

He slit its throat twice and threw it into the courtyard and it dashed around, its broken neck gushing blood.

The courtyard was now filled with chickens with severed necks, running and striping the ground with blood and collapsing here and there. Many of the wikala denizens had come, I didn’t know when, and bought chicken from that Etaita so Sayyed would slaughter them while he was at it. Finally Sayyed wiped the blade of his knife on a rag that Etaita had given him, then got up and went to the corner where he had thrown his chickens and gathered them up. Then he took out of his side pocket several bank notes that he rolled into a ball and gave to Etaita who put them into her side pocket without counting it. The others did the same thing, as if they had agreed on a price that she had no right to discuss. Sayyed Zanati started going up the stairs carrying in his two hands a huge quantity of slaughtered chickens. I followed him with my eyes from where I was seated on the mastaba next to Shawadfi, with a third-round teacup in my hand.

So this is Sayyed Zanati! Thus said Shawadfi's eyes as he pointed toward the staircase in a gesture of adoration as if Sayyed were a maiden with whom he was very much in love. I said, "What else does he do?"

He said with a delight and envy filled with admiration, "He's got a tool!"

I felt shame creeping all over me.

"Tool, again?"

"He's a valiant man who deserves all good things, quite admirable. With men he's more manly; with vile men he's more vile. With women he is more delicate than cigarette paper and smoother than a razor blade. If he senses a roughness in one of his women he scrapes it off to make her smooth again. He is an artist when it comes to scraping off roughness in human beings without shedding a drop of blood. I envy him this talent. The toughest police officer cannot stand a single round with him: he is an artist at eating them and nibbling on their bones and yet they offer themselves voluntarily to him to get drunk and use their flesh as mezza. Had it not been for him, this wikala of mine would have been shut down by now. He knows the holes in the characters of police officers and he stops these holes in his own artistic way: sometimes with money, sometimes with women or sweet talk, and at times by handing their chiefs big cases they wouldn't dream of cracking even if they fucked themselves. And yet he never betrays anyone. So, how does he figure out these cases? You wouldn't believe it. He reads the newspapers word for word and studies the crime reports published in them and finds out the ins and outs and uncovers the suspects, then goes to the person in charge and submits to him papers in his own handwriting in which he says: "Since so and so was such and such and that happened because of that, hence the crime is such and such and the motives are such and such arising from this and that, therefore the perpetrator is so and so. Or, you, government, have to go to such a person for he has the key to the whole case or to such a place where you'll find the evidence." The man's brain is a jewel, my friend. If he had gotten an education, he would've been Minister of the Interior by now."

He became more mysterious to me: "But you haven't told me what he does exactly. And that 'tool,' what is it?"

With great enjoyment he started rolling a cigarette from the sabaris pouch: "A morsel that's disclosed cannot be eaten. Houses are secrets, my good man. If you like to live here, you will find things out on your own. As for me, I don't say anything. As I sit here I can see everything that takes place in these rooms even when the doors are closed. But ultimately I am the big door that protects their secrets and covers their nakedness. They know that I know and therefore no one conceals anything from me. They believe that any problem they find themselves in or that they have among each other, I will solve in the end. In other words, it must be presented to me at the end of the day. They conceal from me some problems and differences thinking that I am not aware of them. And I don't ask them: what have you done about this, that, or the other? Because I am certain that each of them will come on his own and sit where you are sitting and say, "Amm Shawadfi, I've got something to tell you." I don't open my mouth, letting his faucet leak out all the musty, hidden water. He tells me what I already know before he says it. Of course I don't have a crystal ball but all the news comes to me here without my seeking it. It comes to me through quarrels, through rebukes, through grimaces and frowns, through eyes averting eyes, through people volunteering to explain what they see. They tell me what happened in the lands of Hind and Sind and countries where they ride elephants! I have never in my life said to anyone: 'What's the matter?' or 'What happened?' or even 'How are you, so and so?' There are sentences that I've never said. And what do I need them for? We Arabs like to open our saddlebags, especially when we are resting. We love to vent and let it all hang out. What's the moral in all of this: Don't ever, ever take me for a fool or think I am gullible about anything. That is, if you want to win me over and at the same time enjoy peace and quiet!"

Etaita passed in front of us holding an empty bottle heading for the gate.

"Evening."

Shawadfi fixed her with a glance: "The alcohol?"

"Yes."

He let out a deep growl that must have meant something, since she understood and waved the bottle, opening her toothless mouth in something that was meant to be a smile: "You know that I only love tea made on the alcohol burner."

He said very slyly: "Of course, of course, Etaita. I only hope that we get to taste that tea if only once, just one sip."

She pointed to her eyes: "One sip from this one and one sip from that one, for you, sipping man!"

He waved with his arm: "Okay, Etaita, go ahead."

She went out.

"What's up with Etaita, Amm Shawadfi?"

"I think you saw for yourself."

"Yes, but I saw her selling candy to children."

"That's her original job."

"But, the chicken?"

"That's her job on the side. A smart person plays more than one game. You find them in every mess. 'Every adventurer gains pleasures and he who weighs consequences dies of regrets.' Haven't you studied this verse in school? If you haven't I'll give it to you now for free! Listen to what Shawadfi says: if you want to do something, do it, even if the world gets ruined in the process. If you keep thinking and thinking, the time will slip away from you while you're still thinking. Then every Tom, Dick, and Harry will have taken the express while you are bringing up the rear. You, for instance, you come to live in the wikala even though you're educated. There must be a purpose in your mind. At this point I advise you to seek counsel. Consulting is also very important for someone your age. Advice is precious even if you don't benefit right away. It's an asset that will come in handy when it is most needed. The world is full of good, experienced people like myself, so you should share your project, your story, what you plan to do. Our Prophet has commanded to us that we give sincere advice to whoever asks us. Take that young man Abd al-Aziz, for instance, Abd al-Aziz al-Qassab, the one who lived in your room before you. He never asked for advice. He was full of himself, maybe he thought he was Suleiman the Wise. I watched him many nights, certain that he was hungry, thirsty, naked, and cold and had a thousand problems that racked his brain as you could see from the conflicted glitter in his eyes. I hoped he would sit where you're sitting now to talk to me about his worries so I could help him, but he never showed me his face. He howled in pain all by himself. I too ended up taking pleasure in his pain, leaving him alone, maybe things would turn around for him. But there he is, no longer here, all but forgotten. I really wanted to help him, on condition that he speak to me. I also wanted to keep him because he was a quiet tenant that made no trouble. Anyway, may God be kind to him wherever he is."

Etaita came back with the bottle filled with the crude red alcohol with that strong, overpowering smell. In her other hand she carried a package containing tea, sugar, chewing tobacco, and snuff. Under her arm she carried two loaves of bread, a bunch of radishes, and a paper bag of ta'miya. As soon as Shawadfi saw what she had he shouted at her, pointing at the radishes and ta'miya: "Do yourself some good, woman. You make so much money every day, buy yourself a couple of eggs and boil them, or half a kilo of meat, or even a can of salmon!"

She stopped, raising her eyebrows: "What d'you mean? I swear by your honor that you will smell frying chicken after a little while. This is just a snack until I finish cooking."

"Of course I'll smell the frying chicken but not from your room, Etaita, but from those that earned it. Anyway, the most important thing for us now is to wait for your alcohol cooked tea."

"By all means."

She hurried to her room. By twisting my neck slightly I could see way inside her room in the corner. I noticed that she dashed inside, pulled a little sack and tipped it over a small pot and raised it, whereupon some corn kernels trickled down in the pot. When that was almost filled, she held the sack and returned it to the basket. Then she picked up the alcohol bottle and poured from it on the corn until it was covered by alcohol. She kept an inch or two of alcohol in the bottle, then poured it into the alcohol burner. She picked up the earthenware water jar and poured some water on the corn. With her left hand she picked up the rusty teapot and poured some more water in it, shook it energetically, then filled the pot with water and placed it on the alcohol burner and lit it with a match. She searched in the package until she found the bag of tea which she opened and poured completely in the pot and looked again in the package until she found the bag of sugar and poured it all also in the teapot on top of the tea. Then she picked up a small tin cup and a tin mug that used to be a can of salmon. She washed them and set them by the burner. Finally she turned around and began to stir the pot of corn with her hands, then covered it firmly and sat down to her meal of bread and ta'miya and radishes and began to chew very patiently.

The smell of the alcohol was very strong and wafted through the whole wikala as if it were a primitive liquor distillery. Etaita brought the tea, holding the cup and the mug in her hands. As she came close to us she motioned Shawadfi with her chin, muttering through her toothless mouth: "This fancy cup is for the apple of his mother's eye, since you wouldn't know how to hold it, Shawadfi. Drinking from it wouldn't give you pleasure."

She offered the cup to me and the mug to Shawadfi. I had one sip of the tea and was instantly intoxicated by the delicious strong taste. Shawadfi noticed my pleasure and he made a gesture with his eyebrows approvingly, saying, "Ah," and continued to slurp: "May you continue to prosper, Etaita. And may God provide you with good chicken at every intersection. I mean good people, good woman. I mean the kids who buy candy from you. They also are chicks."

He continued to slurp as Etaita observed with a mixture of satisfaction and pride. Then she waved, egging him on to hurry up and finish: "Go ahead, drink and give me the mug." I gave her my cup saying, "Thank you, Auntie Etaita."

She beamed with happiness: "May you always drink in good health. Whenever you want to drink tea, just call me. Anytime! If you're hungry, I'll feed you; if you're naked, I'll clothe you!"

Then she looked at Shawadfi and added in a suggestive tone: "And if scattered, I'll gather you!"

Shawadfi fixed her with a lewd glance which he then redirected to the place between his knees at the waistband of his pants, then aimed part of the glance to her eyes, saying, "Behave, woman! You toothless hag, what's wrong with your kind? Loose from cradle to grave? Here, hold it tight!"

He meant the mug, of course, but his lewd tone meant something else. She snatched the mug with affected force and left happy with her newly acquired feminine coyness.

Etaita

"If you can't find a job, be a judge!"

The proverb rang in my ears as I was reclining on the mastaba in my room, having had more than my fill of sleep, but not knowing where to go. It was Etaita that I heard, teasing Shawadfi as she was leaving to start her day. It was as if I made a momentous discovery; I jumped off the mastaba, shed my gallabiya, and put on my shirt and pants, then my shoes and dashed out. I bade Shawadfi good morning and noticed that he was engrossed in twining a rope of palm tree fibers with great dexterity.

I kept a long distance between me and Etaita, letting her lead me wherever she wanted. It occurred to me that I could spend a beautiful morning for a few piasters, having a hot ful sandwich and a cup of tea with milk at a coffeehouse. What could be better than that? I could also watch people scurrying around in panic on the way to their offices, factories, stores, schools, and trains. It was as if I were telling myself: here I am enjoying a beautiful morning in the city, unpressured by panic or fear, not panting to be on time for an obligatory appointment. Most likely the fact that I had the money for the sandwich, the cup of tea, and the cigarette in my pocket gave me this sense of absolute happiness. My only enjoyment now was to observe Etaita and see how she was managing her life; how she left her house every morning like an employee going to work somewhere in the city and came back at the end of the day having earned enough to buy some bread, a bunch of radishes, and some ta'miya. She was undoubtedly saving a lot; for whom did she save, why or for what occasion was she saving? Only God and maybe also Shawadfi knew. I got exhausted and became a nervous wreck following her. More than once I looked but couldn't see her as she disappeared in the crowds or inside one store or another, buying the merchandise that she would display at the entrance of one of the alleys. It was as if that nice she-devil was deliberately leading me to show me the real ancient Damanhouri alleys that I'd often wished to see but which I couldn't imagine seeing without a guide like her.

As for the neighborhood where we ended up, it was the Abu al-Rish neighborhood. I knew it and walked in it many times for a long time. But what had previously appeared to me to be the entrance of an ancient house, revealed itself now as the entrance of a very deep and wondrous alley. It was as if I had entered an enchanted city in the true sense of the word. I found myself suddenly inside a cell that extended like a crack in the very heart of the city, in a corner of one of her invisible innards: two rows of Mamluk-style homes, all similar on the outside and each three or four stories high, the first floor made of bricks while the other floors were made of wooden lath encased in mud then white-washed. The windows were narrow and rectangular with gray, rusty wooden mashrabiyas which time had given attractive, sweet features. The doors were gates that looked very much like the gate of the wikala. As you stood facing the alley from a distance, you felt that you were entering a free-standing house that came to an end a short distance from the wooden balcony with an iron railing that seemed to block the final space facing you. As you walked toward it you felt that you were heading for it alone and that you would be received like a guest who'd been allowed to go deep into the house. After a short while, however, you found yourself going beyond it without knowing it, distracted from it by a second, third, or fourth row of balconies of the same shape and slanted position occupying the space to the right or to the left. Thus the house appeared to be front and center. You'd also be distracted by the modern highrises that extended along the two sides of the alley as if they were a cosmic décor specifically designed to contain that ancient world in a long, meandering crack. You'd also be surprised to find tiny grocery stores, tailor shops, fabric stores, and carpenters' shops displaying nothing more than equipment and a counter, and tile shops with very short entranceways and deep cellars. Then you'd find that very cute coffee house that used to be a sidewalk below a door that was originally a window in front of which the ground level rose and turned it into a door, from which you descended into a cool, intimate parlor from the floor of which rose steam smelling like the water of gozas and shishas that were constantly emptied there. Your nose would also be greeted by the smell of the kerosene stove humming sweetly under the chafing sand top where hot drinks were constantly prepared and by the smell of the burning brewed tea and by that of fresh ful from the next store or from the pot on a ful cart passing by, or in the plates before the workers having their breakfast and munching on onions in an appetizing way. You couldn't also help noticing the smell of the smoke-colored bathwater just dumped down the drain in front of you by a beautiful, busty young woman in a simple dress, her body shimmering in a delicious amber light, her buttocks swaying from a well-built figure and rounded legs, carrying under her well-endowed arm a large, empty water can. She would then disappear in a side alley or inside a house or maybe at the public tap set up nearby in a narrow opening in the street with large cracked tiles and lots of water from the tap and on the ground. Next to it would be the tap operator, sitting on a small wooden bench, fastidious about his appearance and possibly named Usta Hassan, turning on the tap in an equitable way for a bevy of young women surrounding him, chewing gum, twittering unintelligibly, and laughing in a sudden wantonness, evoking beds, comforters, and coverlets and a delicious rose color shaking from head to toe. They would be accompanied by the calls of vendors as if in duets or well-orchestrated arrangements: "Praise God for you, sweet one!" That "sweet one" would be grapes or figs or pomegranates or onions or tomatoes or fish or watermelons, sold on carts going through the alleys. The women would call from the windows behind the mashrabiyas, asking about the prices, or haggling patiently before coming down to buy. When they did they might be shocked by the bad quality of the produce, whereupon they would back off like well-fed tigresses, strutting in their house gowns with red, rounded bare heels that looked as if they hadn't touched the ground before.

I almost forgot all about Etaita since the alley sucked me in, pushing me to its faraway bottom. Blocked by a huge building that might have been a cotton ginnery or a tobacco factory, I kept going back and forth until attracted by this café where I threw myself, not out of fatigue but out of vehement longing, like a baby going at its mother's breast after a long absence with only a bottle of artificial milk. The chairs were made of braided straw on short wooden legs, some with armrests and some without. There were small tables made of reinforcing steel topped with tin sheets worn out by time or use. I sat inside for a while and I felt utmost joy as I saw people in the alley as mere legs and feet with or without shoes, loitering or hurrying up, stumbling or moving gracefully between carts, bicycles, and pallets on wheels moving Coca-Cola bottles. The workers in the café had begun to have their breakfast and they beseeched me, in the name of the Prophet, to join them. I ate with them for free. I wanted one sandwich but I ended up downing two and a half loaves with the irresistible ful, onions, gargir, limes, and pickled turnip and spicy eggplant.

"May it be as delectable as it is good for you," said the dwarf as he smiled, seeing me pat my belly to indicate that I was full. Then he said in a soft and friendly voice, "Tea?" I said, "Yes," then added, "How much do you charge for a shisha?" and he said, "Don't worry about it." Then he hurried toward the polished primitive counter and poured tea in a large, very clean and shiny glass on top of three lumps of sugar that looked like domino pieces, then he filled a larger glass with water. He pulled out a shiny yellow tray the size of a notebook and placed the two glasses on it and came toward me. With a rag attached to his apron with a pin, he wiped the little table and put the tray on it. He turned around and pulled out a shisha and blew into its mouthpiece, emptying its water. He then took the bowl apart and filled it with water and reattached it, then blew into it again until he adjusted its gurgling sound. He brought it and placed it in front of me in its elegant, decorative glory, with a pair of small brass fire tongs attached to its pan by a chain. As soon as I tried its gurgling sound, the dwarf brought the big bowl filled with lit embers and pressed it on the water bowl to fit, then put on top of it the brass cover that protected it from wind or rain so the tobacco wouldn't burn or go out before it would be smoked. Then he looked at me and asked, "Can I be of service?" I felt very grateful and expressed my sincere thanks by raising my right hand parallel to my ear in a military salute, not mockingly but very seriously. I was in a very delicious serene mood, finally at peace with myself and beginning to savor the beauty of the morning as it ripened slowly in the heat of the forenoon, as Galal Mu'awwad's deep voice read the news as if talking to himself without agitation. In the midst of this deep feeling of pleasure and peace of mind unburdened by any worries, I remembered Etaita. I jumped to my feet and debated the matter. Then I remembered the chairs on the sidewalk outside. I ordered more tea and sat in a wonderful corner between the wall of the café and the wall of the adjacent house, jutting out the width of the sidewalk, as if it had been prepared and waiting for me alone for a long time.

Thus I leaned the small chair in the hollow of the corner and sat by myself. The first thought that occurred to me was of sitting intimately with a book to decipher properly. I felt that I would have such a sitting countless times in the future and that gave me indescribable joy.

There she was, Etaita, squatting on the ground at a far away street corner without any passers by around. The spot clearly was more like a light shaft in a dead end. Etaita was displaying her candy on a board on top of the crate, holding a fly swatter to keep the flies away from the candy, her eyes hardly settling on one spot, looking to the right and to the left in a childlike stealthy manner. Then she would drop the swatter and her hand would sneak to her lap and come out holding a handful of corn then bend to one side and scatter the corn in the alley with great deftness, then grab the swatter again and a short while later scatter some more corn and she kept doing that until she ran out of corn. Then she sat up trying to forget the whole matter and started to hawk her candy in a naïve but carefully measured manner, urging the children to come and taste the royal banana, and various types of candy. It was clear from her voice that she hoped no one would hear her and no child would respond.

The dwarf brought the tea and placed it before me saying as he avoided eye-contact with me: "The first tea is on us. This, you'll pardon the expression, is our way with every new face as movie people might say. We'll start the tab with this tea with this shisha. Shall I get you another pipe of tobacco, sir?

"Everything from you is good."

"May your days be good."

He turned and left. As soon as I finished stirring the tea, I found the mouthpiece of the shisha extended toward me. I sat up to accommodate it and leaned back on the wall looking at the street which suddenly filled with old men and some able-bodied men and youth hurrying, holding prayer beads. I followed them with my eyes and saw them entering a door faraway to the right with greater enthusiasm. Then I saw the tailor removing the garment he was working on from his lap and getting up and the old grocer crossing the counter and leaving the store for a child to watch over it. I heard more than one voice repeating in various places, "God is greater and might is the Lord's." I felt a sudden animation filling the whole air with a prayerful atmosphere and imagined that I had neglected to do something of extreme importance, that I should hurry up and join the others. I was, however, wrapped up in my own form of worshipful prayer, puffing on the shisha and taking in the cool mid-afternoon breeze. I saw young men wearing fancy shirts and the latest fashion of tight-fitting pants and shoes with high heels with metal taps, and shoes producing a squeak resulting from air pressure to create rhythmic music as they walked. I also saw busty girls coming back from school hugging their school bags and snazzily dressed women that were undoubtedly going on dates at al-Ahli or Baladiya Cinema or the Government Employee Club garden or Mahmudiya Canal or the Students' Café.

I remembered Etaita again and I looked at the street corner but didn't find her there. I felt some panic, like a child who had lost his mother in the crowd. I almost shouted out to her in fear and consternation. I laughed at myself and got up and called the dwarf. He asked for three piasters. Quite a bargain. I gave him three and a half piasters. He returned the half piaster, thanking me and saying, "Beg your pardon. We don't accept tips. We own the place."

I patted him on the shoulder gratefully. I hurried eagerly to the street corner. I saw the alley strewn with a large number of chickens, passed out drunk from the alcohol that the corn had absorbed the night before. Etaita was busy grabbing them by the legs three or four of them at a time, throwing them into the crate until it was full. Then she began to stuff the rest into the basket and draped an old gallabiya on the crate and another on the basket and placed the basket on top of the crate then rested her knees on the ground and with great deftness she hoisted the load with one hand on top and another beneath and leaned it on her knee; then she adjusted it and put it on top of her head and got up the way a camel did and turned to leave. I turned my face quickly and headed for the café. After a short while I looked at her and saw her walking in confident, measured steps without a care in the world.

Getting Acquainted

I got addicted to visiting this alley, which was like an amazing magical pocket in the body of the city bulging with fat spots. One afternoon as I was dawdling away, getting ready to leave the alley, I saw him coming from the other end staring at me in a way that made me suspicious. So I decided to challenge him by staring back at him, but he smiled as he approached me. He looked familiar.

"Good evening, sir."

"Good evening. How are you?"

"Can I get you anything here?" he said with a mysterious wink that told me there were things here that visitors might be after, but I looked at him with increased suspicion. He grinned: "Beg your pardon, don't you remember me, sir?"

I began to study him, an old, toothless man, thin like a reed with a blue linen gallabiya, and a forehead stained with coal dust and sweat. He took out of his coat pocket two twisted cigarettes, offering me one and putting the other in his mouth.

"Thank you, thank you!"

"My wife will be divorced if you don't light it. Please!"

"Okay."

He lit it for me and, in a show of familarity, he led me by the armpit:

"Come drink some tea. It's a happy occasion to see you here."

When he saw that I was reluctant and surprised, he stopped, shouting in protest, "My dear sir. Have you forgotten already? It hasn't been so long since you wrote up my marriage contract with your own blessed hand, with Shawadfi at the wikala."

I couldn't help shouting, "How are you? Bridegroom? How's marriage?"

"Wonderful, thank God. God has given me a really good woman, a great helpmate! Thanks to her inheritance and mine too, for I am a lucky fellow."

I walked with him for a while, awkwardly. He said somewhat candidly, "I thought you needed something from here, so I said to myself to look after you before you fall into the hands of this rotten bunch!"

"Something like what?"

"Like smoking a couple of pipefuls."

"Of tobacco?"

"Of hashish. Of the whole area, this alley has the motherlode of hashish and opium. There are ruthless guys and very sweet guys here, it's just the luck of the draw and your just desserts!"

He let go of my arm and pointed as he turned to the entrance of a dilapidated house that looked from the outside as if it were a ruin. That, however, turned out to be a little clearing resulting from the collapse of an adjacent house, with rubble rising and covering the path to the house and hiding its entrance. We went to a large inner courtyard ringed by several rooms, all closed with the exception of one to the left, from which, in addition to the fragrant smell, there arose the noise of laughter, humming, and gurgling. He bent over my ear and said, "I work for the man who owns this joint. We serve the choicest stuff. I'll fix you two perfect pipefuls."

I looked at him in surprise: "You said in the marriage contract that you are an undertaker!"

He let out from his toothless mouth a coarse laugh that reverberated in his chest like the neighing of a horse and said, "Medicine has advanced so much, my dear sir; now death is a rare occurrence. It's now my wife's season. She is doing a very brisk business. She helps five women give birth on a single day. A woman would give birth and nine months later she'd give birth again. Egypt's women, knock on wood, get pregnant after forty days! God has blessed their wombs."

He went in ahead of me: "Evening, everyone."

Those sitting looked at him in suspicion. The gurgling stopped for a short while charged with unspoken tension, then the gurgling sound returned when the man led me close to the counter and sat me down on a rickety bench. He told the man standing behind the counter: "Ten pipes here and one tea at my expense; the gentleman is with me."

He turned around and pulled a goza from the water barrel and began to blow into the goza to let out some water and adjust it. He leaned it against the wall next to me then went to the large brazier and chose a large lump of live coal that he began to grind in the strainer. In front of me were three men who were obviously brokers in the vegetable market, talking about what they had done that day as if they were talking to a complete stranger who was interested in the minutest details, even though they had all experienced and lived through the whole thing together. Near them was a young man, about twenty, with a pipe of tobacco laced with hashish, waiting for the waiter who was changing the water in the goza. Next to the door sat an emaciated man, wide awake, with nothing in front of him.

The owner pushed the glass of tea on the marble counter top next to my shoulder, saying somewhat gruffly, "The tea." I nodded in thanks and began to stir the sugar with the spoon. The undertaker man came and crouched in front of me on the floor and took out from behind his ear a piece of hashish the size of a peanut and began to cut bits of it as big as the shell of a small seed and placed them on the bowl. He presented me with the mouth reed of the goza, saying, "Good evening!" I held it by the tips of my fingers and puffed lightly; he urged me on by hitting the edge of the strainer against the reed, so I took a deeper puff. Then he hit the reed again so I puffed as hard as I could then let go of the reed as clouds of thick blue aromatic smoke came out of my mouth and nostrils. It was indeed good smoke. I felt the owner looking furtively at me in surprise and envy. He didn't think I was such a consummate smoker of hashish or at least that was how I interpreted the way he looked at me. When it came his turn to smoke, he held the mouth reed and puffed steadily as the gurgling sound of the goza rose as if it were the sound of a car engine when the driver pressed the gas pedal. He pointed at me and asked the undertaker, "Who's the gentleman? Where's he from?"

The undertaker hesitated in confusion, so I hurried to say, "You know the bursar of the mudiriya?"

He thought a little: "I think his name is Hagg Mas'oud?"

"Exactly. Hagg Mas'oud al-Qabbani."

"What about him?"

"He's my sister's husband and I am so and so, a student."

"Welcome! You seem to be a veteran hashish smoker."

My vanity was aroused: "Next to our village is a small village most of whose denizens sell hashish. In our part of the world it is almost free. Everyone smokes it and doesn't smoke it at the same time because when it is not there, no one seeks it."

"How much is a piaster's weight?"

"About ten piasters."

"That's nothing!" they both said at the same time. The owner added: "Here, it is twenty-five piasters for the choicest quality."

The undertaker said, "Take me to your village once or twice."

"With God's help!"

The owner said, "By the way, I know that village and I have relatives there in the Ge'aidi family. Do you know it?"

I waved my hand as if to say it was quite well known: "Misbah al-Ge'aidi, Hagg Musallam al-Ge'aidi, Shaaban al-Ge'aidi, and Ali al-Ge'aidi!"

His face lit up and he exclaimed: "Yes, Shaaban al-Ge'aidi, his mother calls my mother cousin."

"So, we are related by marriage!"

"And I am at your service, at any time. My place is your place."

The ten pipes were finished, so I got ready to get up but the owner motioned me with his hand to wait: "Ten more from me. My stuff is better."

"That's enough; I am high."

He waved his arm and made faces with his fat features like the actor Hassan Fayiq's face: "As long as you come from around Ghalawsha, you never have enough and you never get high. I know your type!"

As he bit the hashish to flatten it with his two fingers to spread over the molasses-cured tobacco he added without pausing: "But where did you meet this guy?" and he pointed to the undertaker.

The latter said, "The gentleman here is a friend of Shawadfi of Wikalat Atiya. They are bosom buddies."

A shocked astonishment shone in the owner's eyes. I felt very embarrassed: "It's sheer coincidence, I swear. I met him only very recently through a friend, I mean, an acquaintance."

"I thought he was from near your village. By the way, he is quite a genius at storing!"

I was alarmed: "Storing what?"

"Hashish. But it seems he's gone easy on that now. Some time ago he was quite an expert at hiding the stuff for the big dealers. If the government inspected every little crack in his wikala, they wouldn't find anything even though the hashish was perhaps under their feet and eyes. They've often searched there and even dug up the ground. In the end they gave up and let him store as much as he likes. He's quite colossal. May God protect you from him. He gets out of the tightest spot like hair out of dough."

The undertaker had begun to shake with embarrassment and apprehension. He looked at the owner trying to warn him not to go on, and when he couldn't, he addressed me, saying, "I haven't told you anything that you've heard. And I haven't heard anyone tell you anything. Please, I can't stand up to Shawadfi!"

The owner burst out laughing gaily and the undertaker was overwhelmed in a funny childlike embarrassment, saying, "There's no need for that, Me'allim Nonn."

But the owner fixed him with a sly glance: "Don't be such a coward. Tell the gentleman how he used to hide the goods." Then he addressed me, pointing at the undertaker: "This friend of yours used to work for a big dealer, may God grant him safety in jail. His job was to bring the goods from Shawadfi's store to where the delivery was to take place. Tell him so he would know how mighty Shawadfi used to be. He's been cut down to size now, so he's no longer frightening."

At that point the undertaker opened up and seemed like an unthinking big naughty boy: "You know where he hid the goods? Deep down the sewage drain under the second threshold of the wikala, the one that opened up at the cattle pen. The wikala has a shed next to the water pump where the denizens' mounts and the cattle they take to the market in the morning are kept. In another part of the wikala he also used to hide stolen goods. I had to come in like someone who came to drain or to clear the wikala's septic tank. A sewer system had not been installed yet, so I'd put on old rags and come with two buckets and a pole, and attach one bucket to each end of the pole and make it into a yoke that I carried on my shoulder, one bucket in front and one in the back. I'd scoop up the shit from the tank and take it away to dump it in a distant field or a deserted area where a child or a beggar or a woman selling radishes would be waiting for me. I'd give them packets of the stuff wrapped in fabric and adhesive paper and placed in leather pouches. The goods would be distributed in holes built into the walls of the tank inside so a person going down to clear or to drain it could place their feet. Let's forget about him, may he be cursed."

He stood holding the cleaning rod to clear the goza with great care and enviable energy, considering his age and health, as he continued to speak in a voice rendered hoarse by opium—which gave one a dry mouth and caused the voice box to shake as I read in an article in the Arabic edition of *The Reader's Digest* at al-Houfi's bookstore. The undertaker seemed to have found a topic of which he was enamored: "Oh, yes, my dear sir. This wikala has eaten up my life. I've hated it a thousand times but I could never abandon it. I had many opportunities to live in respectable houses for reasonable rent where landlords gave you a month or two or three to pay. But this dump robbed me of my reason. It's as if somebody had cast a spell on me. Anyone who stays there for more than a month falls so in love with the place that he cannot leave even if they offered you a room at the Muntaza Palace. There are people who have been living there for the last forty years. A tenant leaves either evicted or dead! You ask me what makes it like that? I tell you, I don't know. Perhaps because it's like the world in a box. Maybe it's because it's like the movies. But my mind tells me it's because life in it has a different taste, because you can do whatever you like, whatever you can't do in a different lodging house. No one criticizes you or interferes in your affairs or bothers about you. If he finds out that you, begging your pardon, are a thief or a mass murderer or a highway robber or even a pimp, he wouldn't despise you or fear you or bother you."

He finished washing the goza and changing its water, so he propped it up next to me and began to grind the live coal in the strainer energenti-cally and swing his arm with the strainer as if it were a swing at great speed without a single ember falling off. Then he crouched in front of me and extended the mouth reed toward me: "The wikala, my dear sir, is a state unto itself. Its king and owner is Shawadfi. He is its Gamal Abdel Nasser. He seized it from its owner, Atiya and the Ministry of Awqaf just as Abdel Nasser seized the rule of the country from King Farouk. Except Shawadfi is smarter than Abdel Nasser because he got it without any army or a blessed revolution. To tell the truth, my dear sir, he is better than Abdel Nasser when it comes to ruling the wikala. He is wily and cunning, blue in the tooth as they say, and you don't know what his religion is. They say he is a Copt from Asyut. Others say he is Jewish, judging by his character. Still others say he is a true Muslim. As for he himself he says his ancestors are a mix of Turks and Arabs, that his great grandfather was one of Sultan Abd al-Hamid's old eunuchs. No, I take that back. That was a rumor spread by Atiya who used to own the wikala. When some mischievous people asked him about the truth of the lineage, he snorted and said, 'What business is it of mine if my grandfather was a eunuch? What matters is that I have an organ that I can ram into ten women standing one behind the other, going from ass to pussy. I can hoist all of them and swing them as the ten of them are strung on it!' Shawadfi is a rare gem, my dear sir, a joy to those who understand and love him. Only those who love him cannot only tolerate, but enjoy his anecdotes and his various moods. It's enough, dear sir, that in the wikala he rules over people from so many races and religions."

He took the mouth reed from me to finish the last few puffs. He held the smoke back in his nostrils, creating a squeaking sound like a car suddenly braking. Then he added through the smoke pouring out of his mouth and nose: "Listen, dear sir, in the wikala there are ghagar, halab, tatar, and nawar."

"So what are the ghagar, the halab, the tatar, and the nawar?"

"A ghagari woman, for instance, goes around the fields as a ghaziya to dance and serve her gang. She sells her body by the inch and the handspan to come back at the end of the night fully fed. That's how the ghagar are."

"So, what are the halab?"

"They are very chaste when it comes to honor and the body, but their women rob men of their considerable fortunes by using infernal tricks."

"And the tatar?"

"The most rotten! Their women specialize in robbing classy ladies by devilish means. Their men specialize in stealing the washing from clotheslines and collecting sabaris."

"This leaves the nawar."

"God help us! They are the lowest bunch. Both their men and their women sell their honor. Actually, they have no honor. But somehow, they are always in demand. People hire them for all kinds of schemes, for scaring people away, for disgracing others, for murder and perjury in courts of law, for kidnapping women unrelated to them, and for offering their women to strangers. With them anything goes."

He took a deep drag on the goza and added: "May God protect you, my dear sir. You seem to be from a good family, so how did you and Shawadfi cross paths? Only the lost and strays like us and those running away from the government, the law, and society ever fall into his hands."

I didn't know whether the nice undertaker had made me hate the wikala or made it more appealing to me. My heart began to tremble upon hearing the stories but at the same time my imagination caught on fire and made me want to run to, not away from, the wikala, as if it were the only place that could put out that fire.

The owner, Me'allim Nunn continued to replenish the hashish in the goza generously. The evening peered from a narrow hole in the ceiling. From a window facing me, the high-rises with their bare red-brick backs looked like the strong muscles of a stomach that sooner or later would consume us. I fixed my sleepy gaze inside the room on the faint light coming from a mantle-lamp hanging from the ceiling that I didn't notice being lit. As the undertaker was escorting me to the middle of the alley and then to the end, I felt as if we were coming from an ancient time where history had totally stopped. I only felt back in Damanhour when I began to stagger, dissolving in the air as I crossed the raised bridge parallel to the railway station, on my way to the wikala.

Dumyana and the Monkey

I was certain that I wouldn't be able to sleep easily that night because I had slept all day long on the beautiful mastaba, a very deep sleep during which I didn't see any dreams at all, as if I were temporarily dead. It was long after midnight. Shawadfi had put out his kerosene lamp and pulled his worn out blanket over his head and was fast asleep. The door to my room was ajar and the way I was lying down I could see the whole inner part of the courtyard and parts of some of the upper rooms, most of which were open and lit. You could hear some sounds of people staying up. Some were playing cards or getting drunk or making love or arguing or planning things or discussing calamities that might befall some innocent people tomorrow or the day after tomorrow. It seemed I'd gotten addicted to lying on the mastaba at the same time every night and that I'd tended to go to sleep early in order to wake up and watch these rooms and their disconcerting secrets. And even though I had spent several nights in that condition, I was still at a loss, like someone standing on the shore of a vast and deep sea, unsure which spot would be safe for him to take a plunge. All spots looked safe and the waves calm on the surface, but I was certain that calamitous dangers lurked under that calm, quiet surface. All the rooms were exciting so I found myself moving at lightning speed like a frightened bird from door to door without settling on which room to start focusing on.

The wall facing me as I lay down on the mastaba began to mock that quiet moment. Behind it there rose thudding and disturbing noises that wouldn't give anyone lying on the mastaba the opportunity to sleep. I felt I had to get up and awaken Shawadfi whom I felt could silence that thunderous noise roaring immediately next to my ear. I felt I was justified in complaining since it was a nightly occurrence. I had at one time thought it was something incidental, but it was a complete elaborate ritual that lasted for a long time, sometimes two or three hours at a stretch. It must be that my neighbor Dumyana trained her four monkeys only in the middle of the night. I jumped up in anger and took several steps toward Shawadfi's mastaba. I called him in a gentle whisper: "Amm Shawadfi! Amm Shawadfi!"

He kicked his blanket and sat up, his legs still stretched out: "Who? What?"

"It's me, so and so."

"What's up, so and so?"

I sat on the edge of the mastaba, leaning over toward him and muttering in a low, angry voice, "I cannot sleep, Amm Shawadfi! There is an earthquake in the room of Dumyana, the monkey woman! It's as if it's all coming down on my head. The walls are shaking and the windows are rattling."

He growled in a way that told me that he was certain I'd make that complaint one day. And even though the threshold of the gate was totally dark, I felt a sardonic smile forming on his lips as he said slowly, "This crazy woman is up to no good! What's in her nature cannot be changed. Talking to her, even beating her is no use. I am keeping her only for old times' sake. I can't bear to see her dragging her monkeys, looking for a place that would let her move in with her four wretched monkeys."

He pulled out the sabaris pouch and began to roll a cigarette and in less than one second I saw it lit and between his fingers. He didn't put it between his lips to drag on but instead he made his hand into a fist and placed his mouth on the edge of his fist and sucked. The cigarette glowed and smoke came out of his nostrils filling the air with a sharp acid smell. He went on to speak calmly without raising his voice: "It's the old goddamn monkey! He his giving her a hard time because she is giving him a hard time. He's justified, my friend. Isn't it enough that he's having a hard time all day long with whoever rents him? He's the only one providing her support, feeding and clothing her and giving her a roof above her head. And yet that whore is cruel to him. I wonder how he can bear her! One of these days he's going to lose it and tear her flesh apart!"

I was in desperate need of a cigarette and by then was wide awake. I lit the half cigarette I had saved in my pocket two hours earlier. I tried to influence him: "You must give her a stern warning! You must make her train the monkey in the daytime and leave the night for us to rest. In all honesty, I can't understand what kind of training can cause the earth to shake like that and produce a noise like thunder."

As if in solidarity with me he said, "It's a hell of a training regimen. The old monkey's always rebelling. Always refusing to obey her orders. She beats him with the cane on his sides and he jumps from one corner to the other, hurtling in fear and dashing around as if he were a rock falling from a mountain top to the plain below. I know that, dear sir, and have heard it myself. She holds the chain in her hand, yanks it, then lets him go, and as the muzzled monkey dashes about, she drops the chain and it drags on the floor behind him and she tries to chase him from one corner to the other, crashing against the younger monkeys that are tied by the neck to sturdy stakes attached to the floor. In the end she catches him! She's a truly formidable woman, my friend. In her life she has worn out five husbands as if each of them were a pair of shoes. Of those I saw three who died in this wikala of mine in that room of hers, one after the other. The last one was a wise, good old man who told me that her flesh was tough as nails. The night that he spent with her, his belly against hers, he would wake up feeling that the flesh of his belly had melted and become as thin as filo dough! The healthiest of the bunch was a young man that she finished off in just two years. Originally she is a nawar through and through. All the nawar come from the environs of Sinai. She's nine feet tall and as wide as a door and her buttocks fill a whole gunny sack and each of her thighs is as large as a camel's thigh. When she quarrels she can defeat a whole town with just her tongue and if she has to beat somebody, she uses a club like men, and her knee and her head or a hoe or anything she can lay her hands on. Her face is always full-blown like a ball and neither folds nor wrinkles because, as her last husband who confided in me told me, she rubs her face with bull semen. I don't know, my dear sir, where this she-devil gets bull semen! In her childhood and youth she grew up eating exotic foods and to this day she goes to the markets at the end of the world to buy them for a lot of money: wolf livers and hearts, eagle eggs, and horse penis. Besides, she is such a good cook there's nothing as delicious as her cooking. She's also generous; whenever she cooks something special, she sends me some. Sometimes she'll send some of that food to her close friends in the wikala. And she serves huge portions. May God protect you from her! Try to win her over to your side, that'd be best for you. She can be useful and if she trusts you, she can lend you money until times are good again."

He pulled the cover over his legs to indicate that the meeting was over. When I didn't get up, he stretched out again pulling the cover toward his face. Then he said to end the discussion, "Anyway, it's almost over. As soon as you reach your room and stretch out, the monkey will be exhausted and will give in to her."

He completed pulling the cover over his head, totally covering it, and it didn't take him long for his breathing to become regular. I got up to go to my room in quiet steps. When I entered the courtyard I confronted an extremely beautiful sight, a dazzling landscape drawn on the courtyard ground with threads of light escaping from the slightly and fully opened doors on both floors, intersecting like threads of fabric, creating circles, domes, minarets, arrows, and exotic shapes like imaginary dolls or female jinnis with their hair down. The sigh created a precious-looking blanket covering a large portion of the bodies stretched out in the courtyard under the arcades, the rest extending for long distances getting more delicate as they went further. The threads of light got intertwined with the enveloping dark mass. The shadow of the water pump, with its rectangular concrete basin, however, looked like a deserted tombstone. I began to pace through the landscape treading its shapes and formations parallel to the feet of those sleeping. The light creations climbed on me before I stepped on them. They clung to my feet and chest and head until I crossed them to the dark strip. I went back and forth several times, clasping my arms behind my back like an Arabic teacher between seats in a classroom during reading classes, stopping from time to time and turning in the opposite direction. On such a turn I fixed my gaze on the door of Dumyana's room and I noticed a very thin beam of light coming from a hole, which I figured most likely was one where a lock used to be that was removed to replace it with a padlock. That was something that was done to all the doors either because the tenants lost the keys or because newly moved-in tenants were afraid the old tenants may have held on to their keys. I followed the beam of light to the door and found the hole to be as big as a red milieme, but I turned to my room and entered. As soon as I went in I could hear the thudding sound but now it was muffled, as if it were nearing the end: a quick patter of feet then a sudden collapse and a strong sudden shaking that soon came to an end. I stayed where I was, gluing my ear to the wall for many minutes, enveloped in a false silence broken by the clear sounds of frogs croaking in the distant fields, playing cards cracking in some rooms, matches lighting cigarettes, or liquid being poured into glasses. Then a new sound soon rose, dominating. It was the sound of a strong, drunken hissing filling the throat but so thick that it came out of the nostrils, roaring, or muffled playfully. My legs began to shake and my toes curled in my flat rubber flipflops and then I started shaking all over, my breathing quickening, and I could hear my heart beating. I rushed out and on tiptoes I sneaked two steps and found myself in front of Dumyana's door. I looked through the hole and was aghast at what I saw. I suppressed a scream so forcefully my heart almost stopped beating. I nearly collapsed on the floor from the shocking sight but I soon clung to the door, forgetting everything as my legs got wet: Dumyana was like a corpse, lying on her back, her neck craned forward like the trunk of an ancient sycamore, her knees widely parted with her legs bent over them with an amazing physical adroitness. The old monkey was stuck between her thighs, his red buttocks going up and down, the same way he mimicked a peasant woman kneading dough. She was holding him by the waist to be able to move him, pushing herself onto him to reach him and pulling him toward her to make him reach her. They were at it for many minutes; the monkey frightened, surprised, and acquiescing in pain, making shrill noises followed by growls and whinnies then panting, hitting his shaking tail against the floor. As soon as she let go of him, he pulled himself out, his front legs collapsing on the ground, looking at her in a frightened, suspicious way then jumped away, cowering in a far corner.

I withdrew, backing away to my room and threw myself on the mastaba, lying on my back trying to calm my quickening heartbeats, feeling very sick.

So Early in the Morning

As the sun rose, the courtyard of the wikala began to fill with all kinds of people. A loud din rose, dominated by the sound of the water pump which people turned on to wash their faces and feet. Each person operated the pump for another; most of them dried their faces and hands on the edges of their gallabiyas or just left the water on their faces and hands to be dried by the air. Then the crowds in the courtyard began to thin out gradually. In a few minutes the last person was leaving, shaking the water off his hands. Those were the ones that slept in the open air on the floor for one piaster. Then a cool morning quiet overtook the courtyard, accompanied by fresh scents. And that lasted only a few minutes after which life spilled over the courtyard.

The sights began to follow one another in rapid succession before me through the opening in the door. There was a very respectable-looking effendi, a pasha wearing a very expensive, fashionable suit, over which he wore a fancy gabardine overcoat. He had a pair of very shiny shoes and was holding a leather briefcase with shiny buttons like a briefcase that belonged to a judge or a cabinet minister. He looked like someone belonging to the upper crust, with a clean-shaven face, combed hair from which wafted jasmine eau de cologne. A few steps behind him was a lady who looked like Hind Rustum, only more curvaceous and somewhat modest in dress: the silk dress showed only the front of the luminous neck also partially revealed by the translucent silk shawl. The sleeves fitted snugly around the wrists. The shiny sandals showed heels like unblemished silver coins. On the whole, the figure resembled those of the houris whom we often hear described. The lady also displayed jewelry, presumably gold, everywhere: bracelets on the tender wrists, rings on the fingers, a necklace on the chest, and earrings in the ears. Like any respectable lady she was holding a black handbag. Did such respectable, magnificent people really live in the wikala? There was another distinguished looking gentleman and next to him a lady that looked even more chic than the other one. Then there was the village headman, wearing a cashmere gallabiya, a black broadcloth cloak on his shoulders, and expensive natural leather open-heeled shoes on his feet, with a bright red fez with a black tassle on his head. In his hand was an ebony cane with which he kept his dignified pace. Next to him was his truly sheltered and virtuous wife, or so it seemed. She was wrapped in a dark Austrian crepe with elaborate ruffles that managed nonetheless to indicate that a real lady was under the finery, not to mention the face that shone under the shawl with a fine long nose and long, spiky eyelashes. Oh my God, what's all that? Then there was a very tall, blond young man wearing wool flannel trousers, a shirt, and a hand-woven, sleeveless woolen jersey. He looked like a university student carrying, as he did, a fancy folder under his arm. That woman was undoubtedly his mother, walking next to him wearing a modest loose-fitting milaya. She must be a hagga, going along with her son on a trip or to visit a saint's tomb or to buy him something.

The rooms began to let out onto the courtyard all kinds of people going about their business in the most respectable and dignified ways, so much so that it was hard to believe that there were such distinguished people in the wikala. Meeting any of those people, you were bound to show them their due respect, and feel awed by the manner in which they carried themselves, had not Shawadfi addressed every headman, pasha, bey, or chief merchant by the title they truly deserved: “Goodbye, Playmaster!” “Beautiful morning, Slippery!” “May God be with you, Joker!” or “My heart goes out to you, son of a bitch!” and so on. This drove home to me the point that the rooms of the wikala were nothing but the wings of a stage and here were the actors going onto the stage wearing the costumes for their roles. This inspired me to get up and put on the costume for a role to play. It was at that point that I came face to face with a fact that depressed me to no end, so much so that I almost let out a deep and pained groan: I had no role to play on any stage, not even that of an extra. I found myself bursting into a fit of weeping that I struggled hard to make sure no one outside the room could hear. I became aware that I’d become totally penniless and that I hadn’t eaten for many days. I saw in the mist my middle-aged father, leaning on his cane as he got up and sat down and yet going to work for a living in the city every day, his tired, almond-colored eyes speaking volumes of disappointed shock to me. I saw my mother saving chicken eggs to sell so she could give me an additional ten piasters for my pocket money. I could see her eyes burning with tears over what had become of me. I also saw my grandmother, my mother’s mother, underwriting my clothing and rent in this city, by sending money from a distant village where she lived. I could see her not having heard of my expulsion, nobody had the heart to tell her. She still believed that I was about to graduate. I saw my colleagues who had now become teachers working for the ministry of education and drawing a salary every month and receiving respect from everybody, whereas I had so salary, no position, no house, and no existence at all. Even Wikalat Atiya at which people turn up their noses—I would not be able to stay here; I might even be kicked out in a few days. I had given up on checking from time to time with my friend Muhammad Abu Sinn. What should I do? Where should I go? Why did I have to procrastinate until I found myself suddenly forced to look for a quick, temporary solution?

Badriya came to mind. I liked the idea of calling her: “I am Muhsin, the hairdresser. Can I talk to Miss Badriya, please?” I looked for the telephone number and I found it. Again my heart sank to me feet in pain when I realized I didn't have the piaster I needed to make the call. I crumpled up the piece of paper and put it into my pocket. I collapsed and sat on the mastaba, as if I were sitting after a whole year of standing on my feet.

A very fat shadow crept through the sea of hot yellow that the sun pushed to the middle of the courtyard. A moment later, the midwife passed. Behind her crept another shadow, moving perpendicularly toward me, with a nice, childlike smile revealing his toothless mouth. He exclaimed in a sad, pained tone of voice, "So, you've fallen into the trap, my good man? Don't worry! Don't worry! I knew you were going to fall in love with the wikala. Now I am not going to pray to God to rescue you from it, for that will never be, if you don't mind my saying so. This is the only prayer that God Almighty never responds to. All I am praying for is for God to protect you from it!"

My tears had not dried yet. The undertaker saw them as something different. He stared at me suddenly and wondered: "You've just gotten up! It seems you've slept soundly for a long time!"

His second sentence felt like a slap on the face, so I replied, "Yes, and I am still asleep."

"You don't have school today?"

"I have a study break."

"Good. I too have a break today. My job begins after sunset, for I work days one week and nights the following one. My wife's gone on an errand and if she's successful, there will be a big treat for you. She is doing some matchmaking: the bride is rich and the bridegroom is richer."

"God will certainly give her success. She's a clever woman."

"Pray for her, dear sir. It is not as easy as you imagine. True, the bride is rich and she'll shower her groom with furniture and furnishings and food and savings, but her looks . . . may God forgive me for saying that. She has a beautiful figure and can land the best catch, but her face, again God forgive me!"

I found myself saying in jest, having remembered: “Her lips are huge.”

“Exactly! You’ve hit the nail on the head!”

Then he added right away, taken by complete surprise, “Well? Do you know her? How?”

I went on with my improvised jest: “Her house must be in Sagha Street right in front of the famous ful restaurant?”

He looked skeptical and confused: “Did you talk to my wife? Did she talk to you about her? This is a secret that only she and I know!”

My shock was greater than his. I wanted to end all doubt, feeling that for the joke to be complete, the two persons must end up being the same. I said, “And the proof is: her name is Badriya.”

The undertaker’s jaw dropped and for some time he remained silent, shaking his hands and his head in disbelief. He seemed to think that I was some kind of jinn or sorcerer. Then increased tension showed in his face as it displayed awkwardness, fear, and gaiety. I sensed that he was now quite seriously suspicious of me, that something was bothering him and he was too embarrassed to confront me. I egged him on: “If you want to say something, say it!”

He affected a nice, embarrassed smile, then burst out, “I am afraid, sir, that you might be a detective or an officer. In any case, I haven’t told you anything and I guarantee that my old lady hasn’t told you anything either. So, how in the name of God who brought us together without prior arrangement, did you know about it? By the way, I personally have seen the bride only once. All our dealings have been with the mother. And, truth be told, she is a very generous woman. We’ve lived at her expense for months and years; we’ve eaten their food and worn their hand-me-downs and spent from her cash gifts. This gallabiya that I am wearing on my day off, is the gallabiya of her husband, Hagg . . .”

I interrupted him, “Hagg Mas‘oud! And Hagga Wadida?”

He stood up in alarm: “Listen, dear sir, this woman comes from a good family; that I can’t deny. But she wants to marry off her poor daughter by any means. My old lady hasn’t promised her anything or encouraged her in any way, but she has known her for quite some time when she was working in a neighbor's house. It was the lady who kept enticing my wife, asking her to find a good catch, a husband. And you don't really need to twist my wife's arm in this respect. She has been looking for a respectable husband for the daughter in hopes of a hefty reward and finding a good lawful match. My wife and I, dear sir, are good people and we don't want to deceive or con anyone. We've never done that."

He offered me a Hollywood cigarette. I declined, saying I hadn't had my breakfast yet. He threw it into my lap: "We'll have breakfast together in a little while." He lit the match and brought it close to me; I lit the cigarette, I took a drag, and right away felt that delicious buzz.

"Are you, sir, in vice? I mean the vice squad or in the secret police?" he asked, almost inaudibly.

I laughed against my will: "What are you talking about, my friend? I told you that day we met at that café: I am a student. And frankly, just to put you at ease, the institute has expelled me for missing so many classes. And now, I am looking for a job."

He looked at me from the corner of his eye, his suspicion mixed with merriment, sarcasm, and apprehension: "Ah, there you go! Proving that you are in the secret police. Anyway, it doesn't matter. I can help you to find out whatever you want to know about the tenants of this wikala one by one, on condition that you take care of me. I am a poor man and I'd like to earn my living with the sweat of my brow. Don't be deceived by my work at the joint. I only work there day by day, but why am I telling you this? I can bet my arm that you know it all already."

A wicked thought occurred to me: to leave the undertaker in the dark, letting him go on believing I was a secret police officer. Perhaps I would gain from this rank that he would bestow upon me, so widely that perhaps I'd gain some respect! But it didn't take me long to visualize myself surrounded by everyone making fun of me when the police arrested me for impersonating somebody else. I saw that a barrier had risen between me and everyone; that they were treating me cautiously and feeding me lies.

Even if someone like Shawadfi could believe that false rumor, I shouldn't accept the position in which the undertaker insisted on placing me. He suddenly said as if to bribe me, "What would you like to have for breakfast? Today you are my guest from beginning to end. And by the way, if we have breakfast here, Shawadfi will share with us, so it'd be best if you get up and change so we can have breakfast in town anyway we want. Let me buy you the breakfast of my choice."

"Thank you for this generous invitation, but I'd like you to be certain of my true identity, the one I told you about the day we met in your café."

He shook like someone stung: "He says 'my café.' Dear sir, I told you I am just a poor man."

"I mean the café where you work."

"If you want me to quit, I'll quit without the least regret. I'd find myself another job. I'd go to the undertakers I used to work for; they'd be happy to see me go back. God always provides and a resourceful man like me will always find a way. A noble soul is never humiliated, my good sir."

I admitted to myself that he was a resourceful man, also a dutiful man whom it would be stupid to lose when I needed everyone's help. So I went up to him, smiling, and placed my hand on his shoulder very affectionately: "My good man! You think an officer or even a lowly detective will find himself in my situation, without a cigarette to his name and no money for breakfast?"

He raised his face, fixing me with a piercing glance that was full of hope nonetheless: "They do that all the time, dear sir. That's their job, as you know best. You, sir, told me something that no one else knows, so, how did you come by such information?"

"My friend! Don't you remember the day your boss asked me about my village and what I was doing?"

"Yes, I remember."

"Don't you remember that I told him that Ḥagg Mas'oud al-Qabbani, bursar of the mudiriya, was my cousin's husband? I actually said she was my sister. Try to remember."

A gleam of joy shone in his eyes and began to spread little by little, then he shouted: “Yes, that’s true. I swear it is true. You said that indeed!”

“And Hagga Wadida is my first cousin which makes me Badriya the bride’s maternal uncle, almost.”

The skeptical gleam in his eyes disappeared completely and he looked calm and serene. He swore to divorce his wife if I didn’t get up and change so we could have breakfast in the best restaurant at his expense. And, despite our skepticism about how serious the oath of divorce was, I went along and we had a meal of ful at the restaurant near my cousin’s house. We visited the place where he worked and he sat next to me, as a customer this time, entitled to be served by a waiter like himself and to criticize and draw his attention to how service should be. We spent a nice day on the whole and we agreed to meet in my room on the same day the following week, if we were still alive, as he put it.

The Monkey Adds Up the Take of the Day

I became fascinated with the mornings in the courtyard of the wikala, watching them as I lay down on the mastaba in my room. They were enchanting mornings that changed their colors slowly and beautifully from slate to chalk to rose to gold, all redolent with fresh scents. During the slate phase of the morning, I was engrossed in reading the diwan of Bayram al-Tunsi, captivated by his descriptions of old Cairo alleys with their people, their contentiousness, their mud, and their horny outspoken women. I heard Shawadfi's voice addressing someone at the gate, saying, "She's in the second room to your right as you go in." Then loudly in a gruff voice: "Someone is asking for you, Dumyana."

Dumyana's door opened and she came out shouting, "Hello!"

She walked to my room so the man could catch up with her. Then she looked into my room, her smile mollifying her dark, full, craggy face.

"Good morning, young man," she said to me.

I sat up: "Good morning, Auntie Dumyana."

The man came into sight in front of me. He was a young man of about thirty, with a rusty face, crude features, and shabby clothes. He had on a woolen cap under which his hair cascaded like that of a woman. Around his neck he had a threadbare scarf with faded colors. He had on peasant-style open-heel shoes, but white like those worn by market men of the city. He held in his hand a thin bamboo cane. He was somewhat tall, thin, and dry. As he and Dumyana stood in front of my door they looked like a pillar attached to a grey mountain boulder.

"I am yours truly, Abd al-Hasib al-Shabshiri," he said.

"I know you, deary, and I have since you were a little boy. How's your father and brothers?" she said amiably.

"I come to you from Amm Hassan Zarzur; today he's not feeling well and couldn't get up. So he sent me to make the rounds with the monkey in his place. He reminds you that you have as a security deposit for the monkey a Tram-brand pocket watch and a gold ring."

"That's okay. Go in and get him. But remember you must be here by sunset, you hear?"

"With God's permission."

He left her and went into her room. A short while later he came out leading the old monkey who came out waddling, exhausted and indifferent, and in a bad mood. Abd al-Hasib had acquired a small tambourine.

Dumyana sent them off, saying, "May God make it easy for you and open up paths in front of you. May you return in triumph, I beseech the Prophet!"

From his mastaba, Shawadfi said in a voice everyone could hear, "Give this poor creature something to eat, woman. Slaughter a rabbit or a chicken for him. Have pity on this poor exhausted animal dragging his feet!"

When the monkey was in front of him, he said, looking at him in pity, "God give you strength, champ! Supporter of widows and orphans! Doing your duty like the best of men. Go play the peasant woman kneading and a bride for the headman's sons and dance as much as you like. You'll get into paradise!"

Dumyana shouted at Shawadfi in a threatening tone, "Stop it, friend, or I'll let him come back and slap you around!"

She started moving her hips to the right and to the left, tauntingly, then she disappeared in her room.

The morning was now in its chalk phase when the sky cast onto the courtyard clouds that looked like curdled milk. At this point I was thinking that perhaps I had seen Dumyana somewhere else before, but when I picked up Bayram al-Tunsi's diwan, I remembered his poem about Umm Khalil, so I started looking for it eagerly on the pages.

"Peace be upon you."

I raised my head to find the undertaker coming in, carrying a big paper package that he placed on the mastaba. I sat up, filled with a feeling of embarrassment, maybe regret. The undertaker went out toward his room and I heard him exchange a few mumbled words with Shawadfi but I didn't pay much attention. In a few minutes he came back carrying several things: an alcohol burner, a tin can that was originally a can of the cooking fat people called 'Dutch ghee,' a brass shisha of the kind called 'buri' which was a type of free-standing goza with a flexible smoking tube made of plastic with red and green stripes. He bent down to the floor then placed things next to each other, then rolled up his sleeves and began to talk gleefully as his cheeks contracted and expanded when his lips moved in his narrow, toothless mouth: "Today we'll have breakfast like well-off, well-fed people. Every day we eat ful and ta'miya; let's for once do what the rich do. They are no better than us. We can have a spread like theirs."

He unwrapped the package: there was feta cheese, rumi cheese, and bastirma, each wrapped separately in paper, then two eggs and a small can of corned beef, and six loaves of hot pita bread, a packet of Ghazala-brand molasses cured tobacco, a small packet of charcoal pieces, and an *al-Ahram* newspaper. He spread all of these things on the mastaba carefully, then backed up a little and looked closely at the spread like an artist casting a final glance on a painting he had just finished.

"It can be breakfast and lunch in one!"

He removed the little opener attached to the corned beef can and fixed it in the edge of the groove in the can and turned the can until its top came off, then he dumped it in the pan and broke the eggs on top of it and placed the pan on the alcohol burner, which he then lit, and began to stir the contents of the pan with a clean dry stalk. In a few seconds the corned beef and eggs began to sizzle aromatically. He left it for a short while and went out shouting, "Come on, Amm Shawadfi, the food is ready!" He went to his room and came back carrying a tea kettle and two tin cups and two plastic containers of tea and sugar. He removed the pan from the burner and put it aside then placed the kettle on it, then he put the pan on the mastaba.

The undertaker sat on the edge closest to the door while I stayed where I was. Shawadfi sat squatting on the floor, saying "In the name of God, the Merciful, Most Graceful." Contrary to what I had expected, Shawadfi was the first to finish eating. He didn't even finish one loaf of bread. As for the undertaker, he ate two, and I had two in addition to the piece Shawadfi hadn't eaten.

With tea, the coal was lit and Shawadfi went out in a hurry to resume his extra job that made him a lot of money: braiding palm-tree fiber into ropes for boatmen, building contractors, and fisherman. The undertaker offered me the mouthpiece of the shisha with one hand and *al-Ahram* newspaper with the other: "See what's in the paper! It seems very grave things have taken place. I saw people crowding around the newspaper vendors eagerly, vying with each other as if trying to buy some bread. The whole town was in an uproar. I didn't like what I saw, especially that people were muttering and murmuring unintelligibly. Some vendors looked quite distracted. So what's the matter?"

I took the newspaper and spread it out. On the front page was a row of photographs of men, some bearded and some clean-shaved, under a banner headline: "Members of Muslim Brotherhood Secret Organization Arrested; Caches of Weapons and Explosives Seized; Papers and Documents Confiscated; Lists of Prominent Public Figures Most Likely Targets of Assassination." I read this out loud while the undertaker listened with great interest and from time to time made quick comments indicating that he understood what the Secret Organization of the Muslim

Brotherhood meant and the relations between the members and the "Nasserist Revolutionary Government" as he called it. I read to him all the news on the front page, then spread the paper between my arms and it was now close to the undertaker's face. All of a sudden he screamed as if he'd suddenly caught on fire: "That's him! That's his picture! Hurry up, Me'allim Shawadfi! Come see your friend!"

He rushed out fearfully and anxiously to call Shawadfi. The latter jumped off the mastaba and hurried in.

"Which friend, my good man?"

The undertaker snatched the newspaper and pointed with his finger to a picture in the middle, shouting: "There he is, Abd al-Aziz Effendi!"

Shawadfi shouted like someone who suddenly discovered that he'd been had: "Son of a bitch! Yes, indeed, that's him. I had him figured out right. I am never wrong about these things."

He began to study the picture carefully then gave me the newspaper asking me to read what it said and sat on the edge of the mastaba, all ears. He asked me to read it again, then, please, just one more time. Then he raised his arm as if declaring his innocence before the prosecution: "Okay, the wikala has not been mentioned by name in the news. Do you think that the name will come up in the interrogation? And suppose it did, what does this have to do with me? Do you remember what I told you? It didn't feel right about this man; I felt he was hiding something. One learns so many things and yet one doesn't learn everything. This here is a fellow who was able to deceive me, to pull the wool over my eyes. Only God knows how many more like him are deceiving me!"

He looked at me from the corner of his eye and I felt hurt by that glance, yet I smiled and said in jest, "May God protect us all, Amm Shawadfi. Leave it all to God."

He began to get up then apparently remembered something, so he sat down again: "I'm thinking that I should get up now and burn all the junk he's left behind which I put in a sack in the storage area. Or do you think I should deny knowing him at all? What do you think?"

I said cautiously, "Don't do anything of the kind. The government knows that he used to live here, there's no doubt about it. If you try to deny that you knew him, you'll make them suspect you. They'll look for the reason you're doing that. You don't need them to search and give you a headache. You've said a wise thing: what business is it of mine? Yes, what business is it of yours? This is a wikala and people of all kinds live in it. Are you responsible for your tenants? That's point number one. Number two is the stuff he left behind. You can win over the government if they come to ask you what you know about that person, in as much as you've associated closely with him for a long time. You should tell them, 'I swear by God, your Excellency, that I didn't know anything about him because he spoke with no one, and that he vanished without paying what he owed. These are all the things he's left behind. Take them, they might be of help.' In that case they will thank you, instead of beating you or condemning the wikala."

He had begun to watch me in great anticipation as if he were taking in every letter I said, in the hope that I'd give away my true identity. At that moment I was harboring a secret wish, that I could convince him in a few days to show me the stuff left behind to examine, in the hope that they'd give me some information and details of that exciting world which had always tickled my imagination, the world of secret, anti-government organizations and the hoarding of contraband, such as leaflets and weapons, and training to carry out political assassinations. That had always been fascinating for me ever since I had seen the picture of Essawy, murderer of Ahmed Mahir pasha, in the newspaper standing like a knight or a lion as people watched him in amazement and admiration. That was why I opted to leave Shawadfi in suspense about my identity. There was no need to overdo it in reassuring him about me. Let him go on guessing who I really was. Perhaps that would enable me psychologically to have such an influence on him that he wouldn't hesitate to show me Abd al-Aziz's stuff and not to grumble when I was late with the rent. I found myself telling him in a confident, commanding tone of voice, "Do what I tell you. Forget the whole subject until they summon you for interrogation. God be with you! Have no fear!"

I discovered that I pronounced the words "have no fear" in the tone of someone saying, "I am with you! I will support you and rescue you from any predicament!" That made Shawadfi stare at me with blood rippling under his unkempt face. He seemed to be on the verge of shaking, as though he were growing smaller, like a vicious cat tensing up with fear and anger at the same time. He nodded submissively. His hands were placed on his knees like a guilty school child. He raised them tentatively and said, "Okay. Whatever you say. We've got nothing to lose, anyway!

He looked tensely at the shisha and began to sniff for hashish, affecting surprise as if he didn't know what we had been doing, and muttered in protest, "I don't think we should be doing this now. Our dear friends might descend upon us like a catastrophe, as you know!"

It occurred to me to floor him, especially after I noticed that the undertaker was getting frightened and was about to gather up the smoking stuff. I extended my arm in a confident gesture that seemed to say, "Everything stays!" Then I told Shawadfi, "It's my responsibility. This is my room. If they raid it with me in it, I am the one responsible, not you."

"When the sparks fly, we'll all catch on fire, my friend."

"I know what to say to them."

The undertaker fixed me with a glance, flashing back to our previous conversation as if telling me, "Haven't I told you you're one of them?" I smiled and suppressed a loud laugh because I was sure no one would come or inquire. Yet Shawadfi stayed with us, smoking with great relish, as if he were afraid to go alone to his mastaba by the gate. We kept talking about Abd al-Aziz over and over again saying the very same things three and four times in a row, dwelling on the same traits, making the same comments. The undertaker would tell his stories and observations about Abd al-Aziz for the hundredth time without adding anything new. Shawadfi, who at one point objected to smoking, kept forgetting and asking the undertaker, "Why'd you stop stacking the shisha?" and the undertaker would say, "We ran out of tobacco," whereupon Shawadfi would go get a packet of tobacco. Then he'd ask again, "Why'd you stop stacking?" and the undertaker said, "We ran out of hashish," whereupon Shawadfi got up and disappeared for a few minutes, then returned and dropped a large piece of hashish in the undertaker's lap. At that point, the undertaker and I exchanged frightened glances as Shawadfi said, "And you'll return the rest to me." The undertaker, winking several times said, "Of course, of course." Then he cut a piece with his fingers without Shawadfi noticing and put it under my pillow, as if looking for something. Then he resumed stacking the tobacco, hashish, and charcoal skillfully and enthusiastically and we diligently smoked up a storm.

The daylight was coming to an end and the sun lay down in the courtyard under a delicate gray sheet when there was a knock on the gate. We all came to in great consternation and Shawadfi stood up with difficulty and went out to the gate. We both followed to the door of my room to see who was knocking. When Shawadfi opened the gate, the old monkey came in dawdling, his high, red rear end shaking, followed by the man who had taken him in the morning.

"Curses on you, your owners, your keepers, and your handlers!"

Abd al-Hasib stopped in protest but Shawadfi yelled at him to get in. Abd al-Hasib was shaken up and his face turned red, but he followed the monkey.

Dumyana had heard what was going on, so she came out of her room and met the monkey in the middle of the way bending to embrace him eagerly. The crafty old monkey settled in her embrace and involuntarily began to shake his rear end back and forth, which made us all laugh. Dumyana picked up the monkey's halter and jerked it a little, whereupon the monkey moved away a little and circled around her. She said to Abd al-Hasib, "Where's the money?"

Abd al-Hasib reached into his side pocket and took his hand out clutching a fistful of ten piasters, five piasters, silver two-piaster pieces, piasters, half-piasters, and coins of even smaller denominations. Dumyana took it all in her palm and with great adroitness sorted them out in descending order: first the ten piasters, then the five, the one piaster, then the half piaster pieces to the smallest coin, making a line that started in a large circle closer to the wrist and a small one near the finger tips. With a quick glance, she added up the total then raised her eyes to Abd al-Hasib's face in a look of angry disbelief, which meant that an ugly scene was about to ensue: "What's this, mama's boy?"

Just like that! Abd al-Hasib hid his fear and embarrassment with feigned affection: "What does mama have to do with it? Come on, let's go inside to talk."

Dumyana let out a resounding snort then nudged him gently in the shoulder. He swayed then straightened up. She went on to say, "There's no inside! What do you mean, inside? This here is a woman's room. How can a man go inside? Let's settle the account here in front of everyone!"

Abd al-Hasib undid his scarf, then re-wound it: "As God is my witness, this is what I made."

The old monkey had stood by her legs and now moved between them as if getting ready to separate them if they came to blows. He began to follow the situation in a very good-humored way. Dumyana, waving her hand at the monkey, said, "His outing brings in two pounds a day and on market days, five."

"Search me, aunt."

He held his gallabiya's side pocket and began to shake it whereupon the clever monkey jumped suddenly on Abd al-Hasib's chest and reached into his vest pocket and amazingly brought out a whole pound, then jumped from his chest to Dumyana's.

We were dumbfounded. Dumyana said triumphantly, "See that, thief? The monkey has been counting the take to the last piaster. That's what I've taught him myself! He saw you making change for someone and put the pound in another pocket and didn't forget. Now show me all your pockets!"

Abd al-Hasib gave in to her rough hands, which went through his pockets and one of them brought out a fifty piaster note that she kept waving at his face as he stood there, silent with a faint smile on his lips.

"Don't you dare tell me impudently that you had it from the beginning. I know you and I know your father. You've always been beggars with not a single red millieme to your names. Thanks to this hardworking monkey, you held fifty piasters for the first time in your life. Here, take it. It's your wage for the day. I give it to you freely. Now run off and don't let me see you again, ever. As for the one who sent you, I'll deal with him!"

She stuffed the bank note down the collar of his gallabiya and turned around dragging the monkey to her room. Shawadfi was reclining on the hard straw pillow leaning on it with his right elbow, following the incident with the utmost enjoyment. As soon as Abd al-Hasib left with bowed head, he shouted in a gruff gleeful voice, shaking with emotion, "See that, undertaker? If somebody took you yourself on an outing, he would have robbed you blind!"

The undertaker shouted through his small, toothless mouth, "Well I haven't been raised on such expensive fare as he has!"

Then he followed me inside, laughing and saying, "The monkey has sobered me up," as if finding sufficient justification to light the charcoal and resume smoking.

The Midwife and the Undertaker

The undertaker said, "You must be saying to yourself, dear sir, 'This stupid man has a primary occupation, that of undertaking. So why does he abandon it and work as a server in a joint, opening himself up to risk?'"

I told him that actually I was not thinking about that at the moment, but that undoubtedly I was going to think about it at some point or another, even though I wasn't really concerned to know the reason since everyone did whatever they liked so long as they made a living by the sweat of their brow. However, he stared at me in a way I didn't understand, then added, "The story is, one likes to vent. Venting is very important, my friend. You vent to me and I vent to you and this way we both get rid of our heavy burdens. Or would you rather keep it all in? I don't think that about someone as smart as you. Begging your pardon, you're intelligent and streetwise, and, since you've made it to Wikalat Atiya, you're quite sharp."

It was obvious that he wanted to tempt me to tell him my life story. We Egyptians used this infernal method to find out each other's secrets. The safest way to get you to talk about yourself, where you're from, and where you're heading, was to start by telling you things about my life. It didn't matter whether those things were true or not but rather how well they were told. The more cleverly told the more truthful they sounded. Of course it would be wonderful if you were completely truthful, then the person sitting with you would catch it and, without knowing it, he might relate to you the minutest secret details of his life, especially if you made him feel that his secret was safe and that you were equals.

I smiled, saying, "You said it, dear sir, you hit it on the head. The long and short of the story is that I originally was not an undertaker. I was a farm worker, going around in the fields for hire, carrying my own equipment: a hoe that I carried on my shoulder for tilling, cleaning drainage canals, and digging irrigation canals. I was quite a worker; I supported my old father who had a bad spleen and my crippled mother. That mother of mine, dear sir, was a beauty queen. Unfortunately she was born with what they call infantile paralysis. If you saw her sitting down, you'd see a very beautiful young lady, but when she walked, your heart would break when you looked at her. To make one step she had to thrust her chest forward as she pushed her arms as hard as she could, which caused her body to shake so much you thought all parts of her body were glued together and that they would come apart in the air, her arms to one side, her head to the other side, and the rest of her body somewhere else. Her upper body seemed to separate when she wanted to move her right foot one step in order to drag her left foot easily behind her. Everyone praised her beauty but no one stepped forward to marry her, except my father who was a true man who understood the beauty of God's creation, even with a disability. He said he'd marry her and God would provide for both of them. My father used to guard threshing grounds at harvest time in return for a portion of the grain. My mother bore him four girls, each as pretty as the moon. But for a long time they remained unmarried because the young men in the village were afraid that they'd bear children with infantile paralysis. My mother fixed her sights on the top of the mosque minaret at dawn, noon, afternoon, sunset, and night, catching every word of the call to prayer to place on their wings innumerable prayers and supplications of her own. She thought that the words of the calls to prayer flew into space to the Creator of the sky and earth, so they were like postal carriers that could carry my mother's messages to God. All she wanted was for God to protect the honor of her daughters by sending them good husbands who believed in God's will and decree. And, you know, good sir? God did not let her down. He blessed my four sisters with four good observant Muslim grooms: one is a school teacher, the other a messenger in the same school, the third a modest grocer, and the fourth a worker in the flour mill of a nearby village. That left me with my mother, my father, and a younger brother who is now a worker in Kafr al-Dawwar who's doing well. My father contracted a disease of the spleen because he drank water from stagnant drainage canals and ponds. It got so bad before the end that he looked like a water tank with a head, arms, and feet. At that time I was on the point of being conscripted, and I would've been had they not exempted me to support my father and mother. Work in our village was seasonal, and between seasons it was drought, hardship, and idleness. I had become a full grown, large man when the cholera epidemic afflicted the village suddenly. God's wisdom willed that the first man to die in the village was the undertaker who washed the dead and covered their bodies with winding sheets. He was a relative of ours since my brother-in-law the grocer was his nephew. People were afraid to touch him, but I went in without fear, removed his clothing and washed his body with soap and rubbed it with the loofah, wrapped him and asked him to say hello to the angels. On the same day another man died and people were also afraid to touch him. So I said to myself that I should complete the job and I summoned courage, where from I don't know, and did the job. On the second day, five men died and right away people said, "Bring so and so," and they sought my help and I obliged. I said to myself, one dies only once. So, I removed their clothes and washed them and sent them on their way too. My father and some other people tried to dissuade me from such dangerous bravado, but my mother said, "Don't be afraid, my son! No harm will come to those who do good. And that which is done for God's sake is never in vain." Cholera finished off the village then another kind of cholera arrived under new names such as the Axis, Mussolini, Hitler, and al-Alamein. Bodies kept coming every day from here and there, killed in the war and you couldn't find the fathers, mothers, or uncles. All they said was, "Come Abd al-Fadil, come Abd al-Fadil." I became an undertaker by default, getting paid by the community. I earned a good reputation for being fearless and unsqueamish. I was the best in washing the bodies of casualties: with my caring hand I would gather their body parts on the wooden slab and wash each part separately and recite the shahada dozens of times, then arrange them skillfully and artfully, adding cotton supports to bring the parts together as if they had never been severed. Then I would wrap the body in a shroud in such a way as if it were a hard cast, keeping its shape and figure so that the whole body in its entirety might meet God. The owner of a big undertaking business offered me a job in his licensed establishment that had a big sign and bookkeepers and three hearses and a catering furnishings store. He also had his team of Qur'an reciters of different classes. In other words, he offered full-service packages. Expensive? Yes, but it spared you many troubles, the least of which was getting the death certificate, which for you might be difficult, but for him quite easy in view of his extensive contacts with officials of the ministry of public health. Therefore, the dead who got his package deals had no problems with death certificates or suspicion of foul play or doctors. That's not to mention the pomp with which your dead would be surrounded—as though he were a bridegroom on his wedding night! The business owner was a hashish and opium addict and he liked me so I became his constant smoking companion and purveyor of good quality stuff. To tell you the truth, he was very generous with me. But he died. He died after I became an opium addict through and through. His sons had gone to college and become doctors, engineers, and lawyers. They had brothers who inherited their father's profession but were too ashamed of it because of pressure from their educated brothers, so they specialized exclusively in the catering and furnishings businesses. As for me, I placed my trust in God: some undertakers hired me and others not, so I did not have a steady job. In the meantime my body clamored for opium every day. I went to the dealers from whom I used to buy for my boss and they took pity on me from time to time, giving me a lick on the wrapping paper that I'd then boil with the tea. Then in time they began to send me on errands to deliver for a reasonable commission. I didn't lose my teeth because of opium alone, dear sir, but because of fear. And, thank God who saved me from the clutches of the police every time I almost got caught. Then I met Sabiha, my wife, the midwife, a good woman worth her weight in gold and better than a whole tribe of men. She was married to a sick beggar who died. She came to my boss to seek his help washing and covering his body in winding sheets but he kicked her out telling her his establishment was for humans, not animals. I hated him at that moment and wished he would die in the desert and be eaten up by vultures and wolves. I took pity on the woman and I sneaked out and ran after her and did my duty by her husband and paid for the shroud from my own money, then I collected it from the good people who attended the funeral. The woman didn't forget me and began to invite me to lunch or breakfast sometimes and to tea several times. When she found out that I was living by myself in a hut on a roof in Shubra Damanhour, she moved in with me. We began living together as man and wife without marrying at the hands of a ma'zun who would have asked us for birth certificates and the like. She enabled me to stop the delivery errands and got me the job at the joint where you saw me one day. That was many years ago. The revolution brought people prosperity but it brought me and those like me ruin. The bulldozer came one day and razed the neighborhood where the huts were, since that was government land. The government then subdivided it and offered it for sale to those who could afford to build a new neighborhood. There was nothing before us except the wikala so we came here and it offered us shelter in peace until a good-for-nothing boy who knew me and Sabiha came to visit the wikala. He spent the night in the courtyard. In the morning I saw Shawadfi's face change and he asked me for an official marriage contract. It was either that or we each had to spend our nights in the courtyard away from each other. He pressured us and we confessed the truth and he took it upon himself to solve the problem as you know firsthand. Anyway, let's go back to my father. I received a telegram saying to come at once. I went back and found out that God had been generous to him and provided him with a good burial. Two weeks later I went back to the village by chance and as fate would have it, I gave my mother a decent burial. From that day I became repelled by the profession of undertaker. I began to find the bodies of the dead disgusting and that smell, which I never smelled even when the bodies came in rotten bits, I began to smell when the bodies were intact. And yet, dear sir, I swear by God I have no objection to going back to it at any time. It's quite lucrative, dear sir. This is my story from the day I was born till today. So what's your story, buddy? I'll listen to you."

Thus he left me scattered everywhere his story took me. I began to take deep drags on the shisha as if seeking the right answer there. As soon as the torrents of smoke came rushing, cool and moist, from my mouth and nostrils, I was convinced that I should reciprocate and tell him my story. For the only way to prove to men like him, who belong to our good-hearted people, that you have become someone worthy of their friendship is to talk about yourself just as they have about themselves. Isn't that our way? Anyone sitting with a group of people speaking of a situation or predicament he found himself in or an anecdote about himself, is bound to find another who would take up the thread and relate a similar or even more poignant situation that happened to him. It is quite likely that if there's enough time, everyone would tell a similar story reinforcing the general drift and reaching the same conclusion. So the undertaker was not poking his nose into my personal life or trying to spy on me. He just wanted me to open my heart to him and reassure him about myself, since I would give him the freedom to see me as it should be, from what I tell him about myself just as he did.

I had gathered some threads of certain events in my life and begun to think of the right approach and the right formula that would keep him from misunderstanding me, when I found myself spared that task as we suddenly saw her in front of us in the middle of the room: Sabiha, the midwife, wife of the undertaker according to the piece of paper which Shawadfi dictated and which I wrote down one day in the past on the mastaba by the gate.

"Evening."

And without waiting for permission or answer, she put down a large basket, like those used by fruit vendors, that she had been carrying on her head. Then she put down her even larger rear end next to me on the edge of the mastaba. Then she bent toward me with her laughing slim face: "Evening, young man. I swear by the Prophet that my heart has loved you ever since you wrote our marriage contract."

I remembered the mission that she had been on as the undertaker mentioned some time ago. Several months had gone by without my bothering to ask what happened to that; the undertaker, in turn, didn't mention it again even though he had been spending all his daytime days off in my room. My heart beat so fast and so loudly that I imagined the two of them saw it with their own eyes. I smiled involuntarily, however, when I saw the undertaker shrinking as if he were an apprentice sitting in the presence of his master. He looked cute as he devoted his full attention to the shisha and added a small piece of hashish, as big as a chickpea, on the tobacco and arranged the fire carefully around it like a necklace. Then he brought the mouthpiece close to Sabiha the midwife, exclaiming seriously, without smiling or embarrassment: "Good evening, master!"

Sabiha fixed him with a side-long glance, full of enchanting, crude, and lascivious femininity mixed with mischief: "A most pleasant evening, naughty little mama's boy!"

Then she laughed out loud like the most experienced male hashish smokers, presenting me with a proud cheek as she continued to laugh. Then her face contracted as she held the mouthpiece expertly and began to take a very slow drag. When she was done I figured out the sexual significance that she had created by the way she puffed, the crackling of the fire, and the gurgling sound of the water. She indeed deserved to be called master! She exhaled thick smoke, turning her face in my direction, staring at me with semi-lewd eyes. It was then that I realized that every woman had something attractive for someone. The appeal of this woman was especially in her eyes and in her sense of humor in general. The femininity flowing from her eyes must have made it possible for those living with her to forget her fat, ungainly figure that looked like a two-legged water buffalo. Expecting her to be merely a water buffalo, however, you'd be greatly surprised by her good humor, sweet talk, and wisdom, so your attitude toward her would change and you'd develop great admiration for her. Her eyes were not full of femininity only but radiated with intense ingenious intelligence. She was now staring at me. I joked with her saying what people in my village would say under such circumstances: "Are you measuring me for a gallabiya?"

She moved her chin back closer to her chubby neck and jiggled her eyebrows: "Nonsense! I am measuring you for a royal suit!"

She extended her open palm to strike mine as two men, confirming a joke or a dig, did. Then she said, seriously, "You look like people that I know and from whose house I've just come. Praise the Lord: the same blood. The same nostrils and eyes. Had it not been for the huge lips there, I would've said you were one of them."

My heart beat faster. This woman was so intelligent and perceptive! And also because she went back to the topic I wanted to know how it ended. I felt the undertaker's eyes moving between me and her in disbelief and when I met his glances, I thought I saw confirmation in them. I became aware of my voice asking, "By the way, how are they? What did you do there?"

"May God not deprive any of us of weddings and nights of joy!"

The undertaker couldn't wait anymore and he exclaimed in great joy, "I was sure of it the moment I saw you! And it isn't just the goodies you're carrying. The way you looked told me God has granted you success."

She slapped her own chest proudly: "What were you expecting? This is Sabiha you are talking about. Everywhere I go, good news follows. I thank God and praise His grace! Any house I enter witnesses a wedding. I bring the bride and the groom with these hands of mine, from a distant place to marry as destiny would have it in a distant place. I swear to you, young man, and I don't have to swear, there are brides and grooms that I had pulled out of their mothers' wombs and when the time came I married them off to one another. It's I who brings each of them their perfect mate. God has chosen not to give me any children but I am the mother of them all. Thank God and praise the Lord a thousand times! Contentment is granted to those who are content. My needs are simple: food, cover, and shelter. That's all I need and the good Lord has never made me ask for them, but always gave them to me before I raised my face to Him. You know, young man? I am ashamed before God and cannot raise my eyes in His face, because I don't pray regularly and I don't know when He will guide me to the right path so I can fulfil my obligations on time. Please, God, guide me for the sake of the beloved Prophet Muhammad!"

The undertaker looked at me as if to say, "This woman is blessed by God," then he said to her, "So, did you bag the groom?"

In a sarcastic, reproachful tone she said, "Nonsense! I gave him a gift and I gave her a gift. I caused each of them to fall into the well of honey. The groom is a good catch and the bride is a good catch times two."

"What does he do?" I asked eagerly.

She said, "Secretary under Ministry Waqf."

In some embarrassment, as if he were a pupil correcting a minor infraction by his teacher, the undertaker said, "She means Undersecretary of the Ministry of Awqaf. So it was him! I am happy for him and for her. He's a good man."

"Do you know him?" I asked.

He pointed at his chest, exclaiming, "Very well. I served him. I forgot to tell you that I worked for some time in the caféteria of the Ministry of Awqaf. I brought tea and coffee to the employees. It was I who introduced my wife to him. He asked me once if I knew a lady who would clean his house and wash his clothes, since he was a bachelor. I said I did and sent my old lady the following day because I was certain that he was a virtuous man and pious too. Can you imagine, good sir, that he remained a bachelor until he became undersecretary? It's because, if I can be frank, his appearance also leaves something to be desired. He has long bowed legs and walks with his legs apart as if he were a boy just circumcised. His face is also not very pleasant. Whenever anybody who had business in the ministry sees him for the first time, he tells himself right away that his business will not be done so long as this grim faced man is there. But as soon as he talks with him, he finds out how sweet he really is. Someone who, as we say, if you place him on a wound, it heals. He may get up from his chair and go with you to the office where they've given you trouble and chide them and pat you on the shoulder, asking you to blame it all on him. And he spends all his salary ordering tea and coffee for his many visitors. He smokes a hundred English imported cigarettes and drinks large pitchers of coffee every day.

The midwife added enthusiastically, "And at home, young man, he would be happy if I cooked for him and finished the food with him. He is very polite, clearing his throat before coming in and knocking on any door before opening it and never opening it unless he is sure no one is inside. He is going to make the young lady happy. I also told her and her mother as he told me to do: he will retire in three years; true, although he is quite healthy. You know something, young man? I really came to truly respect this man and became certain that he came from a good family when the following incident took place: the Hagga, the bride's mother, was willing to go in secret and buy the shabaka out of her own money then give it to him and he would then give it to the bride. The Hagga was quite happy with the bridegroom since people would say that he was a high-ranking official in the ministry. When I told the man about that he smiled and laughed in a good-natured manner and said, "No, the father of the bride is a friend at work and I don't like to start by lying. I am not poor, thank God. As is proper, I will buy the shabaka with my own money in the presence of the bride and her mother. Then after the shabaka is bought, her mother can buy whatever she wants to give her daughter while it will be known to everyone that my shabaka is such and such a thing." He also said that, out of love for the young lady, he will have a big wedding in the Government Employee Club and will take her to Mersa Matruh or Ras al-Barr for the honeymoon. Thank God! Did you know, young man, that I have been working on this project for the last three years and maybe longer? Such things do not come easy! But no matter how long it takes and no matter how hard I work, my greatest joy was when the ululation sounded at the beginning of the ceremony. Today was the most beautiful afternoon that I've seen in more than two years."

"So, the engagement actually took place?" I hurried to ask.

She rolled her eyes as if to tell me how stupid I was. Then she said in great delight, "We wrote the marriage contract! You can taste the sweets now. I have more than twenty wedding candy boxes. Empty, these boxes can fetch a lot. You can put tobacco or money or jewelry in them. The groom was afraid they'd change their minds and the family of the bride was afraid *he* would change his mind. It was all yours truly's work. If only you had seen the dowry money as he counted it as the father received it! Now I've seen what a hundred-pound bank note looked like. Wow! What a sight, young man! Like a jewel, and big. He counted many of those and every bank note, Hagg Mas'oud would stall while counting to be greeted by ululations, and this way the neighbors would keep track. May God bring us all joy! God is capable and generous!"

She bent over the basket and began to search in it, making loud scratching noises. Then she turned to me holding in her hand a crystal box wrapped tightly in cellophane, tied with gold and silver threads. On top of the box was a small strip of paper on which was written "Badriya—Shaaban" and under that the date and the words, "May your turn in happiness come!" My hand trembled as I examined the magnificent box stuffed with candied almonds and other fancy kinds of candy.

So Badriya has gotten married! Finally, Badriya is married. I kept mumbling that to myself in a daze. It seemed I said that in an audible voice, since the midwife began to beat her chest in disbelief, "Do you know her, young man?"

The undertaker shouted as if giving color commentary on a soccer game: "The woman's gone senile! The gentleman is Miss Badriya's uncle. Almost her uncle. He is her mother's first cousin."

The midwife's eyes grew wider, shining with affection tinged with disbelief or skepticism. She said, "Come on! Tell the truth now!"

"I swear by your honor, it is the truth."

The midwife seemed very embarrassed; she was obviously struggling to decide what to say and what not to say. Finally she spoke without embarrassment, "May you always be exalted in God's eyes, young man. It's a rich and generous family. Good people! Do they know that you are the Hagga's cousin?"

I burst out in uproarious laughter. I almost embraced the midwife's head and kissed it as I would an impish little boy, but she added, "Does Hagga Wadida know that you are living in Wikalat Atiya? She'd be shocked if she found out!"

I hurried to say, "That's why I beseech you not to tell her! Not her or the Hagg, or Hawwas, or Badi' or Karam or Yusriya or Shukriya or Badriya. You shouldn't even make it appear as if you know me at all."

Amazement was compounded in the eyes of the midwife: "It seems you're telling the truth, young man. You've just listed all their names for me. I told you you looked like some people I know. Praise the Lord! No, no, young man. I will not broach the subject at all. The world is made up of secrets and no one knows what lies behind the walls of houses or the walls of chests and hearts. What's certain is that there is a story in all of that, I'm not stupid. If you are from the poor branch and your cousin is from the rich branch, you've got to remember that true riches lie in the soul. Don't worry, my darling. From now on I will cherish you in my heart. Look at what time does. Praise the Lord!"

She bowed her head absently for a long time as if she were preoccupied with very complicated matters. But then she raised her head looking at me obviously quite moved. In a voice of pure motherly love she said, "Did you have supper, my darling?"

The undertaker said in childlike happiness, "Ask him if he had lunch."

The midwife stared at me with her wide eyes shining in a mysterious way that puzzled me. I was puzzled because I felt that the perceptive midwife knew what happened between me and Badriya at a magical moment behind the back of the whole universe as if it were merely imagined. But the midwife began to make childish exciting gestures with her coarse fingers, as her thick mouth said several times, "I'll feed you Badriya's cooking!"

She started staring at me again, adding in a faintly mysterious, suggestive tone, "You know Badriya's cooking, of course. It drove the bridegroom crazy as he ate. All those creamy, fried, roasted dishes or those stuffed with green wheat and nuts, all the boiled, stewed and grilled varieties, not to mention the dessert, all the baklava, harisa, the sponge cake, and the basima. She gave me some of each. You know, young man? This girl's heart is like an oven that's always hot. She's the best of them all. She has enough kindness for a whole town. The bridegrooms who missed out on her, missed all that's good. How I love that girl!"

The undertaker waved impatiently, saying, "You've made us too hungry as it is. We want to find out for ourselves. Come on, prove to us with irrefutable evidence, as the lawyers say, that Sitt Badriya is the number one cook. Open your bag and show us."

She gathered her faded shawl in her fist, waving: "Come on. Come with me, young man."

"Come where, woman? Bring it over here. Go heat it up there and come back here and we'll give you two pipefuls of Shawadfi's generosity. And, please, don't forget his share of what you have. He's been quite generous with us the last few days, giving us hashish that cost him nothing."

The midwife leaned on her knees and got up. The undertaker got up himself and helped her carry the big basket chock full of things and clean, expensive clothes made of wool, silk, and poplin. When he saw the clothes he beamed, saying, "And we've got fancy clothes to boot!" When the midwife passed by us to go out the door, he slapped her with his palm on one cheek of her large buttocks, saying, "You bring us nothing but goodness and blessing, the only love of my life!"

With the other cheek she tackled him on the legs and he fell down like a palm tree, then staggered as he clung to the mastaba, laughing. He became suddenly energetic, undoing the core of the shisha and shaking it hard, then dumping the water outside the door, saying, "The smell of this water will poison the mosquitoes and repel them from a distance." I began to throw the candy box in the air like a ball then catching it. I don't know why I imagined that I was playing with my heart. I put both my palms on it and pressed it. Was it out of vexation or the desire to hold it? I don't know. I remained like that, my head bowed absently, until the undertaker's voice brought me back: "Where've your thoughts taken you, my friend? It's as if you've attended the wedding! Look at that luck! Look what we learn!"

I stared at him for a moment then slipped the candy box under the pillow. I stretched my legs and felt unsteady so I laid on my back with my eyes closed. I went into the sea of darkness as if I were a wooden board drifting slowly with the current on the dark waves to an unknowable destination. All that was left of me was a mere twinkle, like the glimmer of an ember under a mound of thick ashes, wishing it could meld with the wind, looking for my body to bring it back to life. It seemed to me that a very long time had passed deep down in the thick of an unknown journey of which I remembered not a thing at all. Then I heard the murmuring of voices floating over my head in which I distinguished the undertaker's voice: "Leave him now. He will come to in a few seconds. We smoked a lot on an empty stomach. It also seems the news shook and stressed him."

I clung to the clear voice that I knew and reassurance pulled me out of a bottomless well. I opened my eyes with difficulty and was surprised to see myriad specters with countless shadows. Then I soon discerned that there was no one with me except the undertaker and the midwife. She bent over me staring at my eyes while grinning from ear to ear across the mounds and furrows of the flesh of her cheeks and temples. She reached out and held my hand with one of her hands, and my shoulder with the other one. She helped me to sit up. I was now wide awake as if I had just awakened from a deep sleep. I saw the low table on the floor groaning with aluminum plates and two clay pots that were redolent with Badriya's delicious intoxicating aromas. I jumped to the floor sitting at the low table but the midwife deliberately kept me stuck to the mastaba.

"Easy on the young effendi, woman. Let him breathe!"

She stuck out the tip of her tongue and jiggled her eyebrows, making a playful right fist which she ground in her left palm. The undertaker shook his head as he sat opposite us, mumbling, "A really crazy woman." He pulled out three spoons, two wooden and the third aluminum. He gave me the metal spoon and planted one in the plate nearest Sabiha and kept the other one in his hand. In unison we said, "In the name of God, the merciful, the compassionate." I ate with gusto as if I were tasting Badriya's flesh and her breath that had the flavor of cloves. She appeared to me with every morsel with her big eyes that showed the shyness of a peasant woman under the shiny veneer of a city dweller, suggesting intelligent emancipation and eyes that were full of kindness and simplicity. My heart was squeezed like kneaded dough in my chest. My eyes welled up with sharp hot tears that I kept wiping with the back of my hand suggesting they were caused by the hot and spicy food. That bothered me because at the moment I wished I could burst out crying loudly, sobbing. The midwife's eyes, however, suddenly shone as if she had uncovered a grave secret. For a few moments she looked to be in a daze, her eyes popping out, focusing on the mastaba, exclaiming, "In the name of God, the merciful, the compassionate! Thank you, God, for making things so clear to me!"

She reached with her fingers and began to feel the blanket, the comforter, and the pillow. Then she nodded and muttered as if she understood everything. Finally, she began to pat my shoulder kindly: "I do not begrudge you, sweetie. This comforter, this blanket and pillow. You know, young man? They were promised to me. Badriya promised that she'd give them to me after asking her mother's permission. You know something, young man? I can tell their bedding apart from all the bedding in the entire world. You should laugh and be surprised. Two, three, four weeks ago, Badriya called me to her room and said to me, 'If mom asks you if I gave you an old comforter and a blanket and a pillow, say yes and I'll find you others because I've given them to a poor relative.' Look at that luck, young man! See how God arranges things! I did not believe but God wanted to show me that she was telling the truth. She's such a good girl, all kindness and a big heart. She had kept the matter of this bedding hidden from her mother for a long time until she sensed that her mother was looking for it. Anyway, you or I, it's all the same."

She patted me again on the back as I kept looking at her in utter amazement, feeling that I was totally under siege. It seemed that Sabiha saw the beginnings of a breakdown in my eyes and began to pat my back with her crude palm: "Cry as much as you like, my dear young man, until you feel better."

I immediately began to sob.

Zainhum al-Atris

Until the morning I had not figured out the reason for the unusually huge crowds at the wikala. The courtyard was filled with people of all different kinds. It was also quite noisy, the hubbub rising, then falling, only to rise again. There were over three hundred men and women, not counting the children. And they were all shouting at the same time, so loudly and shrilly you would have thought that they were fighting, that at any moment clubs and cudgels would be wielded, but you soon heard laughter and sarcastic banter.

It was difficult for me to take a step outside the door of my room because bodies had curled, crouched, squatted, and gotten stuffed into every available space in the courtyard. From time to time I stood by the door of my room, casting a glance on the ground covered with human flesh in various postures: sitting, stretched out, squatting, lying down, lying flat on the back, standing and sitting on stuffed sacks, or on the railings of the arcades. There were donkeys, braying and spraying and eating, their mouths buried into feedbags hanging from their necks. There were some small pushcarts piled in a faraway corner behind the water pump. Strangely enough, nobody was upset with anybody else: there was not a single shout of protest, perhaps because of the deafening din in the courtyard. What occurred to me at the time was that the crowd was gathered for forced labor or had been rounded up as migrant workers in some large estate or another. Naturally it was impossible for me to fall asleep during that racket. However, I wasn't upset or alarmed. To the contrary, I felt the same delight and cheerfulness one felt in the middle of a crowd celebrating a popular mulid.

I felt suddenly companionable. I wished I could wade through the crowd and choose a group to stay up and drink with all night long. There must have been quite a few among the crowd from my own village. I noticed that Sayyed Zanati would appear standing with a group, shaking hands with them, but I didn't know whether he was welcoming them or saying goodbye. Then he would disappear and I almost forgot about him only to see him re-appear, squatting in the midst of another group. With one group I'd see him engaged in a very serious conversation as far as I could tell from his general demeanour and features from a distance, and with another group I'd see him joking and laughing boisterously and hysterically. He was not the only one who stood out. Many of the wikala tenants whose faces were familiar were standing in the midst of different groups as if they were erect alifs rising above long lines of short and bulging other letters in the Arabic alphabet. Finally I saw Sayyed Zanati going through the crowds toward his room, holding between his fingers a large wad of old, oily and dusty pounds which he was counting quickly, mouthing the count without a sound as he stumbled among the bodies and kept his balance with great skill.

Then Sheikh Zainhum al-Atris appeared coming from the gate, straining to see with his bleary eyes, trying to lift his constantly stooped body on a crutch. Around his lips, closed on a toothless mouth with a lower jaw drooping like a baby's sock, light streaks of saliva glistened as they went down his thick mustache dangling on both sides of his mouth, singed by cigarettes. The sheikh not only smoked sabaris cigarettes but hired many homeless children to gather the butts which he then bought for half a piaster a mugful. At the end of the night he came back carrying a full sack from which he sold to the tenants, especially Shawadfi.

That, however, was not Sheikh Zainhum al-Atris' occupation. His real occupation was begging, in an old-fashioned, formal way that was nonetheless successful and lucrative. He always had on a faded turban with a green shawl, or one that used to be green a long time ago. He always used one oath that he never changed or amended because, as enjoined by God Almighty Himself, he didn't like to swear. His favorite and constant oath, which proved that he was telling the truth, was "By the life of Sheikh Atris," his master whose green turban he wore as one of his veteran disciples and dervishes. He had devoted his days to one type of begging and his nights to another. He would go out early in the morning to make his rounds in a well-known circle that took him days, sometimes as long as two or three months, to cover. After that he would begin his rounds again. He would take the houses of the city, one by one, one neighborhood after another, then the far suburbs and the neighboring villages. And even though people knew him well and didn't need to hear anything he had to say, I saw him more than once during his rounds at the doors, carrying some sacks with his three sons, Ahmed, Atris, and Ali bringing up the rear, each carrying something else. He would knock on the door of the house, shouting, "God's people!" He would pronounce the words fast and indistinctly and whether "God's people" in the house came slowly or right away, he would start delivering his usual daily speech: "May God spare you being in my situation. May He multiply your blessings. Good people of the house, your generosity is well known. May God grant you, on the Day of Reckoning, merits equaling the number of hairs on your heads. Each good deed multiplied ten times. Life is transient, good people, and only good deeds remain. Blessed be he who feeds the hungry, clothes the naked, and is hospitable to strangers. The true wages and reward are with God, my masters. If you want favor with Sidi al-Atris's blessing, be generous to his sons and his disciples."

I followed him many days in the late morning as he repeated that same speech tirelessly, even after someone from the house came out to give him alms, he would take it and turn around, completing it in a soft voice and when he moved to the next door he raised his voice using the same words and phrases. The alms he got were usually one loaf of bread or two, with one or two pieces of plain cheese. In ful and ta'miya restaurants he got some ful or ta'miya. When a sack or basket filled up, he would leave it with one of his sons at any intersection until he finished his rounds and came back. Around sunset he would come back to the wikala, carrying a cloth saddlebag swollen in front and back, with a large sack on top. Each of the sons would be carrying a sack or a basket or an old gallabiya with its ends tied. Coming back to the wikala, he would stop at the gate to pay customs duty: some fresh loaves of bread or some pastry or any delicacy, accompanied by blessings from Sidi al-Atris, then very proudly going in, moving his crutch rhythmically with Shawadfi's prayers for him, using the same words that he himself had used to win over the people who gave him the alms.

I was preoccupied with a persistent question: where did all those tons of loaves that he gathered every day go, bearing in mind that he and his family bought nothing but fresh bread from the store or the bakery? The room he lived in with his sons could not accommodate all this bread, especially since he also had a wife and three marriage-age daughters, Amina, Ruqayya, and I'timad, in addition to a toddler girl named, interestingly enough, Dahlia whom they nicknamed Duldul. I asked him one day about the reason for choosing this European name after Amina, Ruqayya, and I'timad. He smiled a faint smile that always got lost in the wrinkles that crisscrossed the uneven skin of his gaunt face as if muddy after a long drought, and said, "By God, I . . . I don't really know, master. But, the world is making progress. It seems I heard it on the radio. Maybe I saw it in the movies. There was a beautiful girl whose name was Dahlia. I liked it without knowing why, master. I swore if I'd have a daughter to name her Dahlia. But I think, and God knows better, that the name means 'dangling.' Like the fruits of paradise that will be so close that you can reach with your hand even while lying down, may you and I see that day. What do you say I roll two cigarettes for you and make you some tea or, if you like, we can have lunch?"

I felt that he was sincere in his invitation as he said it while earnestly pushing me toward his room as if I had already said yes, which I did. I didn't wait for him to repeat the invitation since I wished to see his room by any means. He too felt my wish to accept and pushed me, so I went in.

His room was directly next to Etaita's, between hers and that of the midwife and her husband the undertaker. It was slightly bigger than my room and Etaita's but that made a big difference. Right in front as you entered, against the wall, was a solid angarib of palm branches which he proudly told me he had bought a long time ago in Sudan when he visited Khartoum in the company of the grand sheikh of the Atris order. On the angarib was an old blanket made in Fuwwa and a pillow that was a sack filled with straw. Near the angarib was a squarish box, somewhat elevated, with a conical cover, of the type sold in city markets and furniture stores as part of a bride's trosseau, even though armoires had begun to compete with it and outsell it even among poor peasant women. The box was colored and striped like a zebra, full of clothes and objects. When opened, the smell of cheap scented soap escaped from it. Next to the box was a tray of dulled aluminum on which sat four elegant earthenware water jars with broken necks, which chilled the water and made it look so delicious you wanted to drink from it the whole time. Next to that, in the deep corner stood the mountain, yes, a mountain of dry bread arranged so artistically that the person arranging it deserved a Nobel prize in patience, precision, skill, and talent for construction. The 'mountain' was so sturdy that the children leaned on it with their backs as they sat down. Two of them might fight and wrestle with each other and hit the mountain without it collapsing or even swaying, but might actually lacerate one of their heads. When they saw how much I admired the construction of the dry bread mountain, they told me that that was little I'timad's job after primary school. They also said that she planned, God willing, to go to secondary school, then on to college. Her father had sworn on the life of Sidi al-Atris to support her until she became a doctor, or an announcer like Amal Fahmi, announcing her encounters on the street for Cairo radio, especially since I'timad had a speech defect like the announcer.

The room was also, however, big enough for a large frayed mat on which they could all stretch out comfortably. In the corner opposite the bread mountain stood a Primus brand kerosene stove with two legs, the missing third one replaced by half a brick to maintain the stove's balance on the floor. The stove was encircled by a sturdy iron stand that could carry any pot no matter how heavy. Next to it were three aluminum pots of different sizes; a burnt, rusty pan stained with acrid oil; a colander; two clay casseroles; and about five tinned, colored metal plates. From under the angarib there peered a medium sized wash basin.

His wife Rihab looked more like a peasant's dovecote: thin on top, with more girth toward the bottom. She was tall and had a protruding belly with large breasts hanging down under a black gallabiya. She had a dark complexion like burnt clay. It was obvious she had come from a long line of nouris, but she had such a pleasant, uncomplicated face that she appeared to be very young. Her eyes were big with a very thick line of natural kohl close to the eyelashes. In the middle were black pupils floating in a sea of sugar-cane juice—white, but, like marbles, the pupils were so trained to knock off the marbles of your eyes and move them out of the way that you could practically hear her eyes hitting yours. They begged you passionately, seeking your help, perhaps to save her and her children from this ravine, telling you with wordless eloquence, "Protect me, may God protect your honor! Help me as much as God enables you to help, but if you can't help then at least help by not harming me!" Yet you would notice in their depth shades of ancient harlotry that perhaps went back all the way to mother Eve, accomplished harlot. However, you would not answer the call of those shades, at least not at first. The danger was there and if you stayed long enough and got used to her as she got used to you, all the previous suggestions would fall from her radiant eyes, leaving behind only those shades of ancient harlotry, which she didn't confirm by any movement, word, or gesture. The fact that she was totally unaware of all of that would provide the utmost excitement. The dirty clothes, the low standard of living, and the filth all around you and the overall mess might repel you in the beginning, might prevent you from thinking of her as a woman, but you'd soon fall into the eternal trap, finding yourself perplexed as you began little by little to think of Rihab, wife of Sheikh Zainhum, as a woman. But you'd soon discover that filth and rottenness could have an exciting, animal-like aspect. For, just as descending the stairs could be easy, so falling low and giving in to poverty and decay could soon have an exciting, delicious, familiar taste.

I forcefully banished that woman from my mind, but I wasn't able to do the same with her daughter, Amina, the bride approaching twenty whose supple figure was like that of a dark, delicate gazelle. She had her mother's eyes and the richly expressive face of her father, on a reed-like body topped with two ripe, pointed spheres. The waist was more like a barely visible elastic band leading in the back to two globes sloping down, graceful thighs to bamboo-like calves and well-rounded heels. She was standing next to the door washing the tea things after we'd eaten rich peasant fitir with aged cheese in mish. The side view of her gaunt face with pointed nose, with the light and shadow of the faint kerosene lamp cast on it, gave her the look of an ancient Egyptian peasant woman like those one saw in history books sowing seeds or feeding chicken. Her mother Rihab had sat on the mat, her thighs parted and one of her knees stretched and the other folded, in front of the lit stove making a familiar, soothing, purring sound. Next to her sat Ruqayya who was three years younger than Amina but more on the chubby side with hardened featured that made her look more like a thuggish boy. Seeing her one thought she was hiding a pen knife or a lockpick under her armpit. As for I'timad, she sat on the angarib, leaning on the wall, holding a homework notebook and pencil, studying out loud as if to prove to me how smart and deserving of schooling she was. Near her, little Dahlia slept. I refused to sit on the angarib and instead sat on the floor next to Sheikh Zainhum who squatted next to the door inside. The sheikh kept reminding me of his generosity by repeating a line of poetry that I didn't know where he learned:

The good are generous to us with their money
And we are generous with the money of the good.

The smell of the cigarette butts, burning for a second time, stank up the room.

I wanted to get up and out because I felt that Sheikh Zainhum was on pins and needles to start his evening rounds, during which he practiced other kinds of begging. He would go out after performing his ablutions and combining the noon, afternoon, sunset, and evening prayers together. Then he would wrap himself with the remnants of a tattered ancient shawl that must have been worn out by a good rich man before he bestowed it on him. It was made of soft cashmere speckled with pea-like dots, maintaining its original colors as if it were new with that new wool smell, even though it was really strips connected with frayed thread within its folds. When he folded the shawl and wrapped it around his neck, however, it looked intact and it lit up the sheikh's face who looked then like a man who had seen better times. He would then proceed in a dignified manner with his head held high, unlike the daytime humble, bowed-head appearance. He would make the rounds of different stores and shops: fabric stores, grocers, apothecaries, fruit grocers, tailors, and high-class cafés. He was quite an expert at picking out store owners from customers and guests. He would make a beeline to the owner right away, his eyes wide open in a pleasant, affectionate smile. And since there was a gray spot on the black of the right eye, he looked pitiable. He would greet the store owner warmly and the latter would reciprocate even more warmly. In a short while the store owner would discover that he had overdone the welcoming in a manner that would soon cost him. He would stare at the eyes of Sheikh Zainhum waiting for him to make his request known, but the sheikh would just stand there, out of the way, his hands resting below his chest like someone in prayer, bowing his head and mumbling unintelligibly. The owner would soon give in to what he had figured out right from the very beginning and open the cash register going through the coins looking for a half-piaster or a piaster to give to him. At that point, Sheikh Zainhum's voice would rise clearly: "May God grant him his wishes! May God make him even more prosperous! May God diminish the prospects of his competitors! May God defeat those who envy him and devastate his enemies! Amen."

He would be finishing that last sentence on his way out onto the street within earshot of the owner of the store next door who would take it as a good omen and open the cash register and finding a coin right away so as to spare the sheikh the trouble of coming in and waiting. By the end of the night, the sheikh would go back, his pockets jingling with many coins. He would then stop by an egg store, not as a beggar this time, but as an honored customer in high spirits and head held high. And, like any respectable customer he would pick and choose from the eggs ten large ones that he would ask the salesmen to put in a paper bag. Then he would push his hand into his pocket ostensibly to take out a piaster to pay for the eggs but in reality to jingle the many coins to tempt the salesman to ask him for the change. Usually the salesman would take the change off his hands in return for bank notes that would be easy to put in his wallet or the box in the room.

The sheikh's wife, Rihab, was also always at work, accompanied by her daughter Ruqayya who was therefore always a little spoiled. Rihab had employers in various parts of the city to whose houses she went on specific days of the week, washing all the family's clothes, sweeping and mopping the floor, and washing the windows. Some other families also made her cook, so Rihab would go out and buy the vegetables and meat and fruits leaving Ruqayya to do the rest of the housework. As for Amina, she alone was in charge of their own household, cleaning and fixing meals until the mother and Ruqayya returned around mid-afternoon from their day jobs.

Sheikh Zainhum had finished his prayers while sitting next to me without kneeling or prostrating himself, just inclining his head at every kneeling or prostration. Then he said hospitably, "Would you like some more tea, master?" I thought he was giving me a hint to leave, so I started to get up but he held on to me and said, "Make tea, Rihab," and she replied, "Okay, Zainhum," and began to light the stove. I was surprised at the way she addressed him. It seemed I expected her to say "amm" or, at least, "sheikh." Then I noticed anew how young she was and how old he was.

I was certain that surprise appeared clearly on my face since he cast furtive glances at me then said, "Were you surprised, master, that she called me 'Zainhum'? It was I who got her used to saying that. Is she not my woman, master? She must address me by name just as I address her."

I said to clear my conscience, "You have work to do and I am keeping you from it."

"Let's drink the tea and go."

"Just as you like."

He took out of his gallabiya's side pocket a ten-piaster silver piece. He poked at the edge with his thumb and it split into two coins attached to each other. He turned one over and, lo and behold, it was covered with layers of strong-smelling opium. With a match he extracted a piece as big as a chickpea that he brought close to my mouth. "Open your mouth," so I did and he inserted the match into my mouth and I closed my lips on it. He took a piece for himself then stuck the two coins together again and put them in his side pocket and said, "By the way, master, it was I who raised Rihab, my wife. She used to call me 'father.'"

"How, Sheikh Zainhum?"

His eyes grew quite a bit wider. The gray spot in the center of his right eye looked like an island in a black ocean. I became certain that his eyes had always been wide and that the crinkled wrinkles around them looked like the wrinkles of the band on the pants' waist, hiding an invisible elastic and when it expanded the eyes seemed wider and when it contracted they seemed smaller. It became clear to me that the deceptively small eyes were the result of strenuous training, since the wideness of the eyes surely reflected an experience of misbehavior and devilishness and a long exposure to bad nights and worse misery and a time laden with anguish, repression, and defiance. It occurred to me to ask him about the spot on his eye and how it came about. Was he born with it? Or did it result from illness or injury? Then I focused my eyes on it in such a way that he noticed. He pointed at it with his finger and spoke about it using words I had expected: "This one, master, goes back to naughty days. We were taking loot, which we had stolen from the camp of the English. We were confused and in a hurry because our take was huge. I bent my head under the barbed wire to alert my companion to do the same and as soon as I upturned my head, the barbed wire snatched this eye. I screamed like a dog hit suddenly on the head by a stick. I kept squirming and convulsing on the ground while my companions dragged me away from the camp. I went to the hospital and stayed there for a whole month receiving treatment."

He finished rolling a cigarette and offered it to me. I almost turned it down because of the stifling stink of the butts but I was dying for a cigarette because of the opium, so I took it. When I lit it I felt a strange pleasure at the sharp, hot stinging smoke but I was too disgusted to inhale. As for Sheikh Zainhum, he took pleasure inhaling and even greater pleasure continuing his story: "The story, master, begins in Suez where I first opened my eyes in a huge house that had hundreds of children of all ages. There were dozens of effendis whose only job was to kick us and spit in our faces, night and day, in rows, in classes, and in shop sessions. I didn't know that a child could have a father and a mother! That's because ever since I became aware of the world around me, I didn't see a trace of them, and the same is true of those who were with me. I found out that the house where we were was called Zagazig Orphanage, that we were all bastards born out of wedlock who had been found at mosques' doors and in garbage cans. Some of us were brought there by our own families who then forgot about us. I was quite a boy! From early on I knew that the world could be taken only by the strength of your arms. A world that was like a whore that fell in love only with those that had strong, hard hearts. Thus I made my mark among the boys. I got what's mine and what wasn't mine by sheer strength: I hit, I scratched, I tackled, I stole, I lied. It didn't matter to me. The amazing thing is that everybody liked me and denied me nothing, without my having to resort to violence. Even the clerk of the orphanage began to fear me. I asked him where I came from and he looked in his big ledgers and said that twelve years earlier an English soldier had found a foot-long piece of flesh wrapped in mulberry leaves discarded in the camp trash can, so he handed it over to the Suez police. The Suez police sent it quickly to the Zagazig orphanage. Everyday I would sweet talk the clerk until he told me new things that were preserved in the papers establishing my parentage. He said that at the time I was found, there was a rumor that one of the English soldiers had raped a poor girl from Suez and that she'd become pregnant. When she gave birth, she took the baby to him but that he kicked her out, whereupon she threw the baby at his feet and he threw it in the garbage. She set herself on fire and the police came and investigated and wrote reports. I was very upset at that story because back then my eyes had some blue color. The son of a bitch of a clerk spread that story among the boys who began to taunt me by it. He was taking revenge on me because I wouldn't go along with his depravity. He used to hire out boys to the English soldiers and to some pederasts. He would choose a boy he liked and gave him one night off. Anyway, all the kids in the orphanage were children of adultery, but that's not the big issue. The shame of it was for the one who had fornicated with the mother to have been a blue-eyed Englishman. I got fed up with life in the orphanage, so I ran away. I worked as a porter in railroad staions, a shoe-shine boy working for a man who gave me the box and the material and to whom I gave all the take of the day each night, and he gave me whatever he felt like giving me. But I was still very vexed at that low-life Englishman who had had his way with my mother and thrown me in the trashcan. I said to myself: You should go home; so go back to Suez, maybe you'd be able to avenge yourself against your unknown, low-life father. I fell in with some no-good unemployed men from Suez and I was very happy when I found out they made their living robbing the English camp. I threw in my lot with them enthusiastically and they gave me all the difficult tasks and I carried them all out. When my blue eye was scratched by the barbed wire, I got very mad. I decided that revenge should be double. So I'd steal and then go back to burn or kill. Yes, sir! Once I went to the depot where they kept their weapons and to the food warehouse and the barracks where the soldiers slept. I had three kittens, beautiful but with blue eyes like them. I went in with the workers and hid when they left until night fell. I had hidden the kittens under my clothes next to my chest. In the middle of the night I sneaked to the gasoline barrel and turned on the tap, doused the kittens, then let the gasoline flow on the ground. At each door I set one cat on fire and let it run like crazy. When I was outside, at a distance from the camp, I looked back and I saw the fire consuming everything: wood, tents, ammunition, oils, and grains. And yet the sight of the camp in the morning did not satisfy my desire for revenge despite the carnage and the wholesale death. So, I and my ne'er-do-well companions would set ambushes for the drunk officers and send prostitutes their way to lure them to out-of-the-way places, then we would jump them from behind and attack the officers with their pants down, sticking them with knives in the side of the heart or the neck and taking their money and things we could sell or wear, and then be on our way. Then the revolution of 1919 broke out when I was in the prime of youth. The whole world turned upside down, and we made very good use of it: killing, beating, burning, and looting. The English soldiers began roaming the streets with guns and cars, killing people and razing houses to the ground. Back then I met the dear departed Uraibi and his wife the dearly departed, Gall al-Khaliq. Yes, her name was Gall al-Khaliq but they pronounced it Gallkhaliq. Originally they were Bedouins from Sinai. Uraibi worked in the English camp with the Egyptian workers. We met during the demonstrations and he began to visit me in a hut that I had built for myself in the midst of the fisherman's huts. He was a good man and one of the dervish followers of Sidi al-Atris. His sweet talk about al-Atris and his miracles and his covenant and his place with God totally won me over. I fell in love with Sidi al-Atris and began to go to his zikr sessions with Uraibi and we would engage in zikr, and listen to preaching and sermons and words that moved the heart and filled it with submission. You could say I became one of the dervishes of Sidi al-Atris, never skipping a prayer. The sheikh of the Atris order, God have mercy on his soul, was like a saint. He took us to Sudan and the Hejaz to meet our Atrisi brothers. The sheikh of the order, God have mercy on him, also loved me, so I became his faithful servant, following him everywhere, always by his side. He wouldn't let anyone else serve him and wouldn't eat unless I was there. I only became homeless when he died. The good folks took pity on me for a while then forgot about me. Uraibi got me a job at the camp. It was hard work but I did it. Then the world, never constant, delivered me the second blow when my friend Uraibi died, leaving behind his wife Gall al-Khaliq and a seven-year old daughter. I took pity on the woman and her daughter; I took them under my wing and protected them from the wolves. I married Gall al-Khaliq to raise her daughter. She left the rented room and moved to my hut turning it into a piece of paradise. Life went on sweet and smooth. I went to my work and Gallkhaliq went to hers, making a living by washing clothes, cleaning houses, or selling vegetables. Rihab kept growing into a young lady and when she called me 'Aba,' it was as sweet as honey! But the son of Adam is by nature greedy. What need did I have of being a father when I had Rihab saying it at all times and when I bought her nice things whenever I had extra money. But it was greed, master, on my part and also on Gallkhaliq's part. We wanted to have a boy or even another girl to strengthen our bond. And it came to pass, master. One marches to one's preordained fate even when he thinks he is trying to achieve his own happy goals. Gallkhaliq got pregnant and the birth was premature, like a catastrophe, two months early. The woman lay down to give birth and never got up. She was stricken by that accursed thing they call childbed fever. The mother and the baby both died and it broke my heart in several pieces, master. May you never see what I've seen! We ended up alone: Rihab, myself, and time. How could I leave her all day to serve the blue-eyed low-life? The devil, as they say, is clever and Rihab was nubile. Should I have taken her with me to work? The blue-eyed beasts would eat her up! It was quite a problem. She was going to be gobbled up by the blue eyes or the black eyes. I would finish work and return like a madman and, at work, I was there only with half a mind or a quarter mind. When performing the dawn prayer I beseeched God to send her a good groom to protect her. I almost spoke to people offering her in marriage. The only thing that prevented me from doing that was pride and fear of cheapening the girl. This want on for five years until the little one approached thirty. I lost patience worrying about her and her responsibility. But it was fate, mister. On a blessed and pure night I broached the subject to her, with fear and a trembling heart. And Rihab, just like her name implies, welcomed the idea. I took her to the marriage resigtrar and I told him the story from A to Z and he wrote the marriage contact for us in accordance with God's law. That's the story, do you like it or does it need some work?"

"It's a beautiful story, Amm Sheikh Atris."

"Had you said it needed some work, I'd have made you do all the work yourself," he said with a smile.

In jest, I said I was willing to do any work and he said with a big smile, "Some other time."

Then he got up and so did I and we both left, he to his rounds and I to my room.

Hours

Just as it happened this time and every time the courtyard became unusually crowded, week after week, I saw Sheikh Zainhum al-Atris coming toward the gate as I stood by the door of my room watching the intimate crowd. He spoke with Shawadfi for quite some time. He was carrying a small, coarse cotton sack clearly half-filled with cigarette butts that he had bought from the street children. The crutch came in handy as he used it to nudge people to clear a path for him to get to his room. I followed him with my eyes. The door to his room was ajar and a faint light came from within. As I was busy watching him, I heard someone breathing and saw some shadows approaching and a rough hand nudging me in a friendly way. I was startled, then I saw that it was Mahrous, the radish vendor.

"Hello, Mahrous."

"I have been waving for you for a whole hour but you were not here."

"I didn't see you. Honest!"

He pointed to the pump: "I saw you from over there and when I became certain that you wouldn't see me, I left the goods with someone to watch and came over to say hello. I have a pushcart that I rented for one night to take to market tomorrow. Is this your room? So, you live here? That's very good news! Do you have tea equipment?"

"Sure do."

I escorted him inside. The undertaker had left with me simple teamaking equipment in the hope that he would spend more time at my place, rather than staring at his wife the whole time, as he put it. When Mahrous sat next to me on the mastaba, I told him I had the equipment but unfortunately no tea. He took out of his pocket some tea and sugar wrapped in an old newspaper. Then he began to rinse the mug and the two cups.

"I only spend market night here every week."

"So how come we haven't seen each other?"

"I asked about you a million times. By the way, Shawadfi has been trying to find out stuff about you. He rolled me two cigarettes and asked me so many questions about you I thought it was strange and I asked him whether he thought I was Sheikh al-Hara. I gathered from him that he was afraid of you, thinking you were a naïve secret police detective. I assured him that you are a good, but poor, man. I told him I'd seen you one day sleeping on the sidewalk. He growled and nodded and thanked God that you turned out to be a good man as he'd figured out since he saw you the first time. But I don't think he believes me, because he forgot what I told him about you and asked me a second, third, and fourth time. So much so that I myself became confused and ended up also thinking you were secret police. You, begging your pardon, understand so many things and you don't look homeless. Do homeless people read books and discuss politics and art as you do? Frankly, I also began to smell a rat. So, if you are secret police, do me a favor and get me a job with you. I can be a very good detective! I can track down anything!"

I laughed: "Can you track down ten piasters, as a loan?"

He stared at my eyes intently as he poured the dark strong tea: "Really?"

"I am so penniless! I have no job and my debt to Shawadfi has grown so much I am afraid he'll evict me any moment now."

He waved his arm in front of my face, saying, "Have no fear on this account. He'll never evict you. He never gives up what's his. He might keep you prisoner in this room until somebody pays your debt for you. Then, he'd let you go. But he's not going to do that now until he's made sure you're not secret police. He imagines that you are overdoing this poverty bit to convince him you're harmless. You can count on me to encourage him in his belief."

"What matters now is: are you going to give me ten piasters or not?"

"I'll give you five; that's all I can afford. On condition that you wait until the end of tomorrow's market, from my take. Before leaving, I'll drop by and leave it for you. Am I supposed to support you as if you were a lost son of mine? That's all I needed in this world!"

He laughed so hard the cup shook in his hand and he said in his warm, sincere peasant tone, "I swear that I am pleased to have met you. I had no brother, no sister, and no friend. And those I wanted to be my friends turned out not to like mawwals, to be dull in spirit. You be my friend and I'll protect you with all I have, so long as you are sincere in your friendship. Here. This is a two-piaster piece to have breakfast, drink tea, and get two cigarettes. I've tried need firsthand and I know how humiliating it can be. May God never show us humiliation!"

He put down his cup and got up: "I am going back to my produce to sleep next to it and spray it with water. See you tomorrow."

He left before I could answer him. The two-piaster piece had settled in my hand like a big treasure. I began to make big plans for it then was immediately overcome with the opposite impulse not to spend it any time soon, to keep it for a long time. Perhaps if I could hold on to every piaster that found its way to my hand I'd have a whole bunch of them. It would be even better if they were shillings or, better still, ten-piaster pieces. Then I'd pay Shawadfi who'd then deduct them from my debt, which I'd come to dread adding up in terms of so many months' rent. I couldn't trust Shawadfi's patience because I knew what he was really like; he wouldn't forgive a single millieme. I felt that his silence, the fact that he hadn't demanded anything, was a sort of fattening up of the calf before slaughtering it, that it placed me in a situation in which I would accept any job he told me to do to pay off my debt and keep body and soul together. I knew that if I bore the pangs of hunger, I couldn't bear his final burst of anger, the extent and consequences of which only God knew. Besides, I could no longer bear sleeping while walking the streets of a city that I'd begun to find boring, that I'd even almost come to hate even though it had tolerated me day and night without a policeman or a boorish, inquisitive stranger bothering me. But where could I get myself a suit of thick skin to protect me from the stinging night cold, especially since the month of Tuba was on the way? My body was now trembling just remembering, so what would happen if it actually came to pass? I was willing to pay anything now to find out what Shawadfi was planning for me. What was the secret plan he had either prepared or was on the point of preparing for me? Was he about to put it into effect? But, what if I were to blow this whole city, leaving Shawadfi in the lurch, as my predecessor in the room had done? In our village the proverb says that when things got too tight, one should "change the thresholds," in other words, find a new house or a new village where you could make a living. My beloved city of Damanhour had turned its back on me. Maybe it was unlucky for me. I came to it full of pride and hope but it tolerated me only as a homeless, lost wretch. Thank you, my city, anyway. You haven't been as hard on me as I have been on myself. At least I found in you those who helped me cope with some of my hardships and worries. I found in you a literary society and an intimate café that housed it and served as the only family that could understand me. It was the only place that did not get disgusted by my shabby clothes or turn up its nose at my uncouthness, or measure me by what I owned, spent, or wore, or by what position I occupied. One of these days I must find within its nooks and crannies a path that will take me where I want to go—to be a writer someday. So, you see, dear Damanhour, I couldn't forsake you no matter how tight things got. Besides, besides, how could I forsake you when you have Badriya's heart? How could I have forgotten that? How could I forget that I had fallen in love with Badriya? I was now as certain as I was alive that I loved you, Badriya! No, I wasn't in love with you because you, unlike your family and despite knowing what they felt about me, had pitied me and given me, behind their back, a pillow, a comforter, a blanket, and a sheet. You had also given me a large sum of money that was too much for your pocket money. But even if that were enough to prove your noble heart and warm feelings, that real proof was what I felt when I was totally inside you. It was only now that I recalled that fantastic magical moment which I wouldn't have believed if somebody were to tell me about it even though I had lived it myself. To tell the truth, I couldn't describe that moment: how could a fetus describe its mother's womb while still part of it? Goddamn it! Goddamn it! Goddamn whoever has taken her away from me. Yes, I am extremely selfish and I cannot help it. God damn him, Badriya, if he ever made you feel, even deep down inside him, that he was condescending to kiss your huge, beloved lips. Your lips are more tender and delicate than his crude feelings and thick skin. If he were truly enlightened, he would have knelt down to your lips, pouring kindness and hot feelings flowing from the mounds of your unreachable and yet accessible eyes. Oh, Badriya! Badriya! Badriya!

Thus the day broke. I became suddenly aware of the slate color that painted the walls of the room through the window glass. The hubbub that only a few moments ago had filled the space, sinking away deep into a far corner of the universe, now rose and its sounds became clear: the calls, the chimes, the lowing of the cattle, the humming of the stoves, the jingling of the horses, and the rumbling of the carts. I stretched as I sat up, then got off the mastaba. I opened the door and found that the courtyard was almost totally empty even though the atmosphere was still redolent with the cool, fresh morning smells of fried eggs, ful, ta'miya, parsley, gargir, limes, and milk. All the doors were ajar except for the undertaker's and the midwife's, which was wide open, humming with a burning stove and noisy movements. Sheikh Zainhum's room was also half open and there was movement there as well.

It was only a moment before I saw the undertaker emerging, wearing a clean white elegant outfit. He had shaved and obviously taken a bath a short while earlier. In his left hand he was carrying a round, shining brass tray on which were arranged some glasses. In his right hand he was holding a very large, blue zinc-plated kettle from whose spout steam poured. He walked very slowly toward the gate, a cigarette dangling from his lips as he mumbled something that may have been the conclusion of a prayer. I figured out that he was taking the kettle and glasses to the market and that when he sold out he'd come back to the room to find that Sabiha had prepared for him another kettle and clean glasses to take back to the market. I went out to the edge of the arcade and stood opening my chest to the cool morning breeze. I felt my eyelids parting and getting rid of a light sticky discharge. I looked into the distance, going beyond the far wall of the courtyard, settling like an anxious sparrow on the railing of the balcony of the opposite house behind the wall, separated by a public street. The white, rose-cheeked halabi woman was leaning her elbows on the railing, her face shining like a genie in the midst of a thicket of blondish hair. She raised her soft hand through the receding wide sleeve of the house gown and waved to me in a quick greeting. I returned her greeting, imagining happily that the whole world was pleased with me.

Goodies for the Sheep

I saw a flock of sheep crossing the street in front of the wikala gate. It went on for many, many minutes in a seemingly endless procession. Then there appeared two shepherds and several boys each holding a long, flexible cane. Then a gaunt-faced man, with thick features and a dark brown complexion around whose lips a thick, pointed mustache dangled, got away from the flock. He had on a rounded cap like an upturned casserole and had a narrow forehead and narrow eyes. With blinking eyes the shepherd looked at the entrance of the gate then tapped it with the tip of his cane, calling out, "Amm Sheikh Zainhum!"

As if the sheikh was waiting for him, he came out right away: "Come in, Abu Hawana!"

The shepherd came in, saying, "Good morning, Me'allim Shawadfi!"

He sat in front of him. Shawadfi was fanning the burning cobs under the tea mug with the edge of his pants and at the same time throwing into his mouth a few morsels of some food or another that he was taking from a corner in the wall. He said through his busy closed mouth, "Happy day, Abu Hawana! You came just in time."

The shepherd lifted his cap and took out from underneath it his tin tobacco case and opened it, taking out a piece of opium the size of a ful bean wrapped in cellophane. With his nail he removed a scrap, which he proffered toward Shawadfi's mouth. The latter reached out two fingers and took the scrap and put it on his thumbnail waiting until he finished eating. Sheikh Zainhum had caught up with them, smiling, his eyes focused on the shepherd's nail and the cellophane wrapper. He exclaimed, "May we have a blessed morning, God willing!"

The shepherd's nail, covered with a scrap of opium reached him and he opened his mouth and closed his lips on it and sucked it, smacking his lips, saying as he sat on the edge of the mastaba, "Save your tea, Shawadfi. Tea will soon come from my place. Quick, boys!" He shouted, looking toward the courtyard.

Shawadfi yelled at him, "Behave, Zainhum!"

The sheikh shouted toward his room, "Okay, boys. Forget it."

He reached out to take the cup from Shawadfi. The shepherd, sipping the tea in obvious pleasure, said, "How are things this week, Amm Sheikh Zainhum?"

"God's blessings are abundant."

"Can I have a look?"

"Sure."

He went ahead of him toward his room, cleaning his throat in an exaggerated manner. He went in: "Good morning, Umm Ahmed!"

"Good morning to you," replied Rihab as she stood in a far corner. The shepherd looked at the corner where the mountain of dry bread stood and began to survey it with scrutiny, from bottom to top and from right to left, bending his head to examine the corners and see how deep they were, almost counting the layers loaf by loaf. Then he turned to Sheikh Zainhum, wiping his mustache with his hand: "Blessings on the Prophet, Amm Sheikh Zainhum!"

"Blessings and peace."

"More blessings!"

"Blessing, peace, and prayers."

"I offer you ten tens."

"Look carefully before you speak."

"I looked enough."

"Then you are doing me and these toiling boys an injustice. This is the sweat of many days for me and my sons in the heat of the day, from neighborhood to neighborhood and from house to house. You want me to sell that for ten tens? Even if I had stolen it, I wouldn't accept this price. Take it for nothing but don't strain yourself and say ten tens. This is haram. This is really haram, my friend!"

The shepherd waved his arms in the air in a gesture of extreme generosity: "Ten and two?"

"Take the swift train, maybe you'll catch up with me."

"Ten and five and not a millieme more."

He combined that with moving toward the door at a deliberately slow place. The sheikh egged him on to leave by suggesting that accepting such a price was impossible by saying, "Stay and have some tea."

"Thank you. Thank you!"

He started dragging himself slowly and nonchalantly as Sheikh Zainhum, on his heels, repeated confidently: "Good bye. You honored us, Abu Hawana."

As the shepherd was about to get out of the gate, Shawadfi stopped him: "Come here, Abu Hawana!"

The shepherd returned at once, then sat down: "Yes?"

"Have you forgotten that tea here is served three times, you stupid Bedouin? You had only one. You think no one is keeping track here, that you can come and go as you please? Here!"

The shepherd took the teacup laughing: "Each of you is a shepherd and each shepherd is responsible for his flock."

"But how would you leave unsatisfied? How much did you offer him?"

"One hundred and fifty piasters, an educated man's salary for a whole month."

"And how much are you asking, Zainhum?"

"Sixty tens."

And he marked the sum with his finger, pointing in the air. The shepherd shouted, deeming the sum too much: "I could buy a whole ardeb of barley and fava beans!"

"I beg your pardon? This is better than two ardebs of barley and beans. Your sheep will eat for more than a month. This is pure good fodder. Wheat mixed some with milk and some with bran. You know what I am saying."

Sheikh Zainhum concluded with a confident, decisive look. Shawadfi intervened to end the discussion: "Say your prayers for the Prophet that neither of you will ever see."

"Prayers to the Prophet," they both said. Shawadfi told the shepherd, "Let's split the difference. Pay him thirty tens."

"That's too much, Amm Shawadfi!"

"Believe me you'd be the winner! Don't miss out on this bargain. The bread that you'll take weighs more than two ardebs of choice flour. I personally wet the bread and eat it and it is like cream. When your sheep eat it, their skins will be like silk."

"Would you take the twenty tens, Amm Sheikh Zainhum, may God make it up to me?"

"May God make another arrangement."

"Make it twenty-five tens, Abu Hawana, and don't say another word."

"Whatever you say, Amm Shawadfi. Here it is."

He took out of his gallabiya's side pocket a large handkerchief and untied a knot at the edge and a wad of money came out. He took two and a half pounds and threw them in Sheikh Zainhum's lap. The sheikh showed some hesitation but a firm glance from Shawadfi put a stop to that. He put the money in his pocket and said, "You can take it!"

The shepherd got up and shook hands with Shawadfi's slipping him a silver ten piaster coin then left. Sheikh Zainhum looked in his side pocket for a ten-piaster piece but could only find two shillings which he gave to Shawadfi. He opened his tobacco case and started rolling a cigarette. As soon as he was done, the shepherd came back accompanied by two strong young men carrying two large empty sacks containing two smaller sacks. The empty sacks went in and came out full six times over the course of more than an hour. Sheikh Zainhum observed them somewhat resentfully because he felt he was not paid enough, as he had not correctly estimated the value of what he had. But he followed the sacks coming out with a viscous smile, repeating in a certain tone, "It's all to the good. It's all to the good. It's all a matter of fate. May the sheep enjoy it and may it prove healthful."

After a while Dumyana came out wearing a see-through black dress over another one light in color, her face shining under the sequined headkerchief, with her shawl set back on her head and draped over her shoulders. She held the halter of the young monkey, which kept sneaking around, jumping up and down, thinking he had attained freedom but, harshly restrained by the chain, withdrew next to her. She said good morning and slid out of the gate. Shawadfi murmured, "The poor monkey is exhausted!"

Zainhum commented, "Little sticks exhaust mountains of kohl."

She was followed by Etaita carrying a cage full of chickens on her head. Then there appeared coming from the direction of the water pump a thin, tall young man whose pants were stained with paint. He had on a sleeveless T-shirt and the muscles of his forearms glistened with sweat. He was heading for the arcades, where he turned at Sheikh Zainhum's room then went up the adjacent stairs to the room above it. He opened the lock and went in. Sheikh Zainhum mumbled, "The one with the brush! Isn't he done yet?"

"I wish he'd be done with this world! He's been working on last market's loot all night long. He's the only one whose presence in the wikala is a threat. He is exposing me to danger for nothing. If he doesn't behave today, I'll give him over to the police myself, but not here in the wikala."

The young man came out of his room carrying a new can of paint from its wire handle. He cleared the stairs, coming down in two leaps. He went toward the pump and took a sharp turn to the left and disappeared. I was totally intrigued and decided to follow him, but discreetly. I picked up the towel quickly and dashed out to the pump whispering, "Good morning," raising my hand without waiting for a reply. I turned sharply as the young man had and that turn led me to another turn in the opposite direction. I found myself in front of a small gate, partly independent from the wikala even though it was part of it. It had two stories with several windows and mashrabiyas. The gate was ajar. I bent my head to look inside. I found something that looked like a stable or a large shed that had a door leading to a back street that went through to the heart of the market. There was another door in a sidewall that opened out to the distant farms. I saw several cows, water buffaloes, and donkeys tied to stakes in front of a trough with remnants of dry bread, undoubtedly from Sheikh Zainhum's supply. The young man was busy stirring the paint with a look of disgust on his face, apparently from the paint's smell. He began to add some liquids to it that he stirred in, then sniffed again. Finally he stopped and held a flat brush used to paint doors and windows and went to a donkey standing by itself with only its rear end was visible. The donkey's color was as white as cotton. As soon as the young man got close to it, the donkey shied and tried to bolt away, making a loud noise with its nostrils. When its neck and head and front upper part came into view it was all black. The young man held the donkey's neck and twisted it to one side and he began to dip the brush into the paint can and paint the body in even strokes, joining the black parts with new black paint until little by little the white areas began to disappear altogether. I cast a quick glance at the cows and buffaloes and noticed that most of them had bright colors, and that a red cow had white stripes on its head and neck. As for the donkeys, some of them were glistening, and obviously the paint hadn't quite dried yet and in a short while they would roll in the dung and dust and would get even darker in color. I was immediately certain that all of these donkeys and cows were stolen. I withdrew on tiptoe, going backward to the pump, which I pushed calmly and quietly in order to listen in on Shawadfi and Sheikh Zainhum whose voices rose suddenly in the midst of delighted, sustained laughter. Zainhum was saying through his muffled laughter as if he were going to die any moment, "You're too much! You specialize in selling stolen cattle to their original owners. I am afraid one of these days you'll sell us all, one by one, to ourselves!"

Shawadfi replied with a tremendously confident seriousness, "Don't worry. I'll never do such a lame thing because I wouldn't find someone willing to buy the best among you for one millieme. But, in all honesty, I myself am willing to pay all the money in the world for your eldest daughter Amina. She's the only gem in my wikala. As for the rest of you, you belong in the trash or the dung heap!"

The sound of a strong fart, melodious and muffled, rose like a musical note played with skill. Shawadfi yelled in a growling voice, "You're so goddamn disgusting! This is people's sweat and toil rotting inside you. If it had been your own sweat and toil, it would have been fragrant! Since when didn you last take a shit?"

"Since I saw you."

With sarcastic cynical vexation, Shawadfi said, "It promises to be a glorious day, God willing. We started with rotten farting, perhaps it will end in fragrant shit. Get up now and change the omen. Get us a customer or two. Before noon we will open the door to the fields and any customer can come in and inspect and poke as much as they like."

In a tone of serious protest, Zainhum said, "Why should I kill myself working while the master is enjoying himself in the arms of the slave girl? Let him get up and do his job. Why do I have to do all the work? So that in the end he'd give me the price of a pack of tobacco? I don't need it. Why should I place myself under suspicion for nothing? Me'allim Ramadan by now must have sold the whole lot at night without us noticing."

"No. He only disposed of Widad the belly dancer's stuff. Three pieces that came through her about a month ago. Last night, owners of these pieces came to me. They arranged to spend the night then broached the subject to me. Their cattle were stolen two months ago from their fields in broad daylight. They made the rounds of the markets in different villages and towns looking for their property. Finally they came to our market; they might have recognized the animals. They asked me, since I was familiar with such a big market like the wikala's, if I had heard of such an incident and they expressed a readiness to pay a reward. I denied knowing anything about it but during the night I sent them Ramadan Eraiga to talk to them about it. Before dawn that devil had already gotten the reward and advised them to go back to their village, because, before noon, they would find their cattle tied in the very spot from which they had been stolen. Right now, stupid, he's not having fun in the arms of the slave girl but watching his underlings take back the cattle!"

I heard the Sheikh's knees cracking as he got up.

"In the name of God!"

At that moment I passed by them on my way to my room. I changed my clothes and went out without any particular destination in mind. "And God's peace and His mercy and blessings on you," said Shawadfi respectfully without a hint of sarcasm or ill-intent. That reassured me somewhat, but it also terrified me.

A Messenger from Hell

The delightful noise and crowds of the market greeted me. I was coming from downtown where I had spent the night walking around aimlessly, getting away from the boring, stifling atmosphere of my room in the wikala and avoiding Shawadfi and his sharp, painful barbs. It was a little before noon and I didn't want to enter the wikala despite my unplanned return there. I turned right toward the distant fields. The market was huge and seemed endless, with displays squeezing together, selling grains, sugar cane, fabrics, vegetables, birds, and things that one would never think of at all. Crowded blocks of humanity: between every two vendors were more vendors and around each vendor several crowds, reflecting proven sales tricks: a person buying fabrics would buy accessories from the next vendor and, seeing the ring maker nearby, would also buy a ring. Around the butcher stand gathered vendors of onion, gargir, and tomatoes. In the distance was a cattle, sheep, and donkey market in an enclosure surrounded by barbed wire and crawling with guards and landlords collecting usage and storage charges according to the area occupied. That particular portion of the market had distinct smells of dung extending over a large area reminiscent of the smells of milk, cream, ghee, and boiled meat. I turned again with the wall of the wikala, then made a third turn toward the front of the building that looked like an annex, even though it was part and parcel of the wikala. There I was looking from the outside at the gate I had seen from the inside, a very heavy solid gate sinking into the sloping earth as if it had become part of the hardened soil. This building apparently used to be the animal shed where travelers going to the market and staying at the wikala during its golden age brought their animals. It was a huge structure that our era could never produce now in its solid, intricate, and beautiful shape and which to date had maintained its form. It was truly regrettable and funny that such a huge historical edifice should end up in these despicable times being the private property of someone like Shawadfi who ruled over it and turned it into a den of vice with money flowing into his hands. Finally I reached the end of the wall where a narrow agricultural road went through, splitting the market grounds into two sides, one of which was blocked by a gigantic gate, and blocked on the inside by thick solid steel rolls.

I crossed the agricultural road to the other half of the grounds at the end of which was the animal market. I saw Ahmed, son of Sheikh Zainhum, and his brother Atris standing by the side of the road in front of a basket covered with tattered rags. Then Sheikh Zainhum himself soon appeared in front of some vendors' displays delivering his usual incantation that worked like magic, especially on non-local vendors who sought good omens even if they had to pay dearly for them. One of them gave him two handfuls of pressed dried dates wrapped in newsprint. Another gave him a piaster. Then he stopped in front of the butcher stand, holding up the lap of his gallabiya. The butcher threw strange things into the stretched lap: some bones and offal, lung, spleen and intestine parts and scraps of head meat that he was supposed to throw to the dogs sitting nearby growling viciously at Sheikh Zainhum. Some dogs followed the sheikh, wagging their tails, thinking perhaps he was getting the stuff for them.

I stood to look at the vendor of shawls, handkerchiefs, and plastic bracelets around whom stood many women, girls, and children. Immediately next to it were the clothiers, a long row of tent-like structures with trellises in the form of small shops of canvas, stretched on poles and iron and wood partitions dug into the ground. As soon as I stopped there, I saw Muhammad Abu Sinn all by himself, busy rearranging his fabrics hurriedly and awkwardly. When I greeted him he was tongue-tied with surprise. He stood straight and shook my hand warmly. Then he pulled me inside.

"Are you alone here?" I asked him. He said he always went to the market by himself and that was the worst part of it.

"I wish I'd known. I'd have come at dawn!"

"Okay. Roll up your sleeves and help me. Are you busy?"

"No."

"Well then, it's God's will. Stay with me!"

Many customers began to come in greater numbers because Muhammad began to devote his full attention to them. No customer stood before Muhammad Abu Sinn and left without buying, even if he didn't want to and even if he didn't have enough money, for the negotiations revolved around what money the customer had. I didn't know what magic Abu Sinn wielded to put the customer in a serious buying mood. He besieged the customer in such a way that buying became a casual customer's real desire. This had an effect on me: I got very busy going up and down, bringing rolls of fabric, spreading and displaying them as he got busy negotiating with the customers about wools, linens, and silk, aiming for big sales. And while he was busy measuring, cutting, and wrapping I focused on selling small and fine items such as shawls, handkerchiefs, buttons, skeins of yarn of different colors and the like, for which there were many customers.

"In the name of God, the merciful, most gracious! Is that you? How are you?"

I raised my eyes from the bolt of black diaphanous silk fabric. I was drawn into two pits of fire in the middle of which was a little round piece of coal. Were those two eyes or the wings of a terrifying bird from hell? The kohl was loud on the edges like ash expelled by the eyes filled with azure and tinged with the color of twilight, a reflection of the red in her smooth cheeks. Oh my God! What wild beauty! Was she one of the brides of the Nile or a siren genie? The tattoo was a small green spot in the middle of her chin, a sequined kerchief encircled her rose-colored forehead revealing a lock of shiny brown hair. The mouth was big and the teeth smiling with a delicate gap in the middle. The lips were full like two ripe strawberries, the figure tall and slender, full but not flabby. Everything about her body was clearly delineated and seductive: the breasts, the torso, the well–rounded hips, it all showed clearly under a white dress under another diaphanous black dress with ruffles on the lower back. On her chest was a necklace of genuine carnelian and in the ears two gold earrings in the shape of mincing knives and on the wrists a number of bracelets that didn't jingle because they fitted tightly around soft, full wrists. I looked at her as if in a trance, imagining that she had come from the world of delectable fairy tales on an urgent mission. Finally my dry mouth managed to say, in a voice in which I tried to mimic Abu Sinn's warm, sincerely affectionate tone, "At your service, my lady!"

Her glances bent a little bit, overpowering me. I bent my head under the weight of the searing electricity and when I raised my eyes again I saw her smiling and pointing to a bolt of silk: "Let me see this fabric."

I took the bolt from the middle of the shelf and brought it to the counter. I spread it as professional salesmen did. She said in a totally businesslike tone of voice, "How much is a shawl from it?"

Abu Sinn was busy writing down some calculation on one of the cardboard slats you found in the middle of a fabric belt. He replied quickly while carrying on with his calculation, "It's eighty piasters, most esteemed madam, but for you, only seventy-five. Shall we cut one or two?"

She turned to look at him and her eyes looked even more captivating: "I was going to order one only but because you are so nice I'll have two: one for me and one for grandma."

With great pleasure I began to measure the fabric. Each shawl was two meters and a half. Before cutting with the scissors, I looked at her and moved my finger a few inches beyond the mark. She smiled and stuck her hand in her bosom taking out a small black leather purse. She took out a few crumpled banknotes and paid while I wrapped the two shawls tightly in paper that had the name of the store printed on it. When I handed her the package, she said in a whisper, "I recognized you but you didn't recognize me. We're neighbors! At home I greet you from my balcony and my grandmother lives in the room directly opposite you, above Etaita's room."

I was taken aback. I was afraid she would continue to talk about the wikala in front of Abu Sinn. I reached my hand and shook hers affectionately: "You're welcome! Good to see you. Goodbye."

"What's your name?"

"So and so."

"I am Widad. My grandmother's name is Qut al-Qulub. If you come across somebody here who'd like to write his name on his forearm or draw the tattoo of a lion on his hand or chest, bring him to her. She's the best tattoo artist."

"God willing."

She turned and left like a tigress. Under the ruffles of the dress and above heels like silver, two delicate silver anklets with jingles, together with the tapping of her slippers created a well-pleased and pleasing sound. Muhammad Abu Sinn followed her departure with a glance from his eyes hiding under the canopy of his eyebrows, then nudged me and whispered, "Who's she?"

I told him that I lived in a room in a house in the Shubra Damanhour neighborhood for a hundred and fifty piasters a month and that that woman apparently was a neighbor of mine. He asked me how come I didn't recognize her and I told him that I only returned to my room in the middle of the night so the landlord would not see me and demand several months' worth of back rent. He wrinkled his lips in disgust: "Back in the slums again, are we?"

Then he waved nonchalantly but with a tone of regret, adding: "It doesn't matter in any case. God willing, everything can be fixed. Had I known you were so clever and resourceful, I would've given you a job with me. It's not too late, anyway. You can work with me afternoons from five to ten in the evening and you can come to the markets three days a week."

I was so ecstatic I didn't say a word. I just nodded gratefully, because actually he was not asking me to agree but deciding what would happen to the letter. Then it seemed he remembered something. He asked me suddenly, "Why didn't you attend Badriya's wedding?" It was as if he held my heart with a pair of pincers then pulled it. I collapsed on the counter.

"Did Badriya actually get married?"

"It was a big wedding. Everyone in the alley attended and the whole street stayed up till the morning. The wedding tent took up the whole alley. There was a stage and artists and banquets. The newlyweds went to Ras al-Barr for their honeymoon. Your whole village came and the street was filled with peasants and BB guns!"

I became quite chagrined and rested my head on my palm: "I didn't know when the wedding was because I haven't seen them. May God grant her happiness."

"She's a good and sweet girl. The whole street loves her. All the girls in the neighborhood danced in front of her. It turns out the groom is a relative of yours, by marriage. He comes from the village of Afifi, right next to your village. He's been a dear brother for a long time, a good man who deserves her, the kindest that I've ever met in my life.

"Praise the Lord. That's what I hope."

He looked at his watch and said, "Lunch time."

He pulled out from under the counter the amud of several small interlocking pots, fitting vertically and held together by a handle. He undid it and we found that it contained beans, mulukhiya with meat, rice, and pickles. We also bought four loaves of bread from the market. A short while after finishing our meal, the undertaker, with his little portable tea service came in and poured tea for us. As soon as he saw me he almost fainted: "You know each other?"

"Of course. We're friends."

"Praise the Lord!"

He didn't add another word, to my relief. When Muhammad fished for some piasters to pay him, the undertaker restrained his hand in protest: "Don't. Tea this time is on me. I swear by God I am not taking a single millieme."

Then he took the two empty glasses and left. I thanked God he didn't mention the wikala and I decided when I met him to warn him about it. Then the sales traffic grew gradually lighter and Muhammad went to the prayer rug and performed the afternoon prayers. When he was done he got ready to call it a day. He calculated the day's business on paper and gave me three pounds, saying, "Pay your debts and get your affairs in order until you get paid in a month and a half. I am not going to include half of this sum as part of your pay because it is part of the money God has entrusted me with for such a purpose. May we be owed and not owe."

As soon as we finished tying the bolts to each other and putting small items in cardboard boxes and securing them with thread and ropes, we heard the rumbling of a two-horse-drawn flatbed cart making its way then stopping in front of us. An old, bearded driver with a prayer mark on his forehead got off: "I am four minutes late."

"You came right on time, anyway."

We began lifting the packages and boxes to help the driver carry them on his back to place on the cart. When we were done, we looked around on the ground to make sure we hadn't forgotten anything. Muhammad felt his pockets to make sure he had his wallet and keys and he called the overseer and surrendered to him the trellis and the counter. Then we got on the cart and sat on the boxes. The driver tugged at the bridles, and the horses proceeded with the cart rumbling on. We passed by the gate of the wikala stable, which was open and totally empty. Near the gate Sheikh Zainhum was arguing with a tall, thin, dark complexioned man with hard features who was wearing clean clothes and moved with a slightly slanted shoulder. I figured he must be me'allim Ramadan Eraiga. When we reached Muhammad Abu Sinn's store on Susi Street we found it quiet without the usual crowds. I remembered that all activity on such days moved to the market. Muhammad's nephew had opened the store and hurried to help us take down the merchandise that the driver took to a warehouse inside and left it untied and unwrapped in preparation for the next market two days later in another location.

I stayed in the store for a short while then returned to the wikala, filled with delightful new sentiments. With a confident heart I sat with Shawadfi and asked him, "How much do I owe you, Amm Shawadfi?"

He waited for a while, glancing at me quickly as if surprised. Then, confidently: "Nothing! Did I ask you for anything? Have I offended you somehow? Don't worry about it. Even the government itself is hard up and penniless sometimes."

"Today God has been good to me. I don't like debt. It keeps me awake at night. So, how much do I owe you?"

He thought a little, raising his eyes to the ceiling: "Nothing much. Surely it's not worth worrying about."

"Well, how much?"

"Keep it now. Spend what you have. I can wait."

"I cannot spend when I owe you even one millieme."

Slowly he rolled a cigarette and lit it: "Okay then. Give me five pounds and then you'll owe me the nights of this month."

"Well, here's two pounds. In a few days I'll give you the rest, one pound at a time, until I can pay in advance."

He slipped the two pounds into his pocket and I hurried to my room where I wrote the date and the amount. I lay down on the mastaba, full of renewed hope, as if I were waiting for thousands of beautiful things to start happening right away.

The Flame and the Wind

The air in the wikala in the late afternoon was unparalleled: the large courtyard turned into a vast store for the sun from which the day borrowed its light and heat. As the day advanced, the sun stingily hid from it in the corners, nooks, and crannies, receiving delegations of wind rushing in from everywhere to the courtyard and which sifted and refined them, turning them into a sea of refreshing coolness. At such moments of autumn days, all the rooms in the wikala's two stories opened their doors as well as the upper parts of the windows overlooking the street or the vast expanse. At such moments between the call to mid-afternoon and sunset prayers, the me'allims would have been up from their siestas and would have washed away sleep from their faces by a couple of glasses of cheap booze or some hashish and a small lentil-sized piece of opium, then ate a light snack. Most of the underlings would have finished the day's work and come back to join the gatherings and bring some liveliness to them in preparation for reconciling accounts in an agreeable atmosphere, to avoid any problems or clashes. There were twenty rooms in the two stories, each one housing a family. Each of these families was related by something stronger than blood kinship: the bond of chasing a penny using devilish methods without violence and roughness. It was here that loopholes were invented, that tricks were used to circumvent the law and render it useless, and the most heinous crimes were committed under the auspices of that very law. They would now be at their happiest, the courtyard reflecting everything taking place within the rooms, in addition to the different aromas echoing the gurgling of the gozas, the clanking of glasses, the muffled laughter, the ringing voices of the women, and suppressed preludes to reckless moans of ecstasy, together with Umm Kulthum's voice plaintively repeating, "You are unfair to me!" All of that, together with clouds of smoke the color of the sky created a tent of unbelievable peace and security, as if all those beings were fetuses lolling about in the womb. That was how I felt sitting in my room, enjoying it all. It was as if, sitting like that, I had, for the first time in my life, achieved a moment of genuine, secure solitude coupled with beautiful relaxation. Ever since I bought that bamboo chair I discovered the joy of sitting like that especially in the late afternoon, receiving the twilight with equanimity: I'd place the chair at the entrance of my room, stretch out my leg, leaning it on the edge of the arcade, resting my elbows on the arms of the chair, and losing myself in reading or daydreaming of all kinds of mysterious mazes and enchanting paths. All that serenity and enchantment emanated from trusting where the next meal was coming from, with a pack of cigarettes, a glass of tea, and a secure place to sleep indoors.

I soon noticed, however, that the pleasure of sitting in that place at those moments was always accompanied by twisting my neck to the left so that my eyes could cross the courtyard ascending to that angle that the wall of the wikala made with the balcony of a house opposite the wikala. The house and the wikala were separated by a street and yet it seemed to me from where I was sitting that it was part of the wikala, as if the wikala extended a crooked arm embracing two adjacent balconies above two adjacent balconies. My eyes were focused on the upper balcony from which only one half was visible and whoever was in it looked as if they were coming from a corridor in the wikala itself. It was there that the genie of the fairytales with her wild ferocious beauty appeared every late afternoon, sitting in that very corner directly facing me, also crossing her legs, smoking the goza like the most experienced men smokers. As one pipeful of tobacco was burned up, she would remove it and dump the embers into a brazier that was undoubtedly before her although out of sight, picking up another pipe and placing it on the goza and arranging the burning coals on top of it using the tongs patiently and with a steady hand. She would stay like that until the call to the night prayers, whereupon she would disappear from the balcony. I'd be dying to know what was taking place inside the apartment but she would reappear around midnight in the balcony lit by a faint lamp on top of the lamppost in the bend between her house and the wikala. She would be wearing a nightgown of light satin with sleeves just short of the bracelets on her wrists, her blondish hair down on her back gathered on top of the head only by a red kerchief. She would resume smoking the goza whose blue smoke mixed with the kohl of her eyes like eyes in a dovecote.

That was Widad, the dancer, who had introduced herself to me in the market in the stall of Muhammad Abu Sinn the day she bought two shawls from me, one for herself and one for her grandmother the skillful Syrian tattoo artist, Qut al-Qulub. I learned from the wikala that she was a dancer but I didn't know how to initiate a conversation to start a real relationship. When our eyes met she smiled and I smiled. That was it. And despite my interest in her, all I could find out was that her grandmother lived in the room directly opposite mine above Etaita's room, and that she and Etaita were the oldest tenants of the wikala, predating Shawadfi by a long time. Her room had been quite popular on all market days when peasants came from villages all over to get tattoos of lions and other adornments as well as their names on the backs of their hands, forearms, chests, and backs, and sparrows on their temples. However, the tattoo industry had fallen on hard times since the spread of education and since most villagers began to be embarrassed by sparrow tattoos as a sign of backwardness and naiveté. A new occupation came into being, practiced by rural barber surgeons, specializing in removing tattoos by using hydrochloric acid, which most of those who had tattoos welcomed even though it left behind ugly disfiguring scars. As for Widad herself, I heard that she rarely danced at weddings. Perhaps when people mentioned that, they were commenting on her behavior and the way she moved after she had abandoned weddings or weddings had abandoned her. When Shawadfi noticed that someone was eager to talk about her he would say, "It's none of our business. Let's change the subject."

It was not easy for me to do that, for that graceful mare was speaking to me in a mysterious language I couldn't ignore and kept me sleepless at night as I brought her to my bed using all tricks of the imagination.

Today, as I got ready to settle in my chair to look up at her balcony, I suddenly saw her, in person, coming toward me from her grandmother's room. She was wearing a green and red chintz dress. Almost all the parts of her body were coming out, for even though the dress was not tight, it was her body that contained the dress rather than the other way around. The black shawl draped down her head and shoulders did nothing to diminish the rosiness of her complexion. And when I remembered that she was from imported slave stock my imagination lit up with passion and thirst for adventure. I also remembered the Druze mountain and Suwayda and the way Byzantine blood had mixed with that of the Ghassanid in the land, the veins, and the minds, and this made the fire rage even more fiercely in my repressed imagination. At that point she had gone down the stairs and crossed the door of Etaita's room and turned around, going out of the arcade. Now she was facing me; her eyes actually rested on me. As she was leaving the arcade, with the courtyard between us, I grew very confused, like a mouse transfixed by a cat's gaze until the cat pounces on it and devours it. That was what happened to me; she was pouncing on me, the jaws of her eyes were clamped around my head, lifting me off the chair then dropping me, rocking me and swaying me to the right and the left. The smell of soap scented with her feminine body and the gum she was chewing turned me into a lost fish tossed here and there in the heart of a tumultuous yet nonthreatening wave. I began to climb the waves of delicious sensation only to be tossed down and pushed to climb an even higher wave that almost landed my head between the two unrestrained breasts like two handfuls of dough, slightly flattened except for the pointed nipples whose freckles I could see through the dress. I was holding a book, maybe *A Thousand and One Nights*, and a hashish cigarette. Under the chair was a glass of tea that I had forgotten and which had been cooled down by the breeze. The gaps between her snow-white teeth grew wider, as did the red space between her jaws. Everything had grown so quiet that I could only hear my own heartbeat interpreted by the explosive sounds of her chewing gum. She had gone up the arcade and the two breasts were squeezed upward out of the chest like milk boiling over the neck, hitting the brandished eyelashes, and descending again lower on the neck, blending with the red flame.

"May I?" she said with amazing boldness. She was pointing at the cigarette between my fingers with her fingers holding an imaginary cigarette. I understood what she wanted right away and was shaken but I composed myself sitting up in the chair: "Of course! The cigarette and its owner at your service."

Then I got off the chair and went toward her offering her the cigarette even though I could have just extended my arm. She ignored my slip of the tongue and took the cigarette and took several deep drags, letting the smoke out of her nostrils. Then she returned the cigarette to me: "How much did you pay for this hashish?"

As if I were quite an expert at buying it even though I bought it so rarely that I didn't know how much it really cost, I said, "A friend of mine buys me a quarter piaster's weight for seven and a half piasters."

She knit her brows in surprise and her face turned even more red as the kohl deepened around her eyes: "Your friend is cheating you. If you want to buy, tell me and I'll buy for you when I buy for myself. A whole piaster's weight is twenty piasters, sometimes three shillings. I buy from a woman who sells me at wholesale rates and she doesn't expect a profit."

I said without thinking, "Okay, then get me a piaster's weight."

"That'll be twenty piasters."

I had committed myself. I didn't hesitate but went into my room right away and took twenty piasters as if from my own flesh and cried over it in silence even though I visualized a piaster's weight as a considerable quantity, easily lasting a whole month. But that didn't mitigate my agonizing separation from two silver ten-piaster pieces that I put in Widad's palms that were as soft as butter. To alleviate my sorrow, I said to her, "Please make sure it is good quality and the weight is correct."

"We will taste it together; if you don't like it, we'll return it."

"When will that be?"

"Come have tea with me at my house after the night prayers. I am going to change now and go downtown and come back around that time. I'll come out on the balcony when I arrive, so you can come then."

My heart almost split with joy, "Okay, see you at the appointed time!"

She stood straight smiling then her laughter rang out: "Appointed time? You're using bookish words!"

She started walking with a very self-confident swagger. When she got close to Shawadfi at the gate she greeted him: "Evening, monkey-man!"

He was asleep but he turned his back to the wall and putting his arm under his head: "If only that were true. Only an old monkey like me can do you any good."

She responded with a loud laugh that popped like a firecracker as she glided gracefully away.

A Halter of Palm Fiber

She appeared on the balcony immediately after the call to the night prayers. It was as if the whole universe had lit up, for at that moment the universe meant only that area occupied by the balcony that seemed an extension of the wikala. I sensed her appearance before she actually made it. For, despite the distance and the noise around me, I was almost certain that I heard the rustling of her dress and the jingling of her bracelets on her wrists and the anklets around her ankles. She wanted me to feel her presence so she leaned on the railing of the balcony with her elbows and fixed her glances on the door of my room and stayed like that for a long time even though, hiding myself from Shawadfi in the crack of the door, I had signaled to her with my head and hand that I had seen her. Then I turned around and looked for something proper to wear. It was the first time for me to face such a situation and I stood, helpless and dejected at the quality of my apparel in general. I was very annoyed yet that feeling didn't last a long time as I soon developed an attitude that was totally different and defiant. I decided to go out as shabbily dressed as I could. So I wore the same gallabiya and flip-flop sandals I had on. I closed the door and left.

I greeted Shawadfi who was busy braiding palm fiber ropes. He lifted his eyes to me smiling and, out of the blue, said, "On her neck a halter of palm fiber! You've gone to school, friend, so did you learn what a halter of palm-fiber is? I'd be willing to bet a lot that you don't know what it is."

The truth be told, I didn't know what it was. I hated myself and thought that a fitting punishment would be to admit that I didn't know rather than taking pride in ignorance. Thereupon he roared with laughter: "Palm fiber, friend, is what I am holding in my hand now. The rope I am braiding of palm fiber is a halter of palm fiber."

I was very happy to learn that meaning but I said in an attempt to avenge my wounded pride, "But what's the occasion, now?"

He stared at my eyes in a frightening manner: "Such a halter you will see around your woman friend's neck."

I relaxed, smiling faintly: "What woman friend?"

"The one you're going to now."

I forced myself to laugh naively as if I were telling him, "You devil, you." but I thought it best not to beat around the bush because he could see and hear everything and it didn't make sense to try to fool him.

"She's not my friend. I asked her to get something for me. Actually, it was she who offered to do it. I am going there now only to get what she got for me."

He interrupted me, waving his rough fingers at my face: "Of course, of course. Going there you will do nothing more than that anyway. I know that, my friend, and I am as certain of it as I am that you're standing in front of me. I just wanted to tell you a joke that you might find refreshing as you go; I mean, as you come back."

"Frankly, Amm Shawadfi, I didn't get the joke. Why don't you assume I am stupid and also explain it to me?"

"Didn't you study in school some Qur'an that said, *And his wife, the woman carrying wood, she will have on her neck a halter of palm fiber*?"

"You mean the Sura of the Flame: In the name of God, Most Gracious, Most Merciful: *Abu Lahab's hands will perish and he will perish. His riches and his gains will not spare him. He will burn in a flaming fire. And his wife, the wood-carrier, will have a halter of palm fiber on her neck.* God Almighty has spoken the truth."

"That's the one. See what it says about her neck?"

"Yes, what about the neck?"

"This friend of yours, my friend, is like that woman carrying the wood: there is a rope or a halter of palm fiber around her neck. And the end of that rope or halter is in an unknown hand. What I am trying to say is that there's a rough rope around her neck."

"But I . . ."

"Go ahead, my friend. God be with you. My heart is also with you. I wish you a happy evening. Pray for me while enjoying it."

I crossed the gate feeling frustrated and thwarted as if I had before me a rich gourmet meal that was burned and I had to throw it into the garbage. Yet what happened dispelled my fear of the adventure and instead of taking shaky steps, I was encouraged to go forward like someone going under cover of darkness bent on some mischief, someone who, when suddenly the road was lit up, he straightened up and continued walking like a regular person with no evil intent. Thus I was not concerned that anyone should see me entering Widad the dancer's house at such a time of night when there was no other man in the house. I was overcome by a feeling of indifference, as if I were going to visit a patient in a hospital.

As soon as she opened the door for me, high waves of strong perfume engulfed me, almost taking me down a fathomless whirlpool. Her soft smooth hand held mine as she pulled me inside in a manly welcoming gesture that did not become her at all: "Come in! Welcome!" The door closed. We were in a box-like square parlor whose walls were adorned with pictures of Farid al-Atrash, Asmahan, Muhammad Fawzi, Laila Murad, Laila Fawzi, Samia Gamal, Tahiya Karioka, Hind Rustum, Shukri Sarhan, and Kamal al-Shinnawi cut from *al-Kawakib, al-Sabah* and *Akhir Sa'a* magazines. On the floor were two Asyut-style chairs and a sofa and a small table. The wood was dull and faded but the upholstery was clean and had colored covers. On the right wall was a wooden shelf under a picture of Yusif Wahbi on which sat a large Philips radio, and beneath it, closer to the floor was a picture of Amina Rizk between pictures of Sabah and Shadia. The parlor looked as if it were the entire apartment and it felt cozy, a place where one could stay for a long time.

"Would you like to sit here or on the balcony? It's up to you."

"Wherever you like. If there's need for sitting down."

"I invited you to tea and I keep my word."

"Let's sit where the shisha is. I love molasses-cured tobacco."

She motioned me over her shoulder to follow her as she proceeded coquettishly. I followed her, my eyes glued to the two lively magnetic globes ahead. There was a narrow corridor: to the right a small kitchen next to a small bathroom. Facing it was a small room with a brass bed with posts and a light pink satin mosquito met. There was also a dresser with several rectangular drawers and shiny brass handles. There was a bamboo chair and clothes hooks nailed to the wall from which hung some nightgowns and dresses. Next to the dresser was a small door leading to a second small room that had a second door opening to the corridor. In that room right in front was a cot. Oh, my God! I stopped, shaking all over, feeling like someone surprised to see himself in a closed metal cage with a rabid dog or an irate lion. There was in front of me a beast in human form, with two very big eyes shining and gleaming endlessly. Around the eyes was a face as sweet as the purest honey with chestnut-colored tresses, unbound, covering a delicate head connected to a longish neck that looked like a newly planted tree. The veins of the neck connected to the shoulders and the chest looked like roots in an emaciated body. The shoulders were broad, supporting full, round breasts and two long straight arms. The chest ended in an extremely skinny waist as if it were a line in a cartoon, growing even thinner as it ended with tiny feet like those of a baby. There were no legs at all which meant that that beautiful body couldn't stand or move. It also seemed that the body had no mind at all as the face kept looking blankly around in a total daze as if it were that of a plastic doll. The arms waved haphazardly in whimsical movements.

Widad had stopped on the threshold of the balcony, her features now undone in a faint, sad smile.

"Why did you stop? Are you frightened? Your face's turned yellow. It seems you have a weak heart. God help me!"

Widad was now moving quickly toward me, holding me gently by the hand to prevent me from reeling. Then she led me calmly to the balcony and sat me down where she used to sit, so that my head was below the railing. Then she said as if resuming a previous conversation: "This is Raghda. She had infantile paralyisis. One day when she was four she had a fever. I had to run an errand for work. I left her with her grandmother who fell asleep, leaving her alone. As soon as I came back from the errand I carried her, burning with fever, to the doctor, in the fever hospital and he started calling me names and almost called the police on me. He said I had neglected the girl until her brain burned! That day I let that stupid doctor have it. But from that day on she has been growing up but her mind stays the same. She's now twenty but has the mind of an infant. She doesn't speak, but screams and groans and moans in pain. I can tell from her voice what's bothering her and I act accordingly. Poor girl! May God take care of her and of me."

She sat cross-legged in front of me on a small cushion, almost touching my foot. She held the tea kettle, but then she said, "Would you like to eat? I have some grilled fish. I invited you for some tea but we can have bread and salt together."

She got up with agility, disappeared in the kitchen for some time then came back carrying a palm leaf basket on which was a plate with four grilled fishes and two soft peasant loaves of bread. She sat, placing the basket in front of us. I got off the chair and sat down next to her and she moved a little to make room for me, ending up half in the balcony and half on the threshold. I ate one fish and half a loaf and two turnips by way of sharing bread and salt with her which might strengthen our budding relationship. The food, though modest, was quite delicious but seeing the helpless angel in the other room took away my appetite for the food and almost prevented me from having a good time that evening. When I took the first sip of tea I realized that Widad had poured it for me in a glass that had remnants of opium that had been dissolved in it. So, she must also be taking opium. Or she must have invited someone who did, to tea earlier. Slyly I asked her, "Do you have any aspirin?"

She said with refreshing simplicity, "Would you like a bit of opium? I got a small piece that a girlfriend gave me for headache. I took a tiny piece and I have the rest."

She extended her thumbnail to the gold bracelet and scraped from it a black piece the size of a grass seed. She brought it close to my mouth and I took her thumb between my lips and picked up the opium with the tip of my tongue. She then prepared the goza and cleaned the pipe then stuffed it with Abu Ghazala brand molasses treated tobacco from al-Hinnawi factories.

"Did you want to taste the hashish?"

"Of course. Where is it?"

She reached her finger into the narrow space between her bracelets and her wrist and slid out a cellophane wrapped object the size of a lipstick case, which she gave to me. I liked its appearance and size. Then I unwrapped it and the smell of fresh hashish wafted like intoxicating perfume. "Good quality and quantity," I said, smacking my lips, as I began to cut pieces from it to add to the tobacco. The bracelets jingled in her hand as she extended it to stop me: "Just a moment. Take your first turn from mine."

She took off her ring and removed from the setting of the stone a piece of hashish as large as a marble from which she started to cut with her snow white teeth into big 'signature' bits. This surprised me and put me to shame, for such big signatures (as the pieces of hashish added to a pipeful of tobacco were called) were more to be expected from a big me'allim seeking a strong, quick high. Besides, I would appear stingy when I began to use my 'initials' only, adding only a piece as big as a seed's shell, instead of a full signature, let alone being able to keep up with her smoking on this level. I found myself saying, "This is quite a chunk: you are signing your whole family name!"

She laughed half-heartedly: "Actually, I use my seal. That's my way. I don't like to go to bed with hashish in my hand. Hashish must be lit up all at once. The best place to store hashish is in your head. If your head fills up and overflows, store it in your friend's head. That will give you pleasure too."

When the pipe I had signed myself was just about done, the small space had turned into a fragrant paradise full of peace and serenity. The aroma of a third or fourth tea working its way into my nostrils, coupled with the smell of burning coal, all rocked my head, which felt as if it was rubbing against soft velvet. She extended her bracelet-adorned wrist with a hand that tempted me not just to kiss but to eat it up. She held the cup of tea by its handle. With one hand I took the cup of tea and placed it on the floor and with the other I kept her hand, caressing it tenderly and gently with trembling hands. She withdrew her hand very gently, blushing deeply. That emboldened me so I held her hand with my hands and began to press it passionately. Her eyes sparked with anger that threatened to melt the kohl on her eyelids. I relaxed my grip and she pulled her hand away, saying in a decisive warning tone, "I invited you to tea only. I offered you food so that it might be the bread and salt that cements respect between us."

Beads of sweat rolled down my back and on my forehead: "I am sorry. I couldn't help it."

She stared at my eyes with piercing, smiling eyes: "If you want me, then you'll have to marry me the way God and His Prophet enjoin."

I felt dizzy, then I came to feeling short of breath, trying to smoke in a normal way to cover up the confusion that robbed me of the ability to respond properly. My head was so empty I was frightened. I tried to figure out what was happening to my head at that specific moment but I couldn't hold on to anything and say I was thinking of it. Her voice was now feeble, with no resonance to it. The gold bracelets had gotten somewhat stuck in the fleshy part of the forearm as she raised her hand at an angle to pour the dark crimson tea into the cup causing it to foam gradually: "I see that you're speechless. You're all like that. You prefer to steal the fruit from the garden fence as you pass, especially if it had ripened and fallen off the tree on to the ground, or the edge of the fence, even if it were blemished, or unripe or even rotten. It's all the same to you. But God forbid that you'd want to buy it from the fruitgrocer's display. That'd be costly. I've been bitten, stung, broken, and rent apart. And the reason? My kind heart. I only felt the sting when the poison had taken. This poor little girl lying there around my neck? Her father dropped her into my belly then totally disappeared. He was a maddah who memorized poems and wrote some himself. He made the rounds on his donkey. Sometimes I went with him to sing the praises of the Prophet in the villages, stopping and performing in front of every house. We'd come back at the end of the day, loaded with food and money from the nation of Muhammad which has always loved the Prophet and which has always been good. He was one of the tenants of the wikala, living in the room next to my grandmother. I met him when I was young and naïve and fell in love with his youth and his sweet talk. I married him before I knew anything about his past. When he disappeared and was gone for a long time, they said he had been running away from a vendetta and had fallen into the hands of his enemy. They also said he had escaped from a life sentence in prison and they caught him and sent him to Tura. This daughter of his was on my lap. I married many, many times. Each marriage lasted less than a year at most. The longest was for a year and two months and he was the most despicable of them all. He would sell me secretly to headmen and notables without my knowledge, so he could eat opium. He made so much trouble for me and when I wised up to what he was doing, I got back at him by arranging an ambush for him and when he was arrested he had to divorce me against his will. No one had ever gotten anything from me except in a lawful way. All my husbands couldn't bear with me because of the girl whose appearance bothered them and who took me away from their embrace at night so I could make her stop crying or take her to the bathroom. My last husband suggested we bribe the doctor to give her an injection that would rid us of her. That's why I showed him no mercy. But now I am determined that whoever thinks I am beautiful should marry me the lawful way and provide for all my expenses and my daughter's expenses: food, clothing, and medical treatment. If he doesn't like the kohl, he doesn't have to use it. We'd just be friends who look after each other."

I wiped my sweat with my gallabiya's sleeve: "Right you are! From now on I am your loyal friend."

"And I am your servant at any time. Whenever you need hashish like this, let me know and I'll bring it right to you."

It was close to midnight when I left her house. I walked alone chasing my shadow extending in front of me in the faint light of the quiet street. It seemed to me that I'd walked for a long time during which I forgot all about her. I was surprised to see the gate of the wikala as if I had severed all relations with it for good. It seemed strange to me, as if I were entering it for the first time in my life. That weighed heavily on my heart and yet I knocked on the gate and pushed it and went in.

Markets! Markets!

Before leaving the store, Muhammad Abu Sinn told me not to take my time going home because I had to get to bed early that night to get up at dawn, for the following day we were to take the two-horse drawn cart to the market in Mahmudiya village, to be in the midst of the market at sunrise at the latest. There we would spread sackcloth and oilcloth on a spot and arrange bolts of fabric of all kinds and sit in the middle under a large umbrella also of oilcloth behind a low wooden table that would serve as a counter separating us from the customers.

At the market the driver would leave us and perhaps get a job or two—sometimes three—moving stuff, then return to us just before the call to the mid-afternoon prayer to take us back to Damanhour. We would, in the meantime, have packed the merchandise while waiting for him.

Muhammad Abu Sinn knew that every village whose market we went to had its own clothiers who might have the exact same merchandise. But he also knew that a visiting vendor was always enticing to the village people, since he might have good qualities, service, and honesty that the local merchant might not have. And yet Muhammad Abu Sinn did not depend on that proven fact alone, but placed his trust in God first and foremost. He believed that hard work would be rewarded and that, if God were to send business his way to cover the driver's and my expenses, he would have done a good deed that deserved merit from God. But he always earned more than just merits with God, for he had come from a family of cotton and indeed all kinds of fabric merchants. One of his maternal uncles owned a large underwear factory. His other maternal uncle owned a towel and upholstering material factory, let alone the family's other stores, old looms, and outlets specializing in making cheap rugs from tailor's scraps.

Therefore Abu Sinn was quite an expert in managing his market, stocking it with items that complemented each other. He guaranteed, for instance, that skullcaps, underwear, large handkerchiefs, upholstering material, brides' trousseaus, black shawls and pleated wraps, which he got from his uncle's factories at cost, had a large profit margin that gave him flexibility. The same was true of plastic bracelets, buttons, dress trimming accessories, and handkerchiefs embroidered with spangles and sequins, which were very popular in the countryside. So he took a large supply of those with him but took very little in the way of wool, broadcloth, linen, and expensive silk. He also made sure to pack enough cotton cloth of various grades for men's and women's clothing and small items and notions like shoelaces, boxes of polish, socks, scarves, and sandals. He also resorted to a very clever trick that never failed: instead of taking a whole bolt of broadcloth or English wool for abayas, he would measure and cut cloth for one abaya or gallabiya or two which he would then wrap in shiny paper and hide in the merchandise. Invariably someone would come by and ask, "You wouldn't happen to have fabric for an abaya?" Whereupon he would shake his head in regret as if the man had asked for something impossible. Then he would stop him after a little bit of affected hesitation done very skillfully and suggest to him that good broadcloth for abayas was rare those days and that, as an honest merchant who feared God, he would not trade in the bad fabrics readily available at other merchants, because he did not believe in overcharging customers since a person did not have an abaya made to order everyday: "But it seems you're a good man and your money is pure. For I have, by chance, one abaya that I have secured from the black market for a man who ordered it the market before last but has not shown up yet. So, it seems it is all yours." That way he would manage to arouse the man's curiosity and would pull the package in question, opening it gently, letting the smell of the new, expensive cloth fill the air, influencing the man even before he reached out and touched it. The customer would begin to ask about the price, now prepared for some sacrifice without feeling bad about it, especially since Abu Sinn would not exaggerate the price but would tell him that he had bought it for such and such an amount and wanted just his sweat, in such and such an amount. Usually the buyer would deduct the sweat amount which Abu Sinn had tacked on to his profit, so he would end up getting what he had planned to get all along.

The job was hard on me and I usually returned very tired but Abu Sinn took care of all the aches when we returned, getting us a dinner of kabab or spending the evening at Elaishy's house until late at night getting refreshed by the enlightened and novel ideas which Elaishy picked up from Taha Hussein's *al-Fitna al-Kubra* or Aqqad's "Genius" series or *I'jaz al-Qur'an* by Mustafa Sadiq al-Raf'i, overcoming Abu Hantour's ideas which had stopped at the medieval thinkers and commentators. After that we would go home and sleep in as long as we wished so long as I was at the store by time of the call to the sunset prayer to relieve Abu Sinn's nephew who would go home to study and get up early. I would stay in the store until closing time.

Widad's Mother's Genie

That night I had planned to go directly to my room to sleep until dawn, but my desire to spend the evening at Widad's house was strongly tugging at me and pulling my feet to bypass the wikala gate toward Widad's house. Then it occurred to me to just keep going there so that Shawadfi would not notice. Widad's face was always full of fresh, delicious femininity, and sitting with her in the balcony for some time, surrounded by blue smoke, provided me with rest and relaxation sweeter and healthier than tossing and turning on the hard bed.

Thus I stayed with Widad till close to midnight and had a beautiful time during which all my tensions ebbed away. Widad had begun to get used to me and no longer put up a strong barrier between us. She did her best to be natural and I did my best to stay within the bounds of propriety and good intentions. It seemed that as time went on, she had come to realize that I'd given up on trying to have my way with her, so she ignored it if I brushed against her accidentally or stretched my knee as I sat and rested it on her thigh for a short while. She didn't even mind if I embraced her and kissed her quickly upon meeting her or saying goodbye to her.

My nostrils were still filled with Widad's feminine scent, which combined baby milk with sweat and cheap perfume, when I opened the wikala gate and went in. Shawadfi was still squatting on the mastaba, smoking voraciously looking like a mass of black fog lit in the middle by the glow of the cigarette: "Peace on you," I said and he responded enthusiastically and pressed the button of the night light, which barely drew faint lines on the blackboard of darkness at the entrance of the wikala, something that he rarely did, contenting himself with the kerosene lamp: "Welcome! Welcome! What a beautiful night!"

I knew right away that either he couldn't sleep or was waiting for one of his endless secret and mysterious messages, since, from where he sat, he took part in weighty matters taking place in faraway villages and towns even as they were happening. He was a devil in the full sense of the word and he had to be capable of being in two places at the same time. And even though I didn't feel up to it, I couldn't ignore his invitation so I had to accept, even if only for a few minutes, to remain on his good side rather than incurring his enmity, which I couldn't afford.

I sat next to him and right away he reached for the brazier, removed the cover of ashes and placed the tea kettle on top of the embers. I waved my hand in gentle protest: "No, please. Do me a favor. I want to sleep if only for two hours. We have market tomorrow. By the way, would you please knock on my door shortly before dawn?"

He stared at my face with eyes as sharp as a wolf: "You have a market and yet you spend the evening at the wood-carrier's house? I heard your footsteps coming from her house. What a sissy! What unmitigated sissiness! Drink the lousy tea and get the hell away from here!"

"Thanks!"

"No need to thank me."

"Thanks, anyway."

Then, as he fanned the flame with the edge of his garment: "What do you think of the hashish that Widad buys for you?"

"Excellent! Never had better in my life! Good weight and higher quality. Do you know the woman from whom Widad buys?"

"I know the man who sells her wholesale. But these days, we have a little spat going on. In time, though, he's bound to come back to me, then you can have more of that good stuff."

"Widad can buy you some."

"Widad can buy some for a poor boy like you. Me? I have a different setup when it comes to kind, weight, quantity, and price and everything. But that Widad is a good girl anyway. Many a time she brings me a little spot or two of that hashish. As for me, I've often given her many a spot."

Thus he was dragging me to talk about Widad. I thought of torturing him by intimating to him that I'd had Widad, despite his certainty that I couldn't. The moment I was about to speak, however, I imagined Shawadfi rebuking her for what he heard from me, resulting in a big loud scandal. So I got tongue-tied right away. I wanted to give him a hard time, so I said, "Widad is a good woman indeed. Poor, too. May God help her. She's a chaste woman, I can bear witness to that before God. And, just as you said, it turns out that she does have a halter of palm-fiber on her neck!"

A very sly fox, that Shawadfi squatting before me, ready to pounce on my head at any moment. He was smiling as he said in a suspicious hissing tone: "So, the two of you are in agreement?"

"Agreement on what?"

"She too told me she had an errand tomorrow."

"An errand?"

"That's why she got rid of you early! What time is it now?"

"After midnight."

"Whoa! Whoa! Have you already gone to sleep, friend? It's still early. The news summary was on the radio a few minutes ago." Then he took out his old watch tied to a lace attached to a buttonhole in his vest. He lifted the cover and stared at it in the glow of the cigarette: "It's ten fifteen."

"That's strange."

I remembered that I was at Widad's house at about seven in the evening. He returned the watch to his pocket and began to pour the tea good-humouredly: "It's a very strange world. Can you imagine, my friend, that Widad is re-living the same story as her mother, except in reverse? Thank God you haven't seen her mother, otherwise you'd have fallen so hard for her it would have gotten us in major trouble. She was extremely beautiful. No moon or sun or stars are beautiful enough to compare to her. She was a gypsy from Aleppo. Or maybe a Bedouin. God alone knows. But she was very good at telling fortunes, reading coffee dregs, and doing magic and casting spells using slippers. She was possessed by a genie named Duqdush. As soon as he started possessing her she'd begin whirling, I mean, engaging in zikr: *God's alive! God's alive!* and swaying right and left even while sitting down. She'd do that for half an hour, an hour, two hours until she'd achieved a trance whereupon no one could stop her. If anyone tried she'd become more frenzied and her shouts of ecstasy would grow louder. When she pronounced the word Duqdush, we knew that the genie had arrived and was done possessing her and was now just sitting and talking to her. She would answer him and talk to him about strange things: about stolen property, lost children, damaged fields, burned crops, or about someone treacherously murdered. Then she would reply to herself in such a sly way that we understood it was the genie Duqdush who was now telling her to look in such and such a place, or go to such and such a charitable fountain or visit the tomb of such and such a sheikh. Or he'd say to bring a hoopoe's egg, the wing of a black dove and the pupil of the eye of a just-slaughtered ox and knead all of that in dough, stick it with pins, and throw it into the river, and everything would turn out for the best, the original perpetrator would become sick and gaunt and thus be found out. It was all a con, of course, but the stupid people believed her and they came to her from the countryside. Thereupon her mother would tattoo them with the likenesses of lions and birds.

"God have mercy on Safiya! She made more money than most men. She was a thief and a bloodsucker but, when it came to what you are thinking about, she was chaste. Not a single one could have his way with her, lawfully or unlawfully. I could talk freely with her and I'd ask her point blank: 'How is it that you, woman, are depriving your body of the joy of this world?' She would say that if a man mounted her, he would humiliate her and she would become his slave and her will would be broken, but that the man who would break her will had not been born yet.

"I knew many respectable men who were prepared to marry her the way God and his Prophet enjoin us, but she lived only for her daughter and her mother and the memory of her husband who was one of the most dangerous burglars in Egypt. Strangely enough, he was a poet storyteller with a rababa who toured the villages telling and singing the story of Abu Zeid and Zanati Khalifa. People in the villages would invite the rababa storyteller for a night or two or even a whole week to eat and drink and sleep in luxury so he could free Abu Zeid from his captivity. During that time the poet storyteller would comb the house and get to know everything in it as well as all its ins and outs. He'd also get to know what was worth stealing. Then he'd come back to carry out his plan, without the rababa this time, alone or with others depending on how great the loot was. A few days later, he'd come back to the same family in the same village, carrying the rababa. As the evening progressed he'd hear the story of the misfortune and he would advise them to go to Sheikha Safiya who had special powers! She would ply her trade and convince them that she'd found out who did it and act as a go-between to get the stolen property back. That way she'd get a reward in addition to her fees. But, as the saying goes, when two jars collide, one breaks, as they taught us in school in the old days. Our friend was caught by the owner of the house as he was climbing the wall to open the door from inside to sneak out with his loot. 'Who's there? Who's there?' the owner said and he shot the poet storyteller dead. It was not the genie that possessed the late Safiya but it was she who possessed him. None of her victims knew that she was the storyteller's wife but she went and got his body as an act of charity and had him buried in the charity graves.

"Then she began to work alone. The headman of a village called Sharnoub whose own name was Sharnoubi fell in love with her. He had a red face and two chins and rode around on horseback and had tons of money. The headman Sharnoubi spent a huge fortune on Safiya to sleep with him one night but he didn't have her. She asked him to marry her lawfully but he was afraid of his wife and his grown children. He asked her to become his common-law wife in an Urfi way to avoid the scandal, but she wouldn't. He didn't give up. He sent her to Hijaz and she made the pilgrimage to Mecca at his expense. He bought her the house that Widad is living in and bought all the dresses and gold bracelets that Widad is wearing. He would spend fifty pounds a night on her when things were quite cheap. She dined on nothing but pigeons, rabbits, chicken, and turkey. He began to sell his land in secret to spend on her. The poor man had no bad habits until she taught him to smoke hashish, eat opium, and drink liquor every night to stay in continual ecstasy in the hope of a promised night that never came. He had nothing more to sell; even the horse he sold and replaced with a sickly, manure-carrying donkey. Finally he had no choice but to marry her the way God and His Prophet enjoin, officially and publicly at the hands of a ma'zun. But the poor guy didn't enjoy it even for one hour. His eldest son who had been following him appeared from nowhere and emptied his gun into the newly-wed couple.

"The old tattoo artist raised Widad the same way she had raised her daughter but Widad had a kinder heart; she had inherited the heart of her father the poet, who wouldn't have been a burglar had it not been for his accursed wife pushing him. It's easy to fool Widad and that's why she has suffered a lot and lost almost everything. This wikala has seen so many tragedies. As many tragedies as it has bricks. Life is indeed a bitch, and time a traitor, and the two amount to nothing!"

He burst out laughing wildly. Sleep was almost totally gone from my eyes. I pushed myself up and said goodnight and ran to my room as the courtyard still echoed with his maniacal laughter.

In Broad Daylight

By mid-morning the market's business was reaching its peak. Customers came from everywhere and I devoted myself full time to selling small items such as bracelets, handkerchiefs, and the like. Muhammad handled the big sales, taking the money, and keeping track of receipts which he did with an indelible pencil that he kept behind his ear and a small piece of paper from a crude notebook. He never threw away any of the pieces of paper but folded them back so he could review the whole day's take at the end of the day from those scraps that he alone understood. By about two in the afternoon the demand for small items had abated as women, girls, and children left. There was greater demand for underwear and pieces of fabric popular among workers of Mahmudiya factories.

I began to have some time to observe the market and the crowds. The market was set up on several acres of land adjacent to the village near the Mahmudiya Canal, surrounded by a barbed wire fence. The vendors were arranged in rows and corners separated by pathways big enough for pedestrians, beasts, horse-drawn carts, and pushcarts. The clothiers' row gave its back to the barbed wire to one side and its face to the barbed wire on another side. Behind us appeared the village with its flour mills and candy factories, surrounding our back in an arch of various primitive bends, protrusions and twists, interspersed with poorly constructed minarets, wretched balconies, and chimneys with blackened tops suggesting that they were inhabited by huge snakes. To our right was the Mahmudiya Canal that went through the city of Damanhour reaching Alexandria and beyond. It appeared far away in the distance and from it only very small triangles, white and gray anchored on the banks or deep in the water, were visible. The breeze carried to us the smell of the fish, the vitality of the fishermen, the noise of their quarrels and singing, and the smoke of their fires. Reaching us were also groups of fishermen or sellers carrying Nile perch and catfish in wet, fresh, living, cheap basketfuls.

Before us the agricultural road was only a stone's throw away, and to our left green and red farms stretched endlessly. Muhammad Abu Sinn bought a basketful of fish from the agricultural road and the vendor grilled it for us. Limes, bread, radishes, gargir and pickles were brought for free from our fellow vendors. We ate with great appetites as if it were the meal of a lifetime. As I was carrying a newspaper wrapper containing the remnants of the lunch to throw in an iron bin attached to the barbed wire overlooking the road, I saw a dancing woman wearing a flimsy dancing outfit that revealed her body, with a milaya half covering her, on a donkey. Behind the donkey, a drummer carrying his darbukka under his arm and another man carrying a tambourine, hurried along. The dancer was swinging her legs on the sides of the donkey, egging it on. I remembered my friend Widad and smiled, following her until she disappeared in a small cloud of dust. I withdrew my glances from the horizon and started on my way back when I caught sight of Ramadan Eraiga in his cashmere best and his brown shoes and large Saidi turban on his head and cream-colored silk shawl on his shoulders. To his right was a man and to his left another, all walking in a nonchalant manner, their eyes focused cautiously ahead of them. The surprise left me tongue-tied and transfixed: what brought Ramadan Eraiga here today? Did he have business in the market? Did he come to steal or to sell previously stolen merchandise? A thought flashed through my mind that made a connection between him and my friend

Widad. I became certain that the dancer who passed by a few minutes earlier on a donkey must have been Widad.

I went back to the display unable to focus clearly. Immediately after mid-afternoon prayers, the cart rumbled from a distance and we began to pack the merchandise in boxes then tie them with twine. The big display was transformed into a collection of firmly tied boxes. Two of the market porters, who always appeared at the right moment, helped the cart driver load up the cart, adjust the load, and secure it to the cart. Then we both rode the cart sitting on the boxes. The cart proceeded with us as if we were two inspectors surveying conditions around us.

We got on the flat agricultural road, the sun having enveloped us with a cruel orange curtain. Then the market moved away and with its barbed wire looked like the remnants of letters written in pencil before erasing some of them and scraping the others off. Then the village sank in a far away slope, her buildings joining masses of clouds. The road became narrow and uneven and we began to teeter as we sat. I knew it was a short junction that would soon lead us back to the paved road along the Mahmudiya Canal, so I suggested to Muhammad to get off and walk that bit behind the cart, which was now proceeding very slowly. Muhammad thought it was a good idea, especially since it was time for him to relieve himself after the midafternoon prayers and to get ready for the sunset prayer.

Muhammad went down to the bank of an irrigation canal because he had to wash himself and his penis ritually after relieving himself; he may also have availed himself of the opportunity and performed his ablutions and performed two prostrations to thank God for the market ending without problems and pray that the day end well by finishing the journey safely. As for me I went toward an old sycamore to hide myself and squat to relieve my belly from the load of fish. I soon saw that that would be impossible because there was a group of men gathering near a waterwheel a stone's throw away. I saw a small squarish mud-brick building of the kind peasants used to spend the night in or in which to keep their animals as they stayed up for irrigation at night. I found it more fitting to hide in the shadow of its back wall. I passed by the men and the surprise roared as if a gun with a silencer had been shot inside me: it was Ramadan Eraiga and the two men, trying to untie a rope tying a water buffalo and two cows to a stake in the ground. Finally Ramadan brought a knife out of his pocket and severed the knot of the rope. He gave the buffalo to one of the men and the two cows to the other and pointed at the road. I thanked God none of them had seen me since I was in a low point in the ground hidden from sight by the wall of the hut. I squatted, lifting my gallabiya and doing my best not to fart, otherwise I'd be given away. Were Ramadan Eraiga to see me now, it wouldn't be unlikely that he would stab me. The wind was carrying to me the sounds of drumming on the darbukka and the tambourine in the rhythm for dancing. The jingling rhythm was so clear and so delightful that I was shitting to music. I wiped myself with a leaf of a castor oil plant hanging down next to the hut wall. I got up and went around the waterwheel from the other side and I saw, at another slope and another waterwheel, a group of boys, old men and children. The body of the dancer was slithering within the circle they had made around her. They were all clapping as she staggered and swayed on the chests of the two old men, her mouth and legs wide open as the old men screamed impetuously, "Whoa!" and one of them brayed, "All that for a few stalks of clover for your donkey? Take a half acre of clover!" A third one pawed her chest and shoulders with his palms ravenously, shouting in loud agony as if summoning a distant hope: "Just tell me where it is and I'll fetch you the milk of a sparrow!" I went down the slope, approaching the circle. It was Widad! Yes, my friend Widad in the flesh, her arms and chest bare, the contours of her belly going up and down with great expertise. I stopped at a distance on a pile of rubble and manure, staring at her, stabbing her with my eyes in her heart, her belly, and her legs. But her eyes were lowered and she had bent over backwards, arching her back with her hair coming down the legs of one of the two shameless old men. As she righted herself up, our eyes met. She gasped in terror, her eyes sparkling madly. She hit her chest with her fist and shouted "Oh my God!

That's impossible!" I immediately turned and ran toward the road, panting and my legs shaking. I felt as if someone were chasing me, trying to arrest me. Then I reached the junction of the road with the rough terrain. As I had expected, Muhammad Abu Sinn had performed his ablutions and performed two prostrations for the road and stood there looking around for me. Smiling, he said, "I thought you went to watch the dancer."

"I only saw her from a distance."

"What's wrong? Were you running?"

I felt I was going to tell him everything that happened in a rush: *Do you remember the woman who bought two shawls from us in the market in Damanhour and I told you she was my neighbor? It turned out she was the dancer!* But I didn't say anything.

At the beginning of the paved road, the driver was waiting for us, so we got on our way. A quarter of an hour later we passed by Ramadan Eraiga walking alone, slowly as if he were a village elder inspecting his fields. After about one kilometer, we passed the two men leading three water buffaloes and four cows, walking so calmly and confidently as if they were merchants leading their own cattle. I figured out how the infernal game worked: Widad would choose a specific spot to begin dancing, in return for two bunches of clover for her donkey and a couple of loaves of bread for her two musicians. Thereupon the boys left by their families to watch over the cattle would gather around. As they watched the dancer, Ramadan Eraiga and his men would be able to untie the cattle and lead them away. As they got on the public road, he would be just another man leading his cattle back from the market or the field.

The Tomb Below

Widad stood frozen in her open door, fixing me with her scared, humiliated, yet belligerent eyes. It was as if she were looking in my eyes for the true intentions behind this visit, as if I were visiting her for the first time. She was visibly frightened and confused even though many days had passed since that incident. Her brows were knit in a pained look as if asking: *What do you want from me? Why are you spying on me?* But she didn't say it. Instead, she said hospitably, "Come in, please," and opened the door wide. I went in, heading for the balcony, avoiding looking to my left so my eyes would not see that disfigured, tormented creature. Yet I did catch a glimpse of her, for the girl had eyes that caused you to grow eyes in your side, your back, the back of your head, everywhere, making you see that anxious, non-comprehending look of childlike pain. She looked as though she were waving her arms almost jumping toward you, beseeching you for something or another.

I left my shoes next to the door and sat down on the floor. The space above in the open door was filled with an apparition of pure rippling honey reflected on half the wall of the balcony. She said in genuine affection as if she were my wife welcoming me home after a hard day's work, "Would you like to eat?"

I hesitated. I didn't know what to say. She rephrased the invitation, "Let's have supper together."

She looked at my eyes in the light sneaking through the corner of the balcony above the wall as though it were spying on us. Dinner was indeed ready. The basket came with a casserole of stewed meat with potatoes, tomato sauce and garlic and onion, with rice and bread and radishes and pickled eggplant. I ate with great appetite which she encouraged by pushing toward me big chunks of meat, selecting for me slices of eggplant, and trimming radishes for me, urging me to eat until I swore I couldn't anymore. The tea had been brewed on the glowing charcoal in the brazier. She said, "Would you like to wash your hands?"

I followed her to the bathroom. I washed my mouth and hands with scented soap as she stood holding the towel. I dried my hands, then she draped the towel on her shoulder.

"Delicious dinner. May your hands remain healthy."

She blushed gratefully, lowering her eyes as she turned down the wick of a lamp to bathe the tent of light in shade. She looked more captivating than the pictures of all the seductresses that hung near the entrance of her apartment. Yet she looked very miserable, very vulnerable, good at heart even though she tried to appear tough. Despite the strange life she was leading, she seemed not to know much about life. She was so naïve and helpless and the additional burden of her crippled daughter seemed to place her squarely among the truly miserable. I found myself patting her on the shoulder for the first time and it seemed my hand conveyed what I felt toward her at that moment for she turned into a little girl awaiting this gesture for a long time. She threw herself into my chest, resting her head on my shoulder, seeking genuine affection and kindness. When her shaking subsided somewhat, her chest began to settle on my chest. I embraced her gently, then harder, whereupon her solid frame seemed to dwindle as if it had been filled with air. I wiped her tears with my handkerchief and before lifting it from her cheeks she grabbed my hand and planted on its back a passionate kiss of gratitude. I withdrew my hand quickly. I noticed that during those moments I had forgotten that she was a woman or perhaps I forgot that I was a man, that I desired her with all my being, for that particular vein which always throbbed whenever I thought of her did not move. I felt a rare calm and peace, however.

When we sat drinking tea and smoking the shisha, her eyes were sending me vague telegraphic messages that I took to mean that she was somewhat anxious. I found myself saying, "Consider it as though I didn't see you that day."

She said in a rattling voice, "My heart stopped that moment. I fell to my feet. I fainted. People were thinking of running after you. Why did you run? You made me suspect in their eyes, but I told them when I came to that you were my cousin and that you didn't know anything about my profession. I had fainted by choice so they would be busy with me instead of running after you. For in the countryside, when somebody runs, people run after him without knowing why he's running. They think there must be a fire that needs to be put out. They think a cow has fallen into the well of a waterwheel and must be pulled out. They think it must be a thief they have to trip up and apprehend. Anyway, how did you end up catching me in such a mess? Were you spying on me? By the way, I thought so and I was happy and I loved you even though I was so extremely vexed with you that I wished I had a dagger to plunge into your heart. But thank God it didn't come to that. How did you follow me from Damanhour to the Mahmudiya countryside?"

I laughed in confusion: "I didn't see only you. I saw Ramadan Eraiga also, untying the cattle from the stake and giving them to two men with him. I also saw him with them on the agricultural road, coming back with the cattle."

She made a motion with her hands as if moaning and brought her fingers close to her chest in a gesture of ripping her clothes. Then she started wailing, her face and lips quite pale: "What a catastrophe! You were spying, of course. I heard you were an undercover policeman. More than one person at the wikala told me that when they found out you were spending evenings with me. I didn't believe them. It seems I am an idiot! Of course you're undercover. There's no doubt about it. Is it the vice or the felony division? I swear by God who brought us together without prior arrangement, that I am a poor woman, minding my own business as you've seen with your own eyes. Frankly, I buy hashish for you as a favor, on the one hand and on the other hand, the woman gives me a little bit for myself. I don't buy for anyone else but you. I said to myself, 'Girl, he looks like he comes from a good family, like a good guy who's fallen on hard times, so help him out instead of him letting him get into trouble if he falls into the hands of the treacherous government! But I swear to God I am stupid and naïve. Look at me! Many men have betrayed me. They just want to eat my flesh for free. Don't be fooled by my baring my shoulder or shaking my body in front of some kids. It's a hard way to make a living. But to lie down and open myself for anyone to come inside me and humiliate me as he wishes, as if I were just a rag with which he wiped his shoes? That never happens and will never happen except in a lawful marriage. My grandmother, Qut al-Qulub, has planted that in me and said that whoever takes something easily from you, you'll lose him as a man and as a useful friend. She told me that a woman, no matter how much Time has wronged her, will always have something to help her out in a pinch. If gold is good to men in a pinch, word of a woman's honor spreads among people until the time comes when a man who truly appreciates it comes along. If he doesn't, the woman would die noble and chaste of body and as a result, God will forgive the rest of her sins. You, for instance. You desire me, you want to devour me. I also desire you. But that wouldn't please God and I won't do it and I believe you also no longer want it. I am the easiest woman to marry and the easiest to divorce. When I get fed up with my hard life, I get married. And when I get fed up with my husband who turns out to be a lowlife, I get divorced. I've always had bad luck. I never had a good husband. How can I meet a good man when my path is not good? Twenty years ago I was young and dainty. I danced with entertainers in weddings and in bridal processions. Each night ended in a fight over fees and distribution of wages and money gifts. After that came a worse fight when the customer wanted me to go home with him. The manager of the company would then stand up to him, not to defend me but to take me himself! Even the drummer jazzes up the music for me in the hope of stealing me away from them all. Even the guy giving the wedding party and all the guests harassed me until I began to resent my own body. Did I have a sign on my body saying that I was easy and waiting for anyone to beckon to me? It was quite a dilemma. I spent many years with the awalim without respite. And their money seemed to be jinxed! I spent it all on the crippled girl, on someone babysitting her until I came back for my grandmother can't stand seeing her. Rotten luck and scandal even when I don't compromise my honor. The biggest sign of bad luck is opening my eyes and seeing you standing there in a faraway place!"

She gave me the mouthpiece of the shisha with a gesture of vexation that nevertheless counted on my friendship. I took a deep drag then said through the thick smoke, "Listen, Widad. You bought two shawls from me in the market. So I am not undercover this or that. On the contrary, I hate police of every stripe even though I have no dealings with them. I just don't like them and hope that God will keep them away from me. I was a student and I am going once again to study at the university as a student at large, with God's permission. I come from a village in the Gharbiya province but I came here in the hope of staying with my rich cousin, married to an important man here, but I wasn't comfortable there and lived alone. Then an incident prevented me from continuing with my education, so my family got mad at me and cut off my stipend so I came to live in this wikala for the time being and started working for that clothier who sold you the two shawls. When I saw you in a dancer's outfit, dancing for the children, we were coming back from the Mahmudiya market. I was relieving myself when I came upon Ramadan Eraiga untying the cattle, then I ran into you dancing. And, by the way, I saw you passing by the market riding your donkey, followed by the drummer and the tambourine player, then after a short while, Ramadan Eraiga and his two men."

"It's my bad luck, I tell you!" she said with conviction. Then there was a spark of alarm and apprehension in her eyes: "Did Ramadan Eraiga see you?"

"No."

"And neither of the two men?"

"Luckily, no."

"Did you talk about it in front of Shawadfi?"

"I didn't open my mouth in front of anyone."

"Thank God! I am good and kind hearted. Don't you ever let Ramadan Eraiga know that you've seen him. Don't whisper to Shawadfi or anyone else in the wikala. God! Forgive me, God! You see me now doing a good deed, God! I am not snitching but it's a good deed I am doing for your sake, God. Listen, my friend. There's a big tomb below the wikala."

"What'd you say?"

"A tomb! A tomb for burial of corpses."

"Whose corpses?"

"Those they get rid of. Good for nothing boys whom their mothers have cursed. They come to spend the night in the wikala and fall under its spell. One of them gets delusional about his youth, his daring, and his reputation for mayhem. The devil makes him think he can rule the wikala in Shawadfi's place by humiliating him in front of everyone, and take control of him and the rest and the whole wikala as Shawadfi himself did with Atiya. Shawadfi, however, is as sly as a fox. He gives the boy a false sense of security, then sneaks sleeping powder into the tea and the cigarettes. In a few minutes the boy keels over next to him. Shawadfi then finishes him off with a handkerchief and suffocates him. Then he carries him down into the tomb. The tomb doesn't need any digging for it has a secret opening with a cover like that of a manhole. It used to be a well originally, built under the animal shed. It has a built-in ladder connected to a distant deep area underground. In a few minutes the corpse would disappear and no one is the wiser. Soon the mouth of the well disappears under the animal dung."

The shisha mouthpiece started to shake between my lips and I myself began to tremble like a bird under a pouring rain. It was highly likely that Widad was trying to frighten me so that I wouldn't tell what I saw and word would never reach the government. It was even more highly likely that she was telling the truth, which was more probably because she sounded sincere, agitated, and frightened. Besides I wouldn't put it past Shawadfi, who was quite capable of it, otherwise he wouldn't have become ruler of the wikala with all its denizens of hardened criminals and miscreants.

"If you are lying to me, Widad, you will lose me for life. I am a peasant who is very loyal and who pays with his life to defend his friends and what is right. At the same time I pay with my life in vengeance against whoever betrays me or makes a fool of me. If your purpose is to frighten me so I wouldn't speak, I am not going to speak on my own anyway. It is part of my character and comes from my genuine peasant upbringing. If you just want to frighten me, you're only succeeding in making me more obstinate. I know that they're all a treacherous, criminal bunch, but I have a brain that I can use when the need arises to save myself from those with evil intentions. So, be truthful with me, Widad, out of respect for the bread and salt. What you've just told me: is it true or just a silly, made-up invention? I want to know, just to look out for myself."

Widad got up in agitation. She ran down the corridor feverishly, then came back holding a piece of bread: "Pardon me, I don't have a copy of the Qur'an. I am afraid my apartment is not sufficiently pure to be spared being burned by the glorious Qur'an. But his bread is exactly like the Qur'an."

She broke the bread and placed it on her eyes, then said in an emphatic, strongly articulated voice, "I swear by this blessing that God has bestowed on us, that these two eyes of mine have seen the corpse being carried to the animal shed and Shawadfi coming out after a while shaking the dust off his hands and feet. In the morning I looked for the tenant of the wikala from my grandmother's room and I knew who was missing. I kept looking for him many days and he never appeared again. I am certain that he's been buried. With these two eyes which will be eaten by worms, I've seen death and burial several times. Circumstances always work in Shawadfi's favor! In this dirty land of ours, circumstances work in nobody's favor except Shawadfi's."

I sobered up. All the hashish I smoked evaporated from my head and left me with pain in the muscles of my chest and a shortness of breath. Smiling, trying to assuage my fear, Widad said, "You shouldn't be afraid like that! Shawadfi, after all, doesn't go out of his way looking for trouble. So long as you are good and truthful and honest with him he will bend over backward to be of help to you. You should pull the wool over their eyes. You've got a brain as you've said yourself, and they are not very bright, I agree with you. So, use your brain with them at all times. Open your eyes and see everything but close your mouth. Hear everything as if you've heard nothing. The proverb says if you go to a country that worships a calf, cut the clover and feed it. Tenants of the wikala and the good-for-nothing government worship Shawadfi because he's good for them and brings in a lot of goodies for them with no effort on their part. You, too, should cut the clover and feed him. He is very patient and is trying new things on you every day."

From somewhere nearby, a radio was on and we heard the clock striking, then the announcer Hemmat Mustafa announced midnight in Cairo. I got up: "Good night!"

She followed me to the apartment door. I paused to say goodbye. I hugged her so hard I could hear her bones cracking. She moaned and involuntarily her moans were feminine and electrifying. I had such a hard-on I almost pierced her. She separated me from her gently and whispered, smiling earnestly like a friend doing a friend a favor, "I'll introduce you to a woman that you'd like, Sundus the gypsy, whose room is next door to my grandmother's. I bet she can make you forget me. Have a beautiful night!"

When the breeze greeted me on the street the hashish that had evaporated came back to my head and played games with my senses and emotions, taking me from peaks of delight to depths of fear and terror.

The streetlights looked more faint and I saw myself handcuffed by the police to Widad, Ramadan Eraiga, Sayyed Zanati, and Zainhum the beggar. I saw my head bashed in, a corpse carried to the animal shed to disappear forever in a bottomless deserted well. The fields around the wikala sent a cacophony of sounds combining wolves howling, frogs croaking, waterwheels bellowing, water cylinders rumbling, shadoofs grunting, grasshoppers scraping, ravens cawing, and curlews calling. And yet I had no desire to enter the wikala, as if I were standing before a cell where I was sentenced for life and where, if I got in, I wouldn't be let out, ever. So, I stood, my hands in my pants' pockets, taking in the cool fresh air. A few minutes later, there appeared at the end of the empty street two black masses that kept getting larger until I could see they were two tall, shabbily dressed, unclean men. It was obvious they were looking for any hapless soul. They kept coming closer and when they saw me, they stopped at the street corner. One of them whistled and I raised my head. He made a gesture with his finger, ordering me to go to them, whereupon I immediately knocked on the gate anxiously and fearfully, then I pushed the gate and it opened and slid in at the very moment that the two vagrants reached it and almost grabbed me. I pushed the gate in their face and heard them outside laughing and snorting in poorly feigned indifference.

Whispering

Most workers who lived in the wikala did not work the streets on Friday, except Sundus, the gypsy, who carried a basket on her head and went out. She would wear a dress of gray chintz with small dark green dots, reaching her heels just above the anklets with broad ruffles. In the chest area and immediately below, the dress had pleats and cross-stitches that accentuated the chest, the belly, and the hips, and intimated that, under the clothing, there was a captivating female. The face was charmingly beautiful as if painted by an ancient Egyptian folk artist, lacking smoothness and steadiness in lines but the features on the whole were quite attractive. The face was like a clay plate, the color, texture, and shine of ghee despite the coarse looks. The eyes were somewhat narrow, sharp of sight, with long black lashes, under a forehead that looked like a pomegranate, with thick black eyebrows in front and, on top, a sequined kerchief covering her hair in a traditional bedouin manner and a black velvet shawl. The nose was straight and pointed, raised and pierced at the bottom where one gold ring, shaped like a circular chopping knife, dangled. Between the eyebrows was one green spot tattoo and under the nose, in place of a mustache was another tattoo in the form of two thick lines joining two similar ones in the middle of the lower lip then reaching the middle of the chin. She had a tall, supple figure. Her gait, as she carried the basket had a swagger as if she were a mare on her way to meet her rider, almost coming undone in delight, each part of her body moving separately in complete freedom only to come together and fall into place with the other parts.

Ever since Widad told me about her, I began to look out for her with interest. Then I began to urge Widad to actually introduce us. That took place quite boldly and simply on a breezy afternoon when I was surprised by a light knock on the door of my room. As I sat up I said, “Come in,” and Widad entered with Sundus behind her, carrying her basket on her head. I stood up to welcome them and cleared some space on the mastaba for them, but Sundus squatted on the floor before her basket while Widad sat on the edge of the mastaba. The door was ajar and Widad said in a conspiratorial tone, “Tell the effendi his fortune. Whisper to the sea shells. Strike the sand. Read the cards. Open his heart, his head, bring out all that’s in there.”

The tattoos stretched on Sundus’ face and the distances between them grew longer at the same time. Her fine delicate teeth showed and inside, her tongue flowed in a Bedouin accent with twisted consonants that gushed out in a warm voice resembling that of men in its breadth and timber but deep down retaining its feminine rhythm. She took from under the cover of her basket a wrapped piece of cloth like a handkerchief. She unwrapped it and spread it on the floor. It was a handful of sand and two small shells. She started making lines in the sand with her finger: “Your honorable name?”

‘So and so.”

“And the honorable name of your mother?”

“So and so.”

“It’s written that you live away from home and there’s no escaping what’s been written. The world has wronged you undeservedly but patience will solve everything. God has saved you from a harrowing trial. What was it? Don’t tell me, just say whether it happened or not.”

“It happened.”

"A man who, for you, was like a father or a sheikh or a teacher and had it in for you, filling his heart with evil toward you. Who was he to you?"

"My teacher at the institute. That's truly amazing!"

"You fell in love with a big-hearted human being who was good to you. There sang in the rafters of your ceiling a big rare bird that had little luck. No sooner did it fill your life with fun than the hunter caught it. What is that to you?"

"Badriya."

"There's an old man who had turned his back on you and is angry with you. His back is bent under mountains of burdens. Who is he?"

"Must be my father."

"There's a short woman, fair of face, who worries about you day and night and who takes the morsel out of her own mouth and saves it for you in a safe place. Who is she?"

"It's obvious it's my grandmother on my mother's side."

"You are pure of heart. Easy to get angry, like milk, boiling to overflowing, spilling on the edges of the vessel, losing nothing but itself. You're like the prickly pear, thorny on the outside but your heart is full of seeds that taste like honey. The branch is good but the root is better. Generous of spirit and the generous cannot be harmed. There are always good people who offer you good deeds and good words. God has given you a good insight and given you more than he has given others. The reward is where you're going not how much money you're making. If times are hard now, don't give up and don't complain. Those who make light of you today will revere you tomorrow and those who shun you now will entreat you one day. Luck will smile on you and you'll be saved from misfortune, your enemies will be defeated and your sons victorious. Very soon you will get out of a hole where you've fallen against your will to a high mountain with minarets and palms and trees and roses and birds and dovecotes. Give me your word before God, witnessed by his Prophet and by the day when it turns harmonious and the full moon as it becomes full and the forenoon as it becomes manifest, that you'll remember me with the reward of good tidings and fragrant memories, by God: Amen!"

"Amen!"

I said it as I sat there like a good pupil who repeated the words of the lesson. I felt that she wasn't facile at all, that she was extremely intelligent and quick witted, that she was quite an expert at reading faces and homing in on signs of problems and worries in their emotional dimensions thus getting close to causes and facts. It was quite wondrous that that intelligent illiterate Bedouin had not stumbled in one sentence, that she had an innate eloquence that many people educated in the schools and al-Azhar lacked. Where did she get it from? When did she amass this expertise about the psyche and the ability to guess in such a way as to never miss anything since her words would always contain a big chunk of the truth? She must be an expert on qualities and characteristics shared by many humans with similar circumstances, for her guesses to have echoes with guaranteed results in everyone. Was it ancient pharaonic knowledge that she had inherited from her ancestors just as Sinai inherited the monasteries, the priests, the history, the gold and turquoise mines, and the conquerors' invasions?

I was certain that my relationship with this gypsy, Sundus, would be long and strong. The intelligence peeking through her eyes was sharp and penetrating and had that cool, soft sting that tempted you to conquer it on her bed with an outpouring of pleasure, and to bite the tip of that provocative nose that looked like a red pepper and nibble that long round neck, starting with that amber necklace.

Widad looked at me in a certain way, so I sat up and pulled the wallet from under the pillow and took out a ten-piaster bill which I offered Sundus, somewhat shyly. She fixed me with a fiery glance: "Shame on you! We are neighbors and family!"

Widad said, "Sundus is generous and comes from a generous family. You can return her favor any time you like."

Sundus interrupted: "If he returned it, then it wouldn't be a favor, from him or from me."

Widad nudged me lightly and I said, "But I like to see you a lot, Sundus. Your words are wise and you have insight. Please consider me your brother here."

Widad looked at me from the corner of her eye, making fun of my naiveté, as if I were a pupil who had failed a test. Then she sat up as if giving the correct answer herself: "Anyway, let's spend an evening at Sundus' place. She has a fantastic room and even though it's like a box, she makes it like the world in a box. She has a goza like genuine earthenware water-cooling jars from Qena, which is easy on the chest. And tea from her hands is something else. As for food, when she puts her mind to it you must try it."

Trying to prove that I was intelligent this time I said, "You have enticed me, Widad. Let's spend the evening next Thursday at Sundus' place. What do you think, Sundus?"

"My house is your house, any time."

"Agreed, then."

They left. On my way to the store that evening Shawadfi stopped me and, out of the blue, explained to me how happy he became whenever he saw his tenants liking each other and visiting and exchanging food. Whenever there was bread and salt among them, he suggested, there was no room for betrayal or treachery.

Sundus and Harisa

I asked Muhammad Abu Sinn if he would give me Thursday evening off to go to our village Thursday and Friday. He readily agreed and gave me a whole pound, saying, "Buy something for your brothers and sisters. Don't you dare take it for yourself, otherwise you'll lose what you've lawfully worked for."

It was before noon and I was wearing the clean clothes that I wore for work in the store. I left the store, going deep into the vegetable and fruit market street, off Susi Street. On the corner was Fakharani Fruits, a very clean store that looked like a pharmacy in its façade and glass cases. The fruits were displayed in front and inside in pyramids of cardboard boxes filled with a vast array of different fruits. The last thing I could imagine was seeing fruits that vendors ordinarily displayed in crates and baskets or on push carts, given such careful treatment: each orange, apple, or mango, even each guava and date, wrapped by itself in wax paper and arranged next to and above the others like gems in a necklace. The rows on top were uncovered and looked like cheerful faces peeking from colorful veils. It was a festival of fragrances filling the street without competition except for that coming from the harisa vendor standing by his cart or a nearby corner with low heat under the harisa tray filling the place with the aroma of ghee and vanilla. Fakharani's store had two doors opening out to the main street and a third one to the side street. Its walls and ceiling were covered with mirrors; the ceiling fans were whirring incessantly, and the mirrors reflected their movement and everything else going on in the street, making everyone stop and stare in amazement.

My whole being, however, was focused on the harisa vendor on the far corner at the end of the street where the side street met the main street as if it were a rectangular pocket with two openings leading in different directions. I used to pass this vendor everyday on my way to the institute when it moved from Me'allim Ads's building at Iflaqa Bridge to its own building in Shubra Damanhour. There I'd see the crowds around him: effendis, workers, and bicycle riders, stopping and ordering "a piece for two piasters," "four piasters," "one shilling." The vendor answered each, joking, "For you or are you going to eat it?" Then, using his spatula, he would place a big piece on the plate from which a thin layer of steam rose, then he would dip the spatula into a bowl of hot melted ghee and drizzle the harisa and place a small fork next to it. As the customer reached with his hand to take the plate, the vendor would drop it in a well-trained move, whereupon the customer would be alarmed, thinking the plate had fallen to the ground. It was a joy to watch that show every morning and one of my cherished hopes was to be on the receiving end of such jesting, if only for two piasters' worth. Now the time had come to buy a really big piece, maybe half an oka. That was an extremely good idea and how wonderful it would be to take it to Sundus, the gypsy, a classier, and cheaper, gift than fruit from Fakharani's store, which I didn't dare enter even just to ask how much.

I turned first to the fish market: a dead end off the market street. I saw myself following a Bedouin woman of graceful figure who was walking in front of me, carrying a basket on her head. Her figure and the way she walked reminded me very strongly of Sundus. I knew that Damanhour's vast countryside had many Moroccans and Bedouins who had settled there a long time ago and who came to Damanhour for shopping and selling stuff. I expected that the Bedouin woman was planning to buy some fish. I too, had come to buy some fish for our evening at Sundus' house after which we'd have harisa for dessert.

I looked at both sides of the street, which were lined with a great number of panniers chock-full of perch, gray mullet, catfish, eel, and various other kinds of fish. It was the first time in my life I had stopped in front of a vendor to buy something with my own money. I imagined that all the vendors knew me personally and would not believe me were I to stop before them like a respectable customer and ask "How much?" let alone "Weigh this and give me some of that!" No one would take it seriously at all. Perhaps that was the reason I'd come to feel embarrassed each time I came to stop by a vendor: I'd suddenly change my mind and continue walking, thinking how I could intrude on the vendor boldly, like any servant or woman, telling him to be honest and to give good measure. I thought of giving Widad or Sundus some money to come and buy a meal for that party. It had to be fish and specifically eel because of what I'd heard about its benefits and how it put the body on fire and stoked it with energy. I remembered that at the end of that particular alley there was a vendor who knew me well and I decided to go to him as there were no barriers between us.

He saw me from a distance and he smiled, waving his arm in enthusiastic welcome. As usual he was sitting on the threshold of the last house in the alley, a very old five-story house with rectangular windows with iron bars in front of the glass and shutter doors. The glass, however, was mostly gone, replaced by faded cardboard panels. Some windows were totally boarded up with plywood, cardboard, and straightened tin cans. The house looked as though, sometime in the distant past, it had enjoyed signs of magnificent opulence as evidenced by the decorative details around the edges of the windows, making them remotely reminiscent of royal crowns. The big, high door's two ironwood jambs were stuck to the wall, dust, rust, and dirt having filled the gaps and so the door was open all the time on an old, chipped marble threshold three stairs above street level. To the right was a three-room apartment separated by an identical one on the left, with facing doors by a broad marble entryway. The staircase faced you as you entered and between the two apartments on each different floor was a landing separating the doors, each of which had two jambs topped with glass windows protected by iron bars. On each door was a brass knocker in the shape of a hand holding a small ball resting on a small brass pad. A light knock on the door was loud enough to be heard by those inside even if they were fast asleep. It was a very intimate house, for me.

As soon as I stood in front of Amm Hanbuta, I felt dizzy and had a dry mouth. I shouldn't have come to this house! I had long avoided going to the neighborhood, for in that apartment to the left lived Muhammad Fusduq's mother-in-law with her son, Muhammad Effendi Hasan, chief clerk of the Damanhour Telephone Exchange, and her daughter, Wafdiya, the thirty-year-old spinster. Wafdiya had not married because she looked exactly like her brother who, in turn, was the spitting image of his father as one could see from the framed photograph on the wall. The father was a Nubian police sergeant as shown by a second photo in full dress uniform, who married a white girl from Damanhour named Masriya and the two had three children: Muhammad, Safiya, and Wafdiya. Muhammad Effendi Hassan got a primary school degree thanks to which he got a job as a clerk in the Exchange then began to support the family after the death of his father. He kept postponing marriage until he approached fifty, perhaps because he had no hope of finding a virgin who would marry him since he had a very repulsive fat face with crude features, large teeth and lips, and unattractive hair and eyebrows. He took great care in combing his hair and making it shine and wore a suit and necktie. He was very gentle and nice and generous and a good listener who followed conversations in silence with his eyes and clay-like facial reactions. Next in the order of birth was Safiya, then Wafdiya. The latter looked like him in everything: the crude features, large lips, and buck teeth. She had, however, a nice, tall, delicate figure and a soft, soothing voice. Besides, she was a good cook, economical and resourceful. She embroidered handkerchiefs for her women neighbors and spent most of the day either in the market shopping for vegetables or at haberdasheries buying sequins and beads. She stocked up on bridal necessities. There had been several suitors but no one knew why they developed cold feet at the last moment. And yet she maintained her good humor and was not affected by her bad luck and always said that God knew that she loved her mother and wouldn't be able to leave her, so He kept her by her mother's side. The mother, short and fat, sitting on the sofa, looked at her with profound sadness and pity in her dejected honey-colored eyes. As for the older sister, Safiya, she was tall like her father and like him had two protruding front teeth with a nice gap and thick eyebrows. From her mother she took her ruddy white complexion and delicate features. That was why she was married, early, to Muhammad Fusduq who worked as an usher at the Court of Appeals, but whose real main job was running the subleased Court's coffee concession, which he ran wearing a fez and clean khaki suit and specialized in serving the judges in the chamber.

Muhammad Fusduq was able to save some money with which he bought a few meters in agricultural land adjacent to the Shubra Damanhour neighborhood. There he built a small two-room house with an unroofed parlor. His money ran out while roofing so he used wooden beams, bamboo, and sackcloth instead of a fully finished roof. He and his wife lived in the only fully roofed room which he furnished as a bedroom to which he added a few chairs scattered between bed and armoire. The floor was covered by a cheap kilim on a mat. In that room Safiya would sit all day long, cooking on a kerosene stove or washing clothes or embroidering handkerchiefs that her sister, Wafdiya, had sent her. She would wait for her husband Muhammad Fusduq's return from the court at three in the afternoon to have lunch and then go back to the courthouse from which he would return around nine in the evening. Safiya always liked to say of her husband: "Muhammad went to court!" She would say that so earnestly and simply that one would think that her husband must be a judge or a counselor. As for the second room, he put it up for rent and we were led to it by the agent after many months of continuing to live near Iflaqa Bridge after the institute had moved a half-hour's walk away in Shubra Damanhour. We were four students from the same village, each paying thirty piasters a month. Thus Muhammad Fusduq benefited doubly: one hundred and twenty piasters a month and four young men guarding his wife during his absence in that place far from the city and close to burglars and robbers. He also got to enjoy their company in the evening. He was confident that none of the peasant students would dare bother or harass his wife.

As soon as you saw Muhammad Fusduq and his wife Safiya you immediately believed in the saying "birds of a feather flock together." For he also had buck teeth so unnaturally big that he couldn't close his lips. It was as if he had no lips to begin with. When he laughed—and he was always laughing, sometimes for no reason—it was as if he were a crocodile opening its jaws to catch prey from the air, in a broad dull voice despite his attempts to give it some resonance. Both Muhammad and Safiya were very kind and loving. Safiya would cook and sit waiting for him, knowing that he would be late as usual. By that time we would have returned from the institute, changed into our gallabiyas and begun to munch on dry bread with salt or leftover ta'miya or pickled turnips or mish that we had bought from the village. The two rooms had a door connecting them in addition to the two doors opening to the parlor. That inside door was only closed at bedtime at night. Safiya was always sitting facing that door observing us in sad contemplation. Sometimes her big eyes would wander far away and her features would freeze in such a way that only her pupils would keep moving like a bobbin in the two ponds of her eyes filled with a quasi-frozen liquid as if it were deferred tears or excess tears about to fall. Then she would break the silence suddenly shouting: "Mustafa!" We don't know why she called on Mustafa in particular; perhaps because he was the one who rented the room in our name and he was the one who collected the rent from us and paid her on the first of the month. Or perhaps because he was the only one who seemed to come from a good family, with his handsome prosperous face, his robust health, and his many clean clothes. He was the son of a grain merchant in our village, the nephew of Hagg Mas'oud, my cousin's husband. As soon as he heard his name he replied very politely as if addressing his own mother, "Yes, Umm Ashraf?" And she would tell him in a strong, resonant voice: "Come here, son," in the tone of someone saying "It cannot be helped." When he got up to go to her through the inner door, the smell of cooked food would rise intoxicatingly and we would know, each crouching in his corner on his mat, blanket and pillow, next to the box of his provisions, that she had lifted the lid of the pot to ladle food on to the plate. Mustafa would know ahead of time that she would do that and that he would say no, and yet he would go every time to stand at a short distance. She would have filled the plate with potatoes, beans, or okra with four small pieces of delicious meat on top. She would extend her long, tender arm and clean white chubby hand with the plate and Mustafa would say, "No, thank you. Thank you. We've had our lunch. I swear we had our lunch. Thank you." She would shout in her resonant voice, "Come on. Hold it, don't give me a hard time!" while he would continue to say the same words as we kept exchanging resentful glances behind his back. Mustafa did that because he was totally sure that, after she gave up on him, Safiya would call me, "Okay, so and so, you come here! You don't give me a hard time. You are frank and don't play games," whereupon I would rise and go quickly to her, hold the plate by my two hands and go back with Mustafa behind me. I would take it to my mat and place it on a neutral spot. Mustafa would come carrying a large loaf of bread under his arm, followed by al-Nims then Bahiy al-Din. Then we would sit around the plate to begin munching again.

Quite often Muhammad Fusduq, nicknamed Abu Ashraf, would come in at that time to find us struggling to finish wiping the plate clean with the dry bread. He would look at us with his almond-colored eyes beneath the rim of his fez, putting his hands in the pockets of his western-style gallabiya with a collar, jiggling the coins that were undoubtedly the day's tips. He would open his jaws, laughing: "Oh, you devils you! As if I'd fathered and abandoned you!"

Then he would go to his room: "Evening, Safiya."

We would immediately turn to finishing our homework before Muhammad Fusduq came back to keep us company, counting on our welcoming it for the sake of the tea that he was going to serve us. He would tell us all kinds of stories about what had happened at the courthouse that day, the praise that he got from judge so and so and counselor so and so. When he became sure that we had begun to fall asleep, he would leave us after closing the inner door and get into bed. At that moment we would be wide awake again as we heard the bed rumbling loudly, then in a more muffled way, like volcanoes erupting underground giving us a pleasurable feeling that we joked about on the way to the institute in the morning or during recess.

Finally Muhammad Fusduq wanted to resolve the food issue so a new topic was introduced to our evening conversation and it lasted several weeks until we were convinced.

"You are strangers here and no one is cooking for you. Store-bought food is neither satisfying nor healthy. That is a problem. But we have a solution. I and my wife are willing to serve you for free. You are like our brothers. All you have to do is contribute to the cost of food. Listen, I am responsible for your meals, breakfast, lunch, and supper. You are paying thirty piasters a month each for rent. You can pay only one pound which would cover your rent, your food, and your drinks. Three meals a day. What a bargain! And good food, as you know. What do you say?"

Mustafa was the first to agree without hesitation and after him Bahiy al-Din whose father was a well-off farmer who owned five feddans of agrarian reform land which Abdel Nasser later distributed to those who were farming it. Bahiy al-Din, like Mustafa, spent twice that amount on the movies. As for al-Nims, his mother was a widow who sent him nothing at all and only gave him a basket of cracked dry bread that she saved from her work for some families and somehow got him the train fare and the rent, which was already too much for her. Like me he believed in a proverb that was firmly etched in the memory of our village: "If you've got bread, then salt is a luxury." As for me, my pocket money was barely half a piaster a day. The sum requested by Muhammad Fusduq, for me and al-Nims, was astronomical to which we fell silent as though it were one of those cosmic things over which we had no control and no business even talking about. Yet we were surprised when things got to the phase of actual execution. It seemed that Muhammad Fusduq considered our silence as proof of our approval, so he started planning and organizing the times and kinds of meals for breakfast, lunch, and supper in a way that was luxurious beyond anything we had witnessed in our own homes. Out of generosity and to give finality to the agreement, Muhammad Fusduq began implementing the project the very next day.

We lived in the lap of luxury for three months, eating something different at every meal, and having tea with every meal, with milk in the morning. Our complexions changed and blood found its way to our faces. We became more jovial and peaceful and took enthusiastic interest in our studies. We also became a family and started going with Muhammad Fusduq every few days, especially Fridays, to the mother-in-law's house to have lunch. There Muhammad Effendi Hassan would sit with us through tea, smoking two cigarettes, and then would go to his Exchange. We would stay until the call to the sunset prayers, whereupon we would start back, taking turns carrying the two children on the way. Mustafa and Bahiy al-Din paid their share regularly every month. As for me, I claimed that I was waiting for harvest time when my father got paid by the peasants whereupon I'd pay my share in a lump sum. When Muhammad Fusduq seemed inclined to believe me, al-Nims followed my example and used the same tactic. Muhammad Fusduq would likely have been suspicious of our claims had it not been for something that happened which gave us a few week's respite. Hagg Mas'oud al-Qabbani, my cousin's husband, came to visit us, sent by his brother in the village to make sure that his son was telling the truth about the new system by which Mustafa was getting an additional pound a month. When Hagg Mas'oud was reassured that it was all real, that there was nothing fishy about it, he expressed great admiration for the system and praised the goodness of Muhammad Fusduq and his wife. When talk came around to me and al-Nims's lack of promptness in paying the agreed upon sum, Hagg Mas'oud pounded his own chest valiantly and said through his huge lips that pronounced 's' as 'sh', "These kids," meaning me and al-Nims, "are telling the truth. And anyway, if they don't pay, I will!"

He had lunch with us from the food that his brother had sent with him: a roasted goose and a casserole of creamed rice with veal, with fitir, honey, and cottage cheese. Safiya decided to place all of that in front of us so as not to be accused of greed or expecting any recompense. Before leaving, Hagg Mas'oud gave Mustafa a quarter pound bill as a gift. Then he felt awkward so he gave each of us a silver ten-piaster coin: then felt awkward again and gave each of Muhammad Fusduq's two sons a quarter pound. When he left we all followed to see him off close to his house. Even Safiya got up and saw him off until he left the street and remained standing until he disappeared behind distant houses. After that Muhammad Fusduq's trust in us got stronger to the extent that he let us leave after the exam carrying all of our belongings, with the promise that I would be back in a few days to find out the exam's results, bringing with me my and al-Nims' payments. However, I never returned because of what happened between me and the math teacher. One day, we were surprised when Muhammad Fusduq carrying a bag of fruit entered our house together with Mustafa al-Qabbani. My father had no idea I was in debt to Muhammad Fusduq and when he heard an explanation from Mustafa, he didn't say a word. Then, after a long silence, he said to Muhammad Fusduq, "If you'd like to buy him for one quarter that amount, you are welcome. Actually, why don't you just take him for nothing!"

Then he left him and started prayers. My father had punished me for what happened, so he refused to buy me new clothes, so at the time I was wearing shabby clothes, torn in several places. Muhammad Fusduq fixed me with an enigmatic look that I did not understand, but he opened his jaws, laughing. Then he got up and patted me on the shoulder saying,

"May God make it up to me and to you." He took Mustafa with him and left, his laughter ringing in front of our house for a long time after his departure. That day I found out from Mustafa that it was Hagg Mas'oud who had sent him to our house and given him precise directions how to get there. Then Mustafa told me, as he hid his embarrassment, that his father paid al-Nims's and my debt in celebration of Mustafa's success.

All of that came to my mind as I sat on the low sofa that looked like a shoeshine boy's chair on which Amm Hanbuta insisted I sit as we drank tea. As I was drinking the tea I told him that I craved a meal of fish hand-picked by him. He reached out and picked some perch, eel, and catfish that he put in a large paper bag and closed it firmly.

"May it be delicious and healthy for you!"

"How much?"

"Whatever you want to pay."

"You must tell me."

"Okay, thirty piasters."

"That's it?"

"It's all in the family."

I paid quite readily and I started to get up to go but he asked me to stay, inquiring about my long absence. He mentioned that my colleagues, Mustafa, Bahiy al-Din, and sometimes the one called al-Nims kept coming until recently, a few days before graduation. He also told me a surprising bit of news that he had heard from Mustafa to the effect that Bahiy al-Din and al-Nims, after flunking twice, dropped out and joined a school for military clerks and that each must by now have become a big army sergeant major. I was anxious to leave before someone from the family saw me, to avoid an awkward situation, but the news kept me. I began to ask Amm Hanbuta about details of that school and conditions for applying there; maybe I too should apply. Suddenly, I saw Muhammad Effendi Hassan approaching wearing a gallabiya and staring at us, his whole face turning into a big smile upon seeing me. Amm Hanbuta, overjoyed, said,

"Muhammad Effendi has appeared! I wonder how many years it's been since you saw him last! He's retired now. He's negotiated an early retirement and opened a cigarette and candy stand on the corner of Sa'a Square. He got it from the city through shady deals with candidates of the Arab Socialist Union of which he's now a member."

Then he added with a wink, "And now he's looking for a bride. People get crazy when they get old. This senior citizen is going to kindergarten!"

At that moment Muhammad Effendi arrived and he embraced me very warmly. After kissing me and greeting me and inquiring after my health, the times, and life in general, he turned to Amm Hanbuta and asked him, "What were you telling him about me, you blockhead?"

Amm Hanbuta laughed until his yellow teeth showed: "I was talking to him to find you a bride! That's what I said."

Muhammad Effendi laughed, "You're a bit late. We're talking today about setting a date for the wedding."

He pulled me by the arm toward the house. I hesitated, pointing to what I had in my hands. He swore that the woman whom he had yet to marry would be divorced if I didn't go in and say hello to the family. I had no choice but to leave the paper bag with Amm Hanbuta and go in with Muhammad Effendi Hasan, bowing my head out of sheer embarrassment.

As I turned to go in the door of the house, I caught a glimpse of a man whom I ascertained to be Ramadan Eraiga, who was pacing nervously in front of the vendors. He was stealing glances here and there. Wafdiya opened the door for us. It was obvious she was too preoccupied and too much in a hurry to notice my presence. As soon as she hurried inside, Muhammad Effendi Hassan yelled at her, "Are you blind? Why don't you shake hands?"

She stared at me in shock and shouted, "It can't be! Welcome, welcome! Where've you been all this time?"

She shook my hand warmly then led me to her mother, who was sitting cross-legged on the sofa next to the window overlooking the street. She too shook my hand warmly and asked me about my family. Then

Wafdiya shouted joyfully, "Safiya is also here! Come, Safiya. A surprise for you!"

Safiya came from the 'girls' room,' as they called it, followed by two big children. As soon as she saw me, she shouted in genuine joy, "It can't be! Welcome! Welcome! It's been a long time!"

She shook my hand even more warmly and began to fight off a desire to cry. At that point Muhammad Effendi pulled up a chair that he placed next to his mother's sofa and asked me to sit there, then pulled up another chair and placed it in front of me and sat down. Safiya sat on the edge of the sofa, wiping her tears which had started pouring down in a way that surprised me, since I had not expected to stir up such passionate emotions and warm longing. But Muhammad Effendi Hassan interrupted that line of thinking when he pointed to the big children, saying, "Can you imagine? That low life scoundrel left these two beautiful children and went off to get married! Yes! God was generous to him and he fixed the house and built two more floors and began to collect a princely sum in rent and opened his own caféteria at the railroad station. And then, first thing he did? He thought of marrying another wife alongside this poor woman who had endured bitter poverty with him. And the root of it all? A loose woman with colorful eyes that he met in the courthouse who made him lose his mind. She's divorced and has a bit of money on hand and under the matterss in addition to some goats and cattle and crops. Ever since he knew her, he turned on this one and gave her a hard time. But I am going to make an example of him. I am going to make him bite the dust. He's going to curse the day he was born." Safiya kept crying more loudly and blew her nose into a small handkerchief. Wafdiya brought in a tray with two bottles of spathis which she placed on a small table, and left in a hurry to the girls' room, which I was now facing. The door opened a little and I saw something that shocked me and caused me to freeze in an idiotic glance: Sundus the gypsy, in the flesh, was squatting on the floor in front of a wash basin filled with the smoke of burning frankincense rising around it as she was busy going through things in her basket. I thanked God she didn't see me. Wafdiya closed the door behind her. Muhammad Effendi Hassan said, "Lunch, Safiya. Let's eat something, the ustaz and me."

"No, please. I'll take a pass on lunch. I have an important errand."

"Something quick, whatever is available. Come on, Safiya!"

"I must go right away!"

"Okay. Safiya!"

I sat down again and Safiya took the tray and went to the kitchen, then came back a little later with two cups of coffee. At that point the girls' room was opened a little and out came Wafdiya who went toward Safiya and whispered something in her ear. Safiya said, "Okay" then took from her neck a gold necklace that had what looked like yellow olives. She also took four thin bracelets off her wrists and a ring off her finger and an earring from her ears and gave them all to Wafdiya.

"I am coming after you."

"Okay, Safiya. You can go."

She nodded to me and said, "Excuse me."

"Go ahead."

She went to the room and went in with the two children at her heels. I noticed that by now the room was totally dark. Muhammad Effendi Hassan looked at me knowingly with a sarcastic smile: "Women's stuff and nonsense! Retarded people! But some people have to make a living!"

"What's the matter?"

He hesitated for a moment, looking at his mother, whose head had bent over her chest and her eyes closed. She had fallen asleep. He bent toward me, saying, "This gypsy woman has played the two girls for fools. For a whole month now. She's convinced them of a strange recipe to solve both their problems: one wants to snare her fiancé with a spell to make him grow more attached to her and the other wants her husband to come back to her, to love her again and be faithful. Do you see how stupid women can be? But, can I tell them that this is nothing but a con game and useless trickery? They wouldn't listen. Well, it is not my business. And, anyway, who knows? God Almighty reveals His secrets to the weakest."

"But why did Safiya take off her gold?" He waved sarcastically and said in a snorting tone, "The spell is called the *mushahra* or the 'divulgification' of the gold. The magic has to be done in a darkened room. The gypsy woman says that gold holds a grace secret for those who understand its truth. By the way, I heard this kind of talk a long time ago from wise people. The gypsy woman told the two girls to prepare a pitcher of water on which dew has fallen and she adds things of her own to it. Then she puts the gold in the wash basin and casts a certain spell on it in addition to frankincense and benzoin into which she whispers words known to her alone. Then she dries it and returns it to its owner who wears it and her luck mends and the person in question is put in a good mood. Between us, I do not believe in such superstitions, but who knows? Maybe they'll bear some fruit. And, let me tell you, this gypsy woman once read my fortune and she was truthful in all she said about me and my situation and my personality. I tell you this woman turned me around. I had, in jest, asked her to cast a spell that would make a certain woman whom I loved fall in love with me. She asked Wifdiya to bring her one of the personal effects from that woman's clothing. Wafdiya gave her a handkerchief she had been embroidering for her. And what do you think happened, ustaz? One week later that woman agreed to marry me! It is very strange, indeed. One doesn't know how the world works anymore."

He took a deep drag from his cigarette without the muscles of his face moving and his broader smile revealed big protruding teeth that accentuated the look of idiocy etched on his face. I felt a desire to leave quickly before Sundus saw me thus indicating that we knew each other, so I stood up right away asking to leave. Muhammad Effendi Hassan got up and shook hands with me asking me to come visit again since that visit did not count.

I found a large crowd standing around Amm Hanbuta. I stood waiting for him to be done with a contentious customer. Actually, I was waiting for Sundus to come out so I could follow her from a distance. Then I saw Ramadan Eraiga loitering nearby, pretending to be looking for a good fish bargain. Suddenly Amm Hanbuta got into an argument with three effendis whom I soon figured out were one Ministry of Provision inspector and two aides. Amm Hanbuta kept trying to convince them that he was selling his merchandise for less than the official pricing list, showing them samples of his goods and the price sign that a customer had caused to fall under the fish, as he said. He asked some customers standing there about his prices. Then, very boldly and with extraordinary agility, he held the effendi's hand like someone seeking friendship: "I swear by these ten, Effendi, I haven't lied to you!"

He meant the ten fingers each of which God has given a unique print, but at the same time also meant the ten piasters that he secretly slipped into the effendi's hand. The latter took it, half folded and hid it with a notebook that he placed on top of it, and began writing some information then took his companions and left. Amm Hanbuta saw them leave and murmured, "May it feel like fire!"

At that moment Sundus came out of the door of the house carrying the basket on her head, going through the crowd in the street without looking right or left. Ramadan Eraiga bumped into her and, with amazing speed, she reached into her side pocket and took her hand out, with the gold jingling. She thrust her hand into Ramadan Eraiga's fist who thrust his own hand into the pocket of his vest and dashed into the crowd, disappearing from the face of the earth. As for Sundus, she started walking at a deliberately slow pace, calling enthusiastically, "Fortunes told, sand. . . !" Then she would stop and repeat her call many times as if deliberately announcing her presence to those in the house she had just emerged from. Then we heard a harrowing cry followed by Muhammad Effendi Hassan emerging in a hurry, panting and shouting:

"Catch her before she disappears! Quick! Get her! Catch her, the thief! The swindler! The bitch!"

He dashed about in the crowded market until he collided with Sundus. He gripped her by the shoulders then pulled her hard by her collar: "Come here! We need a few words with you!"

He began to pull her and grudgingly she walked with him until they disappeared in the apartment. Right away I figured out what might have happened and I froze in my place, trembling. Yet I wanted to stay and try to find out what really happened. I remained standing with Amm Hanbuta, bewildered and quizzical for more than a quarter of an hour. Finally he made room for me on the bench and cupped his hand around his mouth saying, "Two teas, Abu Gamus."

I recognized Abu Gamus whom I used to know. He hadn't changed. He came with the teapot and glasses on the tray, swaying playfully. Amm Hanbuta pointed at him and at me, saying, "You recognize him? He also grew up, but he's still swinging like the sissies of Benha! People don't change!"

Abu Gamus, unconcerned, did not comment. Rather, looking at my face he shouted in welcome, "Hello, effendi! Where've you been for such a long time?"

He handed me the glass: "The tea's on me, Hanbut!"

Amm Hanbuta waved as he gave him two piasters and said, "A kite never throws chicks!"

To my surprise Abu Gamus took the money and dropped it into the pocket of the faded apron without objection and turned and walked away.

I was about to finish the tea when Sundus came out adjusting her appearance. Her face was swollen and she looked badly beaten. She had some lying tears in her eyes. She went on her way avoiding looking at anything. When I took the bag of fish and got ready to leave, Muhammad Effendi Hassan emerged, aggrieved, striking his palms against each other in disbelief, on the verge of tears: "What a catastrophe that came seeking us which we did not seek! I don't need any more calamities, God! We searched the woman everywhere, even in her private parts and we didn't find a thing! How can that be, people? Could the goldsmith have cheated us to begin with? How can Safiya, resourceful and smart, be cheated? The truth be told, she's been apprehensive from the beginning. I told her, Safiya, this is women's non-sense! She was afraid but she went along! As soon as the gypsy woman left she took off her gold and weighed it in her palm after she grew suspicious. She said the gold was somewhat heavier and coarser to the touch. I held it in my palm and weighed it. It was heavy. I looked closely at the stamp. It wasn't in the place where it had been before. It's our gold and we know it piece by piece. I knew right away that it was just gold-plated! But it was exactly the same arrangement: same strand, same bracelet, same earring but the gold is not the same gold. Could this gypsy woman have magically changed it? For a month she has been coming once or twice a week, inspecting it, counting the pieces, measuring and whispering. We should have handed her over to the city police but I took pity on her when we were searching her. She took off everything. Piece by piece and shook herself and withstood punches and kicks. Think with me. We caught up only three minutes after she left. It doesn't make sense that she got rid of the gold in lightning speed. Where? How? She hardly moved away from the house. I am going crazy! All my life I've been afraid of scandal and look at me now, scandal comes to my own doorstep! Tell me what to do. What do I tell that son of a bitch, Fusduq? Could it be that he was the one who cheated us? When? How about Wafdiya's gold? I wish I hadn't let the gypsy woman go. But, what can the wind take from the bare tiles? We deserve what happened to us. This ruin is just punishment for being retarded sons of bitches who believe in superstitions. Oh, my God! I am willing to pay the rest of my life to know how what happened happened. But, if she were the one who did it, would she have stayed without running away? She herself asked us to take her to the city police. I am going to go crazy. I am going to be paralyzed. True, only the truly sighted get taken!"

The sound of wailing and face slapping inside the apartment was overlapping with Muhammad Effendi Hasan's voice. A short while later, Wafdiya came out wrapped in her black milaya and behind her came Safiya also similarly wrapped. Muhammad Effendi saw them off in exasperation: "It's no use! Don't strain yourselves! It's fake gold! The plate has come off parts of it. Any goldsmith will laugh at you! Where're you going, you miserable bitches! Oh, my black fate!"

He strated trying to rip his clothes off but Amm Hanbuta clamped his hands, shouting in the warm eloquent tone of people from Brullus and the special way in which they pronounce the *qaf* sound: “Don’t lose faith in God, my friend! Is it going to be both death and ruin? Say whatever you want and vent but don’t rip your clothes, for that’s like denying God’s bounty!”

Muhammad Effendi Hassan kept screaming in vexation then he hurriedly followed his sisters. Sundus’ voice had moved away while I remained, frozen, not knowing what to do. The earth was spinning and I was at the heart of a serious dilemma. If I spoke and revealed what I knew, I wouldn’t be safe from accusation. It was even most certain that I would seem like a partner whose conscience had suddenly awakened and he confessed and gave away his partner. All circumstances would confirm this suspicion for everyone: what brought me here today, out of all days, after a long absence in which I had developed a generally bad reputation? What was the connection between me and Sundus? What I would say would turn the world upside down, on my head. I would have to lead the police to the wikala, and the police would arrest some of the inhabitants. I wouldn’t be able to live in the wikala after that. I was now convinced that Sundus had deceived these poor naïve people and kept visiting them until she memorized what their gold looked like and bought fake copies of it with the help of Ramadan Eraiga whom I had seen with my own eyes take the real gold from her. But can I say that or admit it? Would anyone have mercy on me? Would the police respect me or even take pity on me? I didn’t think so at all. A man couldn’t be honest inside a milieu of corruption and wrongdoing. Honor could not be an individual affair in any case, even if someone like me, who wanted to become a writer who spoke of morality and ideals. Even if one were to choose to be honorable and to live by a code of honor, it seemed to me to be impossible to achieve by mere choice or sheer practice, otherwise I would be a silent partner in the crime at hand.

Thus I held the bag of fish and staggered in the streets dragging my feet in defeat and pain and dejection, having lost my enthusiasm for everything. I wished the earth would open up and swallow me, saving me from these agonizing thoughts. But the earth opened up and revealed Muhammad Effendi Hassan grabbing Sundus by the hand and going to the city police station. Bringing up the rear were Safiya and Wafdiya and some passersby and children in school uniforms. I followed them until they entered the station and got into the sergeant's room on the public street overlooking Sa'a Square, with two long open windows behind iron bars through which the sergeant himself appeared sitting upfront at an ancient desk with the gunrack filled with rifles. To the back street were two other windows, but they were closed. I stood under one of them eavesdropping while holding the fish bag and the harisa packet. This fish was supposed to be cooked by Sundus herself this evening and we were supposed to eat it and have harisa for dessert, in her room in the wikala. So what calamity happened? I felt I should throw the fish away for it seemed to be at the root of the disaster. As for the harisa, I could nibble on it by myself. I remembered Widad. I'd give her the fish. I moved to the opposite sidewalk and walked next to the wall of the park, passing the municipal public library and the fire station. In front of me was the Damanhour Court of Summary Justice where my friend Muslim al-Maghazi the writer worked. This building had always drawn me to pass by it and go to the back, on the right, to the Messiri Café, but I turned on the main street, to my right al-Mu'ati schools and after that, Frum's elegant photography studio, on the corner of a side alley that led to Cinema al-Ahli and the bicycle rental shop whose customer I had been for a long time. I passed once again by the harisa vendor and moved automatically to his sidewalk. Then I passed it to al-Banna Bookstore, then Susi Street and the Mudiriya. Then I hastened my steps and walked in the direction of the tail of the city extending in the open space abutting the distant fields.

Exhaustion

I saw Widad's head over the edge of the balcony. I snapped my fingers and she looked down. I signaled that I was coming up there and she withdrew her head.

Handing her the fish bag and the harisa packet I said, "It seems Sundus has forgotten our appointment tonight. Her room is closed; she must have gone out to work and God knows when she's coming back."

She seemed to know Sundus' plans for the day in detail as she said quite confidently, "She's coming back. She's on a nearby errand downtown. She hasn't gone out to work, because to do so involves a long trip and different towns. She knows about the appointment and is getting ready for it. She has a little errand downtown of which some good will come. She's a poor woman, but from time to time, not often enough, God sends some good her way."

I pushed her inside: "It seems you know her errand!"

"Yes. She doesn't hide anything from me. I am her only friend here. I keep her secrets and she keeps mine. Don't worry about it. When the time comes you will find the light on in her room. We'll see it from here."

"Are you sure she'll be back in time?"

"Unless she's run over by a car, God forbid!"

"Or if she encountered a problem, for instance?"

"She doesn't encounter problems. She can get out of the tightest spot like a hair out of dough. She's quite a nawar, you'd be proud of her. Throw her into the sea and leave her there. Put her head down there and you'll find her floating two meters away. She's quite a fighter. If you want to give her a hard time, she'd give you a catastrophic time. But she's good and kind and her heart is as white as the whitest cotton fabric. She's not treacherous, but she knows how to avenge herself. She'd beat you with the same weapon that you brandish against her. So, don't worry. Sundus will be here on time and we'll spend the evening at her place. Are these things for her?"

"For all of us. Why don't you go ahead and cook the fish before it goes bad. And this is a packet of harisa. Why don't you bring it all with the fish for the evening? I'll go lie down for an hour or two. We'll meet in Sundus's room."

"Why go? Go on the balcony and stretch out to your heart's content. Sleeping while you smell the cooking is good and it fills your head. Go and eat rice pudding with the angels until I awaken you to go."

"That's a good idea."

I went to the balcony and took off my shoes, then removed the seat cushion and folded it beneath my head. It didn't take me long to fall into a deep sleep. When I opened my eyes as Widad shook me, I had forgotten everything in life, as though I had just been born. I was still in a stupor as I slipped my feet into the shoes again and staggered to the bathroom to wash my face.

As we sat around the low table digging into the fish, fried and in tomato sauce, Sundus said, "Today I had a terrible experience that I could never have imagined having, Widad! One goes about one's business not knowing where catastrophe might come from. Just like that! I was walking, minding my own business when, out of the blue, a man with a fat, ugly face grabbed me by the shoulders and started raining blows on me and kicking me! Behind him were two vulgar low life alley-dwelling women shrieking and heaping abuse on me for no reason. 'What's the matter, good folks?' I asked. They said, 'Give back the gold you stole from us! Come to the police station with us so the police will interrogate you!' But, God be praised. Your sister, Widad, has a blameless heart. God sent me a schoolchild that stood watching them as they were beating me. When they dragged me to the police station, I brought along that boy and gave him a piaster. The sergeant opened the police report and that lying man, the son of a bitch, claimed that I had entered their house and performed some magic or deception and stolen their gold and given them false gold instead. What do you think happened next, Widad? The sergeant looked him over and did not believe him. He asked him, 'When did that happen?' And the man said, 'Just now. We searched her; she must have swallowed it!' The sergeant said, 'She swallowed a necklace, four bracelets, a pair of earrings, and a ring? She must be a bottomless sea! If she had done that, she'd have died right away. Find another story to tell!' Then he said to me, 'What do you say to that, woman?' I said, 'Please, sir, may God grant you long life. I am a poor woman, trying to eke out a living. I was walking in the street, when these people started beating up on me. You can see the marks on my face and my whole body. And it is only now that I know why they were beating me, sir. I have never seen them before or talked to them.' The two women started to slap their own faces and the man threw his hands up in the air and pushed me, saying, 'You lying, impudent woman! Now I am certain that you are a thief, by God.' I pushed the schoolboy in his school uniform and his books and said, 'Esteemed sir, this is an innocent boy who doesn't know me and whom I don't know; ask him what he saw with his very eyes.' He asked him and the boy said: 'Sir, this lady was walking and saying that she would tell fortunes and this man ran after her and held her and started beating her with his fists and kicking her and they dragged her down the street to this place.' The sergeant said, 'Anyway, let's search her,' and they searched me and finally the sergeant said, 'Excuse me, folks. I can't hold her here. The lockup is already full of suspects and the officers yell at us when we hold someone without good reason. And anyway, if a new reason should become known to you, come to me and I'll get her from wherever she is, even if she is beneath the earth, for we know all the places that shelter her kind. All I can do now is file a report in which we detail the description of your gold and look out for whoever goes to sell it to goldsmiths. And you, woman, if it turns out that you've done what they say, I'll stick this club up your mother's private parts. Get the hell out of my face, whore! We get nothing from the likes of you except trouble everyday in the countryside, but if I live, I'll get rid of you one by one.' When we got out of the station the man came and wanted to beat me up, so I threw what I had to the ground and started beating them and screaming until I messed them up and tore their clothes. Then I played dead and they left me and went away."

Widad looked at me as if to say "See? Told you!" and got up, licking her fingers. Then she took a plate covered with a clean piece of gauze that we had filled for Shawadfi so he wouldn't give us a hard time and went to him. I stayed with Sundus, looking at her furtively, trying to figure her out. After a short while Widad came back and the party began. Widad washed the goza, cleaned the hose and the pipe, lit the fire then added the tobacco and signed it with hashish. She said we should have ourselves a good time smoking and not to worry because Shawadfi was sitting by the gate like a lion and wouldn't let the government come in before shouting and cursing and making enough noise to give everyone a chance to get rid of whatever the government was after. That way the government had never been able to find anything at the wikala.

We started to unwind and as time went on, Widad kept telling me to relax and feel at home. She told me to change into my gallabiya and took my clothes to my room to bring the gallabiya and I stayed in my underwear until she came back, which gave Sundus a chance to see me almost naked. At another point she told me to stretch out to rest my back and I remembered that I was between two whores each with her own taste. We ate the harisa and caught on fire: we began to laugh hysterically and nonstop and with real feeling, touching and shaking hands. The radio was on somewhere nearby, perhaps at one of the houses adjacent to the back of the wikala, as if it were with us in the same room. Sabah the singer was singing her famous song *Zannuba* to music of the nay and darabukka, whereupon Sundus stood up and enthusiastically took off her gallabiya and stayed in her slip, revealing her taut body with its sensuous contours. She pulled out a shawl and tied it just above the thighs, pressing up her mound, which looked like a pot's closed cover that kept dancing, going up and down, not to mention her breasts and the area under them or her hips, which looked like risen dough as she kept circling around in ecstasy. She held her palms pressed together and snapped her thumbs rhythmically in time with the music with astonishing grace. It seemed Widad got jealous as she too got up and started dancing away. I began to clap my hands to the beat and the moment I got up to take part in the dance, the song ended and the announcer began reading the summary of the news, then the radio fell silent all together. Sundus collapsed in a theatrical manner and I received her in my arms, also theatrically. Then I turned her around and embraced her and kissed her. She acquiesced softly and Widad said with a wink, "I'll make myself scarce! I'll quietly go to my grandmother's room next door. I'd like to hear you dancing!"

She slipped through the door and we heard the rustle of her dress as she sneaked into her grandmother's room and gently closed the door. Sundus reached out and locked her door from inside and we fell to the ground in one other's arms. I began to embrace and kiss her and feel everywhere and she did the same fervently. But she was like someone blowing on an extinguished fire. We took off all our clothes and rolled on top of each other, but nothing happened to me except panting and sweating. The feminine scent came to me, burning my nose, mixed with the smell of sticky sweat, onions and garlic and fish. I'd get taut for a few minutes then the rope would get broken. The call to the dawn prayer was coming at us from all directions as we stretched out next to each other, two naked bodies, one trying to put out the fire and the other desperately trying to stay alive, but in vain. We had reached an unspoken agreement to rest for a while until our nerves could calm down and fatigue depart us, but everything soon disappeared down a dark well. When I came back into being after a long disappearance in the confused unknown, Widad was tapping on the door to awaken us. The late morning was painting the courtyard of the wikala a cream color. Sundus opened the door for her and as I was stretching and sitting up I caught a fleeting glimpse of Sundus moving her finger in an obscene gesture toward me, expressing disappointment, contempt, and shock. It was then that I noticed that I was completely naked. I was greatly embarrassed and hurriedly put on my clothes.

The Incomparable Wadida

"Sit down for a little bit with us, young man. Or does your new love make you forget your old friends? Everything that happens here does so with my blessing, anyway. So, don't think you're something special.

"Sit down for I might need you. Yes, it is true, it is God who helps but let's remember: God makes people help people. I am going to give you such tea the likes of which you have never had. And you'll get a piece of opium in the bargain. Ha! Ha! If you had taken it the night of that party, it would've spared you some embarrassment! Here, don't eat it all now. It's too big!

"Okay Zainhum, get the things. We need a couple of smokes. I received today a piece of choice hashish, brand name 'al-Mushir' after the field marshal with the picture of a rose on the bag. It came in the diplomatic pouch. This, my friend, is known only to big dealers and only for their own consumption. It's not for sale! I am willing to bet anything that you don't know what a diplomatic pouch is.

"Hey? What do you think? I can tell from your faces. Enjoy! Enjoy! But don't get too used to it, it's not available in the market.

"The story, young man—and this is also for you, Sheikh Zainhum—is that big things will happen here at the wikala tonight, and I don't want to be alone when they do.

"I think you remember Wadida, Zainhum, and who doesn't? That virago that only death could stop. She was a gypsy who told fortunes like your poor friend Sundus. But she was also a halabi woman of rare beauty, that bitch, may God have mercy on her soul. One glance from her felled a man on his neck, speechless, to the ground. But fortune telling was not her only profession as you know, Zainhum. People drew attention to her captivating beauty. This country of ours, the truth be told, deserves burning. Yes, it deserves more than what it's getting, because it keeps flattering people—their heads get too big. That's the problem. That's become a deeply ingrained trait in us that we have from birth. Wadida, for instance, did not know that her beauty was captivating until there were too many humbled supplicants at her feet. Every man she met proposed marriage to her, in whatever form, just like Widad's mother, God have mercy on her soul, but she was more beautiful and cleverer. She had a colossal brain that deserved to rule a whole country. Only yours truly knew how to keep her under control, because I knew the secret of her strength so I deactivated it as far as I was concerned. Her secret was her beauty, of course. And, by the way, I am nothing if not an expert swimmer in the seas of big black eyes in a large white face with red cheeks, but I also knew my limits very well, young man. I would never be content with being a stupid child, distracted by a piece of candy or a lick of her cheek, to let her do what she wanted and rule the wikala in my place. I cast the anchor of my eyes away from the shores of her eyes and stayed at a safe distance, content with getting my share of her big profits!"

"When the woman realized how beautiful she was in the eyes of men, she realized that, if she got married, she would be selling herself cheap to one man who might not live up to his expectations in the future, even if it were Gamal Abdel Nasser himself or King Farouk. So, she took off her gypsy garb and put on that of homemakers from good families. I and others did not recognize her as she appeared in the morning, ready for work dressed to kill, wearing a filigree dress, wrapping herself in a red velvet shawl, with a fancy pair of shoes and silk stockings the color of her legs.

She would start off, and waiting for her at the coffee house would be a very well dressed, respectable effendi, one of several bastards that only other bastards could figure out. As the saying goes, it takes one to know one, and birds of a feather, etcetera. Am I right or not, Zainhum Atris?

"The bastard effendi might be Suleiman today and Ibrahim tomorrow, and then Ra'fat or Heshmat or maybe Girgis or Butros! Today he may be dressed like an effendi and tomorrow like the sheikh of a Sufi order or a pious hagg! They may all be the same person but 'at work' they have multiple personalities: each of them can be all the different personalities at the same time or at different times as needed by the job. You can ask Sheikh Zainhum. He is quite an expert. He's their leader. Well, I mean that was a long time ago. This Sheikh Zainhum went on many errands with Wadida, in the naughty old days, of course. And, by the way, we've all been naughty at one point or another.

"Wadida was the master holding all the strings. It was she who chose who'd go out with her on the job. She was quite an expert at picking the men she felt she needed at the right moment; those she could wear on her hand, her feet, her head, or her chest, or anywhere she wanted. She chose the person even at the gloomiest moment. Even at the moment when a person had to arrest her and hand her over to the police, things got turned around somehow: the adversary got so enamored of his enemy, seeking nothing but pleasing that enemy. So, can you imagine what it would be like when the idol himself threw the bait at him and like a clever fisherman caught him in the net? The catch always entered the net with a glad, intoxicated heart and without any resistance. And it was always a precious catch. And just as we hold the mousetrap to shake it with the mouse inside until the mouse bleeds and disintegrates, Wadida did exactly that with her catches. Many a man from a good family, hoping to pluck the roses of her cheeks, or squeeze her or drown in her eyes, ended up one of her lowly servants, even though at home and work they were revered masters. The poor man would remain her willing captive, his personality totally lost to his house, job, and to everything else away from Wadida. Like a cocaine addict he can regain consciousness only with cocaine. Undersecretaries, directors, and generals found themselves running her errands cheerfully and as much as they could. Many such a man was voluntarily reduced to becoming just a doorman, or a lookout watching out for her or a mere companion, a safe friend, an obedient servant, a scarecrow keeping away birds of prey until a stronger man could do his duty inside in a way that pleased Wadida. It is for that reason that Wadida cannot live in a royal palace but loves the wikala, for in it she is a queen, but in a palace what would she be? In the wikala she has a large entourage of men who have all truly fallen in love with her; they all became her dervishes and fervent followers even though they have returned from their errand with her walking on thorns, be it back to their offices, their jobs, or their village boss positions, or their enterprising nighttime adventures. And despite the humiliation, the agony, and the deprivation, they never give up hope about her, even though some of them are married to chaste houris, but it is greed and wandering eyes, young man. Or you can say it's a matter of decreed fate and a gift that God bestows on whomever he chooses.

"The she-devil let them all leave her in despair. No one remained under her control except those who had nothing else left to go back to. Those that stayed she used to help her catch others who in turn would open up new paths for her. She never let them just go as if they had never been there. No, sir, she kept the strings and the ropes of the nets in her hand and pulled them whenever she wanted a new catch or to get out of a tight spot or help in hard times, or get her out of the hands of the police. Each of them had something that he cherished secretly: a hot kiss, a close embrace, a night of pleasure, the stab of an eyelash. So, you can imagine how they'd react if she sent them a special messenger asking them to do something for her.

"You ask me, Zainhum, why I am remembering her now and why I am trying to bring corpses back to life. I had no hand in that: she is back because time has brought her back to resolve a serious problem she made fifteen years ago. Now she has to testify about many complex things.

"Wadida's forays were endless. One led to another and one errand brought about many errands and a deal engendered several deals. You see, young man, she was a lowlife queen that cared nothing for custom, honor, appearance, inner reality, or anything else. What kind of person could someone like that be? She had a favorite hobby that enabled her to expand and prosper; but no matter how much she cleaned up her act, she always went back to her low life nature in the end. As they say: when a whore repents, she becomes a pimp.

"That woman used to go with a respectable looking effendi to Alexandria to stay for some days during which she sifted it, which meant that she stole something from everyone. She chose non-stop buses especially the most crowded ones. She would ride, followed by the effendi and they would squeeze their way to the middle where her perfume and her body would create quite a stir, with everyone trying to get close to her. But she would slip through them easily and, from experience select a passenger that she thought was a good mark, and stand right in front of him. He would immediately cling to her, happy and oblivious, whereupon the effendi would cling to him from behind. While the man was latching on to her, the effendi would clean him out, relieving him of his wallet and valuables in no time and without anybody noticing. When she sensed that the man latching on to her rear end was done, she knew that her friend had done his job. So she pretended to be upset and turned around fixing the man with looks or reprehension and disgust. Thereupon another man who had been following the scene would invite her to stand in his place giving her room at first then beginning to latch on to her, relying on the fact that she would be grateful and return the favor and let him do his thing. And she would until he was done. A short distance before the end of the line, she and the effendi would get off the bus and clear the street right away. They would have to disappear in the small winding alleys or in a cab or a tram or anywhere else so they would never be caught by whoever was pursuing them. As for those who messed themselves up on the bus, they wouldn't dare give themselves away if they discovered they'd been had.

"That's about the buses alone. Now let's go to the beach which they call the plage. One day she goes to Mandara, the following to Sidi Bishr, or Muntaza or Abu Qir. All she had to do was take off her clothes and walk on the beach in her swimming suit. A thousand bachelors would follow her most certainly. Have you seen a group of dogs circling around one bitch? They would fight over her while she just sat there at a distance waiting for the end of the battle and in the end perhaps leaving them and going away not giving herself to any of them. That was Wadida on the beach. One man must win in the battle of seduction, one that she, from his looks, the way he talked, the way he spent money, would be sure was loaded. That would be the one she picked. They would agree to meet somewhere at night after she got rid of her husband, as she claimed. She would go with him to his apartment after they'd been on a spending spree downtown where she'd buy whatever delicacies she craved while the sucker paid generously and with pleasure. In his apartment she would slip sleeping pills into his tea or liquor or some pastry whereupon he'd fall asleep and eat rice pudding with the angels while she was totally awake. She then would pick the house clean of money, clothes, and all valuables, which she would put in bags and bundles. Downstairs in the street more than one effendi armed with switchblade knives would be waiting.

"Then she would go to small neighboring towns such as Kafr al-Dawwar, Rashid, Mahalla, Kafr al-Zayyat, Zifta, and Mit Ghamr and head directly for second-hand clothing stores, as a retail vendor so that no one would short-change her and so that she wouldn't arouse the suspicions of police informers. Then off to the gold market where she would sell jewelry she couldn't use. She sold those pieces that were not her style, such as antique rings and brooches and things that no one would believe she had bought for her own personal adornment. You might think that she overdid the stealing bit, but there was a reason for that. She took even the clothes that the victim had on when he was drugged so that when he woke up he found himself stark naked with nothing to cover himself as he went down on the street. That meant that by the time he was able to notify the police, she would have left town and gone back to her old character as a halabi gypsy with no resemblance to the elegant lady that the sucker would report, if he did at all. Most of them would just keep the matter to themselves.

"From the small towns she went back to the wikala where she would hide her loot for the day her rose would wither and she would have something to live on for the rest of her life. Then she'd spend a day or two or more in Damanhour buying a great quantity of gold plated, Camel-brand bracelets, rings, earrings, and necklaces for almost nothing. She would put quite a dazzling array on her wrists, ears, fingers, and neck. And, don't forget, young man, that clothes and jewelry of all kinds don't fit all people. For you or I may wear a ring or a pair of pants and it may appear plain and ordinary but, if somebody else were to wear it, it would look very elegant. People are of two kinds: showcases or the dark insides of a big water jar. If you put all the goldsmith's jewelry into a water jar it will be buried but if you put it in a showcase, well, you can imagine the difference. Wadida was a showcase in which brass bracelets on her wrists looked like the most expensive pure gold. The same was true of all she wore: whoever saw it wanted to own it.

"She would go to a village in respectable and modest attire with a piece of paper on which was written the name and address of someone who did not exist. It would be better still if the family name were similar to that of a famous family in the village. She'd start asking about the unknown man. The good people would take her to the family with a similar name. They, of course, would be very welcoming, especially with guests and strangers since strangers are supposed to be treated generously, for the sake of the Prophet. 'Come in, come on in, please, lady, have some tea first.' Tea could lead to lunch and lunch could lead to spending the night. From the moment she arrived, she would get them all intrigued with an exciting story that dispelled the boredom of their dull, uneventful days. She told them that she was the wife of ustaz so and so, the one she'd come asking about, who married her a year or two ago and who'd left her with child.

One day long ago, however, he left her to come to this village but did not come back. When a long time had passed and life in Cairo became tight for her, she came to ask his family about him. 'Oh, poor dear! There's no might or strength save in God! May God avenge her! Are people's daughters playthings? See how the bastard deceived this poor woman! Did you ask at the police station? How about the hospitals? Did you open the mandal? Did you visit one of the sheikhs? Did you recite the sura of Yasin the requisite number of times?' She would respond to all of that with wailing, playing very skillfully the role of a miserable victim, coping with all problems of this world and the next one to boot, supported by her elegant, respectable appearance, above all suspicion. Some of these people were good people indeed and generous and they took good care of her. After spending the night she would leave in the morning loaded with goodies that the people had donated to her and her children: food and clothes and money. Some of them, out of the goodness of their hearts, would go with her to a neighboring village where other similar names might be found. They would tell the story on her behalf, in a better way, in a language that the peasants understand among themselves. The listeners would be moved mightily and become very enthusiastic. Some would volunteer advice with great enthusiasm but all would contribute generously with more donations. We would sometimes be surprised to see her coming back to the wikala with many loads of goods being taken off taxis, horse-drawn carriages, or carts. I've often had my share of these goodies and eaten and drank and worn so many unbelievable gifts. One good thing about Wadida was that she was not a scorpion who stung for the sake of stinging anyone who came her way. If the truth be told, whenever she made good in a village, she came back satisfied without hurting anyone. But if she was badly or coldly received, she was not above catching some lowly but greedy persons and conning them: Now, she would tell them, she was in a bad predicament. She didn't have money for transportation and there was no food at home for her children. She didn't like to beg since she didn't need to with all that gold she had. If only she could find someone to pawn the gold with for a small sum of money, she wouldn't mind. At that point some of the listeners would become greedy and start trying to buy that shining gold for next to nothing. So, they would haggle with her. Thereupon she would take out of her handbag the invoice for the gold from the goldsmith from whom she had bought it when she was a bride. The person doing the haggling would be as naïve as a small fish moving freely inside the jaws of a crocodile. She would be the first person to ask to move on to the store of any goldsmith anywhere to have the gold assessed at today's value and then she would discount that price by as much as they wanted. She would insist on that for some time until greed took over and the person would ask her to close the deal in secret for fear of the evil eye. From that point the good peasant or the naïve peasant woman would try hard to reduce the price that Wadida wanted by one fourth. Sometimes there would be some barter involved, while paying the difference. For instance, the peasant woman would agree to take the big necklace and the heavy earring and the ring and would give her the old Qur'an with the chain and the light earring and such an amount of money or several measures of rice or wheat or two sacks of cotton. And Wadida's men would always be waiting to volunteer to help her for the love of God.

"She was a she-devil, both a tatari and a halabi! For her father was a tatari and her mother a halabi. Only God Almighty could handle her. May God protect you from her, young man, even after her death. She had reached the age of sixty but was quite healthy and vigorous and her wild beauty had not diminished in any way. Her daughter Nur al-Sabah was a bride of twenty-two that she bore to her old first husband Turk Khan whom she divorced one year after the birth of Nur al-Sabah. Nur al-Sabah never saw her father because he left for God's wide world and we haven't heard a thing about him since. Yes, sir, young man! Tell him, Zainhum! Tell him about Turk Khan who was as big and strong as a royal farm's mule, with a mustache as big as a scarecrow. His only occupation was at the gambling tables during mulids, where he tossed dice in a cup and customers bet on a certain number and if the number didn't add up or didn't match they lost. On non-mulid days he played the three-shell game, except he did it with cards. He was a dull-witted dolt who drank a mug of grain alcohol first thing in the morning and if he got into a fight he would grab a strong man by the waist and snap him like one would a cucumber. He was afraid of no one and respected no one except Wadida. She was the only one he gave thought to a thousand times before crossing. One time, he wanted to be the man, as any husband would with his wife, and yell at her and tell her to do something or another. So he drank two mugs of alcohol to get up the courage to yell at her, after which Wadida's slipper kept coming down on his head and he had to run and she chased him with the bathroom plunger as if he were a mangy dog. Dogs come back after being kicked out but Turk Khan never returned since that day.

"When she grew older and the daughter grew up somewhat, she lost some steam and her stories came to be as well-known among the villagers as those of 'Our mom, the ghoul.' She started to fear going to the villages for work. And, as you put it, Zainhum, the tough strong men around her dispersed, either by death or old age or by giving up for good. Do you remember those days, Zainhum? Do you remember the day the police arrested her after one of her gigs and she couldn't find someone to intervene on her behalf to get her off? The she-devil paid five years of her life in the women's prison, leaving her daughter Nur al-Sabah in the care of her friend, Widad's mother, who had named her own daughter after her friend. As usual with women she came out of jail repentant, wearing a white shawl. As for her hidden savings, whatever was left after the lawyer's fees and court clerk expenses and gifts to the jailers and special food in jail and milk for her daughter, it was all gone in a few months.

"She went back to her old profession. She carried a basket and went around telling fortunes in the same villages that she had conned earlier. She would come back and tell us how she found that people in these villages were still talking about her old stories with them and how some of the women had asked her in secret if she knew a woman who looked like that.

"On one of her outings she snagged a boy, much to his mother's chagrin. He was an only child. His father spoiled him, almost worshiped him, 'Come Badr, go Badr!' and Badr had free rein of the house as if he were in charge, even during his father's lifetime, who actually preferred him to himself. His father got him engaged to the daughter of a large landowner and paid a big dowry and a shabka for him and the wedding and the consummation were only a few days away. But it is fate, young man. The world, as Yusif Wahbi said, is a big, strange play. Badr, son of Said, two very appropriate names: Badr was the full moon, like a large, engraved copper plate that the rich hang on the walls of their homes. As for the body, it was as stout as the trunk of a sycamore tree and as supple and strong as the branch of an acacia tree. The colored wool skullcap daintily rested on the back of the head and the cashmere gallabiya was a perfect fit. The maroon shoes on his feet and the crooked ebony stick in his hand made him look like a candidate for a headman's job.

"That day he was taking his cattle for an afternoon walk along the bank of an irrigation canal in his village. Fate placed Wadida in his path as she was leaving the village. She fixed him with one glance and the boy fell for her right away. He asked her to stop and tell his fortune. She immediately made up one to his liking and she cast a spell on him that snared him. Whenever she tried to get up to leave, he asked her to stay and charge him whatever she wanted and she couldn't shake him off except after she gave him her address in the wikala. Poor Badr al-Said! He actually came. At the end of the same week he came to the wikala bearing a precious gift of rice, flour, honey, ghee, eggs, cheese, milk, fresh-baked bread, and fitir. He stayed with her for two days during which he was welcomed warmly. At bed time, Wadida spread all the bedding in front of the door of her room so that he would be certain of her honor. But Badr al-Said didn't want to be certain of anything, as he himself said. Whatever she was, whatever she had done, he was a captive and there was no escape.

"The boy set her older imagination on fire, awakened her slumbering emotions, and reminded her of her old kingdom and her previous captives. She also fell in love with him. He started visiting her once or twice a week. Then we were surprised to see a ma'zun coming into the wikala to marry them. Wadida became the legally wedded wife of Badr al-Said! What bothered me was that she brought a ma'zun from outside the wikala even though she knew I could have done it myself. Anyway, young man, Badr al-Said moved into her room and left his well-bred fiancée, his family, his land, and his future and chose to live with Wadida. Her secret was not just her eyes alone, young man, nor her body which was the devil incarnate in a woman's body designed to seduce the most pious men and the most steadfast in faith, in full confidence that, as they raised their foreheads from the prayer rug, if they happened to catch a glimpse of her eye, they would prostrate themselves again for no one else but her. The secret was the whole person and no one knew exactly what it was. Badr al-Said's own fiancée came here to see for herself the one who had snatched him from her and she found that he was justified, even though, would you believe it, young man? Tell him, Zainhum, she was as beautiful as a houri, perhaps even more beautiful, by God. But, do you remember, Zainhum? The poor girl was so proud of her own beauty when she came in and sat with her family next to me on this mastaba, but when she saw Wadida, she became crestfallen right away and her eyes teared and she got up and told Badr al-Said, 'You are right, Badr. For all of your life you've been in love with beauty. I am not mad at you; here's your ring and your shabka. God will protect me and cause me to meet someone who loves the beauty of the person before the beauty of the body, Badr. Thank you Badr for waking me up, for, like you, I used to love a person for his beauty. I believe that you will cherish me.' The girl took her family and left. When she reached the opening of the gate she turned around as the wind blew and caused her clothes to fly back and flutter, making her appear like an arch of a sky-blue cloud, tall and thin with a ruddy face under the sequined kerchief. She cupped her hand above her mouth and let loose a long, shrill resounding ululation of joy that captivated all our hearts. I swear that I can still hear her ululation ringing in my ears, coming from the open space of the gate from a long time ago and not changing in the interim. I can hear her voice now, saying in all sincerity, 'Congratulations, bridegroom!'

"The young woman who amazed me and everyone else left. But after a few months, his father and mother came accompanied by a group of men. His father looked awful and would have moved even infidels to pity, but Badr al-Said was not moved. Illness had taken its toll on the father and he looked humbled and broken as he begged his son to have mercy on him and to go back and look after his possessions and lands and livestock, but the boy would not budge! Had he been my own son, I would have killed him right away, even if he were my only son. Can you imagine, young man, that Wadida herself was moved by the appearance of the old man and began to beg Badr to go with his father, that she agreed to let him visit her one or two nights a week. Badr hit her on the mouth with his elbow and she shut up. I knew from the start that Badr al-Said would not go back to his family, for he had tasted her wine, he had drunk the nectar of her spicy lips and the drug had run into his veins and the only medicine for this drug was more of the same drug. Wadida's beauty was not the kind that you could just possess but one that you had to guard with wide open eyes at every moment. That's what Badr al-Said did, young man. After a few months he got word of his father's death and he went to bury him and came back after a few days. A few months after that he got word of his mother's death so he went and buried her then returned a few days later. Every few months he would go back to the village, sell some property and come back to spend the money on eating pigeons, shrimp, crabs, and fish roe and smoking hashish and drinking liquor which he learned from Wadida and which he acquired from Yanni Kiryakos on Bandar Street. And yet his health was actually getting better and better and that rubbed off on the woman's health and renewed her youth. But he broke her will by his sheer vigor and she came to love him and fear him. For the first time in her life she came to know fear of a man. And now she became modest in her dress, the way she talked, the way she went out and the way she sat.

Badr divided the room with a wooden partition behind which the woman and her daughter slept while he and his friends stayed up on the other side, drinking and gambling until dawn whereupon he sent them home and sent for the woman to spend the rest of the night in her bosom.

"Gambling was his only game and his only occupation. He lost hundreds but won thousands, which he spent on Wadida and her daughter. He made Wadida his mission in life, he truly liberated her and gave her quite an education. He only beat her with a Sudanese leather whip soaked in oil, each beating worse than the previous one. He trained her eyes not to stray here or there. Four or five years later, we were surprised to see the ma'zun coming into the wikala again, going to Wadida's room. We were dumbfounded. We couldn't believe that Badr al-Said dared divorce Wadida. At that point I started getting suspicious. You remember, Zainhum, those days? I began to think of intervening. I thought I finally had a chance to tell him, 'What's keeping you here, now, Badr al-Said? I think you should now go back to you family!' But he didn't give me the opportunity. As soon as I convinced myself to talk to him about the matter with the pretext of disapproving of the presence of a bachelor with a woman and her marriage-age daughter, I was surprised to see the ma'zun entering the wikala a third time to marry Badr al-Said to Nur al-Sabah, daughter of Wadida and Turk Khan. The moment I thought of advising the crazy woman, Badr al-Said was inviting me to the wedding. Not only that but he made the girl choose me as her proxy to place my hand in his at the time of the writing of the contract. As the girl's proxy I demanded my legal right to be alone with her to find out her opinion. Can you imagine, young man? It was the girl who was madly in love with him and it was she who forced her mother to ask for a divorce from Badr al-Said so that she would marry him rather than do the sinful thing with him. I also spoke alone with the woman and found some wisdom in what she said: 'Badr al-Said would not let anyone else marry the girl, that way she would stay unmarried and bring dishonor on herself. So, why disappoint her when I have had my fill of this world? Let her marry him and live her youth with him so long as she loves him and he loves her more than he loves me. And because I love him and love my daughter, I leave her to the one who loves her more than I love her! See the words of the old witch, young man?

"She loves, that is true, and her love is as wild as she is! But whipping can have consequences and doling out breaths to a chest used to breathing freely can have a painful effect. Similarly, lowering the head of someone used to have the final say about everything can also have consequences. No one, not Badr al-Said nor anyone in the wikala knew what the consequences on Wadida's mind would be. Would you believe it, young man? Even Wadida herself did not know that she was planning revenge without knowing it! That's what I think. I believe that she found an opportunity and let someone else act on it.

"Hamu'a, also know as Buri, was a bicycle repairman and owner of a store behind Cinema al-Ahli. He was in his twenties, made a good living, and was a good man but he also gambled, drank alcohol, and smoked hashish. The gamblers brought him to the wikala in good financial form. He had pleasant features, a delicate face, and a ruddy complexion with a touch of European and aristocratic blood. On his narrow forehead the locks of his hair were coiffed in the manner of movie-star posters. He was lean and strong, his hands, cheeks, and the front of his nose dirty with bicycle grease and dust. As soon as he came in, he would go directly to the water pump to wash, for he liked to be clean when he gambled, since his fingers, stained with the sweat of work, would remind him as he paid the money to the winner of his sweating to earn that money. Actually, he seemed like someone who had come into a large inheritance, especially since he appeared to be decent and polite and from a good family. That was why I chose him, for his honesty, to be my representative at the gambling table to collect the commission assessed for every game. He did that in all honesty and sometimes I heard him fighting with the other gamblers for not calculating the commission correctly because of not having the exact change. This Hamu'a, as Wadida called him or al-Buri, as we all called him, I felt he was like a son of mine who had strayed. I often tried to advise him but he never gave me a chance. I felt he was hiding something, and he was, but I only found out about it in the end. It turned out that he was a big swindler who stole and cheated and got adolescent girls to fall in love with him then took their jewelry, their money, and their honor. He also got them to steal money or get it from their families in any way possible so he could pay it as a dowry when in fact he was paying it at the gambling table. He also defrauded companies and took many bicycles on consignment secured by his ownership of the store, and sold them and pocketed the money. Then it turned out that he didn't exactly own the store—it was owned by many heirs. Then he caught the bug of Wadida and her daughter and was unable to resist. At the same time he was unable to outdo or bypass Badr al-Said to get one of the ladies. He tried to win at gambling but lost his shirt. He tried to show off his good looks and he appeared like a sissy so he stopped that totally and began deliberately to forget that he was good looking. He tried to outdo Badr in matters of strength and machismo, but there again he lost miserably because Badr al-Said was stronger and more manly, hands down.

"That old virago knew all that! She told me about it during the quiet times she spent here sitting with me in the afternoon while Badr was asleep. I thought I was quite smart, that nothing got by me, but it turned out that daughters of Eve couldn't be fathomed, not even by Shawadfi. Haven't they taught you in school something in the Qur'an that said that their guile is great? Yes sir, indeed, God has spoken the truth. That woman started working on Buri secretly behind Badr al-Said's back and lit him on fire, even while soothing his soul burning with despair and his wounded manliness. So she would meet him secretly for fleeting moments during Badr's sleep or at the market while buying food. Sometimes she would give him a hug and sometimes a kiss but many times she managed to poison his thoughts: she gave him hope, granted him a new lease on life. She told him that she could give him herself or her daughter Nur al-Sabah or both at the same time, if he was able to get rid of Badr al-Said. She drew up the whole plan for him: to start a fight over gambling early in the evening so the whole case would be a quarrel leading to a killing in self-defense, thus the punishment would be no more than three years in jail which he would serve and when he came out he would marry Nur al-Sabah without paying a dowry or any other obligation. She said she would steal Badr al-Said's switchblade from his pocket and give it to him. He would then hold it by the handkerchief and, during the interrogation, he would say that it was Badr's knife, that he wanted to stab him with it and that he defended himself.

"Early in the evening the boy was insolent to Badr in such a way that he lost his self-control and insulted him. Buri responded with an insult of his own whereupon Badr gave him a punch that almost knocked him out. Badr thought that Buri would be deterred by that blow and would come to him senses, but Buri stood up and aimed a blow with his head at Badr al-Said's face which threw him off balance and caused him to bleed profusely from the nose. Badr reached in his pocket for his knife, when, lo and behold, the knife appeared in Buri's hand wrapped in one of Badr's handkerchiefs. With lightning speed, Buri stabbed Badr in the left side and the whole blade disappeared there. Buri left it and turned around, staggering through the door and down the stairs then ran out of the wikala to the railroad tracks thinking of hiding with his relatives in a faraway small village. Can you imagine, young man, that Badr al-Said was able to pull the knife out of his side then run at top speed like a bolting horse until he caught up with Buri on the tracks before he could cross them, and to catch him? He fainted on the tracks though and the knife flew from his hand and was picked up by Buri who stabbed him repeatedly in the heart. Buri did not forget to nick himself with the point of the knife in more than one place in his body to prove that he was attacked and he defended himself, especially since some people had seen Badr chasing him a long distance while holding the knife that was dripping with blood, thus painting a red course on the ground which the police and the prosecutor's office followed from the wikala in latern light. Buri went to his relatives stained with blood and they wouldn't take him in. On his way back the police caught him and he found out that Wadida had arranged everything: she explained to the police that there had been hostility for a long time between the killer and the victim because of gambling and over the daughter. She stated that the killer had stolen Badr's switchblade and his handkerchief and thus had prior intent. She didn't forget to mention to the police how the victim had trusted the killer with his honor and had shown him peace and love and how the latter tried to betray that trust, but that she didn't tell Badr so as not to drive a wedge between the two friends.

"The she-devil wanted to get rid of the two for good and that's what came to pass. Badr al-Said died and there was no family to release the body to, so it was brought to the morgue, then the refrigerator where it stayed several days away from home. Do you remember, Zainhum? Who do you think, young man, got his corpse in the end? That very poor fiancée of his who gave him back the ring and shabka accompanied with the ululation! She came this time with her husband, the waterwheel carpenter, wealthy from his profession and his land. That virtuous young lady did not forget to stop by the room of Wadida, her rival, to ask if the departed was indebted to anyone, for she was totally willing to pay off his debts. This Zainhum al-Atris, pardon me, Zainhum, was standing there, crying, not over the deceased but in hope of getting some alms. And indeed, the carpenter gave him a whole shilling and he distributed piasters to everyone in alms for the soul of the deceased! It was on that day that we found out that it was the carpenter who bought Badr al-Said's land and his livestock, for, as a neighbor, he had the right to first refusal. We were also told that, despite his purchase, he was willing to return everything had Badr awakened and returned to his village and fiancée. He told us that he married the fiancée to heal her wound! Would you believe it, young man, that he was crying in anguish as he said that?

"The she-devil got rid of her Badr by a treacherous death and of Buri by imprisonment. The court sentenced him to ten years and she stayed in a hell that she wished to escape even by death. Her daughter, Nur al-Sabah, never forgave her for what she had done. The girl was truly in love with Badr al-Said and no other man would take his place. She was on the point of going to the police and informing on ther mother. Their frequent fighting in the middle of the night reached me on this mastaba as if they were sworn enemies inseparably doomed to spend the rest of their lives in one prison cell. That girl, young man! I've never met a more strong-headed person! So determined. So strong-willed! So insolent and with such a hurtful tongue. Many a time I was surprised, as I sat in this very place, to see Wadida coming out of her room wailing as if she were on fire asking for it to be put out. She would try to rip her clothes, slapping her face hard, and swaying so fast that her face looked as if it were burning embers. I'd call her and she would come and throw herself on the mastaba, hiding her face in her hands, crying bitterly. I would try to reassure her with a few soothing words and I'd dissolve a piece of opium in a glass of tea to calm her down. While all this would be going on, the daughter would be leaning on the wall of the arcade, chewing gum coldly and enjoying the sight of her mother. She was so cruel that she didn't leave her alone when she returned but seized on any opportunity to put her on trial again. One ominous afternoon I saw a firestorm leaving Wadida's room and running downstairs coming toward me, flames coming out of its greenish edges. Inside was a sizzling and crackling mass that I soon realized was Wadida's body! I jumped up and pulled the blanket and ran toward her to wrap her and put out the flying fire, but she soon changed her direction to the water pump sink full of stagnant, putrid water and threw herself into it. We could all hear the sizzling sounds followed by a sharp hissing sound like that coming from a deflating balloon. The courtyard of the wikala filled with people from everywhere and the air filled with the smell of burnt flesh. She became like the blackened branch of a tree that had lost its contours after a huge fire. The prosecutor's office came and they examined the scene and ordered that the body be removed. No one stepped forward except me. I lifted a featureless column of drowned coal. We folded a sheet around her and now she is buried in the charity graves five kilometers from here.

"Yes, yes, Zainhum, you are right. But I haven't forgotten anything. I am just telling the young man the story bit by bit, from beginning to end. Now to continue: when we buried Wadida we couldn't forget her. For whole months it was as if she'd never left; we could still hear her and see her. One day, at around noon we were surprised to see a huge blue car with fins moving slowly until it stopped right in front of the wikala gate. A thin effendi got out of the car, stretching in an expensive suit, exuding a strong perfume. He had a white complexion like the heart of a palm tree, with small eyes and thick red hair, gathered like a cluster of dates. He said in a gentle tone, sounding like someone who can give an order to execute you any time he wishes, and with a lisp, 'Good evening.' We all got up: 'Good evening, sir, welcome!' 'Is this Wikalat Atiya?' We all said: 'Yes, can we be of service?' He said, 'Thank you. I wish to meet Wadida Hanim Khan, known as the Tatari lady.' We all looked at each other in shock and confusion, our eyes tearing again. His face turned red: 'What's the matter?' And, for the first time, young man, I burst out crying like a woman, 'May you live long, sir. She died a short time ago!' It was as if I had pushed the crying button: everyone cried as if they had been waiting for a special occasion to do so. The effendi himself began to shake and tremble as if blown by a wind directed at him alone. His features contracted and his face looked like a bowl of dough on which a cat had stepped and messed up. Tears came through his eyes as though through an orange juice press,

"We were even more surprised, young man. Then, crying, he turned to his car as if nothing had happened. 'Come here, sir, effendi! Who are you? Please, have a seat. Get a chair here, boy!' Do you remember, Zainhum? That day you acted like a real man of authority and shouted at your children to bring tea, at once. And, the truth be told, the tea came at once indeed. But, to go back to that effendi. It is so strange, this world! Had he noticed, we would've stayed fearful and cautious with him, but now that he had cried, the barrier between us collapsed. He became like us. Then he sat with us on the mastaba. The Egyptian people are very smart and wise in the ways of the world. So, even though we were no longer afraid of him, we kept quiet, just like that, on our own, without anyone telling us to do so. What occurred to all of us at the time was that this effendi must have been one of her victims and was so overcome by longing after being separated for a long time and had come to seek out his old flame only to find that bitter shock, so he cried. But when we saw that he was still crying, almost fainting from the fatigue written all over his red swollen eyes, we were confused as to his real identity. 'Beware, you sons of bitches; don't say anything stupid that might bring us trouble of any kind!' was the wordless message our eyes told each other.

"We remained silent for a long time and whenever I caught a glimpse of the effendi's face, my heart broke. For on his face was written such misery as would be enough till doomsday. He looked as if he had died then was taken to where accounts would be settled and when they handed him the account book in his left hand, he knew and sat waiting for the arrival of the guards of hell who would consign him there. Love alone couldn't do all of that to a person, my friend! Finally I couldn't hold back any longer so I bent toward him and said, 'Where's your faith in God, sir? We're all going to die! So why don't you tell us who you are so we can get to know one another?' He looked at my face and the faces of all present with eyes that were as dull as if they were two frogs on dry river banks. Then he threw in our faces the bomb that was so loud that we didn't hear it, even though our bodies trembled then flew off and landed with a thud on the ground, causing us to lose our ability to think. After a moment the sound of the explosion died down so we asked him again, all of us bending toward him scrutinizing him very closely and inquisitively. 'So, who did you say you were, then?' With trembling lips he said, confirming it: 'Yes, I am her son! Her only son. More than ten years ago I started looking for her everywhere and by all means. I knocked on every door and looked through every window and clutched at every straw in the midst of the waves. My father is a Lebanese millionaire who owns farms and estates and big department stores in Beirut. He is the chairman of a political party and is married to more than one wife, each of whom lives in her own palace and he has children by each of them. As for me, I live alone in the palace of his mother, my grandmother. Every summer I come to Egypt where I spend the whole summer looking for my mother, since no one had told me anything about her. I've never even seen her. It was my grandmother on my father's side who gave me information on my mother in a niggardly fashion: she would tell me something, a word, every few years, one that would shake my life to its foundations as I waited for another word a long time later. Strangely enough, my interest in my living Egyptain mother made me interested in my father's past which might guide me to something leading me to my mother. I found out that my father started out a poor destitute merchant who was an immigrant from his original country, Palestine, which was occupied by the Jews and that when his life got better in Cairo, Egypt, he married a woman named Wadida al-Raggal who used to live in a city named Damanhour. My father lived with her in that city in a neighborhood called Abu al-Rish since at that time he was trading in sackcloth and cotton-ginnery byproducts, such as seeds, which he sold in distant markets. My father loved money and my mother a lot, but they were always fighting because of my father's constant travel and his love for money, which competed with her for his affection. My father was always traveling, from harbor to airport to railway station to truck stop. My mother got fed up and nagged him and threatened to ask for a divorce. Then I was born and my father began to humor her and bide his time until he was able to arrange to take me and his money away for good. When the 1948 war broke out, I was a child in nursery school and my father used to go to work and spend some nights away from us. During that time the story of my mother got etched in my mind. I came from school one day and found my grandmother crying her heart out and I found out between sobs that my father had married a woman and set her up in a faraway palace. I heard her badmouthing my Egyptian Tatari mother. I saw some letters that my mother had sent to my father before they were married and knew that they had had an amazing love story. When I came to Damanhour a year later, those I asked said they hadn't heard of Wadida al-Raggal but knew a Wadida Turk Khan who told fortunes for a living. They said that I bore a great resemblance to her but that they didn't know where she had disappeared to. I asked some people here to search and write to me in Beirut. There I pestered my grandmother with questions until she admitted to me that my mother indeed told fortunes. That's why I couldn't wait when I received a letter saying she was living in this wikala with her husband Turk Khan. And now you tell me that she is dead! I wish I hadn't started on the journey to begin with, so I'd have had peace of mind. But now where can I get that peace of mind, good people?'

"That's what the effendi said, young man. I didn't miss one word of what he said nor can I forget. His condition was so moving and that's why I memorized what he said since I repeated it for the police and prosecutors dozens of times. After the effendi said what he said he burst out crying hard and the blood kept burning under the skin of his face. Whenever he wanted to get up to leave, his legs failed him and he sat down again, broken hearted. Then he said in a weak, rasping voice: 'Did the dearly departed leave behind anything? Is she in debt to anyone? Does she have children and a husband? I want to see anyone, anything of hers!' I said, 'My son, she has a daughter whose name is Nur al-Sabah who was married but whose husband died while she was still a bride and she hadn't taken off the black shawl. A friend of hers who lives behind us took her in to look after her. She's all that's left of the deceased. If you like, we can call her. He said he would love to see her and befriend her. As soon as he said that several people went to Widad the dancer and brought the two: Widad and Nur. What a sight it was, young man! This life is a riddle that we don't understand, Don't tell me schools and learning, it's a matter of seeing and experiencing before anything else,

"Widad and Nur al-Sabah stood in front of us, one picture divided into two halves: totally covered in black dresses and black shawls. You couldn't tell one from the other. So, who led the effendi to his sister, daughter of his mother whom he had never seen in his life? No one, I swear, young man! It was he himself who stared at them with his strong eyes then immediately threw himself on the bosom of Nur al-Sabah in tears. She started patting him on the back. I was quite taken aback: I swear, I looked at the two faces, the shape of the jaws, the look in the eyes, both identical. The effendi told his sister Nur al-Sabah, 'Sister, my name is Khalid Ibrahim al-Nu'man.' Nur al-Sabah said as she shook his hand, 'You're her son, Khalid? How are you, dear? She's talked to me about you only once and after that told me never to mention you! But I've caught her many times talking and crying in her dreams and saying, 'Bring my beloved son, Khalid.' And one day she woke up from such a dream and slapped her face and rent her clothes. God have mercy on her soul! There were many things in her life about which I knew nothing. So, you're her son? Welcome, my beloved brother!' The effendi said, 'I came this time intending to live with my mother for good because I am fed up with life in Beirut without a mother, especially since my father is busy with his other children whose mothers he loves. They all despise me. So, where do I go now? And to whom shall I turn? Listen, sister, I brought with me all my money and clothes, which are now in the hotel where I am staying in Cairo. I am going to go get them now and let's find somewhere to live here together until God decides what to do with us.' We followed him to the car to bid him farewell. It was one of those Cairo rental cars with an old driver who was fast asleep. The effendi reached with his hand to open the door but he staggered and his torso bent, then he fainted and fell to the ground. We gathered around him turning him right and left but he was as limp as a rag. The boy had died! We were questioned and the police raided us several times. The police investigations said that the effendi had committed a heinous act: he had killed two of his half-brothers in a moment of blind rage, as he was a drug addict and had been mentally disturbed since his childhood; that he went to all kinds of clinics and mental hospitals. When he killed his brothers he was acting out a crazy play using a gun stolen from his doctor. They found out in Beirut that he had sneaked into Egypt to hide at his mother's place after stealing his grandmother's savings and her jewelry. During the autopsy they found that he had ingested a large amount of painkillers, sleeping pills, opium, and hashish mixed with chocolate that caused his heart to stop. His father refused to take the corpse; so it was a big predicament!

"What a sight it was, young man. Nur al-Sabah who had clutched at a straw of hope to lead her to a safe landing found herself inheriting from the dream nothing but a dead corpse! But she rose to the occasion. She accompanied her brother's body like a valiant man and buried it next to her mother. We all, of course, considered it a bad omen to open the new tomb on a body that had not settled yet, but there was nothing to do. After that Nur al-Sabah lay down in her bed for many days in the care of the wikala women but she was in a bad way. One day we were surprised to see her come out, her hair dishevelled, hallucinating. She sat in the sun in the courtyard, absently, with saliva running down the corners of her mouth. She had lost her mind, pure and simple! She started going out naked at night shrieking for no reason, scratching her face, and heaping dust on her head. We would restrain her and force her to put on a dress, but she would rip it off and she did many other crazy things. She'd dance and wiggle her eyebrows at the kids, laughing all the time and throwing stones at people. The squad car came and took her in a straitjacket to the mental hospital at al-Khanka! Widad, God bless her, began to visit her once a month, then every two months, then three, then twice a year and every time she would come back with no hope that her dear friend Nur al-Sabah would get well.

"Now, you must be asking yourself: why is this man telling me this long story that no one has been thinking about? But don't rush to judgment, young man, you'll soon find out the reason."

The Mirage

The night had begun to get very dark even though it was still early. The ten o'clock summary of the news, read by Hemmat Mustafa, was still being read in the distant radio although it sounded as if it were nearby. The gate of the wikala opened after a light, symbolic knock. A thin man wearing a shirt and pants came toward us with open arms, shouting gleefully, "Amm Shawadfi! It's been a long time! The living are destined to meet again!"

He rushed into the arms of Shawadfi, who got up to welcome him warmly, embracing him and patting his back with his rough hand as he said, "How are you, buddy? Thank God for your safe arrival! I received your message today and I sent back my greetings with the messenger and told him I was awaiting you eagerly."

Then he let him go and he came over to me, greeting me, then turned around and hurriedly shook hands with Shawadfi again, without noticing the presence of Sheikh Zainhum al-Atris, who was curled up next to the mastaba on the ground leaning his back on the gate wall. He sat between me and Shawadfi on the mastaba. His whitish, chapped face was emaciated, with prominent jawbones covered with a thin layer of dust. There was a hint of defeat in his eyes and humiliation hiding a secret rebelliousness. He was constantly blinking as if protecting himself from the light or receiving it in a rationed manner. It seemed to me that I had seen him before, for he looked familiar even though I couldn't place his many images in any recognizable frames. He seemed to be fun-loving and attractive despite the repressed aggressive spirit radiating from his eyes and expected from his tongue.

Shawadfi pulled the brazier and got busy breaking the carbonized cobs and lighting them by rolling a page of an old newspaper into a cone which he then lit and blew on through the narrow end. Shawadfi said as he pointed to Zainhum who looked like some rags discarded in the dim corner: "You didn't say hello to your old friend! Has jail made you forget your friends?"

He got up, opening his arms and shouting, "Sheikh Zainhum al-Atris? What a surprise! Please forgive me, Abu Atris, for my eyes haven't become used to the light yet. How are you and how are all the children?"

He threw himself on Zainhum, kissing and embracing his as they kept repeating, like children enjoying the game, "How are you? Good!" until Shawadfi shouted, "Okay, enough already!" Then he looked at me nodding as he pointed to him, "This is Hamu'a al-Buri, our old friend!"

"Welcome!" my heart shook as I spoke, out of curiosity. Al-Buri sat, patting his knees, looking in the direction of the arcade at the upstairs room, shouting in a gleeful, joyous voice, "Good evening, my heart's desire! I am home!"

Then he turned to Shawadfi, "How are things, Amm Shawadfi. I swear by God and Sidi Abu al-Makarim, I miss you very much!"

In Shawadfi's voice there was a tone of a gentle, warm sadness that I was surprised someone like him, with a special tomb for his adversaries, was capable of: "Everything is fine, Buri. Everything is decreed by fate and no one gets more or less than what God has decreed for us."

Buri said gleefully, "I sent you the messenger from the security directorate while going through discharge procedures. I said to myself that you would rejoice at the news and perhaps prepare a home-cooked meal!"

He pointed to Wadida's room, the glee now gone from his voice, replaced by a dark tone hinting at an evil recess deep down inside, "No light in the room! Did they hear the news? I don't think they heard that I've been released from prison today. Can you imagine that I haven't gone anywhere? From the security directorate to this place right away. See how things are arranged? From here to prison and from prison to here. Would you believe it, Amm Shawadfi? In prison I saw nothing, remembered nothing but this threshold, this room, and the eyes of Nur al-Sabah. There was nothing else on my mind. My cellmates were all from here and among them were some who spent the whole night in my bedding in my arms. I swear by Sidi Abu al-Makarim that while asleep I'd extend my arm to embrace the person sleeping next to me and I'd imagine that I had embraced their actual body. But you should never forget this. Freedom is a real joy. You might eat dry, plain bread or go about naked and praise God that you're healthy and covered. I swear by Sidi Abu al-Makarim that spending ten years on one cheek was longer than a million years. I will try to get interviewed by Amal Fahmi on the program *On the Street Corner*, for I have a lot of good things to tell her, but mainly to request Umm Kulthuum's song *I Am Not Coming Back to You* and dedicate it to jail. Never, ever. May God spare us even talking about it! Tomorrow I marry my heart's beloved and joy and begin a new life. I have my skill, thank God. I'll work in any bicycle shop or I'll set up a stand on the agricultural road to fix tires and God will give me the gift of settling down and I'll make it again, so long as I am beside the joy of my heart, Nur al-Sabah, the light of my eyes, God will guide me to the right path and will make me good again. Please pray for me, Amm Zainhum, for the sake of Sidi al-Atris and tell him that I am a good guy. I owe him a pledge and a similar one for Sidi Abu al-Makarim because I prayed for his help in jail and God sent good people my way. The Muslim Brothers came to jail and they splurged their families' generous visits on us every day. Everything that came in was distributed fairly and we, prisoners in criminal cases, worked in their palce with the collusion of the guards who shared everything with us: they ate with us, smoked with us and drank tea with us. Even prayers: the Brothers forced the guards to participate in them, otherwise supplies were cut off from everyone. What a time! So many imams and bearded guys and words as sweet as honey. Words that never left the heart once you heard them. I and other criminal prisoners didn't know anything about our religion or the world, but these sheikh effendis fixed us. Criminal prisoners grew their beards and learned good words. Some of them started holding circles of prisoners convicted of fraud, larceny, cheating, and counterfeiting and spoke to them about what 'God said' and what the 'Prophet said.' There were prisoners released with me who planned to spend the rest of their lives in mosques. Others are going on the pilgrimage this year, or at least that is their intent. As for me, I'll pray regularly."

When the cup of tea was placed in front of him, Sheikh Zainhum stretched as he sat, then extended his hand to Buri with a small piece of opium. The latter clapped his hands in great joy, shouting, "I love you! What a blessed month!"

He scraped the opium from the Sheikh's thumb with his thumb and dropped it in his mouth smacking his lips. The sheikh then gave each of us a piece and Shawadfi, licking his lips and seeking the sheikh's help in getting out of this predicament which was too big for him, said, "Don't you have a few good words to tell us, Abu Atris? I give up! My brain has stopped working. Pick yours. We want to hear some of your good words. And you, young man, you've seen what you've seen and heard what you've heard, maybe *you* can tell us something useful in the present situation."

Sheikh Zainhum looked from the corner of his bad eye and the white spot began to get lost in dark red spots and he began to scratch his neck behind his head. Shawadfi laughed, waving fingers that looked like hooks, "I tell you to pick your brain not the back of your silly head. What should we tell Buri now? You get my drift? Keep that in mind and say something. Express your longing, for instance. Think of something that will put him and us at ease. We are now like a pregnant woman who wants God to help her deliver without pain. So what've you got?"

The sheikh lowered his eyes to the ground and began to take deep drags on a fat Wings cigarette between his fingers. Then he raised his head looking at it, his lips colored blue from the smoke and clinched in what looked appeared to be a smile. He seemed to get ready to speak. There even appeared in his good eye a gleam indicating he had found the right words to solve that serious problem, and to soothe Buri and prepare him to receive the tragic truth.

The Tale of the Amazing Bird

"Praise the Prophet! There was (and oh, how much there was!) in old times gone by, a good, strong young man called al-Shatir Karim. He was not al-Shatir Hassan that you know about from the tales, because our story takes place in real life. Al-Shatir Karim was a tough guy: if he got into a fight, he beat up all his opponents; if someone upset him on the street, he cleared the whole street; and if he didn't like a gathering, he brought it to an end. No one could stand up to him. He fell for a beautiful girl, the daughter of a poor man and went to ask for her hand, thinking that the girl's father would be so grateful and offer him the red carpet treatment because he had condescended and come to ask for the girl's hand. It was not within the power of the father to decide, but he welcomed al-Shatir Karim warmly and offered him all that he had by way of hospitality and told him, 'O Master of all Shatirs, I am greatly honored to give you my daughter's hand in marriage but you've come too late. For the girl is engaged to her cousin whom she loves and who has loved her since childhood.' Al-Shatir Karim was mightily vexed and he said 'O Chief, since when did a girl have a say in her marriage? And since when did she know how to choose a suitable husband? And how can you, in your own words, say that she is in love? Isn't love a shame and a disgrace, Chief?' The man, now very afraid, said,

‘O Master of all Shatirs, this is what happened. And it is an honorable and chaste love and anyway, the law of God says the girl had the right to say what she thinks of a suitor. And you have proposed to her, so let’s go ask her in front of you, whether she accepts or not.’ Al-Shatir Karim grew even more vexed and said to him, “Frankly, I don’t like to propose and be turned down. I am not used to that. Would you like for that to happen to me?’ The man said, ‘No, I wouldn’t, my son, but I also cannot force my daughter to marry someone. There’s nothing the matter with you, so, if she accepts you, you’d be quite welcome.’ The girl was brought and she said she loved her fiancé and did not add a word to that. Al-Shatir Karim left, very angry and determined to bring the girl to her knees and make her beg him to marry her. Thus he devised a plot for the girl’s fiancé and drowned him. The body appeared a few days later and the perpetrator was listed as person or persons unknown, but everybody knew it was Karim who did it. Our friend wanted to win over the girl’s heart, so he started sending her and her father and brothers gifts from what he had looted in his highway robberies. But the girl continued to grieve for her fiancé, and all lost interest in life. So she kept sending back his gifts. Karim decided to break her will just as he had broken her heart. So he hatched another plot, this time for the father. He did not kill him but arranged to have him wounded and frightened. While the poor father was lying in his sickbed from fright, Karim went to visit him and to promise him that as of that day, he was under his protection and that he was going to exact revenge on the perpetrator. He didn’t forget to hint at his old request. The girl was standing behind the door of the room, listening. When she heard her father say that she was not desirous of marriage, she went in and said that now she was desirous and wanted to marry Karim in particular. She had figured out Karim’s evil intent and took mercy on her father. Karim was very happy and the wedding celebrations lasted seven nights. The bride moved to his faraway house where his mother lived with two of the children of her dead daughter. On the wedding night, Karim found his bride sick. Every night she got even sicker. Whenever he tried to enjoy her he found her a lifeless corpse in his arms, so he would leave her and go out at night, beating the air with his club, oppressing people for no fault of their own, looting warehouses and markets, waylaying traveling caravans, and killing whoever got in his way. Finally, masters, he got tired of the darkness that had taken over every corner of his soul. As he was walking once, he came upon a soothsayer. He squatted before her and asked her to tell his fortune. She struck the sand, whispered to the shells and shuffled the cards. Then she told him: 'There is, in your life, an involuntary prisoner who is going to tear down the walls of the prison. The prisoner will escape and that escape will release bad smells that will rouse the people against you and break your back. So, who is that prisoner?' Everything became black in his eyes and he was vexed at the soothsayer, so he kicked her and left, cursing her father and the evil day that placed her in his path. He decided he did not want to go home, so he kept on walking unaware and without any destination in mind, from one place to the next until he came upon a town that he liked, situated on the edge of an endless forest on the bank of a narrow river. Are you following, masters? He saw on the bank of the river a place where people of all kinds were sitting: fishermen, sailors, peasants, merchants, shatirs, thieves, mercenaries, boatmen, and donkey drivers. He sat among them and ordered a drink like them and started daydreaming about God's creation, enchanted by the beautiful scenery. Yet he noticed that everyone around was talking about one subject. Are you with me, masters? What kind of subject? A single subject. Everyone was talking about a bird of amazing appearance that lived in the adjacent forest but no one knew what it was called and no one had ever been able to capture it.

"Karim was intrigued, masters, but he kept looking at them in disdain. For what kind of bird was it that shatirs could not catch? An eagle? A falcon? A kite? Even if it were a lion with two wings, there was bound to be some shatir who could catch it, for each hunter had his art. But they flabbergasted him by recounting the exploits of shatirs who tried to catch that wonderous, amazing bird without success. See how strange that was, masters? They even spoke of kings and princes and generals who amassed armies and chariots and cannons and came to engage this bird in battle and remained for months and years until they ran out of ammunition and patience and were crippled by long intervals of heat, frost, and travel, so that in the end they went back empty-handed.

"I forgot to mention, masters, that Karim, whenever he tried to get together with his bride, she gave herself to him like an old rag, so his nerves didn't stiffen and he started having doubts about his manhood. So, when he heard this talk of the amazing bird, his imagination lit up and he started visualizing himself having returned to his town in a big procession carrying gifts and money in just reward for catching the bird that armies and cannons couldn't. He saw his bride, overjoyed by his heroism, opening her arms to him, whereupon he would get peace of mind again and recapture his lost manhood.

"So, enthused, he got up and went to the people sitting there, introduced himself, and apprised them of his position among his compatriots. They welcomed him and got him into the conversation about the amazing bird. He said he wanted to see it to try his luck so they said it was there in the forest: 'So go to it and bring it back if you can and we'll give you whatever you want. For whoever is able to catch this bird in particular has the right to become ruler over this country for as long as God wills.' Our friend made his decision right then and there: he got himself ready and headed for the forest, his quiver filled with all kinds of arrows, in addition to spears, shields, and projectiles.

"He entered the forest, apprehensive and trembling, looking closely and examining all the tree branches to study the angles of aiming and how to cast his nets on the bird as soon as he saw it, for his plan was to surprise it before it noticed and tried to evade him. Are you still with me, masters? Our friend hardly went a few steps into the forest when he was surprised by something small and light landing on his left shoulder. Something like a sparrow or a dove or a plover. As soon as he tried to shoo it away, a captivating voice, sweet of rhythm and with words clearly enunciated, said to Karim sarcastically and innocently, 'Why all this trouble, Karim? What do you need these arrows, spears, and projectiles for? It is simpler than you imagined, Karim.'

"'Who are you, beautiful sparrow?'

"'I am it! The amazing bird that you've come to catch! Before you came armies, tanks, and other frightening things. But they all returned empty handed, because catching me is easy and impossible at the same time. For how easy it is for you to grab me with your hand, but how much easier it is for me to fly away from the hellish bullets, and you will never reach me. You, Karim, can hold me in your hand. You don't even need to hold me, for here I am, on your shoulder! If you like, I can get into your pocket and you can take me back wherever you want to; I'll be yours!'

"'So, how come they failed to catch you when you are so easy and available?' said Karim, in shock, unsure whether to believe what he was hearing or not.

"Shrugging its wings regretfully, the bird said, 'Because they failed the test. They always fail!'

"Are you still with me, masters? Failed what? The test! 'So what is this difficult test, beautiful sparrow?' asked Karim. The bird said, "'I will go with you peacefully and contentedly, but only on one condition.'

"'What is it? I welcome it!'

"'We are walking on a long trip; so, it behooves us to amuse ourselves so as not to get tired or bored. I'll tell you three short tales on the way, with three big chances that I will grant you. If you fail in one, maybe you'll succeed in the other and thus we would have a good relationship together till the end. My only condition is that after I finish telling you a tale, you don't sigh and say 'Ah!' in regret. If you say 'Ah!' at the end of the story, I'll fly away and you won't see me. As for the third time, that'll be it. If you say 'Ah!' you will never see me again.'

"Karim laughed and said, 'Don't worry on this account, for I am so hard hearted I have never uttered an 'ah!' even if they gave me a sound beating. Many a time have I been beaten and burned but I never said it.

Am I going to utter it, moved by a story that you or someone else for that matter tells? That will never be, by God!'

"'Okay, we are agreed then. Here's the first story: it is said that a man of means was living on his distant farm with a faithful dog that guarded him and they loved each other dearly. It so happened that the man went out into the fields on one errand or another and his wife also went out. They had a baby that they left sleeping in his crib, guarded by the faithful dog, when out of nowhere a huge snake started crawling directly toward the baby's crib. The dog bared its fangs and pounced on the snake and began to tear its flesh apart until it devoured it and stood in front of the door wagging its tail in joyful anticipation of its' master's arrival. When the master arrived and saw its mouth stained with blood, he thought the dog had gone rabid and eaten his child, whereupon he drew his pistol and shot the dog dead.'

"Thereupon Karim involuntarily shouted in regret and pain, 'Ah! What a pity that the faithful dog is gone and what a rash, stupid man!'

"Whereupon he could not find the bird on his shoulder but heard its voice, 'You failed the test, friend! You have to go back alone!'

"Karim shouted, 'I still have two chances; so forgive me for this one!'

"The bird alighted on his shoulder again: 'Here is the second story: it is said that a man was lost in the desert, staggering for days in the heat. He almost died of thirst and there was no water around to be found. Suddenly he saw in the distance two mountain boulders between which, in a groove, shone a thread coming down from above. He hurried to it and found it to be a thin line of water coming down from an unknown spot on top of the boulder to grooves below it. He said, 'Thank God, the Munificent!' He had a clay bowl which he placed under the thin line of water and kept it there for more than three hours in the extreme heat as the water dripped in the bowl one drop at a time. When the bottom of the bowl filled with a good draught he raised it to his lips whereupon a beautiful hoopoe fell in panic from the sky into the bottom of the bowl, causing it to fall on the ground and shatter and the water to be spilled. He pounced on the staggering hoopoe and trampled it underfoot, pulverizing it. Then he went back to the thin line of water in the rock, trying to open his mouth under it when he saw what he had not seen before: a speckled serpent lurking in the groove with horrible looking eyes and venom driping from its fangs like droplets of water. His heart was broken from grief!'

"At that point Karim shouted without realizing it, 'Ah! There's no power or strength save in God! That wretch has betrayed the beautiful hoopoe that had saved his life!'

"Right away he didn't see the bird but he heard its voice, 'You've failed the test the second time.'

"Karim shouted in supplication, 'I have a third chance and I guarantee that I will be hard hearted as is known of me.'

"The bird alighted on his shoulder: 'Here is the third and last story: there was a talkative hunter who was a chatterbox. That's why he was not doing so well and his livelihood suffered. Good people showed him a forgotten forest with plenty of opportunities but also sizeable dangers where only a wise person, careful with his tongue, would do well. He gathered his arrows and entered the forest and found it to be filled with thorns and precious, pliable animals. Approaching one quarry, however, he saw a human skull discarded by the side of the road under a tree. He stood contemplating it in fear whereupon the skull spoke to him, saying, 'Mind your own business, go on.' He said to it, 'So long as you speak, tell me: what brought you here?' It said, 'Words!' Our talkative friend forgot his hunting and ran to the city. By the time he reached his house, he had told the story. People heard it and it reached the ears of the ruler of the city who sent for him and told him, 'Show us the skull that talks and you'll get a big reward!' He said, 'To hear is to obey!' So the ruler sent the executioner with him to the forest, telling the executioner, 'If the skull speaks in front of you, give him the reward. If it doesn't, cut his throat and leave his head next to the skull and feed his body to the city dogs.' The hunter went with the executioner to the forest, but the skull did not speak, whereupon the executioner cut off his head and left it next to the skull and carried off his body and left. After the executioner left, the skull leaned to the hunter's neck and asked, 'What brought you here, hunter's neck?' It said, 'Words!'"

"Thereupon Karim shouted, 'Ah! Right. Words will do that to you! They'll protect you or else they'll be your undoing! This chatterbox deserves it!'

"He felt his shoulder but the bird was totally gone. He began to speak to himself saying, 'Truly it's an amazing free bird which refuses to be imprisoned in a cage or be at the mercy of the police!' He heard the bird's voice, saying, 'No, Shatir Karim! It's not a matter of a bird fearing a cage or flying away from the police. It's the story of the 'ah!' and an 'ah!' cannot be imprisoned. You, Shatir Karim, even though you're hard-hearted, could not hold the 'ah' in your chest. You think you could imprison it in someone else's chest? Go back and don't think of capturing me again!'

"Are you following me, masters? It's the story of what? The story of the 'ah!' Each of us says it, willingly or against our will. But when he causes it for others, he cannot stand hearing it from them. Shatir Karim, feeling defeated, went back to his community, his head seething with all kinds of thoughts. He began to feel regret for what he had done throughout his life and his ears began to fill with all the 'ahs' in the voices of dozens that he had wronged and hurt all his miserable lawless life. He wished they'd all accept his apology and forgive him but he felt that God would never forgive him. So he pledged to atone for his sins and repent and treat his bride well since he was now certain that she could never be faithful to him because when he killed her beloved, he stabbed her in the heart. Thus she was not his wife by choice but was imprisoned in his house by fear alone. And just as he couldn't suppress the 'ah,' he wouldn't be able to keep his bride a prisoner in his house forever since his bride would not be able to hold back the ah in her chest.

"But he found that the suppressed ah had gone out ahead of him. The poor girl, during his absence, went through his things and found a gold ring that she recognized right away, since it belonged to her fiancé whom he had drowned. She also found many things that belonged to people who had disappeared under mysterious circumstances. She went to those whom she knew among the families of his victims and told them of what she had seen. They all went to the government and made their reports. The government arranged an ambush for him and as soon as he settled in his house they raided it and carried him off to jail as he cried, saying, 'The imprisoned ah must break the bones of the chests and fly off to avenge itself.' Are you still with me, masters? The narrator of the story said that when they placed the noose around his neck because of all the murders that the evidence had awakened, and surrounded him, he was hallucinating about the soothsayer who told his fortune and whom he had not believed and about that amazing bird that he said kept pecking at his eyes and heart with a sharp beak. See, masters, the end of every criminal oppressor. Just as you treat others, so you shall be treated. What you take by force or by crime will injure your health and your eyes. So think what will happen if you take something by treason, murder or poison? Think of that, masters! You, Buri, are welcome and it's an honor for us. Now that you're out of jail in good health, thank God and do not covet what's forbidden. Repent sincerely before God and don't grieve over what's gone. It's all a matter of fate and God will make it up to you. The next one will be better, Buri, that's how the saying goes. May God guide us and guide you, God willing."

The Confrontation

"You son of a bitch! You are really clever, Sheikh Zainhum! May God reward you!"

Thus spoke Shawadfi, waving with his big hand. Then his eyes began to dwell on Buri's face which obviously had now changed completely. His face was relaxed and drooped and signs of aggressiveness had left it. A confused, hurried, and tense glance in his eyes had now subsided into one of total, quiet lethargy. The evil pride and mysterious joy were now replaced by childlike, wretched helplessness. The side of his face opposite me, in the shadow of a very faint light hanging from the ceiling, appeared very miserable, pitifully helpless. There was an absent-minded look on his face that reminded me of possessed dervishes drowned in melancholy and boredom. He glanced very briefly and hopelessly at Wadida's room as if it were the last glance one cast on a grave that entombed the remains of someone that was dear but now gone. Then he hit his knees with his hands and it seemed he was thinking of leaving but wasn't sure where to go. When he raised his face to us, he seemed to be terribly disappointed for not having gotten the reception he had been dreaming of all the years and nights in jail. It also became apparent that he had realized that something out of the ordinary had taken place. The questions appeared in his eyes in a moving way, especially since Wadida's room was engulfed in silence, dark and frightening, depressing stillness all the more poignant because its current occupant was Ramadan Eraiga. Suspicion appeared clearly on Buri's face and it was also clear that he was thinking of an intelligent way to ask about the truth, while at the same time afraid of finding it out. Shawadfi waved his long arm that looked like a palm frond in a gesture of someone who wanted to strike the iron while it was hot: "Listen, young man. You've unjustly killed a gem of a man. And you paid the price, which was slight, considering that you've taken a man's life. Wadida wrecked many homes and got her just deserts also, as God has summoned her to put her on a stern trial and she'll get a life sentence in hell, God protect us! The only poor victim between the two of you is Nur. She has received a touch of God's mercy, may God spare you, and is now residing in the lunatic asylum. She's probably dead by now. Widad no longer visits her, except by chance. The big calamities happened in your absence. And look at you! You've gotten out of it alive. You are the only winner. You still have your health and youth; you can work and get married and start anew and with a clean slate. That's all there is to it. So there is no need for sorrow or anything like that. It is not worth it."

The bulging of Buri's eyes, despite the sparks flying from them indicated that he must have been prepared for serious surprises like that. So his face remained expressionless and his features looked tough for quite some time during which we were enveloped in a charged, apprehensive silence. Then Buri's features began to soften little by little, then tremble and turn red. Then the tears came like rain.

We bowed our heads in profound sadness. None of us said anything. Even I, despite my lack of respect for Buri as a violent criminal, found myself fighting off a desire to cry. His situation at that moment seemed terrible to me. And whenever we imagined that he had regained his calm by falling silent or seeming lost in thought, fits of weeping came over him hysterically, his whole body shaking and convulsing in the midst of exclamations by Shawadfi and Zainhum al-Atris: "Don't lose faith in God! It's no use! Thank God! His decree has been merciful! Have mercy on yourself!" Then he seemed to be getting fed up as if he felt that we wanted to prevent him from doing something that he liked. He got up suddenly saying, "Peace upon you," then dashed to the gate in rash zeal. Shawadfi shouted, "Where are you going, you crazy one?"

"I am going to al-Khanka. Tomorrow's sun will rise on me there, with God's permission."

"Are you crazy, young man? What will you do at al-Khanka? Are you going to report to the conscription board? Sit down, let's talk."

"I need to cry."

"Well, can't you cry here?"

"The dearly departed's grave will not be annoyed by my crying?"

"Nor will this mastaba. Cry here until morning. This is a mastaba and that is a mastaba. There are evil genies and here are good genies."

"I am not going to calm down until I have cried over her tomb and told her what's in my heart! And I am not going to calm down until I meet Nur al-Sabah and see her with my own eyes. I have great hope that God will restore her sanity when she sees me. God is capable of everything and I have great hope in him."

"Do you have any money?"

"Not a millieme."

"So, how are you going to ride the train? How are you going to go to the hospital when you've got nothing? Sit down; let's come to an understanding."

"Walking will do me good."

"Okay, here, take this."

And he gave him a ten piaster silver coin: "Say hello to the two of them. This one," and he pointed with his thumb behind his back toward the graveyard, "and this one," and he pointed with his index finger in front of him, "and recite the Fatiha for us in al-Hussein mosque." Buri extended his hand shyly and took the coin. Sheikh Zainhum had also taken another out and proffered it to him: "This one bears the blessing of Sidi al-Atris!"

He took it. I found myself driven to do the same with great pleasure. I smoothed a ten piaster note and gave it to him: “And this is from me!”

He looked at me with special gratitude, perhaps because he hadn’t met me before and didn’t know yet who I was. I found myself following him as far as the gate and watching him as he turned into a column of dark gray smoke as he went further away into the cemetery, which also looked like masses of dark clouds joining the sky’s clouds at the edges of the horizon’s tent.

The Omen

Muhammad Abu Sinn, to my surprise, dismissed me early. It was surprising because, on such a night every week we spent the evening in Elaishy's room until the dawn prayer, eating dinner and drinking tea and cinnamon and coffee and eating fruits and reading and talking. True, my talking was very limited, confined to expressions of surprise or admiration but their conversation was usually quite wondrous. I'd hear the same Qur'anic verses and the same hadiths of the Prophet that I'd heard in the mosques from preachers hundreds of times but on any given night I'd discover many other meanings that might actually sometimes contradict what I knew. These were sunny meanings that filled the horizon with light and the heart with awe and fear of not living up to the expectations of full religiosity. They pushed you to be more daring in life, awakening in you the feeling that all humans were equal, that you and the ruler of the country were two similar creatures, that each distinguished himself only by piety, following good and avoiding evil. They were meanings that deprived the ruler of that aura of inspiring fear and showed him in the true light of being a human being who could be right or wrong and, accordingly, should be subject to the code of reward and punishment. I loved that particular evening gathering because it gave me a great amount of pithy sayings, Qur'anic verses, and hadiths of the Prophet that I could use in dealing with others, be they colleagues, bosses, or the police. These were sayings, lines of poetry, verses from the Qur'an or hadiths that were so flexible and rich in meaning as to suit every context and occasion. The most enjoyable sayings were those that involved an intereting story and the most beautiful proverbs were those that required going back to old tales or exciting events. As for hadiths of the Prophet, the most outstanding were those that resulted from specific issues or social problems. Some of my happiest moments were those when I suddenly found an occasion or situation or debate to which some of those sayings applied, whereupon I would repeat them as I'd heard and memorized, with as much eloquence and zeal as I could muster. I even took great pleasure in correcting someone's pronunciation of complex and inelegant Bedouin and Arabian names or in pronouncing, myself, such names as Umm Salama, Tha'libi, Ibn Abi Zar'a, Ibn al-Ja'd, Ibn Quhafa, and I don't know whose other Ibn. Interestingly, I found those who listened to me amazingly responsive, paying full attention and lending me their ears waiting for more. When they found out that I ran out of material or that my repertoire was confined to just that one story or saying, they hurried to replenish my supply with other stories that were in the same vein. That motivated me to redouble my effort in acquiring as many sayings as I could. I had come to the conclusion that people in my country are alike in this respect: they either listened very attentively to intoxicating words if the speaker had a rich supply of brilliant sayings or they competed in the conversation by recalling or making up stories and sayings in the same vein and to the same effect. The real star among us—them—was the one who had the largest amount of stories, anecdotes, novelties, and cute expressions. He would be the only one to captivate the hearts and enchant the ears, even if he were a con artist and a fraud. And thus we would go around in a whirlpool in which the only ones who stayed on top were those unburdened by thinking, reason, honesty, and a genuine conscience.

At Elaishy's evenings I discovered the truth of that phenomenon and became certain that those who enchanted us with sweet delicious talk were the ones to whom we gave our confidence and all our money. We even came to trust them with our honor and secrets and to place our fate in their hands. I found out that the most skillful among them were those who were most familiar with people's problems and pain. Their skill showed in giving people vaccine shots of sayings and historical precedents to cope with their maladies and how they ended as the Lord, not the servant, wanted them to end. That then cowed those in pain into transferring their pain and troubles onto the shoulders of providence, thus getting rid of the burden so long as everything that happened to humans had been decreed to happen, that they had to endure without facing up to fate, because to stand up to and to challenge providence was an act of disbelief. Faith meant you accepted pain and endured it even as Job patiently did.

At Elaishy's evenings things got too confusing for my little mind to classify and catalogue. Every evening I discovered a lot of enlightening ways of looking at things but also discovered many contradications. I didn't know whether those contradictions were within the texts or resulted from my and their understanding of the texts and the lengthy, pedantic analyses. But I loved and enjoyed the game of influencing people by polished, carefully measured speech steeped in tradition, the kind that created emotional tremors in the hearts of listeners. I was developing the makings of a bold, articulate preacher who could come in handy if things got tight in this city. Perhaps such a course could help me, as I have seen it do to many, live comfortably and marry the most beautiful pious women. There were many smooth operators in this tradition with a great talent for hiding their original personalities behind the cloaks of preachers or the beards of dervishes or the guise of so-called Islamic thinkers writing for newspapers and periodicals.

I had always looked forward to the Elaishy evening and spent the whole week prepared for it, as did everyone, especially Abu Sinn. But this evening he looked grouchy, with no desire to stay up to begin with. He even seemed reluctant to speak with anyone and replied tersely to questions or remarks. What was more surprising was that he, perhaps for the first time in his life since I'd known him, seemed unenthusiastic about work, lukewarm toward the customers. He was even going to close the store three hours before the usual closing time. In addition, when I looked around I was surprised to see that the huge amounts of merchandise on the shelves had been depleted, reduced to just samples. So where did it all go? Oh my God, I hoped that good warm days would not lead to cold humiliating exposure to the elements.

I did not continue with my disquieting musings because a faint smile on Abu Sinn's face hinted, almost explicitly, that it was just a routine procedure for some temporary reason or another. I contented myself with getting off early and the disappointment of missing out on the anticipated evening. On my way out, Muhammad Abu Sinn called me. I returned from the door and he opened the drawer and took out about five pounds, which he pushed toward me, saying, "Take this." It was much more than I had coming to me and I got more worried, especially when he added, "Spend it carefully and look after yourself." I nodded and began to think how to spend the evening most frugally. I was afraid I might spend too much on something silly so I headed for the wikala, thinking maybe I'd have some better luck with Sundus.

At the gate of the wikala I stopped for a short while then went past it to Widad's house. I realized that I felt more comfortable spending the evening in Widad's apartment than in Sundus' room. Widad's apartment was intimate and out of Shawadfi's piercing eyes. Besides I had become used to seeing her crippled daughter and I no longer shuddered when I saw her except when I was completely stoned, and then only for a passing moment.

Nakedness

The door opened. I saw Widad's face, which looked pale, as if she'd never slept in her life. The eyes were dull, the roses on her cheeks had turned into dry, wrinkled lemons and her smile was like a dead locust on the lips. Something strong inside me gave way as if an electric current had been shut off. I felt as if I were fizzling gradually and was actually engulfed in darkness for what seemed like a very long time, even though I had encountered the crude shining light in the corridor leading to the balcony.

I turned to the square parlor to the left and threw myself onto the sofa, leaning my back on the wall weakly. I was surprised to see someone sitting the same way opposite me on a sofa identical to mine. My eyes were riveted on him as my heart raced. He looked exactly like me! It *was* me. It seemed Widad had placed a large broad mirror in the room. Widad came and sat right in front of me and right next to me at the same time. Looking at her was quite painful. She was wearing a black house gown from which her pale white limbs appeared very enticing despite the emaciation, pitiably devoid of vitality. I found my neck in the mirror leaning toward her chest, "What's wrong, Widad?"

It didn't sound like my voice, that which was singing in my chest in a rhythm and tone that pleased me for the first time in my life, as if I was just discovering it that very moment. For I had never been aware of such warmth, kindness, and affection in my voice before.

"Nothing! Is anything wrong with me? It seems I had too much trouble on this trip. It was exhausting. I haven't caught my breath yet. I've just arrived from the railway station. Imagine that! Only now I feel I made it home. Just one moment. I shall be back right away."

She left an imprint of her faint smile on the surface of the mirror and got up, trying to regain some energy. Her joints cracked like dry, crumbling bread. She moaned and stretched and bent her torso backward so hard that she groaned as she righted herself up. She went inside. I lit a cigarette and began to contemplate the rings of smoke as they curled around my head, climbing it like the stratosphere of a planet that the sun was about to get close to. After a short while I heard the sound of the shower water in the bathroom coming down with a refreshing patter. I immediately visualized her body, naked under the rain. The Phillips radio on its wooden shelf was above my head. I got up and turned around and pushed a button and it came on in a thunderous sound full of static and screams. I turned down the volume until it was a barely audible whisper, then I turned the tuning button quickly, skipping past talk and slowing down when it got to music, when Muhammad Qandil's voice came from the ether radiating warmth and confidence in the midst of the plaintive nay, the beat of percussion, and the lively tambourine, singing:

Forgiveness, generous soul!
A lover's rebuke can wound!
The beautiful are generous
And the generous forgive!

I felt about to cry as the tunes penetrated my feelings. From behind the bathroom door came Widad's voice: "Turn it up a little." I did and her voice came again, "A little bit more!" Then her voice came again after a short while, shouting as if ordering her unruly son, "Get the bath towel from the bedroom." My heart beat very fast as I got up in hurried, almost military steps, went into the bedroom and looked around guided by the light coming from the corridor, avoiding looking at the girl who was fast asleep. I saw the bath towel hanging from a clothes hook on the opposite wall next to the bed. I took it and crossed the corridor and simply pushed the bathroom door gently. There she was standing, naked, the water clinging to her body. In that very small area she looked like a luscious kernel within a hard body. She looked like a houri, with her undone hair down, with broad shoulders and chest, a stout trunk and a waist so narrow as if it had been very finely sculpted to separate the borders of two separate yet connected continents. The lower half flowed from a wide semi-circle, with intersecting arches and divided circles, between legs that looked like two large peeled bananas. I almost lost my senses but held on to exaggerated dignity as if I were indeed her son, too shy to look at her. I gave her the bath towel in silence and she took it with a broad grin this time, glancing at me from under her eyelashes with a defiant and mischievous look. When she saw that I was persisting in pretending to be bashful she pulled the bath towel and turned her back on me, "Thanks!" My eyes popped out and my glances rushed like a gondola pushed by intoxicated winds along her amazingly beautiful back, at the lower end of which her buttocks stood like a large knot at the end of two ropes on two marble pedestals. I remained standing without moving until the bath towel spread around her trunk and her hands grabbed it to dry her legs around and in between them. Then she turned suddenly to see me transfixed in the door whereupon she laughed in delight, "Why are you standing there like a statue?"

"I thought you wanted something else!"

She pushed me with one hand while the other held onto the two edges of the bath towel wrapping it around her body. I held her soft white arm and began to feel it. I was tempted to kiss it, so I did. I kept holding it then began to look into her eyes when amazingly the secret candle had lit up deep inside the black pupil, and life had come back to the cheeks and the lips and the neck had grown longer above the broad shoulders. I was surprised to find that she was now totally in my arms, that the towel was now piled like a ball between us. I began to kiss her everywhere from the shoulders to the neck to the lips to the black tresses of her hair to between the breasts then the breasts themselves. I felt that she had completely given in and that her enjoyment was quite obvious everywhere: in her mouth and eyes and the way her body shook at every touch. After a lot of panting I dragged her to the parlor and we sat on the floor. I was tense like a bow, inflamed as if with restrained anger: I could almost knock down the wall. With tense speed I took off all my clothes and threw them wherever then threw myself next to her, preparing for the vicious attack to come after much burning, painful deprivation. The camel went up the hill and tried to go through the eye of the needle. The first crash knocked him down; his burning blood evaporated and his bones became soft: nothing was left except layers of flaccid skin. With extraordinary patience the camel kept thinking how it could change itself into a thin thread to enter the glowing, living dream that had been all spent, but it was no use. Then the camel died.

A very long time passed as I sat there, my head between my knees, my back leaning on the sofa, lost in endless shame, regret, and misery. I came to as a soft and tender hand was patting my back trying to console me like a kindly mother but in a whip-like voice, "Don't worry about it. It is very normal and it happens in the best families. Anyway, only a short while ago you were one hundred percent. I don't know what happened to you. But, let's eat something and drink tea and smoke a little. Maybe!"

We ate a can of salmon with fried eggs, cottage cheese, and cucumbers and gargir until we were full. Then we moved to the balcony that Widad had draped with a heavy curtain. The fire was burning wildly in the brazier because of the wind, while the smell of strong tea escaped through the spout of the teapot placed on top of it. As Widad laid out the cups of tea in front of us she asked, "Do you have any opium?"

"Where would I get it?"

She smiled and took off the gold ring from her finger and inserted the back of her thumbnail inside the inner cavity under the stone and scraped out a reasonable scrap which she divided in two, extending her finger to me with one and inserting the other into her mouth. She began to suck on it and sip tea with great pleasure then got busy cleaning the pipe, stuffing it with tobacco and signing it while I broke the embers and smoothed them. I noticed that I was smoking voraciously and so was she. She was absent minded and I was not totally there myself. We were both quite miserable and neither of us could dispel the misery even though we consoled each other somewhat or perhaps we had intensified each other's dejection. That was what I thought as my eyes settled lethargically on Widad's face as she exhaled profusely through the mouth and nostrils. She set the shisha aside as a prelude to changing the water and cleaning the pipe for another turn, then she stretched her legs on the floor and the front of her thigh rested on my outstretched shins, as if I was sitting cross-legged. She leaned her head on one of the jambs of the balcony door, resting her chin on her chest and went into deep thought, clasping her arms on her chest with her eyelashes drooping on her eyes. She looked very miserable. I tried to avoid looking at her face as I also tried to avoid looking within. I kept trying to think of something that would take us away from the bottom of that deep well. But a strong tension began to crowd out anything that occurred to me and inside me raged a cursed devil of uncontrolled fury that almost pushed me to hit the wall with my fist, to behead a group of thugs in a fight, to get up and lose myself in a dance or a dhikr, to throw myself from this balcony and drop like a clown in the courtyard of the wikala, or to grab Shawadfi by the neck and pound his head into the ground until his brain was smashed.

At that moment the radio let loose an ear-piercingly loud burst of static, then it readjusted to the voice of an announcer who soon quit to let the music flow in harmony as the string instruments started to tug at our emotions and the percussion to calm and regulate our nerves. Then came Farid al-Atrash's voice, enchanting, sad, and plaintive:

Our beloved are no longer with us
We left them and they left us
Neither they nor we are happy!

I felt tears pouring down my cheeks, strong and copious. I looked at Widad's face and it too was totally engulfed in tears coming down in horrible succession. The last percussion note in the song came as if it were the last drop of tears in that fit of weeping that came over us, washing us as we stood in the rain, naked.

In a few moments our eyes cleared and things appeared slightly brighter. Widad got up to change the water of the shisha and I began to clean the pipe and revive the fire in preparation for a new round. When Widad came back from the kitchen, her face was still covered with tears and I knew that she had resumed crying in the kitchen and there she was at it again, crying non-stop. She sat and began to help me, stuffing the pipe with tobacco and signing it but the tears were dropping on the pipe. I gently moved her hand away and with my handkerchief dried her tears, "You're not yourself tonight, Widad. What happened on the trip? Where were you exactly? Don't tell me nothing happened."

Her tears still flowing, she said, "I have never been as disgusted with the world as I have been today. I hated everything that made us cling to it. A despicable world! If you had seen what I've seen today, you'd live your life for the moment, come what may. It's all going to dust. The whole world is worth nothing. What a pity! I haven't lived a single day. I wasted it all in meaningless fretting about nonsense!"

"What did you see today?"

"Nur al-Sabah! My beloved friend, the dearest one to my heart. I went to her because the hospital was on the way. So I said to myself I should stop there. I wish I hadn't, but that's fate. It was God who made me stop there, for her sake."

She burst out crying and couldn't go on talking. I embraced her and rested her head on my chest. I begged her to calm down and tell me what she saw, in detail. She looked at my eyes with some surprise that I had shown interest in Nur al-Sabah whom I didn't even know. Then her surprise increased and she removed her head from my chest and leaned on the door. It seemed that she was about to embark on a long, complicated story and that she would try to make it as short as possible.

The Law of Madness

"You know Nur al-Sabah? Shawadfi told you about her? Certainly! I don't know why he suddenly remembered her now. It was he who reminded me a couple of days ago. He stopped me and asked me how Nur al-Sabah was doing. I told him I hadn't seen her for some time. And right away I missed her and said to myself that perhaps it was a good omen. So long as someone mentioned her, she must be asking for you. She must need you. Who knows? Maybe she was cured or got better. That same night I got an errand near the hospital and I said to myself: girl, this is all God's plan, to get you there without extra trouble, so, you should go see her.

"How's she doing? Horrible! I always visited her whenever I had the money. The poor woman didn't recognize me. They would bring her to me in the guest area or the nurse would accompany me to her room. She would stare at me with unfocused eyes and smile suddenly and say, 'How are you, good friend, and how are the kids? Are they all right? And your father, is he out of jail or not yet? Your mother is here with us in the village and she says hello. I've just seen her. People in this village cannot stand each other any more. They stab each other in the back. Hello! Welcome! How are you? How come we are next door neighbors and I get to see you only once a day?'

"It's all gibberish and hallucination that breaks my heart. I spend half an hour with her and leave her food and fruits and money for the nurses. For days after I go back, I cry whenever I remember her. I plan to make it my last visit. Two or three months later my heart tells me that she recognizes me and doesn't recognize me at the same time. She never uttered my name or mentioned anyone she knew. My heart tells me to go and that this time she will remember my name and if she says it she will be cured and the rest is up to God and me.

"The day before yesterday I went to her. She was physically sick. They said that she was calm and did no harm. She was holding her belly and having pain. She was having pain like a perfectly sane person, talking about pain in her belly. She asked for medicine and food and asked to be seen by the doctor. She washed the dishes and arranged them and served food and made her bed. She was kind to others and treated them all like her children, even the elderly among them she treated as if they were her children. The nurse is my friend. I mean she became my friend. I gave her a nightgown once, a shawl a second time, and the third time some lipstick, that's not counting the money. And I gave her my address. All of that so that she would realize how dear Nur al-Sabah is to me and remember me by my gifts and when she remembered then she would take good care of her. She also befriended Nur and loved her and looked after her and calmed her down and cleaned her and stayed with her for hours talking like a sane person but she didn't remember anything about her name or her family or her town or anything about her past. When the nurse told her her name and town and family she agreed but soon forgot. If the nurse told her a second time a different name and different information she would agree and not remember what she had heard before even after just an hour.

"When her health improved, her mind stayed absent. She asked for food and ate with appetite and her face regained some of its glow. And after she used to walk in the hospital garden, lost and absent-minded, she started going on walks for recreation and to pick some fruit and laugh at her fellow inmates' weird gestures and weirder words.

"In the hospital they don't all suffer from vicious, evil insanity. Some of them are semi-sane. Among them are very sane people who had a hard time surviving among the almost sane and went to the hospital to find comfort among the insane. Among them also are those who feign insanity to escape a death sentence or any crime or vendetta or any catastrophe. All of these I've seen with my own eyes as I walked in the garden with Nur when the devil was toying with her and when she was oblivious to everything.

"The nurse told me a story that would turn an infant's hair gray! One of the bastards who worked with the merchant who supplied the hospital with food and vegetables fooled Nur al-Sabah. He sneaked inside and enticed her to go with him until they went to a far corner between two trees at the end of the day just before all the patients were checked and accounted for. He did the forbidden thing to her. As time went by and as he did that several times she came to think of it as a pleasant children's game. A cunning woman who feigned insanity saw them and she told some of her visitors who reported it to the administration, but they didn't believe them and threw them out and restrained the woman.

"When the pain got to be too much for Nur al-Sabah, she said so. Her mind came back at the peak of pain and she said, 'I am pregnant.' They made fun of her and laughed at her. The nurse was on her day off. All the women gathered around and started helping her with the delivery, causing her great harm. She fell unconscious and bleeding as they dragged her around like a carcass. The hospital people intervened at the last moment and moved her to the treatment ward. The following day the nurse came and looked after her. On the third day I went to see her stretched out on the gurney near the end of her coma. I sat by her side for a long time crying my heart out at her condition and the way she looked. I wondered why Shawadfi would talk about her, why I saw her mother and my mother in a dream, and why I heard that Buri got out of jail. All of that in one day and one night, so that I might come here and see her in that heartbreaking condition!

“Glory be to God! You, God, are my witness. If I tell not the truth, then strike me mute! Nur al-Sabah opened her eyes and saw me beside her. She stared at my face for a long time. The blood came back to her face and gradually she showed signs of gladness. She raised her head by a span of the hand and spoke! Yes, I swear by God the Almighty she said it herself clearly, ‘Widad? Widad?’ in her old voice that I knew quite well and in the same way that I loved! I couldn’t control my joy so I let out a ululation and bent over her. I took her in my arms and kept kissing her as tears of joy drowned me! ‘O my beloved! You have recognized me? Yes, I am Widad your only friend in this world! Thank God! Praise the Lord!’

“But the joy couldn’t last. Her head fell on my arm. She was gone. We turned her; we felt the pulse; we shook her head! It was no use. She was gone! I was too shocked to scream and my broken heart has been wailing ever since.

“But the worst thing was my inability to take her body to bury it next to her mother. This is what really breaks my heart. True, I am penniless, and transporting her by myself would have been a problem but I swear by God I regretted not having her released to me and I don’t know how I came back and left her there. O, dear Nur al-Sabah, how can this be your end and before my own eyes? I wish I never went and never saw you. I wish I hadn’t awakened that day. I was about to throw myself out of the train window. Praised be the One who guided me and kept my sanity until I arrived.

“My heart is broken and torn. Nur’s body is turning into wood in my veins. I’ve had it with this life. I hate the world and love it at the same time. I am so afraid I want to get out of this condition in any way, quickly. Something in my heart tells me, ‘Girl, live the rest of your life without thinking about anything.’ And something else tells me, ‘O God what would my poor daughter do if God remembered me the way He remembered Nur al-Sabah while still so young?’ My mind answers, ‘Forget these worries, woman, you wouldn’t understand better than God Almighty. And He will look after her and would not leave her a lonely orphan.’

“I am consumed with regret now though. If only the dearly departed had stayed conscious for half a day to tell me what happened to her and her mother’s nest egg. They had a lot! Her mother made enough for several lifetimes. And Nur also made a fortune. Three fourths of what Badr al-Said made from selling his land and livestock, and won, gambling, turned into gold jewelry in Nur’s hands, chest, and ears. She sold a little of it as she told me. And actually I didn’t believe her because she and her mother had this habit of hiding things out of fear of the evil eye and to guard against envy. She loved to hoard gold and only wore it when she traveled on business to earn people’s trust. Nur al-Sabah was my bosom buddy and she lied to me but couldn’t go on with it, so she would tell me the truth the following day. She hinted to me before she fell ill that she was planning to buy a house in a distant town to rent it and live off the rent the rest of her life. She thought of opening a fruit store and she thought of opening a coffee house. All these projects needed money, right? She must have had the money somewhere!

“You know something? My heart is telling me that Shawadfi got the whole shebang. He is like a grave that never sends the dead back. Aunt Wadida trusted him. I am willing to bet anything that he fooled her and found out where the money and the gold were. Anyway, what I am certain of is that he has helped Aunt Wadida to invest some of her money with some merchants, with his knowledge. I saw her more than once receiving the profits from vegetable merchants in the market. A few days before she fell ill, Nur al-Sabah was telling me that she planned to talk to Shawadfi about the money. And that bastard never visited her at the hospital or spoke about the money in front of anyone.

“What can I say? I place my trust in God alone. He will look after me.”

Return Trip

Widad was silent for a long time, as if we were at a funeral. I wanted to end this sudden, depressing stillness, so I sat up in front of the brazier and began to blow on the remnants of the burning coal until the flames lit up again. There were still some pipes left so we started smoking them very slowly. Then I found myself saying, "You said something earlier tonight that was very wise. One should not waste a single minute of his life. So, get up and wash your face and comb your hair and change this dress and come back."

She glanced at me in boredom and disgust and started exhaling very slowly as if she didn't want to waste the smoke. I quickly added, "You have wasted many minutes of our lives and added to our worries. Come on! Let's live in the moment; let's forget everything. The living take precedence over the dead."

She nodded in resignation, "Okay," and got up rather lethargically. She went to the bathroom where she washed her face, put on perfume and makeup and put on a sleeveless, low-cut, see-through nightgown that revealed all details of her body. As soon as she came in like that, armies of ants rose and invaded all my veins. My heart beat so fast it was like a flint that set my blood on fire and energized my body.

We started smoking again. I felt I was a totally new person, as if the mention of death had given me a shot at living, as if I planned to defy the death that was lying in wait for me. Things suddenly looked different, clearer and sharper. I began to feel that I was willing to be tolerant of many things, to disregard many things and to accept events or surprises without the least objection.

Everything inside me became harder and more rigid. The boiling in the blood caused anxiety to evaporate; the veins got inflamed and swollen and left their resting places in preparation for an intimate union. We smoked the remaining three pipes in about half an hour and through the kissing and hugging, rolling and crazy, intoxicated trampling we went from one high hill to a higher hill and from ravines to plateaus and from heights to plains, peaks to foothills; it became clear to the camel in all stoned clarity that it could not indeed go through the eye of the needle. The failure was not abject but the success was not complete. I actually was having a dialogue, actually wrestling was more like it, with the corpse of Nur al-Sabah who, in spite of my having neither seen nor heard, would not forgive me or Widad for trying to attain pleasure on her body or to violate her memory. She was turning in my arms like someone degraded, defeated. Even the copious water from the shower could not snatch Nur al-Sabah's body from my arms or erase her from my head.

I turned off the shower tensely and called out, "Widad."

She came, with puffed body and hair. I asked her, "If we leave soon can we catch Nur al-Sabah before they bury her?"

Widad's eyes widened and she said, "God knows; but what do you mean?"

I began to dry my body, "We can go and claim her body."

"Do you have any money?"

"I have train fare. As for expenses for transporting the body, I have an idea. What do you say we take the press train?"

"That'd be great. Okay. We can stay up until it's time. Get out; let me take a bath. Put on the teapot. It's a fantastic idea. I'll never forget this favor!"

With the call for the dawn prayer we were on our way to the railroad station. Widad was dressed modestly under dawn's gray cloak. I was preoccupied with thinking how to convince some people to transport the body from the hospital to Damanhour for free.

For the first time I found out that the Khanka hospital was different from Abbasiya hospital even though people use 'Khanka' to refer to both of them. They even used the word to refer to anyone with even the slightest mental disorder and to people who spoke slightly out of line, by which they meant that such a person was crazy and deserved to be committed to Khanka. When we arrived at the Abbasiya hospital, Widad told me that the Khanka hospital, located in a town of the same name, about an hour away by car from Cairo, was set aside for the most serious cases, for those patients who posed a danger to others.

At the hospital gate we found many people arguing with the gatekeeper. We asked him about the body of the woman who died the day before whose name was Nur al-Sabah Turk Khan and he said a man inside had come to claim the body saying he was one of her relatives. Widad gave him a silver coin and he let us through pointing to the ward where they moved the dead until preparations of burial were finalized. At the door of that ward our attention was drawn to a man sitting on the lowest step of the staircase, leaning his elbows on his knees and his head between his palms, totally absorbed as if he had died and was totally isolated from everything around him. He looked so miserable it was a pain to look at him. The pool of tears had left a shiny wax-like layer on his face. His features showed signs of deep humiliation. I felt drawn to him and I bent over to see better. He looked familiar. I drew nearer and stood observing him. He raised his head to look at us. It was Buri. Widad gasped, beating her chest, too dumbfounded to talk at first, "Buri? In the name of God, Compassionate, Most Merciful!"

He murmured as he got up feebly, "Widad? How are you, Widad?"

He rushed to her arms, hugging and kissing her. Then he burst out crying like a child who had found his mother after being lost for a long time.

"When did you get out, Buri?"

"A few days ago. I wish I hadn't. It seems I must go back to jail. I don't have anyone left in the world. Freedom is meaningless. Nur al-Sabah is dead, Widad. They say she had childbed fever. My God! Childbed fever only happens to pregnant women who give birth in bad circumstances. So when did that happen to Nur al-Sabah? Don't you think they killed her here, Widad? I hear they kill patients here with injections and electricity if they give them a hard time. But, my God, Widad, you used to visit her; was she dangerous? Did she have fits of agitation? I don't think so. Nur al-Sabah was not crazy. She was in shock. I place my trust in God alone. He will look after me."

He went on crying with Widad in tow like a chorus, as if they were in a weeping contest. I stood between them awkwardly, not knowing what to do. I fought off tears and tried to stop my lower lip from quivering. With great difficulty and in a trembling voice I said, "Why were you sitting here like that? Are you the one who came to claim the body?"

He waved his arms and said in the tone of a helpless child, "They kicked me out! The criminal bastards. They wouldn't release the body to the family. They are afraid their crime would be found out."

"How did they deny your claim? What reason did they give?"

"I don't have an identity card!"

"Oh God! I should've listened! Everyone said I should get myself an identity card."

"I have papers to prove who I am."

We asked to meet the director of the hospital. I showed him the papers I had, which included a birth certificate, a criminal record status sheet, a primary school certificate, and some papers from the institute. I also showed him my name in print at the end of a half-column article in which the writer Amin al-Kholi referred to me as "man of letters," ustaz so and so. I told the director Nur al-Sabah's story in as much detail as I knew. He seemed convinced about releasing her to us. He said, "Did you bring a truck?"

The three of us burst out crying pitiably right away. We told him through our tears that our financial situation was not good and that we had to do that humanitarian deed to bury the body next to her mother. The man took pity on us and reassured us that he would get an ambulance to transport the body at the government's expense. And indeed the man spent more than two hours in telephone calls, shouting and yelling until an ambulance actually came and papers were drawn up which the three of us signed. We were also given a burial permit. The body was brought, wrapped in an old sheet, rigid like a slab of ice. We rode with the body and the ambulance sped off. On the way back I cried more profusely than both of them, which surprised me as I could find no precedent for it in my life thus far.

Widad jumped off the ambulance at the wikala followed by Buri then me. Shawadfi got up and confronted us suspiciously, "What's this, busters?"

Widad shouted, "We brought Nur al-Sabah's body."

In an affectionate submissive voice, Shawadfi said, "Good! May God reward you in the hereafter! Zainhum Al-Atris!" he called out and Zainhum hurried out of his room.

"May it be good, Shawadfi!"

In a soft, hopeful voice Shawadfi said, "Please prepare your room. Nur al-Sabah's body has arrived. May God repay you and keep you healthy." Then his large, rough fingers wiped a tear that had fallen on his cheek against his will.

Sheikh Zainhum shouted, "There's no god but God! To God we belong and to Him we sall return. Make room, guys. We are ready, Shawadfi."

At that moment the driver and his two colleagues in the military-style khaki uniforms and caps had pulled the stretcher with the body from the ambulance. One of them held it from outside the ambulance and the other from the other side until he also got off. They started, one of them giving his back to the stretcher and the other behind him holding the other end. They went through the courtyard to Sheikh Zainhum's room and went in. Right away a warm and sad resonant wailing voice rang out from the sheikh's room: it was the wife and the eldest daughters, acknowledging the somber occasion. Then soon after that Etaita emerged from her room, wailing, followed by Dumyana on the opposite side. Qut al-Qulub, Widad's elderly grandmother shuffled down the stairs wailing in a hoarse, pained voice, "Your mother's heart! "This is unbelievable, apple of my eye!"

In a few moments the courtyard had filled with heartbreaking wails in a large demonstration that, though it created a lot of commotion and agitation among the neighbors, gave Shawadfi a lot of pride and contentment. When the two ambulance operators emerged with the empty stretcher on their way to the ambulance, Shawadfi met them and gave each of them a silver ten piaster coin while shaking their hands, then went around to shake the driver's hand and give him a similar amount. Then we all got busy following the wailing and crying and couldn't hear the ambulance as it left.

It was still late morning and some wikala residents had not left for work yet. That was why Sheikh Zainhum's room filled up with many women from the wikala and some neighboring houses, some of whom had never heard of Nur al-Sabah. Shawadfi's mastaba and the clearing beyond the gate, though expansive, filled up with people from nobody knows where, crouching or squatting. Sheikh Zainhum tapped the ground with his crutch and said in a somber, trembling voice, "Listen, folks, God will provide! The girl doesn't have a shroud and she hasn't been washed yet. This old sheet will not do!"

Right away Shawadfi pulled a large handkerchief from under his pillow. He spread it on the ground before Sheikh Zainhum in a theatrical gesture by waving his hand toward the handkerchief, saying, "Come on guys!" then he put a ten-piaster coin on it. Zainhum twisted and turned, reaching into his inner pants pocket, through the opening in the gallabiya and the tattered pants, taking out a ten-piaster coin which he threw on the handkerchief. Thus the men's bodies twisted and turned as the hands reached for the handkerchief with ten-piaster coins and quarter-pound notes. When everybody settled down completely Sheikh Zainhum got up, bunched the handkerchief in his hand and said, "Ramadan Eraiga, come with me."

Ramadan got up right away and followed him. As an indication that he was busy thinking and wishing to concentrate, Shawadfi pulled the brazier and stirred the burning cobs, adding new ones, and placed the tea mug in the middle and began to roll a cigarette from the sabaris pouch with the pungent smell. As he squatted on the mastaba, holding the tea mug and shaking it over the fire, he was able to send several men to various places for different tasks. In a few minutes the fabric for the shroud was in the hands of the midwife and we heard it being ripped and cut to measure. Buri and others were done digging the grave and preparing it. Sayyed Zanati had secured a coffin from somewhere and the undertaker arranged for a Qur'an reciter.

The courtyard thundered with screaming voices which erupted all at once as the body was being moved to the coffin, then the sound rose even louder as it surrounded the coffin moving slowly in the courtyard on the shoulders of Buri, Ramadan Eraiga, Sayyed Zanati, and the undertaker. The screaming accompanied the coffin following it as we walked toward the grave in a small dignified procession that was quite interesting. In front of the grave, Sheikh Zainhum preceded us and led the prayer calmly and with enviable dignity.

Upon our return and until the evening the washwater sprinkled on the courtyard ground still smelled of cheap soad and carbolic acid. Some mats had been taken out of the rooms and spread on the floor and topped with cushions, pillows, and other items that some neighbors of the wikala had sent. On one such cushion sat a blind Qur'an reciter wearing clothes so dirty that his turban was almost black. But he had a strong, angelic voice with notes so sharply enunciated they felt like a blade cutting through the hearts and nerves of the listeners, taking them up all the way to the seventh heaven and down to the bottom of the earth, as though they were feathers in the midst of a storm. We were a group of men sitting like one family on the mat around the Qur'an reciter, bowing our heads in submission and mumbling prayers for forgiveness and repeating the declaration of faith, followed by deep sighs. Between the reciting sessions there was a lot of talk recounting memories of Nur al-Sabah, her captivating beauty, the sweetness of her temperament, her politeness, and her youth, which she hardly got to enjoy. In a tone that sounded sincere, Shawadfi said, "Thank God we were able to do our duty. She was a good girl even though she lived a life of pain and sorrow. I swear by God Almighty, people, that my heart breaks into little pieces when I see someone coming back to his family and folks after an absence. So you can imagine what seeing a dead body's return after an absence does to me. It melts my soul. I am willing to sell all my possessions to see that body honored. Shaming a living human being is a sin that God does not accept. So imagine what shaming a dead body would be."

Sheikh Zainhum picked up the thread and he gave us a speech about the value of loyalty in God's eyes, the value of neighborliness, respect for long friendship, compassion, and mutual affection. And how his sheikh and leader Al-Atris, God have mercy on him, used to say this and that on such and such a matter. The Qur'an reciter resumed his recitation of a portion of the Book. He concluded his recitation with some short suras after which he called on everyone to recite the Fatiha. We all raised our palms in prayer in a very somber, submissive way. The undertaker got up to accompany the reciter to his house. Ramadan Eraiga left to commit or plan a new crime. Shawadfi went to recline on the mastaba as usual and everybody went their separate ways. I invited Buri to spend the night in my room but he insisted on leaving. It never occurred to me that Widad had invited him until I went out late at night to go to the bathroom across the courtyard and saw their shadows together on the edge of the balcony enveloped in light gray smoke.

Black Dawn

Susi Street and the surrounding area were quite desolate. This was what I first saw as soon as I went beyond the Administration building. The morning was not like previous mornings. There was an unmistakable humid gloom enveloping the buildings, pavements, the asphalt of the road, and the people, even in the pale sunlight devoid of any warmth despite the red sun visible directly above the Administration building.

Traffic was slow and people moved about in a bored and lethargic manner. Even the donkeys and horses drawing carts and carriages had their ears and heads lowered and their eyelids drooping as if they were being driven to the slaughterhouse. The government employee effendis had rolled newspapers under their arms and some of them were looking at the headlines as they walked slowly, confident that others would avoid colliding with them. The workers, craftsmen, and salesmen gathered around ful and ta'miya stands chewing their food mechanically, each keeping to himself and avoiding starting a conversation with the person next to them. The older students were moving individually rather than in groups. It was as if everyone had been dealt a secret, disabling blow that dispersed dwellers of the same neighborhood who used to wait for each other or even pass by each other's houses to walk together and join the other neighborhood youth in a beautiful, fresh procession to Mu'ati Secondary School or the Agricultural School on Mahmudiya Canal or the Vocational School or the Teachers Institute or Secretary School. Today they were walking in such feigned enthusiasm and fake preoccupation that if one of them caught up with another, they'd exchange greetings of the morning as one of them hurried to go ahead of the other, as if to prove that they were not together. Thus everyone looked hurried, panting, confused, and unrelated to the others. As for the young children, their faces did not look as fresh as they did everyday: most of them were frowning and tearful as if each of them had received a beating just before going out. So what happened to the city today? It was obvious that a great catastrophe had befallen everyone while in the wikala we had been busy burying Nur al-Sabah and eulogizing her. Most likely that catastrophe was even more recent.

At the Bosfor coffeehouse I ate a ful sandwich and had a tea with milk and smoked two of the Belmont cigarettes out of the five that I had bought a little earlier. I looked at the clock on the wall in the coffeehouse. It was close to nine in the morning. I was sure that Muhammad Abu Sinn must have opened the store by now, lit the frankincense, set up the glass cases on the sides of the door and sat down to peruse *al-Akhbar* newspaper. The image of him, sitting at an angle, looking at the newspaper reminded me of the paper, for the catastrophe that must have befallen the city must also have been covered by the newspaper in a small corner of the page, away from news of the president and the government. There was a newsstand next to the coffeehouse and papers were hung on lines to which they were attached with clothespins. There was a red banner headline: "Muslim Brotherhood Dissolved." The whole front page was devoted to the story. All the columns had titles in large black letters, underlined. The page was filled with photos of bearded faces wearing fezes, turbans, and skullcaps, with scarred, gray prayer marks clearly visible on the foreheads giving the features a touch more piety than militancy or rigidity. I put off reading the news until I got to the store where I could read it at a more leisurely pace.

I turned on Susi Street. Some stores were still closed. That was unusual as owners made sure they were there early to sprinkle water in front of their stores and to invoke good omens by reciting quasi-magical formulas that each recited to himself. It was unlikely that they had overslept until ten in the morning. Muhammad Abu Sinn's store was also closed for the first time in his life apart from on market days. I was certain right away that Muhammad Abu Sinn had been arrested the night before or maybe at dawn today. I started shaking and my mouth became dry out of fear of the impending danger. I began looking around suspiciously, trying to deny any connection to the store in front of which I was standing. Then I laughed at myself in a sort of bitter way. A feeling that I might be arrested later came over me. I could see the various forms of torture that I'd heard about in political prisons, especially for those accused, rightly or wrongly, of trying to overthrow the government. A rather unsettling thought occurred to me that I should run away as soon as I could and disappear from this city right away. But where to? If I went to my village, I'd still be within reach of the police. But why worry about escaping before I found out what really happened? At that point an even stronger thought occurred to me: *If I look frightened, I'll arouse the suspicion of that secret person or entity following me who knows everything about me.* I found that thought comforting: whoever was following me also knew the truth about me, hence, he knew that I was not a member of the Society and did not partake in any of its activities even though I sat with dangerous key members who had organizational and operational capacities. It didn't take me long to discover how naïve I was, so fear made me walk around aimlessly.

Thus I found myself taking the short cut past the fruit juice store to Sagha Street whose glittering gold and jewelry showcases in the stores on both sides, beyond the stores that sold grains, sacks, and sack cloth, used to delight me. I found myself turning automatically to Hamdi al-Zawawi's store. Amazingly, it seemed that Hamdi's days proceeded with clock-like precision: there he was spreading loaves of bread on a ful tray, about to have his breakfast. As soon as he saw me blocking the opening of the door he hit his forehead with his palm as if to say, "What a good guy you are!" Instead he said, "You always come right on time." As usual I jumped on to the counter right in front of the ful tray. He jumped out and stood by the door shouting, "Another tray, Handouqa," then jumped inside again. He broke the bread and took a piece with which he stirred the ful on the plate, releasing the srong aroma of linseed oil, lime, and the mix of spices. With his mouth full he said, "Did you see what happened?"

"What, exactly, happened?"

"It was the blackest dawn for this town. The government arrested all members of the Muslim Brotherhood and every bearded guy, young and old, at dawn. If only they had arrested them secretly or discreetly! Rather the government used rough and violent tactics. It searched every corner of every house, turning things upside down, making a mess and hurling insults and obscenities at the women and kicking them. The women screamed for help and the children were scared to death and are still frightened. Many painful things! I swear I cried until my head split when I saw, only a few minutes ago, Muhammad al-Khawalqa's children going to school, walking like beaten, humiliated chicks, looking grim and miserable. He's our neighbor. We were awakened by the noise they made when they arrested him. His children and the neighbor's children were screaming in great fear as they saw the policemen storming their bedrooms, humiliating their mother and cruelly beating their father, throwing him into the patrol wagon. How many young children saw their fathers being kidnapped, their mothers kicked to stop them screaming, and their houses messed up and their privacy violated? It's horrible! God would never be pleased with this. Is He going to let them do that to people? I don't think so. His revenge will be horrendous. Your friend, Muhammad Abu Sinn. That sweet man. You should've seen what happened to him at dawn as he got up to perform his ablutions. If he had been one of the outlaws of the south, or even a mass murderer, they wouldn't have grabbed him like that or beaten him or dragged him on the floor with rifle butts and nightsticks!

What's happening to people under the revolution? Suppose they tried to kill President Abdel Nasser and suppose they have a secret organization training young men to fight and suppose they are planning a revolution. You have the power! Arrest them and try them with respect within the law. They are Muslims like you, not Jews and not Englishmen. Besides, why arrest elderly men and students and pupils in school? Sayyed al-Elaishy, for instance, will lose the whole academic year and God knows how many other years. But, I tell you, it's none of our business. It's not as if the country belonged to our father. But it's the children that break my heart. Tomorrow they'll grow up hating religion, the Qur'an, the fatherland, and any government. They will even develop an aversion to the word 'revolution'! If I were Gamal Abdel Nasser, I wouldn't have been concerned about anybody. Why concern yourself, Gamal? You made the revolution and people supported you and loved you and are happy with you, so, why give them such a hard time? Is it a war? Go ahead, eat! Let's enjoy the food we have. Who knows if we'll find it tomorrow!"

Then a long deep silence fell upon us for a long time, interrupted by the sound of crunching green onions as we continued to eat with extraordinary appetite. Suddenly, Hamdi al-Zawawi snapped his finger as though he had remembered something very important, then said, "By the way, the house of your relative was searched. Hagg Mas'oud, your cousin's husband looked very funny. He was not sad because they took his oldest two sons or because they kicked everybody. He was wailing and crying over the jars of ghee and mish that they broke and the sacks of potatoes and lentils that they tore open as they searched for weapons and ammunition. This is such a stupid and foolish government! They think arresting people at dawn is a secret. They forget that the alleys from which they themselves have come are so closely packed with people that if someone at the end of the alley tossed in bed those at the other end, awake or asleep, would feel it. Everyone in the alley knows who has a toothache, which woman is giving birth, and which man beat his wife for such and such a reason. It was as if the search was taking place in our own house. The government, in its idiocy, forgot that people are all connected. So and so is a Muslim Brother and I am not; I am with the revolution, but that so and so is ultimately my relative; my cousin, my brother-in-law, my classmate or my childhood friend. That stupid bitch of a government hasn't thought of that. It hasn't considered that it cannot take someone from his house to jail as if it were pulling a hair from dough. First, because he is not a hair, and second, because his family is not dough. The person they arrest will be bruised and that will leave bruises in those around him. Have they thought of the impact of watching these heartbroken kids walking to their schools? A pox on those who watch and don't feel their pain. Screw the revolution that humiliates children!"

I was quite moved by what Hamdi al-Zawawi was saying. For, despite his apparent nonchalance and his usually cheerful countenance, he was extremely angry, even though he loved the July Revolution and was quite captivated by Gamal Abdel Nasser. At that moment there was quite a buzz in my head, as if dozens of people were fighting very far away, making a resounding but indistinct noise. My mind was trying to get through that din to hold on to a glimmer of peace in the hope of gaining some reassurance. I began to smoke in a sort of oblivious pleasure after everything appeared totally black in my eyes. Going back to my village seemed extremely loathsome to me but inevitable. Everything was conspiring to force me to go back. At least there would be no Shawadfi suffocating me, demanding rent and insisting on knowing everything about me and my life. But it didn't take me long for my head to spin with vertigo, as if it had hit a hard wall, the moment I realized that in this city I could go hungry and naked, sleeping on the pavement like garbage without a scandal, but I couldn't do those things in my village. In my mind's eye I saw my mother sitting in the open door of our house, hiding from sight behind the door jamb, watching the road, waiting for the arrival of an unknown person who never came. I saw her placing her hand on her cheek like someone sentenced to life in misery, wearing her faded black gallabiya, wrapped in her drab shawl, with aged features in her dazzling white face, elongated as if it were a rabbit held by the ears, sighing bitterly whenever she saw an effendi passing by, be he a school teacher or an employee of the health center or the agricultural society. I saw myself running away, evading her as I used to by sneaking into our house from the other door overlooking a narrow alley separating our house from that of my cousins. I had found out from her increasing sighs that my failure in school was the reason for all the bitterness. She had wished to see me an effendi with an official diploma from the government. That wish was about to be granted, and would have had it not been for my disappointing misfortune. I was surprised to find the house smaller and darker than I imagined or could remember. The room we slept in was dirty, small, dark, and damp with walls that had been blackened by the soot from the cooking hearth and the kerosene lamp. It had a stifling smell of urine, old sweat, and rot. The mat was frayed at the edges and in the middle; the old papyrus stalks had grown very hard from age and filth and they left marks on our skin that were visible on our faces, thighs, and ribs as if they were permanent birthmarks. The pillows were hard and oily and the blanket was fortified with pieces of sackcloth and old rags. The fighting began in the dead of the night when our exhausted bodies longed for one hour of deep sleep, at which point huge armies of bedbugs, lice, and fleas moved in squads and circles and concentrations. They entrenched themselves in the inner stitches of our clothing and everywhere in the pillows, to wage marauding raids on our emaciated, exhausted bodies which would toss and turn all night long on relentless fires of stings, pinching, and punching. As our hands extended to scratch, the tips of our fingers would hit their ranks, safe and satiated on our blood, soft and smooth. Our clothes were always speckled with red blood, for our bodies would turn and rub against the floor or the papyrus stalks as they defended themselves, squishing the insects and spilling the blood they had looted from us. The room never saw the sun, and the bedding, if we could call it that, would stay on the roof all day long and the insects would escape from it to safe spots inside the house, until they gathered again and multiplied on our bodies like herds of sheep grazing in a no-man's land. My old wretched, destitute father understood politics. He stayed up at night holding the kerosene lamp from which he lit rolled-up strips of newspapers and passed their flame on the corners of the room and over the mastaba on which he slept. As for the smells in our house, they were many and they stopped up the nose: the smell of the powder distributed by the health center to spray the bedding and the rest of the house; the smell of the blood of the squished and burned bedbugs, sharp and disgusting; the smell of the paper burning; and the smell of the farting young brothers, fast asleep from fatigue, feeling nothing after their skin had thickened so the pinching didn't affect them, and after running out of blood, the stinging no longer bothered them. My father, who understood politics and who at one time was a local leader of the Wafd party in our village but who lost his post after all parties were dissolved, said that Muhammad Hasanain Haykal's weekly article "Frankly Speaking" was not totally frank except in burning a whole squad of bedbugs since its flame rose in the corner, peeling off the bugs from the mud of the wall, causing them to burn in the heart of the flame and we would hear their crackle. My father attributed that, with great pride and confidence, to the fact that Haykal's picture, published with the article, suggested to the bugs that he had been sent by Gamal Abdel Nasser to say that the one who ordered the English occupier to leave our country was just as capable of evacuating and ending the bedbugs, lice, and fleas' occupation of our bodies, bedding, and homes. Men from the health department sometimes came to our houses carrying a big spray like the one we used to water our plants and sprinkle our floors during our well-off days before the revolution, and they would spray our homes and bedding. If you gave them a piaster or two, they left you some of the liquid in a bottle. My father would thank them enthusiastically as if delivering a political speech, saying that that war of attrition should be continuously waged against the occupying enemy until Abdel Nasser came to the rescue with his massive armies and his heroes the valiant Free Officers.

I saw the sofa in the guest room to which I used to sneak every night to escape the hellish room where I tossed and turned from the cold on its bare wood all night long. The last night I slept on that sofa the whole house was sad for me: my mother didn't remove her hand from her cheek and my father turned his eyes away whenever our eyes met. My brother who was learning carpentry boasted that he would have a skill on hand as insurance against poverty after I used to boast about my education in the city. The other brother who was learning to be a tailor was trying to win me over so I would divulge to him my experience with city women, movies, and bicycle riding which they were sure were the causes of my going bad. My brothers who were working as day laborers in the large estate looked at me with disappointment, for they were waiting for the day that I would be employed and get a monthly salary from which they'd pay the grocer and buy clothes. At dawn that day I sneaked out absolutely penniless. I walked six kilometers to the train station in a neighboring village. I took the train, prepared for all eventualities. The train was completely empty, so no one knew I had gone on board. I managed to hide from the conductor in a washroom until Disuq where I got off. I walked back along the tracks and got out of an opening in the barbed wire fence at a street downtown.

I walked around aimlessly and passed by the mosque of Sidi Ibrahim al-Disuqi. I felt he was calling me so I went in to the ablution fountains where I cleaned myself, performed my ablutions, and then went over to the prayer niche and performed the morning prayers. Then I sat next to the pulpit feeling an unprecedented inner peace. In front of me were dozens of students from the religious institute squatting on wooden crosslike stands in great enthusiasm accompanied by intermingling sounds of recitation and running saliva. Some bodies had stretched out in the prayer area and were fast asleep in peace. I looked around a little then extended my legs and lay down on my back with my hands clasped under my head contemplating the domed ceiling adorned with intersecting decorative lines in brightly glowing and delightful red, green, and blue colors. It didn't take me long to fall into blissful sleep rocked by the friendly sounds of the finger cymbals of licorice root drink vendors, jingles of candy vendors, calls of various other vendors and dervishes, the rumbling of wheels, and songs from a radio. Then I felt myself drifting upward from the well of sleep and opened my eyes to the touch of a kindly hand as if it were gently helping me out of the depths. The rows of men getting ready for prayers had formed and there was a rising hubbub. I ran to the ablution fountain and got back in time for the collective noon prayer, then went out with many of those leaving the mosque.

I went directly to a street next to the railway station, then turned on to a side alley at the beginning of which was the office of Abd al-Aziz al-Khibbi, the lawyer, in a damp apartment on the first floor below street level. To the right as one entered there was a room and a parlor right in front with a desk and four chairs that at one time were upholstered but were now quite tattered with broken springs with sunken seat cushions which made sitting on one of them for more than ten minutes excruciatingly painful. On the door of the room was written one word on a black sign, "Lawyer." The door was open and in the room was a much bigger desk and good, clean leather chairs. There was a large glass bookcase filled with bound volumes. On the desk were piles of files, a leather desk cover, a wooden blotter, a crystal inkwell, a letter opener, a ruler, and quills and pens. The room was always empty except for a few moments in the morning and the evening when it would be full of peasants and elders who had eternal cases that would never be settled and they could be heard arguing heatedly.

As for the desk in the parlor facing the street door, that was where Tawhid al-Maghrabi with his fat and prosperous body sat. Tawhid had a round white ruddy face with compact features that made his big eyes appear small. He had an attractive double chin, a dimple in the middle of the chin, and two dimples in his puffed cheeks. He was the closest to my father in looks. He was quick to laugh, quick witted, and quick to capture paradoxes, ironies, turns of phrase, and innuendos. His laughter usually started with a wheezing sound that soon gave way to resounding guffaws, accompanied by a reddening in the face while thinking of an appropriate retort which never missed its mark. He always spoke to the point, and politely, no matter what. He always dressed meticulously: a necktie with a gold clasp that looked as if it were carved on his chest, expensive looking cufflinks, and English wool jacket and pants. His short fez and his jacket were hung on a clothes rack behind him as he sat in his shirt and cross-like suspenders. Men like him had to master the art of looking like effendis faithfully and religiously so that they wouldn't give genuine effendis any chance to find fault with them as outsiders.

That was Tawhid al-Maghrabi, my cousin, husband to Aisha, my oldest paternal uncle's daughter. He was a lawyer's clerk but knew more than his boss about the law, how to deal with clients, the kinds of problems they had, and the kinds of lawsuits to encourage them to file so that they could be fleeced for the longest time. He was also quite widely read even though his formal education had ended at primary level. He read al-Aqqad, Taha Hussein, Mazini, Manfaluti, Ghazali, and Khalid Muhammad Khalid. He bought all the newspapers and magazines of different kinds and read them with an amazing speed. In addition, he had his own well-stocked library at home from which he lent books to my father whenever he went back to the village on Thursday afternoon before returning to his work on Saturday morning. He had debates with preachers whether they were in agreement or not, always trying to convince them that they were hasty or wrong or missing this or that point. Candidates for elected offices and notables sought his support in case they needed it for whatever reason. He smoked at least a hundred cigarettes, the flat Cotarelli kind, a day. He would take two or three puffs on the cigarette after it reached the halfway mark and toss it, then light another one right away with his gasoline-filled lighter. His guests, even non-smokers, were constantly offered cigarettes. He also insisted on offering his clients and guests tea and coffee which were supplied by a coffeehouse on the corner of the main street, so that his clients would take their time and speak their minds which gave him the chance to tighten the noose around their necks. He would convince them that this or that lawsuit would result, at best, in a prison sentence of a few years rather than capital punishment. He would say that, not as someone negotiating about retainers or fees but as a kind brother who was on their side with their best interests at heart. He always called the client "our son" or "uncle" so and so and convinced them to sign the contract, pay a retainer and fees, revenue stamps, bribes for clerks and record-keepers, and tips for messengers and office boys. In a few minutes all of that would be turned into an elegant, typed file, then moved carefully and placed on the lawyer's desk as a new source of income.

I had visited my cousin several times with my father and he had been very welcoming and took us to his apartment in a distant alley east of the city where we had lunch. My cousin Aisha was delighted. I visited him by myself three times during all my years of studying in Damanhour and noticed that he hardly welcomed me at all but rather neglected me for a long time. Then he would ask about the family and how I was doing in a serious and arrogant tone of voice. At the end he'd ask if there was anything he could do for me and when I assured him that I was just visiting, he would give me a silver shilling and ask me to say hello. I never liked to visit him except under extraordianary circumstances as happened that day after the harrowing night.

When I went in he had just come back from court and was reading the newspaper as he drank his coffee. When he felt my shadow approaching, he raised his head smiling his usual congenial smile and was on the point of standing up to greet me. Then it seemed that he remembered suddenly that I was a rotten bully of a boy who had beaten his teacher and got expelled from school, to the disappointment of the whole family. Suddenly also there appeared on his face the results of the meetings my father had had with him during which he complained about the pain I caused his spine. Thus he shook hands with me unenthusiastically with the tips of his fingers, the smile disappearing from his lips in the meantime. Then he withdrew his hand from mine and pointed at the chair as if giving me permission to sit down. I sat next to the desk. He picked up the pack of cigarettes and was about to proffer it toward me, then thought better of it and took a cigarette for himself and lit it, took a sip of coffee, and resumed reading the newspaper, knitting his brow and squinting behind his thick prescription glasses. I was vexed because I needed to smoke a cigarette even though I had decided to turn it down if he offered me one, pretending that I didn't smoke and that my bad character was just a false rumor. But now that he did what he did and proved to me that he thought I had such a bad character no matter how much I tried to deny it or how good I really was, I found myself reaching very brazenly into the open pack, taking a cigarette then taking the lighter and lighting it. Then very insolently and haughtily I crossed my legs, sat back, and began to smoke voraciously in a pleasurable, defiant gesture. I had made up my mind to answer him with the utmost rudeness if he tried to hurt my feelings by word or glance. Luckily he didn't and ignored the matter totally by going on reading, even though the expression on his face betrayed extreme annoyance and vexation. I planned to leave immediately after finishing the cigarette without shaking his hand or taking my leave, but he soon folded the paper and drew a faint smile on his full lips that looked identical to those of his mother, my aunt. He sighed and said in sorrow, "Okay. What's new with you, wretch?"

"Nothing. I was going to Damanhour so I said to myself I should stop because I haven't seen you in four or five. . . ."

He ignored my lie.

"But why travel to Damanhour today?"

"Ustaz Tariq al-Shubashi, principal of the Agricultural School is from our village as you know. He promised to submit a petition on my behalf and try to get me admitted back into the institute now that I have been disciplined for a whole year and learned the error of my ways."

That had never occurred to me before that moment; I don't even know how or why I said it. But my cousin Tawhid seemed to have hit upon an idea that had escaped him until now and he seemed to like it now that he'd discovered it: "That makes a lot of sense! Tell him that Tawhid, son of my aunt, says a very special hello and that he will never forget this favor and will return it, God willing, on joyous occasions!"

Then he got up, gathered the pile of newspapers and magazines and placed it under his arm. He put the lighter in the inside pocket of his jacket, leaving the pack of cigarettes because he had more than one in his pocket and more at home. He left the office calling the office boy and instructing him to open the office and sprinkle its floor at exactly five o'clock. He walked ahead of me with the office boy following. I tarried a little and quickly took the pack of cigarettes and put it in my pocket and caught up with them at the door. I walked beside him as my heart beat in hope and fear of a night that I had not prepared for. Near the station he stopped: "You're going to take the train, of course. You only have a quarter of an hour! Write me a letter as soon as you get there and tell me what happened with Ustaz Shubashi. Here's a quarter of a pound to tide you over. See you. Goodbye!"

I clutched the quarter and shook hands with my cousin and went directly to the ticket window to catch the Damanhour train that arrived early in the evening.

I saw all of that as I sat cross-legged on Hamdi al-Zawawi's counter, smoking and drinking tea in confusion and uncertainty. I was brought back by Hamdi's waving of his arm before my face and by his voice: "Hey! Where'd you go? You must be thinking about jail." I came to with a shudder, but it soon became clear to me that jail was a much more merciful fate or at least not worse than going back home. At that moment I sat up and got off the counter and shook hands with Hamdi. Then I walked confidently, staring with defiant looks at any policeman I could come across.

The Well and its Cover

The news hit me like a large rock falling on my head and knocking me off balance. I almost beat my chest like a woman shouting, "Woe is me!" but I handled the shock with a faint smile by which I tried to conceal a fire that rose in my chest. I found myself looking at Shawadfi, summoning my utmost ability to disapprove: "Have you no fear of God? Why are you spreading this rumor?"

Shawadfi roared with laughter like a mischevious child, "God be praised! Go see for yourself. Maybe then you'll believe it."

"Widad? Married al Buri? How?"

"I don't know! What's so strange about it?"

"It doesn't fit! Cover too small, pot too big!"

"Now you're talking! Exactly, young man. That's what's needed. The cover falls into the pot."

"In that case, it's no cover, then. Both of them need a cover."

"Forget this mumbo-jumbo and go get the wedding sweets. Tonight they celebrate the end of the first week. The successor has ridden at the head of the procession and the mulid will never end!"

"That's the last thing I could imagine. But how did it happen behind our backs? They are very careful, those two."

"You've been missing in action these days. For some time now, you've been distracted and abstracted. I wonder who's abducted your brain? You're hiding something these days. If you reveal it to me, you'd be doing good, not least to yourself. If you hold it in, you'll make your chest a tomb in which the corpses of secrets will rot and everyone who gets close to you can smell them. Always purge yourself, young man. Get rid of it and shake it off. Don't you see the donkey getting down to the ground, wallowing and rolling and shaking it off and braying at the top of its voice out of vexation and pain? It's a poor animal; if it didn't do all that, it wouldn't be able to go back and carry the burdens. It shakes off the pain and the sorrow and the bad luck because it cannot turn around and grab the neck of the person riding it and eat it. Beasts of burden must do that, otherwise they'd just kneel down under the weight and never get up."

His words were convincing yet I had to be cautious with him. The ground on which I could wallow and roll to shake myself off was definitely not Shawadfi's chest. Yet I couldn't help telling him the main problem that was now depriving me of sleep: all my friends had been arrested, even though they were not involved in plotting any assassination. I knew that the Damanhour branch in particular was one of the most important and largest branches, perhaps because of the character of the city's inhabitants. I had heard key members in the organization saying many times that the reason this province had many good Muslims was because most of the inhabitants had Moroccan roots and that they had settled in this land since the time of the Fatimids. Moroccans, by nature, the thinking went, were more inclined than others to Sufism and activism. Thus it was no wonder that al-Sayyed Ahmed al-Badawi, Ibrahim al-Disuqi, al-Shadhli, Mursi Abu al-Abbas, al-Qabbari, al-Qina'i, al-Siyuti, and al-Tartushi and other saints with shrines were all Moroccan Sufis who struck roots in Egypt and acquired high regard and sacred status in the hearts and minds of Egyptians. Hence allegiance to Damanhouris throughout the province to the Muslim Brotherhood and its principles was perhaps more profound than elsewhere because these principles agreed with their character and bent of mind. Thus they were key figures in the main society, providing it with its most important cadres and especially a group of influential speakers who captivated audiences with their goodness, the purity of their hearts, and their excessive zeal in commitment to restraint and wrestling with the self, suppressing its greed and worldly ambitions, and killing the sources of pleasure in it. I would admit that their strictness about what was acceptable and what was not acceptable in matters of religion and worship rose to a degree that perhaps was too cruel for those not following their precepts, but it would be hard for me to accept claims that they were engaged in gang-like activities such as murder, sabotage, and destruction. That might be because I was still looking at things from the perspective of a naïve peasant who assumed goodness in everyone. Say whatever you will about them, but I wouldn't forget that some of them took pity on me and helped me make a living without asking too much of me, without even requiring me to become a member in the Society.

That was what I told Shawadfi, whereupon he sat up and got absorbed in deep thought. Then he started rolling a cigarette, lit it, and began to take deep drags on it. He then waved his arms as if telling me that the matter did not need lengthy discussions, that it had already been settled for the beginning: "Young man, Widad the dancer, Buri, Sayyed Zanati, Ramadan Eraiga, Etaita, Ut el Ulub the Syrian, and Dumyana are not all like you in need of the Muslim Brothers' help. They are Muslim brothers to begin with, with no need to be members in the Society. Didn't you study in school stuff from the Qur'an that said that God Almighty hated parties and partisan groups? So, forget these arguments with which you are cloaking your laziness. All these people that I mentioned make a living with the sweat of their brow and not one of them goes to bed hungry. You, begging your pardon, young man, are looking for chains by which to bind yourself. Isn't it enough that you're just sitting in your small place doing nothing that you have to go get some iron chains to hang around your neck? Education for the likes of you is a waste! And look at you! You failed in school and it's over: are you going to spend the rest of your life crying over a diploma that you didn't get because you were vicious and unruly and because you beat your teacher? Who, besides yourself, says you've been wronged? Forget the whole thing and get yourself a job that can earn you some money. Work is nothing to be ashamed of no matter what; what is shameful is extending your hand to beg and steal. Okay, you can steal but do it discreetly without picking pockets. Do what many do! Do you think prosperous people became that way by being honest? On the contrary, young man: the more money in a person's hand, the stronger the proof that he's dishonest. You believe in the saying about our country, that it's a country of diplomas? I'd like to meet the person who made up this false saying so I could beat him on the head with my shoes. In our country, diplomas and public testimonials are worthless. Listen to this simple story: in a hamlet next to our village in the deep south, there was a man, so poor and penniless, like you, that people, apparently to reverse his fortune or just to give him an apt name, nicknamed him 'Mr. Livelihood,' or 'Abu Rizq.' This poor man was also unlucky so he got married and had children even though he had no work and no skills. When his back was bent under the heavy burden, a member of the rich branch of his family put in a good word with the priest to appoint him in some custodial job in the church. The priest asked him, 'Do you know how to read and write?' He said, 'Yes.' 'Do you know how to do this and this?' He said, 'Yes.' 'Can you come every day at such and such a time and leave at such and such a time?' He said, 'Yes.' The priest ordered that he be appointed right away because he would do the church a lot of good. As he was signing the appointment order, he paused suddenly and asked, 'I believe you have a primary school diploma?' Abu Rizq was taken aback and said, 'No, by God, I never got a diploma!' Whereupon the priest folded his papers and said, 'I am sorry, son, the law says that to be employed here, a person has to have a primary school diploma at the least.' Abu Rizq left, quite vexed, cursing his wretched luck. His wife was more intelligent and was a peddler who bought stuff on the installment plan and sold it for cash. She took him and they left for another village where nobody knew them. Her purpose in doing that was for her husband to get rid of his bad luck.

She trained him in matters of commerce. Big merchants gave him goods on consignment which he paid for after they had been sold. You give and you take and before you know it, you've gotten yourself some money. Abu Rizq followed that principle and developed capital that he invested even while others owned it. One transaction led to another; he opened a store, then a warehouse which kept growing bigger. The store opened branches in all villages and towns and Abu Rizq became a monied man, then a landed owner of real estate, earning titles and friends among the notables and the rulers. Now he walked surrounded by guards and rode elegant horse-drawn carriages and had bank accounts. He started donating to charity and giving to churches and mosques and was beloved by Muslims. The church that had denied him employment had a big reception for him after he donated money to it and the same priest gave a speech in which he anointed him with all manner of blessed holy attention. When the priest found out that the great tycoon was the very Abu Rizq that had applied for a job at one time, he joked with him saying, 'Why didn't you think of a diploma, pasha? That wouldn't have been difficult!' Abu Rizq laughed and said sarcastically in front of everyone, 'If I had a diploma, I would be a custodian at the church!' And this is the same with you, young man: you want to be a custodian in the church and regret the loss of the opportunity. Listen, young man, you want to come tomorrow, pay all you owe me in many months' back rent and still have a lot of money to enjoy life? Let me handle it! But, be flexible, learn how to hustle! Enlarge your brain! Is Buri more resourceful than you? Yes. Is he smarter, more intelligent? He's streetwise and not hung up on illusions like you. He married Widad and considered her a work project. He'll work with Sayyed Zanati and so will Widad. They'll be part of Sayyed Zanati's team. They'll make tons of money! You too, young man, can be part of Sayyed Zanati's team. You are a type of tool that can outdo all other types. Sayyed Zanati will be very happy with you and will give you a big commission. And the harder you work, the greater the commission and the closer you get to him. When you're done with work at the end of the day, you will find that he has prepared for you a dinner of roasted chicken and grilled meat and you will drink with him the liquor that he himself distills for his own use. So? Okay? Are we agreed? Don't hang down your head and dangle your ears like a stubborn donkey! Say yes or no!"

"Yes."

I found myself saying it, awkwardly, but, whatever will be, will be. Let me try this line of work, at least to get to know it, for the desire for experience in my case was stronger than the desire for gain in itself especially in this area. What really surprised me was Shawadfi's enthusiasm. As soon as I said yes he jumped up and, for the first time, I saw him leave the mastaba, saying, "Let's go." Then he walked ahead dragging his feet and strutting like a black mud dovecote, swaying right and left to Sayyed Zanati's room.

Picked Clean

Sayyed Zanati's room was a dazzling little museum. It was the largest room in the whole wikala. It must have been designed for some administrative function or another, for in addition to being large, it had three stories, with somewhat low ceilings. The first level was for sleeping and so was the third. As for the one in the middle, it was devoted to Sayyed Zanati: that was where he sat, stayed up, and received the teams for the settling of accounts. All the walls of the room were covered with well-washed, rose-colored linen drapes interspersed with mirror strips like in a hairdresser's shop that gave the room great depth and width. There was a picture of Gamal Abdel Nasser in military uniform at the signing of the British evacuation agreement in a gilded frame hung on the main wall in front. The room was adorned with colorful crepe paper in branches, clusters, balls, and other fruit-like forms and shapes. On the floor was a clean kilim on which were arranged several large and small cushions. The air was filled with the smells of burned and roasted tobacco, alcohol, ghee, and fried onions.

Sayyed was sitting cross-legged in front on a cushion and two rests, each the thigh of a graceful young lady with bright eyes. These were his recent, younger wives. Close to the door, opposite each other, sat two belles whose faces shone with the amazing freshness of well-groomed, carefree beauty. I knew that the one with the wheaten face and kohl-adorned eyes under locks of hair straying from the sequined headkerchief, with a longish face like a honeydew melon and taut chest strung on two bows under a brightly colored chintz gallabiya, was Haniya, his first wife who was also his first tool and the foundation of his career. It was said that originally she came from Arish, and that, like her family, she was a tracker. Opposite her sat another woman like a panther with a round, rose-colored face with compact features, and a large mouth with fine teeth. Her hair cascaded down her shoulders in black braids. It was as if her face was a lit lamp strung on an invisible thread between clouds of dark shadows. Every detail in her body was soft, full, and fleshy without being fat. That was the second wife, Sittat, who proved to be the real tool. She was a constant moneymaker, of great appeal to village headmen, notables, and large merchants. She knew how to lure and bewitch them. It was she who trained the two recent wives, having chosen one of them to marry Sayyed Zanati, or as cinema people would say, she discovered her. That was the one now sitting to Sayyed's right whose name was Ikram, nicknamed Karamella. As for the one sitting to his left, the fourth one, she was discovered by Haniya in the marketplace of life and was chosen by her to marry Sayyed Zanati, or in other words, was given a job. Her name was Gannat, nicknamed Gannuna. No one of the women was jealous of the others, for marriage for them was a matter of common interest which they built up and nurtured with Sayyed Zanati. They were as smart and resourceful as they were beautiful and talented. They knew that tools must all be one family caring for each other and protecting each other. It was better, actually it was a must that such a family be supported by official documents.

They all got up to meet us with great interest. We all shook hands. Shawadfi sat between Ikram and Sittat while I sat between Haniya and Gannat. As soon as we sat down I noticed two kerosene stoves, lit very low in front of Haniya and Sittat. On the stove in front of Haniya was a large pan filled with tobacco which I immediately figured out was sabaris which was the only kind of tobacco that gave Sayyed Zanati real pleasure, despite the presence of more than one large pack of Belmont on the floor from which Gannat and Ikram smoked. Haniya was stirring the tobacco with a spoon to roast it and get rid of remnants of others' breaths, the smell of urine, and other unpleasant smells resulting from butts being crushed underfoot. As for the other stove in front of Sittat it had on a medium-sized pot filled to the rim with water and in the center of the water in that pot was another smaller floating pot filled with methylated spirits or red alcohol. On top of that pot was a strainer and on top of the strainer was a cover. Over the very low flame the water in the bottom of the large pot boiled, raising the heat on the red alcohol in the small pot which evaporated and joined the steam from the water, which then lit the cover of the pot, and which in turn returned it to the small pot where it fell, drop by drop, like transparent pearls. When the sound of the small pot hitting the larger pot got louder, that was a sign that the water had run out, whereupon the stove would be turned off and the pot left to cool. Then Sittat would bring an empty whiskey bottle and, with a small funnel, fill the bottle with the carefully distilled alcohol. The bottle would then be placed with glasses in front of Sayyed Zanati next to shelled peanuts, lupino beans, lettuce, and mish so he could drink and smoke all night long. Then the one designated to spend the night in his arms would stay, as the other three went to their beds. Thus the day would break with Sayyed Zanati in his place like a king embracing a beautiful woman slaking his thirst with the honey of love while he slaked her with tenderness and virility. By the time the sun had sent its early heralds to the courtyard, passing by Sayyed Zanati through the interstices of the window overlooking the street, all his women would have gotten up, washed and preened, transformed into aristocratic ladies, redolent with expensive, brand-name perfumes, with gold glittering on their chests, wrists, fingers, and ears, in preparation for the day's work. After a little while the men, the rest of the tools, would begin to arrive: a dapper gentleman more handsome than the king, an effendi in the government's employ, a village headman from the upper crust, a contractor or a big merchant. Each of the men would take one of the women and go out for the day's work. Each duo had a prescribed line and appearance, a memorized dialogue and a charted route, all invented and devised by Sayyed Zanati with unique ingenuity as he sat there drinking and having fun, calculating every step of the equipment, almost pinpointing the exact amount of money that this or that duo would bring, depending on the novelty of the idea or the potential of the situation and their ability to arouse emotions or use persuasive arguments. As soon as they left, all the newspapers and magazines would be sneaked in through the window onto the street. He would then lie down on any bed and read them all carefully then sleep soundly until three in the afternoon when he would get up like a horse. He would go downstairs to find that whoever was in his embrace a few hours earlier had prepared for him the wash basin and the water. He would bathe and put on clean clothes and go out and shop for food: chicken, meat, vegetables and fruits, and cigarettes and alcohol. Then he would go back and roll up his sleeves like the best of women and get busy plucking the fowl, slicing the onions, squeezing tomatoes, washing the rice, and heating the ghee. He loved also to check on the food being cooked on the stoves, cooling himself with a glass of distilled alcohol, and, for mezza, sampling the food.

As soon as the sun began withdrawing from the courtyard the tools would start arriving, one duo after the other, punctually. Everyone would be expected to hear the call to the sunset prayers in this room with a margin that extended only until the last prayers of the day. As soon as the duo arrived the woman would open her purse and pour the day's take on a handkerchief spread before Sayyed Zanati. He would then arrange the money and count it quickly and think for a moment, as if checking the figure against an estimate he had made in his head for the job. Ordinarily, if the figures were not identical it would be because the actual amount was greater, more or less. Then he would count the money in a different kind of calculation in which he would set aside the commission which he would fold and give to the man saying, "May you have a wonderful night!" Then he would set aside another sum that would be the commission of the woman who accompanied the man which he would put in one of the pockets of his large leather wallet. Then he would put the rest of the money in another pocket. As soon as everyone was there, the large low table would be loaded with several delicious dishes. Everyone would eat, smoke, and drink tea, then the first half of the evening, what Sayyed Zanati called the lining or foundation, would begin. That part would be arranged around hashish and opium and that would be Haniya's department: she was the expert on arranging, lighting, stuffing, stoking, and cleaning the shisha because she was a veteran smoker and because she also took care of that aspect of Sayyed Zanati's life. The gathering was not simply an occasion to smoke hashish and consume opium but had another essential component that began with the first puff: two packs of cards, always new, combined for rummy over a three or four hour period that always ended with Sayyed Zanati winning all the commissions in the men's pockets. But Sayyed was a magnanimous guy who would not dream of letting them leave after being plucked clean, without carriage fare or money for breakfast, so he would lend each of them a pound which he would get back the following evening. Then they would begin to leave as the clock struck eleven so that Sayyed Zanati would have an intimate evening with his four women. Thus would begin the second half of the evening, the essential component of which would be the distilled alcohol.

Luckily for us—Shawadfi and I—we came at the beginning of the second half of the evening. Shawadfi took a sip from a glass that Sayyed Zanati had placed before him and he cringed when the burning stuff hit his throat. Then he said, "I brought you a tool that can be both a tabla and a tar but it is up to you to use him as one or the other. This is a good boy, I guarantee it. He's resourceful and has been around. He wants to make a living with the sweat of his brow. He's got brains. He used to be in school, almost became a teacher had it not been for his bad luck. What I an trying to say is: he's educated and he'll be good."

I became the target for a thicket of enchanting eyes that began to scrutinize my whole body accompanied by welcome, pride, excitement, and a little bit of resentment. Looking me straight in the eye, Sayyed Zanati said, "I wonder if he knows what we do. You know our work is hard and not everyone can do it. It's not a matter of education or schools. It's a matter of success granted by God. The most important thing about our work is for someone to have acceptability, to be *simpatico*. Acceptability is essential in our line of work, people will believe everything you say and do even if you were a liar and a fraud, even when they know that you're lying to them."

Like a slave merchant trained in the ways of packaging and presenting his merchandise, Shawadfi said, "Look at this guy's face: it has acceptability written all over it a hundred times! Look at this forehead and you'll see a crescent shape. His teeth have gaps in front as you can see. That means he's lucky, God willing."

Once again the eyes kept examining me closely, tarrying over my forehead and my mouth. I began to smile awkwardly. Sayyed Zanati said, "He's welcome! If he needs some money, my pocket is at his disposal. But he must love this work of ours so he can do it with finesse and pleasure like a favorite hobby. If he truly loves it, he'll find ideas to sell people for tons of money. Our work depends on sweet and well-thought out talk and even sweeter acting. If you are, don't get me wrong, talented in these two areas then you'll have a fantastically sweet future with us. So, what are your talents?"

Shawadfi answered right away, "The young man is a member in the drama society at the National Guard. And he's fond of writing stories and novels and he does have sweet talk. More important, he wants to work. Try him with your eyes closed and you'll thank me."

Sayyed Zanati's features relaxed and his eyes, big and with long lashes, gleamed with curiosity, "Well then, let me think of a gig for you. But what did you do before?"

Shawadfi was quick to respond, "He had a friend, a fabric merchant who's a Muslim Brother. He used to help him in the store and he paid him whatever."

We heard a shout of approbation coming from near the door. It was Sittat and she shouted again, "Great! I got an idea, Sayyed Zanati. Okay? The Muslim Brothers! This is a good guy indeed, Shawadfi. I'll train him. Leave him to me. I'll go out with him. I'm going to tell you the idea, Sayyed, and you work on it and cook it. As for the guy, he will know the idea when we carry it out."

Shawadfi waved optimistically, "Thank God! Newcomers bring good with them."

Sayyed Zanati sat back puffing on a cigarette: "Good! Let's proceed, with God's blessing."

Sittat sat up looking at me, as if scrutinizing me for the last time before buying me: "Darling, I have a simple request. Would you do it for me?"

"Of course, of course!" I said truthfully, then added, "Just give the order!"

She turned her face to me with a captivating, radiant smile, then moved her head to throw locks of her hair back and added, "You have clean clothes, of course. And respectable?"

"I've got some. I can wash them."

"No. Sayyed Zanati will buy you a respectable full suit from the used-clothes market. There you'll find clothes that beys and effendis sell after wearing them just once. We'll buy you one or two for cheap and then we'll settle when God sends you from his bounty, God willing. Do you hear me, Sayyed Zanati? You must buy him two suits from the used clothes market. Just to his measure and very chic, with a dress shirt and tie. Can you look at me, my good man?"

I looked at her trying to suppress laughter. I enjoyed the situation, which looked entertaining to me. I drew great pleasure from looking at the big, kohl-adorned eyes of this beauty. What made it pleasurable was my feeling that her eyes were drawing in my eyes and my looks with her own eyes wide open. I felt even more pleasure thinking that perhaps fate was arranging exciting rounds for me with this luscious and attractive woman. She lowered her eyes, saying decisively, "You've got ten days to start working."

Shawadfi said, waving, "A whole ten days? Why?"

Sittat fixed Shawadfi with a look: "This is how we do our business, Shawadfi! It's not haphazard. The man must grow his beard."

"Grow his beard? Why, is he going to be a Qur'an preacher or a grave digger?"

Sittat ignored him and looked at me, "This is what I want from you. From now on, don't shave. In ten days, come and I'll trim it for you to make it like Muslim Brotherhood beards. By that time, Sayyed Zanati will have bought you the suit. Go with him to the market in two or three days to try it on."

"What do you think, young man?" said Shawadfi.

"I agree, of course!"

"Well then. Meet me the day after tomorrow and we'll buy you the best suit that you like and that I like."

Shawadfi said, "Okay then, let's hear the Fatiha."

I almost burst out laughing but I controlled myself with difficulty when I saw everyone, to my surprise, raising their palms toward the sky and reading the opening chapter of the Qur'an with such skilled piety as if they were in a mosque after prayers. Everyone wiped their faces with their palms. Then Shawadfi addressed me saying, "The Fatiha will break a traitor's back." We all nodded in agreement with him and drank a toast to the Fatiha, each one a sip from the same glass. The room had begun to look very intimate to the extent that I felt nailed to my place, not wanting to leave, had it not been for Shawadfi who gave me a secret glance to the effect that everybody had work early in the morning and that Sayyed Zanati had business he had to attend to before dawn. I got up and preceded Shawadfi to the door and the stairs going toward my room filled with many vague, anxious feelings, but I noticed that I enjoyed them even though I didn't welcome thinking about them, perhaps because I was actually eager to get on with it. The only thing I was certain of was that roaring laughter that filled my chest in a manner that shook me to my foundations: I was sure those were the laughs of the one called Satan.

Bearing

The way my face looked in the mirror disturbed and agitated me; I almost denied it was my face. My beard had grown over an inch, completely covering my fair complexion under a coarse blondish fur like that of a sheep that began with two sections next to the ears growing larger as they went outward to the temples, cheeks, the chin and the front of the neck. I had a hard time keeping it and felt the need to get rid of it, scratching it all the time. After a short while, however, I gradually began to forget I had one.

And even after my beard grew longer I hadn't decided yet whether I would join such a group of swindlers and con artists. These, after all, were low lifes whom I was supposed to be against socially and morally and in other respects. Actually, I had wanted to grow a beard for a long time, by way of experimentation or rebellion against my boring, usual appearance. The only reason I hadn't was seeing men of every background growing their beards, either to deceive people or to declare adherence to a certain group. Besides, having a beard would brand me as a Muslim Brother subject to investigation and needless headaches. I did, however, like the sight of my long beard since it gave me the look of artists, poets, men of letters, and philosophers.

Sayyed Zanati took an interest in observing my beard and was happy and optimistic about it. He said that the beard, by looking so good, had reassured him that I was descended from good ancestors since its appearance reminded him of many truly pious sheikhs. The ten days extended to a whole month. By that time my beard was quite thick. Sayyed took me to the used clothes market and bought an elegant suit I couldn't have dreamt of owning, one of those suits that I used to see worn by high society beys and famous fancy dressers made to exact measure. We proceeded in the market, both sides abounding with various types of clothes hung on racks and hangers, renewed in devilish ways to make them appear straight-from-the-factory new. Groups of different people were standing in the middle of the road, taking off their clothes publicly to try new items on for size, shouting and screaming and bargaining and swearing. Here appearances were changed, some completely transformed: uncouth barefoot peasants turned into elegant, respectable effendis; young men from modest backgrounds turned into sons of well-to-do families wearing European-style short-sleeve shirts. Others were turned into clowns. This was a world of marvels that tempted us to buy a gabardine coat for me and a broadcloth one for Sayyed. We also bought a fancy cotton shirt and a poplin one, a necktie, two pairs of socks, and a pair of suede shoes. It all came to less than five pounds—Sayyed gave me thirty piasters to even it out at five pounds. I took off my old clothes to try the clothes on in the midst of the market crowded with countless people without feeling any embarrassment since all those people cooperated to conduct that kind of business with great and amazing ease. Even while trying on something, more than one of the other customers would volunteer an opinion such as: "perfect"; "It becomes you"; "It fits you like a glove"; "It's icing on the cake"; "That's your good fortune"; or "Congratulations!" And if you disagreed with the vendor about the price, someone would intervene to settle the argument with a soothing word that might actually end the disagreement: "Each should give a little," "Let's split the difference," or "Give him that much!" When it was done I saw myself in the vendor's mirror standing next to him like an open door: I looked like an effendi from a good family. Finally I had the bearing before which I had often stood subserviently: from the teacher to doctor to director to undersecretary to all those who treated me and my family so unfairly and so arrogantly. At that moment all anger in my chest awakened as if all the valves were suddenly broken. I felt that a decision was forming within me never to give up that awesome authoritative bearing for as long as I lived, rightly or wrongly, no matter what circumstances or conditions existed. A voice in the back of my head said that our country didn't ask anyone for a certificate or legal documentation or the authority of prevalent custom to do what he wanted or to assume whatever pose, since everything was for sale, either for money or clout or any authority. So why wouldn't I cling to a bearing that would satisfy my vanity regardless of whether I deserved it or not? I had seen or perhaps heard someone say something to the effect that if you were in a country that did not believe in God, no one could accuse you of being an infidel. Actually I could claim that I was in a country that did not believe in honor, except by way of propaganda and false appearances. Thus there was no place for shame.

Sayyed Zanati walked by my side as if he were my personal guard or the manager of my estate, carrying my old clothes, his rosy face giving off a big radiant smile as if he had just finished an artistic masterpiece and was waiting for the crowds' reaction to it, almost thanking everyone who cast an admiring glance toward me. When Sittat saw me she couldn't help letting out a soundless ululation of joy, contenting herself with placing her palm like an umbrella on her mouth and moving her tongue like a bobbin in obvious joy and pleasure. Then she told me to take the clothes off to keep them pressed for when we went on our planned errand.

After I watched the night's settling of the accounts and the usual gambling session and after all the tools had left, our private evening session started with the eleven o'clock news broadcast. I couldn't turn down Sayyed Zanati's invitation for a couple of distilled alcohol drinks, hell's water as he called it. I was able to withstand its burning taste because I'd had a rich dinner with them. Sittat brought Sayyed Zanati's shaving equipment which was quite neat: a razor with a blade as sharp and clean as a barber's, a large ivory-handled brush, a shaving cream tube, a brass bowl, and a strop. To my astonishment I noticed the presence of several issues of *al-Da'wa*, the mouthpiece of the Muslim Brotherhood. Sittat began to persue it until she came upon a full-page picture of Sheikh Hassan al-Banna with his short fez and the meek, dreamy look in his eyes. She kept examining his beard carefully then had me sit in front of her, placing a towel on my chest and lathering the cream with the brush in the bowl. She drew some lines on my face, delineating the shape of the beard as she wanted it. Then she started looking back and forth between the picture and my face, wiping the shaving cream with her thumb from certain spots. When she managed to delineate the parts that would be shaved off, she applied extra shaving cream there and, with great expertise, her soft, chubby wrist kept going back and forth excitingly on my cheek and lower neck and next to my ears. Then she brought the mirror and aimed it at my face: I was taken aback at my appearance; my face was identical to that of Hassan al-Banna. I was amazed at the similarity of the two beards. At that moment I understood why Sayyed Zanati and I spent such an exhausting time in the used clothes market looking for a short fez. When Sittat positioned it in such a way that a small portion of my forehead appeared under it, Sayyed Zanati looked at my face with great admiration then waved his arm assuring us that, early in the morning, Sittat and I would place our trust in God and go to work.

The Wings

The plan that Sayyed Zanati had drawn up for us was broad, but with precise details and sound structure. He supplied us with a number of Qur'anic verses, hadiths of the Prophet, and sayings attributed to Ali ibn Abi Talib, Umar ibn al-Khattab, and Abu Dhar which were often quoted by Muslim Brotherhood speakers. I was quite surprised at how Sayyed Zanati knew those sayings in particular, and no others, to be used by us to help out when and if needed. He conducted a rehearsal for us by impersonating characters that we might encounter or who might argue with us or try to get us to give away our true identities, showing us what we should say or do in this or that situation and which words or gestures might be lifesavers if things got tight or a crisis developed.

Sittat was much cleverer than me in her replies and comments, which reflected extraordinary intelligence. In my naiveté I had thought she and Sayyed Zanati were illiterate. When I noticed to my utter amazement their correct pronunciation of literary Arabic with sound grammatical vowels and emphatic consonants, I thought I was sitting with prominent intellectuals in disguise. My perplexity concerning them did not last long as Sayyed Zanati responded to my visible surprise with a broad smile before telling me that both he and Sittat had primary school diplomas under the old system when students paid tuition and got an education better than those with secondary school certificates of the present day as far as coursework and English and French were concerned. There was a gleam of defiance in his eyes when he pointed downward to the floor telling me that the room downstairs had mountains of literary and cultural books and periodicals that I may never have heard of in my life even though I considered myself an intellectual and a man of letters. Before preparing for his test he listed for me a large number of valuable books that he had read, some in English, several times. He mentioned novels by Charles Dickens, plays by Shakespeare, Ibn Khaldun's *Muqadimah*, and other classical Arabic works and works of modern authors on literature and history and poets. He also mentioned key modern Egyptian periodicals such as *Apollo*, *al-Katib al-Misri*, *al-Risala*, and *al-Thaqafa* for, as he said, his father, still alive in their village of Kafr Bulin, had the highest degree from al-Azhar, equivalent to a doctorate. He also said that when he flunked several times in secondary school, he refused to go back to his village because his tough father would've killed him, especially that Sayyed's education had cost his father a lot of money on the one hand and because people complained a lot about him on the other hand. Sayyed got into many quarrels and was frequently arrested on suspicion of theft because, as he said, he actually stole to cover his expenses. His skill saved him many times but his luck ran out and he was caught by the police red-handed, robbing a grocery store with two accomplices. They offered the police stiff resistance but they were overcome and Sayyed got a three-year sentence. He came out of jail a different person: he gave up his hobby of writing literature, specifically poetry, but he kept reading. He admitted that reading had been very useful to him by expanding his horizons and stimulating his imagination to devise ways to get out of tough situations.

Sayyed Zanati then was the closest to a role model as I could get. Was I bound to follow the same line and have the same fate inevitably? The thought hit me like an earthquake and the earth shook under me right and left. I tried to stay composed. Then I asked Sayyed Zanati almost matter-of-factly, "Of course you wished you continued in your studies to become a prominent poet or writer?"

Very confidently and quite simply he said, "At the beginning it was as you say. But there's not a single homeless wretch that I've met in my life who did not turn out to be an afficionado of literature and poetry and who, because of that accursed hobby, got neither here nor there! One day I saw Bayram al-Tunsi sitting in a coffeehouse, eating a ful sandwich and arguing with the waiter over a half piaster. Seeing him like that was heart rending. At that very moment Umm Kulthum's voice was singing on the radio playing in that very coffeehouse from the 'amal' song and she was moaning 'I found no way to you.' The waiter of course did not know that that wretch who insisted on getting back that half piaster was the poet who wrote that song filled with generosity, light, and goodness. If he knew, he wouldn't have believed that the man truly needed the money. At that moment I dropped that hobby for good. And now, as you can see, I am doing very well. I live just as I wish. Free like a bird. I can challenge the best of them. I eat the best food, wear the best clothes, I do what I please. So, listen to my advice and forget all these costly, ambitious wishes if you want to live a couple of days in security and pleasure."

He sounded quite truthful and sincerely wanted me to succeed in that mission as a prelude to many other missions. Suddenly he said to me as he slipped me a small glass of real booze from the bottle of his two younger wives, "Listen to this opening,

Without speaking I found out what you're planning.
These are your hands
Shake mine!
Why're you hiding it?
The look in your eyes,
The touch of your hand,
Everything about you
Is saying goodbye.
It's over! Goodbye!

He looked at my eyes waiting for my comment. I said in genuine admiration that it was indeed a beautiful opening for a modern song. He said he had quite a few more such songs, some of which he finished and some he dropped. He recited several openings along the same line that only a person experienced in matters of love, prosody, and common expressions could master. He also recited for me some songs he had written for singers at weddings, mulids, and nightclubs some of which had made it together with those singing them to the Alexandria broadcasting service. One of these quasi-folkloric songs began:

Shun me for a month,
Reconcile for a day
Spare me rebuke one day a month!
We're spending our love apart!
Twenty-nine days are quite enough!

I asked him why he didn't submit his songs to the radio, the movies, and records. He snorted at my naiveté saying that the radio was not for the likes of him. He said he was writing for fun and that he had friends, male and female singers in Alexandria nightclubs, who visited him at the wikala and whom he visited at their clubs when he went to Alexandria during the summer. He said that most likely he stayed with them as their guest and it was then that inspiration came profusely. He also said with the utmost amazing simplicity that he was a friend of some high-ranking officers and famous officials in local government. I did not doubt it, for indeed he had an attractice personality that exuded confidence, bravery, selfishness, strength, and virility. Those were actually his salient characteristics. He looked at his yellow Jovial wrist watch with a black leather band as a gesture that it was time for me to leave. As I prepared to leave, he said as if giving me the last bit of instruction, "This work of ours depends on daring and strength of heart and having no fear. Fear is always what points an accusing finger at you. It is what informs the police about you. The police don't know about you. A policeman is not a magician or a wizard who can read the sand and know what you're thinking. Be smarter than him. Don't show him what's inside you. How? Cool, steady nerves. Impassive face. Strong, impervious heart. Measured words. Answering just the question with a single word. That's the first lesson you have to learn if you face interrogation or a police report. If you volunteer one additional letter, that one letter might reveal what's hidden. Learn the plan I explained to you and be unshakable before Sittat; there's nothing to fear on her account."

He shook hands with me. I left, intoxicated with the exciting adventure. It was close to three in the morning. I had to get up at seven so we could leave at eight. I had no desire to sleep, yet I went to bed, and began to review what happened and recall details of the role I would play in the morning in a very interesting and well-made comedy.

Acceptability

According to Sayyed Zanati's plan, there was an observer that we were not supposed to have anything to do with. I wished I were him instead of being involved in an actual role that might get me into trouble. The observer would take the same means of transportation with us as a totally unrelated person. He would follow us every step of the way without anyone noticing that at all. Once we got to work he'd come in with us as a regular citizen. If he noticed that we got into trouble or a passing difficulty he would intervene out of compassion to help us out safely. That would be the case in simple troubles, but he was also qualified to intervene on many astonishing levels, such as fighting on our behalf on the pretext of separating us or helping out a wronged party or running interference for us to prevent an adversary from taking a timely stand against us to give us the opportunity to make a break for it, or by misleading that adversary. If the trouble went beyond his control, or his efforts could not help, such as our being arrested by the police, for instance, he would run back at lightning speed to Sayyed Zanati to tell him about us so he could do something and yet keep an eye on us from a distance. One of his biggest tasks, however, was learning how much we had made, to report it in detail to Sayyed Zanati.

We took the train to the town of Disuq heading specifically for the mosque of Sidi Ibrahim al-Disuqi. It was a Friday and the plan was to attend Friday prayers from the beginning at the mosque and for me to get a place very near where the imam sat before ascending the pulpit. I was supposed to be an Arabic language teacher at a secondary school in Fayyum, let's say. I had come to this town, with my wife, this lady, to visit the saint Sidi Ibrahim al-Disuqi and some of our relatives. A pickpocket, who looked like such and such—according to the description of some famous pickpocket in the town—fooled us into thinking that he was a porter who would carry our belongings to our relatives' address. Midway there he disappeared with our suitcases, which had our clothes and things. After he disappeared, it turned out that he had lifted the wallet from the inner jacket pocket where it had become visible when I raised my arm to help him carry our bags. I had not noticed the disappearance of the wallet, which had my money and identity card, because he had such a light touch. We had gone to the police station where we filed a report that had such and such a number or such and such a date (that, by the way, was an actual police report that we filed at the police station on our way to the mosque). The really bad clincher was that when we did make it to our relatives' house, we found that the head of the family, may the present company be spared, had an ordeal of his own, may God help him out of it (hinting intelligently that he had been arrested as part of the clampdown on the Muslim Brotherhood which was still fresh in people's minds). The problem now was that my wife and I wanted to travel to the far south to be with our family and that we had no money whatsoever.

My wife, Sittat, was wearing very modest and dignified attire as befitting the wife of an effendi who was a high-ranking government employee. She covered her face and head with a white shawl that did not reveal her features distinctly. I had prepared in my head the speech arranged in advance which consisted of certain verses from the Qur'an, part of a famous hadith of the Prophet, and a few well-known phrases that were part of the Muslim Brotherhood's profound and effective slogans. The components were subtly composed in such a way as to get the imam moved by my financial predicament on a purely human level and to take heed of the divine imperatives and religious and moral arguments that put any truly religious person in touch with his conscience. I was also supposed to hint, implicitly, never explicitly, so that the imam would understand that I was a high-ranking member of the Muslim Brotherhood and that I was fleeing the eyes of the government, seeking refuge, and that I was asking for help at that particular time to enable me to escape to a farther place until the present difficult situation cleared up. I had to be successful at that complex role to utilize as much as possible the strong sympathy that common people had for the Muslim Brothers who were, after all, their sons and brothers. Besides, many would sympathize with us not because they loved the Muslim Brotherhood but because they hated the revolution that had terrorized them with military orders.

When the imam came he found me waiting for him next to the pulpit, absorbed in soft-spoken prayers in a state of profound pious devotion. Then I got up and performed some prostrations and moved next to the imam, greeted him, and engaged him in conversation. It seemed that all the discussions I had followed attentively with my friends who were now under arrest started coming back to me and I found my tongue effortlessly swimming in a sea of dazzling, hot phrases that focused on asking God to protect us from the circumstances, conditions, and events on which we were embarking, on signs of misguidedness and corruption, human weakness in the age of materialism, fear of tyranny, and the might of tyrants that had replaced God's place in the hearts. To my great delight I noticed that the imam was responsive to my words on his own and that as he followed them he was supporting them with prayers for mercy and guidance and hope that God would put good people in charge of our affairs. At that point I struck while the iron was hot, "Can you imagine, master, that this and that has happened to us in your blessed town?"

When he showed signs of paying attention, I immediately added, "Know, master, that my name is such and such, that I come from such and such a place and my story, may it never happen to you, is such and such." Then I pointed at my make-believe wife who was standing in a corner at a distance, in the midst of suppressed but noticeable glances that showed signs of quizzical disapproval and mockery. The imam looked clearly touched and chagrined and fixed my wife with a glance that conveyed these feelings. She also was ready and as soon as she received the imam's glances, she bowed her head, and her body began to shake violently as an indication that she was crying for fear of public humiliation, a sign that she had not faced such an unpleasant ordeal before. The imam said in a shaking voice, "Let her move to the women's corner, there. May the unjust be held to account by God! Don't worry anyway. There are many good people, thank God. And, with God's permission, things will be taken care of."

I got up and went to Sittat. I bent over her and patted her on the back gently, whispering in her ear. She brought a silk handkerchief to her face under the shawl and dried her fake tears. Then she leaned on my hand and got up with her head bowed as most rows began to look at both of us inquisitively, focusing on my beard and her white shawl, my short fez that looked identical to that of Hassan al-Banna even in the way it was pushed back a little, and the rich dignified musk-like perfume wafting from both of us. She went where I pointed to, in the women's corner, whereas I went back and sat next to the imam, absorbed in a state of embarrassment and sorrow that I had devised precisely, utilizing the long theatrical practice I had had at the national guard troupe of the Muslim Brotherhood branch in the government employee club in beloved Damanhour. An ingenious thought occurred to me to test my acting ability in that situation, so I lost myself in the role, overplaying it by recalling touching scenes, sad words, and weeping songs. I got so involved that the muscles of my face actually twitched and I bit my lower lip, closing my eyelids so tightly as though I were squeezing a dry lime of which only a few niggardly teardrops fell. Actually, I didn't need more than that. As soon as I took out my handkerchief to dry my eyes, the imam's voice came to me bringing me reassurance and security, "Have faith in God, my good man! Everything will be all right, God willing. God will ease your hardship and ours and will bring us all home safely. God willing, you will always find good people on your way. But let me warn you that the police are all over the place and I am afraid that on your present journey, you might be taking refuge from the frying pan into the fire. Hindawi of Dwair is from a village nearby and you know who he is in the secret organization. That's why the whole region is in turmoil. If you are one of them, God be with you and He won't let you down!"

If was as if he had pressed an electric button; my tears came pouring down, hot and genuine; I couldn't stop them. Deep down I was over-joyed for my passing the test with flying colors!

When the imam ascended the pulpit he gave a very intelligent and clever sermon in which he explained the lack of compassion and the disharmony that were changing society and people as a result of replacing fear of God with fear of others. He inveighed in particular against the dark days and rotten times that subjected us to non-believing colonialism that tormented us and strengthened evil in us even after colonialism had left. He prayed to God to protect the blessed revolution since it miraculously rid us of that colonialism just as it got rid of the symbol of tyranny without shedding a single drop of blood, a sign of God's generosity to the Egyptian nation because the bloodshed was always that of the people. He found an excuse for the revolution for the delay in harvest seasons and prosperity and urged people to go back to principles of compassion and piety as their only safe haven. For in these bad times if we did not have compassion for each other, if we didn't help each other in such a way that the full shall try to fill the empty, then God Almighty would not show us mercy but would set up as overlords over us, those of us who would do evil and shed blood. "O God, hold us not responsible for what the foolish among us have done, Amen. O God, put the good among us, not the evil among us, in charge of us, Amen. O God, be with us, don't be against us, Amen. O God, pardon us if we forget or transgress, Amen." This last amen shook the mosque to its foundations as if it emanated from a mythical creature filling the whole universe, as the whole prayer area of the mosque filled with chandeliers and marble and beautiful ornaments in the ceiling separated the echoes of a . . . m . . . e . . . n in broad blocks of sound aspiring to embrace heaven. At the end of the prayer, with the second *assalamu alaykum*, my heart was racing with anxiety had I not noticed that the imam was hastening to finish the prayer as if he had an important task to conclude before the worshipers left. And, indeed, no sooner did some worshipers get ready to leave than the imam sprang to his feet saying, “One moment, please, good people!”

Everybody paused and shoes were returned to their places while some stayed in the hands of their owners. The imam raised his arm passionately: “Dear brothers in God! May you never experience a hardship! We have here this Muslim brother who, together with his family, was subjected to an unpleasant situation in our town in addition to the fact that his circumstances, to begin with, were hard enough. For, as we know, believers are constantly tested. Right now he is asking God for no more than the train fare to go back safely to his family. Verily God loves the believers and those who prefer others above themselves though poverty became their lot. A believer unto another believer is like a solid structure, each part reinforcing the other.”

Right away one of the men spread a handkerchief on the floor and threw on it three silver ten-piaster coins that made a pleasant jingling sound. Another followed with a quarter pound then shillings and ten-piaster, two-piaster, and piaster coins rained down as my heart danced to the music of the silver’s march of delegates. I bowed my head mumbling prayers like song joining the silver band. The pile of money kept rising and expanding as the heavy red bronze piaster rolled dragging the lighter two piaster pieces aside, making an annex that soon became another adjacent pile. I didn’t know what to do had not the voice of the owner of the handkerchief come to me with an indirect advice, “Pick up your money, Hagg! Are you bashful? Put it in your pocket and wait; a lot of good is yet to come!”

I raised my head to look at him when lo and behold, it was the observer entrusted with watching us, having impersonated one of the worshipers making donations. I began to scoop up the money by the handful and put it in my pockets quickly in a measured way. As those coming from the other end of the mosque saw the pile of money small, they increased what they had planned to donate several fold. Before the last worshiper left, we were surprised to see some bearded men wearing short gallabiyas and suits and caftans come toward us carrying some packets which they gave us saying, "A little something to eat."

I guessed they contained bread and kabab. I thanked them and prayed that God protect them. Then I carried the gift and got up looking around for Sittat whom I saw coming toward me like a dignified goose waddling in studied bashfulness. When she saw the observer standing in front of me, she pretended not to know him. I thought it would be polite and politic on my part to shake his hand and to thank him and his fellow townspeople for being so generous to us. He lowered his eyelids as he shook hands with me pressing my hand discreetly saying, "Go with God's blessing. May your road be safe! Look after yourself. God be with you!"

I extended my arm to Sittat and she took it and we left the mosque. We walked slowly and with dignified steps toward the railway station. We passed al-Sardi pastry shop. Seeing it awakened a childhood's sense of deprivation toward that particular pastry renowned in our village and I almost stopped to buy some but I painted a frown on my face and went directly to the ticket window and bought two tickets to Damahour.

The sun was not yet quite done with the courtyard when we entered, still fully absorbed in our roles in a manner that was difficult to shake off. Sittat was still holding on to my arm and we were still walking in slow dignified steps that were almost dancing with joy nonetheless. The smell of roasted chicken welcomed us, overpowering Shawadfi's shouts of glee, jest, and mockery, "With all these airs, I wonder: did you catch a glorious lion or a lowly hyena?"

Sittat fixed him with a haughty look over her shoulder then kept walking next to me in a dancing, theatrical step. Sayyed Zanati had heard Shawadfi's comments and came out to receive us at the door, his face flushed with joy and optimism. As soon as our glances met, the smiles broadened and the faces beamed. We greeted Sayyed so warmly he was filled with great hope.

We sat down to count the money. It was more than one hundred and fifty pounds, a huge fortune, of course. Sayyed divided it up, giving me forty, and forty to Sittat, thirty to the observer and a few extra ten-piaster pieces that he sent to Shawadfi for discovering me as a good tool. In appreciation of my success, Sayyed forgave me the five pounds for my wardrobe. After his fair divvying up, Sayyed lit a roasted cigarette and sat back saying, "This is the Egyptian people! Every piaster that they paid, they wished were an arrow in the heart of the enemy. It is their way of getting back at the government and of buying for themselves a similar favor if they find themselves in a similar predicament in the future. Thank God for your success! I was sure of it. And this was the sum I had expected. Now you have to get ready for next Friday to do the same thing in another town in a big famous mosque but with a new play which God will help me make up when my head heats up."

Toward the end of the sitting, Sayyed's head had indeed heated up and resulted in many plays. And even though I was not enthusiastic to repeat the performance, perhaps out of embarrassment and perhaps fear, I left after I promised to come in the early morning to go on a quick gig with Sittat. As soon as I threw myself onto the bed my nostrils were filled Sittat's perfume so I summoned her whole body and kept it in my arms all night long.

The Last Night

Sittat was trimming my beard in preparation for putting on the same show the following morning, Friday, at the Ahmedi mosque in Tanta. As her fragrant breath greeted my face, as she approached with her mouth closed firmly on the knot of the thread by which she was removing some thin hairs around my ear and nose, I remembered at that moment that the two of us were alone in the room with its three floors and that I was sitting on the same cushions on which Sayyed Zanati sat. My heart beat fast and my breath raced as though I had suddenly discovered that I was naked in the street or as if I had found something valuable on the street and was afraid that whoever saw me pick it up would demand that we share it or snatch the whole thing for himself.

Sayyed Zanati had left at dawn for Cairo to attend the last night of the mulid of al-Hussein, son of Ali, may God be pleased with them both. It was his annual custom to attend the last nights of the mulids of the important and famous saints: Disuqi, Ahmedi, Hussein, al-Sayyeda Zaynab, al-Sayyeda Nafisa, al-Sayyeda al-Nabawiya, and Sidi al-Qinawi, even the one named Abu Sris buried in a distant spot in a desolate desert across very rough terrain. Sayyed made sure to make that trip in particular because that saint's power was legendary, as attested to by the fact that many, many people from all over the country traveled there without any hardship, most likely to spend a whole week of playing and reveling, engaging in all manner of unlimited debauchery. Mulids, for Sayyed Zanati, as far as I could conclude from many indications, were big markets for his numerous schemes to separate suckers from their money by selling them illusions. The most important reason he went to mulids, however, was for the chance to meet a woman to add to his tools, or a man who would be good at one of the tasks. As for the al-Hussein mulid in particular, his motivation was strictly one of piety and out of love for all the members of the Prophet's family. His annual visits to the mulids of al-Hussein, al-Sayyeda Zaynab, and al-Sayyeda al-Nabawiya were a pledge he had to honor no matter how busy he was. Usually he would take his four wives but this time he didn't want Sittat or himself to miss out on an opportunity for considerable gain, perhaps more than what we made in other mosques and railway stations. So he assured us that we would return from Tanta quite satisfied, God willing, and that we should splurge on a good dinner in Tanta.

Sittat's hand was feeling my cheek gently and softly looking for any hidden hairs that she could pluck with the thread. Her chest was touching my shoulder and resting on top of it. The blood heated up in my veins and I was consumed with irresistible desire. I held Sittat's hands and kissed them in gratitude for her taking care of me. Sayyed Zanati had left me a quarter of a bottle of cognac to put me in a good mood to sleep soundly in preparation for tomorrow's errand. I told Sittat that we should rehearse the play we were going to perform the following day. She got up and got the bottle and prepared some appetizing mazza. She prepared the fire and the goza to have a couple of pipes of hashish, which she preferred to liquor which she considered to be the unclean work of the devil.

We got high, and conversation took us to faraway and unfamiliar destinations. I told her much about events in my life, my village, my family, the girl I loved back home, about my cousin, and the estrangement between the two families. I even told her about Badriya with a passion that almost led me to admit what we had done. I talked to her about my psychological hang-ups with my colleagues at the institute who were from well-off families and how biased the teachers were in their favor and how they treated us with contempt and impatient displeasure, and about the legal problems that had arisen between my father and his nephews over the inheritance of a tract of salty land that was ultimately sold for a pittance to pay lawyers' fees and court expenses that we had borrowed to bring the lawsuit. I noticed that she was listening to me with interest, that he glances were full of sympathy mixed with admiration. She even told me that she thought I had a kind heart. She also told me about herself: her mother was from Kom Hamada and her father from al-Tawd. He had been a sergeant in the army and died in the siege of Faluja in the Palestine War in the late 1940s. Her mother married the former head watchman in a common-law arrangement without official registration because the mother didn't want to lose the pension she was getting from the government every month and at the same time wanted to have a husband who supported and satisfied her. Sittat was sixteen when her stepfather began to notice her and he kept flirting with her explicitly, finding opportunities to be alone with her and to teach her women's things she didn't know. She tried to escape from him but he pursued her relentlessly and seduced her, deflowering her one day in the chicken coop on the roof just as in the movie with Kamal al-Shinnawi and Shadia. She enjoyed it so she kept going for it whenever he wanted. She even started waiting for him every night. He had threatened to kill her if she told her mother or anybody. Then the secret couldn't be kept anymore when she got pregnant. She was secluded at home for fear of scandal. Her mother was mortified and asked her husband to investigate the matter to find the transgressor and force him to pay the price. The painful thing was that her stepfather put her on a horrendous night trial trying to force her to divulge the name of the culprit, any culprit, by listing certain names that he suspected so she could choose one to accuse. She was so shocked, her tongue became tied and she didn't know what to do except cry and threaten to set herself on fire. Out of desperation she told her mother that it was her husband and nobody else that had done it. The mother confronted him and so did Sittat whereupon he beat them up with the club and taunted the woman about her daughter, claiming that both had brought a scandal and shame upon him. He raised his voice angrily rather than wait for rumors to implicate him if he had kept quiet, the idea being, the louder you shouted, the more likely you were to win. The scandal spread everywhere from palm tree tops to windows, and roofs to where women did their wash on the irrigation canal to the flour mill. The poor mother had no alternative but to run away. She thought of death, but being a believer, that was out of the question. She wished the girl had a brother or a cousin who could rid her of the dishonor. One dark day at dawn, the mother placing her faith in God, dragged her and started traveling to a place where no one knew them. They were overtaken by a dark sun like an ember submerged in black coal dust. In the shade of a faraway willow in a distant village the mother sat her daughter down near the abandoned well of a waterwheel. She parted her legs and caused her to lie on her back and brought a green stalk of mulukhiya or sweet potato plant, she couldn't remember, and inserted it all inside her. It was as if a red hot poker had penetrated her and she screamed at the top of her voice. Her mother muffled her with the edge of her shawl and she kept biting the shawl and growling and snarling as the blood kept flowing slowly into the well of the waterwheel. In the flood were some small clotted masses and a large sticky mass slipped through; she knew in her heart that it was the fetus and began to fight the pain, wishing that she'd faint and never come out of it. Yet she saw her mother hurrying to dry her and wash her, scooping up water with her hand from the well of the water wheel and washing. Then she put some herbal stuff that she must have gotten from one attar or another in some kind of diaper and applied it until the bleeding stopped. Then she carried her daughter by her upper body with whatever strength was left in her, dragging her legs on the ground with her braids sweeping the ground as though they were willow branches. She laid her out on her back in the midst of hemp plants and took off her pleated wrap and spread it on top of the hemp plants making a rectangle of shade which filtered the hot stagnant air of the Ba'una midmorning turning it into a cool breeze. Then she sat next to ner daughter crying her heart out, her whole body shaking, making the earth underneath her move in muffled vibration similar to that made by a train coming from a long distance.

"What'd you do that for, Sittat? Shame on you! Why didn't you tell me from the beginning before things went that far? You should've alerted me. But it is that mad dog. May God take our revenge on him! May I live to see his comeuppance! May I see him cut into pieces under the wheels of a train! May I see dogs eating him! Do I deserve this? Why, God? I am a believer and I perform my prayers. I am lonely and poor. Maybe I've sinned without knowing it. You know what it is like for me. Where would I take her now? Forgive me, Lord! For the sake of Your beloved Prophet, forgive me! I call on the Imam, Sayyeda Zaynab, Sayyeda Nafisa, and Sayyedna al-Hussein to intercede for me! Take my hand and get me out of this misfortune. I pledge, if You get me out of this scandal and protect me, I will have a khatma and a celebration of God's good people."

Sittat knew that her mother would know how to handle matters should any passerby become suspicious. During her intermittent unconsciousness she was aware of her mother leaving the basket by her side and getting up and gathering dry stalks, straw, and dry tree branches. She got some bricks that she pulled out of a dilapidated hut next to the waterwheel with which she made an open hearth for cooking. She piled the firewood and lit it and took out of the basket a pot that had a chicken boiled the night before and placed it on the fire and began to blow on the fire and fan it with the hem of her gallabiya until the broth was heated. She removed the pot from the fire and put in its place a smaller pot filled with mughat mixed with sesame and ghee. Then Sittat lost consciousness of everything around her for what she deemed almost an eternity until she felt a hand gently nudging her under the chin, then two hands raising her head from the ground. She sat up, feeling her mother's belly sticking to her back. With her left hand she encircled her left shoulder and with her right hand she filled the ladle and brought it close to Sittat's lips, whispering like a cat meowing, "Drink, little girl, eat!" and she drank. Then she cut the meat of the chicken into little chunks that she sneaked into Sittat's mouth. Then the mother said, as she returned her to her supine position, "There are two other cooked chickens! As soon as you feel hungry, let me know and I'll heat it up for you."

She went to the open hearth and emptied the sugar-sweetened mughat in a large glass and once again held her up and gave her the mughat to drink then laid her out again. The sun was turning red when two men, an old man and a young one approached. The old man came up to the mother and asked her what she was doing in his land. She burst out crying and told him how her husband, so and so from such and such a village, had mistreated her, and she brought her daughter to go to her family in Kom Hamada. The girl, however, was pregnant and the journey was hard on her so she had a miscarriage and now she didn't know what she was going to tell her husband who was working on the road. The old man squatted next to her and sent his young son to the village and he bought a mat, some blankets, a pillow, a midwife, some supper, and tea and sugar. The midwife examined her and saw that she was all right. She gave her something to drink then spread the mat and arranged the pillow and moved her to a comfortable spot with a cover. She sat with the mother and the two got into a conversation and a chat that she could not follow or understand. They ate supper made up of rice and veal and pigeons. The night fell and they lit the brazier and all the friends of the old man and his sons came and stayed up with him next to the waterwheel under the willow tree until the morning. Then they left and the old man's wife and her daughter came carrying corn fitir, curdled milk, cream, thin flat bread, and eggs fried in ghee. They ate and stayed talking until the call to the sunset prayers and the women, with the exception of the midwife, left. After the night prayers the old man and his friends came back and stayed up. Sittat had felt that she had somewhat recovered, so she woke up and ate her fill. She felt that she could resume walking with her mother wherever the mother wanted to take her. It turned out that the old man was a genuine

Bedouin and wouldn't let the mother and her daughter travel alone under these conditions, so he ordered his son to accompany them with mounts to her family in Kom Hamada. That forced the mother to accept going to her family against her will. There the young man didn't find anyone to welcome him and do their duty by him, so he left the two women at the door of the house and returned. The mother herself couldn't find someone to give her a warm welcome since the unfortunate news had preceded her. So they spent a very unhappy night in the house of her family of which no one was left except a doddering aunt and an old cousin who worked as a foreman in the remnants of the estate and hardly ever stayed at the house. In the morning the mother and daughter left anew, destination unknown, until they reached Damanhour, the big city where people got lost and sins forgotten and covered up. The mother sold a gold necklace and earrings that were all she had and bought tea equipment as some good people advised her to do. She settled on a place in front of the Barakat Cotton Gin where she served tea, coffee, cinnamon tea, and anise seed tea to the workers at the Gin and adjacent shops, and cooked lentils and sprouted fava beans for their breakfast. She made the drinks and the food, and Sittat carried the orders on a tray and took it here and there. They looked for a place to sleep and some good people told them about Wikalat Atiya. The night they arrived, Sayyed Zanati had just come out of prison and come to live in the wikala. He made friends with Shawadfi, who gave him this room. The mother and daughter were in the room downstairs and Sayyed Zanati started flirting with Sittat who repelled his advances because of her earlier experiences with men, yet she came to trust his love of her and his readiness to sacrifice for her, so she agreed to marry him in accordance with the dictates of Islam. As soon as the mother was reassured that her daughter was now the responsibility of a strong man, she bid farewell to life without falling ill. She went to bed at night as usual and did not wake up in the morning. Sayyed Zanati gave her a fitting funeral and had her buried in the charity graves. He made Sittat quit her tea job and began to train her in his line of work which she loved just as she loved Sayyed's personality, for he still loved her better than his other wives even though his physical strength was now devoted to the two younger wives. He still took great pleasure in reading to her at the end of the night things that he liked in his books and magazines which she arranged and took care of for him and she fell in love with them also because they taught her things she could never had thought of on her own.

The clouds of smoke filled the room and we were like two fish in a sea of blue and gray smoke. It was an enchanted atmosphere and Sittat was like a large Nile perch quivering with vitality, excited by the storytelling, laughing at times and frowning at other times but all in a good, beautiful humor. As she told the story and as I drank and she and I smoked, she touched me, embraced, and hugged me with a simplicity and a generosity of spirit and self-confidence, as a straightforward, good friend. It didn't occur to me that she was a woman and a desirable female and that I was a young man tormented with long-repressed desire. And yet I felt a very sweet pleasure.

In the midst of this wonderful moment, there arose at the gate a commotion filled with roughness and orders and shouting. Sittat whispered in some confusion, "The government is here! We haven't seen them in quite some time. Anyway, they are not going to do anything to us but they are a nuisance and will give us nothing but worrying and impudence and bad manners. I also give as good as I get but tonight I can't do much to them because Sayyed is not here and they are the kind who respond better to fear than embarrassment. The least they can do is take me to the police station where I'd spend the night in the lock-up with prostitutes and bums. That's why I am going to do this and I won't open the door even if they break it down."

Then she raised her buxom torso and extended her soft and fleshy arm up to the wall next to the door and turned off the light. We were enveloped in total darkness. Expertly she pushed the brazier and the rest of the smoking paraphernalia aside and crept on her buttocks on the floor until she got near me. Her face hit my face and our breaths mingled.

I clasped her neck and we both went down on the floor, stretched out, when lo and behold I found myself in her ample embrace, totally lost in a lining of soft, hot intoxicating velvet. In the hubbub we could distinguish Shawadfi's voice, "You, sir, honor us with your presence all the time! Your Excellency knows that no Muslim Brothers live in my wikala! Only infidel brothers! Only bums and riffraff live here! So why are you doubting my words? I myself would immediately inform you if I suspect anyone! Don't you remember, sir, that I came to your office and handed you the papers of the boy who was living here and whom you arrested? I don't wait for the honor of your visiting to inspect us everyday or so! I wouldn't hear of your taking the trouble!"

We made out the voice of the officer answering him in a vulgar, arrogant, and unfriendly manner, "You, son of a bitch! I tell you, one of the Muslim Brother biggies is living here with his wife. She, by the way, is fat, white,m and has rosy cheeks. He is an Arabic language teacher in Fayyum, that means he is a fugitive! Our informers have followed them and saw them come in here and not come out. They saw them more than once. Shall we not believe our informers and believe a faggot like you?"

"My dear sir, faggot is not me. I am like your father and you shouldn't insult me for any reason! And I am a sick man. If you slap me once, I'll fall dead. May God protect you in your youth. For you are like my son and my children are grown-up like you and they hold important positions."

Sittat whispered as she embraced me tighter, "He's a liar! Nobody knows anything about his family or where he's come from."

"Son of a bitch! You gave *them* the papers, not me as we agreed! What a cowardly low life." I whispered. The hubbub was getting nearer and rougher. There were sounds of pushing, protest, and grumbling. I heard Shawadfi saying, "In this room lives a student of the Teachers' Institute, quite poor and keeps to himself. I've already shown you his papers. Right now he's gone to his village and will come back tomorrow morning. This here is Dumyana's room and you can hear the agony of the old monkey looking for a way out! Look through this wide hole and you'll see everything! This is Mawawi's room, wide open, and here he is lying down like an animal. Search him, maybe he is hiding a Muslim Brother sheikh in his pocket. This is the room of the maddah and his wife and two kids, also wide open. You can search their bodies if you like. This is the room of Ramadan Eraiga who works with you as an informer and you know better than me where he moves. This is the room of Zainhum al-Atris and his children, let's go have tea with them. Evening, Zainhum. And this here is the fortune teller's room and right now she's spending the evening with her friend, Widad. And this is the tattoo woman's room: Evening, halabiya! If you like, she can tattoo your name on your biceps that would be better than your identity card because it cannot be lost or damaged. This room here is Etaita, the candy woman's room. Evening, Etaita. Say hello to the bey! And, by the way, she has good free-range chicken when your Excellency likes to eat fowl. And this is the room of Sayyed Zanati, your beloved friend about whom you know everything, and, oh, well. It's a good thing we thought of that! Sayyed always tells you about everything and you trust him, so ask him about the truth. Luckily he and his whole team have gone to Cairo for the mulid of Sayyedna al-Hussein, may Umm Hashimi's blessings be with us. Here are all the rooms open in front of you, Excellency. Go in to your heart's content. As for the closed ones, we have no business with them because they are my responsibility so long as their tenants are absent. If you think someone is hiding in these two closed rooms, get me a warrant from the prosecutor general and let's break them at his responsibility so I would be in the clear. You are a man of law and you know my responsibility."

We heard a new voice, maybe that of another officer, saying threateningly, "In any case, the wikala is not far from our sights. We'll look out for that man at all times. If he is seen leaving here we will ram this whole pillar up your ass! We will show you no mercy! You will be convicted of harboring a criminal and you will go to jail! Your end will be at my hand, you Shawadfi dog! Let's go."

The hubbub started moving away. I don't know whether it was out of fear and desperation or because of the burning desire and the wind hitting the embers that what happened happened even though it wasn't planned. As soon as the hubbub totally disappeared, Sittat and I had turned into one body, shaking to the core with strong, mad intoxicated pleasure whose hot magic went deep and almost pulverized itself in a roaring fire. The ecstasy seemed to have no beginning and no end, even though there were occasional stops to catch our breath. With the morning light we went to the room downstairs where we washed and had a delicious breakfast in profound silence. And, without a single word but with perfect understanding, I sat in front of Sittat who held the razor and began to shave off my beard calmly and in a good mood. When I looked in the mirror I saw a brand new face, totally fresh and glowing, and redolent with eau de cologne. I got up and put on all my clothes. Sittat got up and gently opened the door a little bit and the morning light came in cool and gray and intimately familiar. She opened the window and rays of the sun came in like honey spread on the floor. Sittat brought the tea-making equipment and lit the stove. We were surprised to see all the day's newspapers slipped through the open window by an unknown hand used to doing that every day. I began reading them with interest and to the accompaniment of the pleasant intimate humming of the stove, I began to read aloud so Sittat would hear. She listened attentively as she extended her hand with the tea-kettle over the stove. We awaited Sayyed Zanati's arrival to tell him what happened so that he might think of a new play for us now that the old one had been exposed.

What a Night!

It was obvious that something unusual had happened to Sayyed Zanati and his wives at the mulid of al-Hussein. For since his arrival he had been frowning quite visibly even though he did his best to relax the muscles of his face and fix them in a broad smile to look normal. But who'd believe him? He forgot those around him totally for long periods that he spent absently absorbed in smoking and drinking. And, like a possessed dervish he interrupted his reverie with a gasp or a moan or a groan that could only indicate a reaction to discovering something new, which meant that be was in a state of intense dialogue with himself—a state displayed clearly on his face in a casual smile or a sudden, inexplicable fit of anger. Things were also falling from his hands either because of poor nerves or because he lost sensation in his hands for a few moments. For the first time he lost at playing cards and it was obvious he was playing only to keep the men around for as long as possible, then he had to agree to their leaving. Even the news of the police coming to the wikala and their putting us under surveillance did not make an impression upon him; it was as if he had never heard it. He spent many hours like that from the moment he arrived. The wrappings around the packages of food that he had brought had written on them that they were from Mudiriya Street in Damanhour and not from Sayyedna al-Hussein in Cairo as he had promised before he left. Those packages were lying next to us on the floor like an unattended corpse. Finally he asked for dinner and the wrappings were opened and the contents, kabab, kufta, liver and brain and salads, were served. We ate with bowed heads and without a word. From that moment, Sayyed stopped speaking and, like a mute, began asking for things with unambiguous gestures that had to be obeyed at once. Finally, Sittat and I got up: "What happened, so and so?"

"Nothing."

"Okay, you, so and so, what happened?"

"Nothing."

"How about you, so and so? Tell us something."

"Personally, I don't know."

"And you, so and so?"

"You know as much as I do!"

"Well, how about you Sayyed?"

"Well, there's something I've been thinking about."

"Would you like us to leave you to sleep?"

"No, I'll be all right in a little while."

And indeed his mood started getting better after the tenth drink and after going through a quarter ounce of fragrant green hashish that gave off thick smoke. His laughter, however, was not clear, his glances were unfocused and his jokes old and silly and not funny, but rather pitiable especially that he assumed they would tickle us with their novelty and the profundity of their meanings so he followed the telling with loud, hollow laughter whereupon we would laugh at his laughter like crazies overcome with inexplicable hysteria. Yet I and Sittat picked up on a thread at which our eyes met with lightening speed that was enough to provide some understanding. We had caught Sayyed Zanati, more than once, sneaking anxious pitiful and desperate glances at Gannuna. So we figured out that the root of the matter had something to do with her. Then the thread began to unravel little by little, very slowly. The secret messenger between my eyes and Sittat's said that we had been preoccupied with Sayyed Zanati's condition and neglected Gannuna's even though she was more deserving of compassion. She was in a truly pitiable condition, her face pale, exerting excruciating effort to appear normal and composed. She was almost totally oblivious as if she were a mother who had lost all her children in one fell swoop in an earthquake. From time to time she would place her hand on her belly in pain and growling sounds came from it. Had we looked closely at them the moment they arrived at midmorning we would have figured out that Sayyed's condition was actually a reaction to Gannuna's unnatural condition. Besides, coming back as they did at midmorning meant that they had missed the big night.

It was getting close to midnight when the hubbub in the wikala's courtyard began to subside among those sleeping outdoors, especially roving merchants and vendors getting ready to set up their displays early in the morning at a market in a nearby village. The noise had dwindled to whispers and soft sounds when the sound of a very attractive crooning rose to the surface. As soon as it could be heard all the other voices stopped as if to ask the singer to raise his voice. All he had sung was the traditional opening of a mawwal in a melody that, in it's lower and upper registers, sounded like an extraordinary feat of vocal acrobatics as if in pronouncing a single 'ah' he had loaded it with dozens of emotions on behalf of thousands of listeners causing it to hum in their chests with all degrees of feelings. As soon as he finished that opening with a clean-cut stop like a period at the end of a sentence, an overwhelming roar rose like thunder shouting "Allaaaah! Again, please, good man! May God reward you! How sweet! A nightingale!" And right away everyone, each of whom had come from a different village or town, turned into a single listener. We heard the sounds of the doors of the wikala rooms open so everybody would take part in listening and applauding. Even Shawadfi shouted from his mastaba, "What a wonderful night! We haven't had anything like that in quite some time. May it be a good omen. For there's a curse of blood on this wikala. And it's about time for some joy. Sing, sing, good man, as much as you like. Tonight we'd like to forget this bitch of a life!"

Right away Sayyed Zanati's and Gannuna's faces changed into all kinds of hues. Gannuna began to lose her composure; she looked worried and her features contracted and she knit her brows and seemed to be in the grip of incomprehensible terror. Sayyed's features froze as if he had died and the smile on his lips looked like a skull's open mouth. Gannuna fidgeted and changed her sitting posture several times. She looked so worried that she tried resting her head on her palm several times a minute. Finally she looked at Sayyed in genuine supplication, bringing her voice up with great difficulty from a distant depth, "With your permission, Sayyed, I'd like to go downstairs and stretch out a bit. I am tired and my head is about to split in two!"

The smile moved between his lips like a dead fish dangling down between his jaws. He nodded as his eyes fixed her with an almost audible glance saying, "So, it's like that then? Okay, okay." And yet Sayyed didn't utter a word. He looked at the other young wife to his right and motioned her with his chin to go upstairs to rest if she was tired of the trip. She complied right away as if she had been waiting for it and was quicker than Gannuna in getting up and even extended her hand to the latter, who clung to it and got up, almost staggering. Through the open inner door right in front, the narrow spiral staircase with rusted iron banister squeaked in the hands of two women, one going downstairs and the other upstairs. We could see a back with a pointed butt casting its shadow on a face with a pointed chest, each slipping away from the other. Sayyed opened his tin cigarette case and rolled a cigarette with roasted tobacco that he kept in a large pouch. Then he lit the cigarette and took a deep drag on it then got up and crossed the room to the door overlooking the courtyard. He put on his slippers and went down into the courtyard, saying that he was coming back in a little while to talk to me about something.

I stayed alone with Sittat and the woman from Arish. As soon as Sayyed made it to the courtyard the woman from Arish and Sittat bent toward each other like magnets, displaying a longing for gossip. Then the whispering acquired tones of ominous rhythm. I had to bend my torso and incline my head toward them to be able to listen. But the voice of the singer had begun to resound and glow with tunes of torment, the fire of love, perplexity, and tragic pain:

If I complain to stone one quarter of what I have, it would melt!
First, to the Prophet, second, to Job!
Third to being away from home!
Fourth to Fate!
Fifth: once a victor, now a victim!

"Wow! More please! May God reward you!"

The voice went on.

A jailer was given orders to kill love!
Watching every crevice and peephole in the cell,
Lighting the prisoner's heart on fire.
I said, please, jailer, give me a chance to see my love.
He said: I've been given my orders.
The judge of love was black.
The one who gave the verdict, a Turk!
You've spared no one, O Time.
So why spare me?
The precious you've sold cheap.
To you, nothing is dear!

There was torment and lovesickness in his voice and a hoarse wailing resounding like the ringing sound of church bells. And despite the uproar that rose suddenly in thunderous admiration, imploring the singer to continue delivering his burning, sorrowful moaning, we could hear Gannuna's wailing crying coming from downstairs, almost breaking our hearts. It was the crying of a tormented human being who had no say whatsoever in her fate. Perhaps *she* was that prisoner for whom the jailer had orders; perhaps her crying was out of commiseration and pity for that prisoner whose complaint to stone would cause it to melt!

It was now easy to see the connection between the singer and his words and tunes and what was happening to Gannuna and Sayyed Zanati. The singer was no mere singer but in addition, a genuine lover, scorched by the fire that undoubtedly burned his heart. The beloved, setting that fire in the heart of the singer was, either specifically Gannuna herself, or she could be in a similar situation. Thus the singing was a broadcast aimed at the prisoner and the jailer, calling for fairness and sympathy.

After Sittat and the woman from Arish had their fill of barely distinguishable gossip in which they used words with missing letters and others that were nasal, I shouted at them impatiently to tell me what was going on or else I'd go crazy. Sittat kept flailing and wailing and beating her chest with her hand. The woman from Arish bent toward me with a withered smile and a mouth dry with fear and apprehension, saying that Sayyed had taken them to the pavilion of the Shadhliya Sufi order as he did every year. The hosts welcomed them and served them the traditional tharid of bread sopped in broth with big chunks of meat. During supper, Sayyed noticed that some of the men gathered around the other platter of tharid were staring at Gannuna in disbelief. The woman from Arish noticed that Sayyed was pleased at first, since he was used to men flirting with Gannuna and their being smitten with her wild peasant beauty, which caused them to lose control. But she also began to get concerned when she saw that Sayyed's face was beginning to change. He was frowning when he saw those looking at Gannuna were bending toward each other, whispering, then looking again, then whispering some more and arguing. Some of them were heard saying confidently, "It's her! Yes, it's her! I am willing to bet my own arm if it isn't her, in person. If people found out it was her, here, it'd be quite a spectacle. It would be the darkest night. Are the folks here? I saw so and so in person here and also so and so. Oh, what a catastrophe! The two rivals and the rival of the rival are all here with us? Are we destined to see the catastrophe? May God spare us the calamity and prevent a meeting! We should tell them! We should *not* tell them. No, we should tell the flesh at least to protect his flesh. I wish we never came here; I wish we never saw. Well, we haven't seen anything. How can we?" The woman from Arish was sure that Sayyed heard all that buzz. As for Gannuna and the other brat, as she called her, they didn't notice anything at the time. The woman from Arish felt that Sayyed's mood had changed, that he'd become worried as he followed that group as they washed their hands and snuck out one after the other, leaving the pavilion even though they were supposed to stay and take part in dhikr and serve the newcomers. Sayyed looked apprehensively but he stayed calm and smiling, greeting people and returning their greetings. He had sat with his three wives in the row on the right close to the street. To his right was Gannuna and to his left the other brat and next to her, the woman from Arish, her eyes scouting the road looking over men's heads looking for a danger she expected to come. And come it did. In about a quarter of an hour they saw a group of young men making their way slowly and cautiously to the pavilion, dazzled by the lights and the noise. Among them were some of those who were eating next to them, winking at the new arrivals as they pointed to Gannuna. As soon as one of them saw her he'd open his mouth in shock and utter an exclamation such as "Yes, it's her of course, son of a gun!" Some would leave right after they'd made sure it was her and others would just stand and stare.

Amazingly it was Gannuna herself who exposed herself without knowing it. She gasped several times upon suddenly seeing more than one person. With every gasp, Sayyed Zanati looked at her and the person and his surprise grew. The singer had started and the loudspeakers had carried his resonant voice and many people began to sway in dhikr to the rhythm and tunes. The pavilion was electrified with the sound and the movement and utterings of "peace and blessing on the Prophet" all the time. But the delegations of strangers coming to take a look at Gannuna's face didn't stop. Every few minutes new faces fixed them with shocked looks focusing on Gannuna's whole body in sorrow, regret, gloating, contempt, or pity. Then a group of five well-dressed, handsome young men came in, dragging a well-dressed, handsome young man like Sayyedna Yusef, but emaciated and weak as if still convalescing from a long, debilitating illness. He stood in front of them like a child happy to find the favorite toy that he had lost and given up hope on finding again. He almost shouted her name in sheer joy but he was bashful and shy, so he closed his mouth the second that he tried to shout. Then tears poured profusely from his eyes and he would wipe them with the wide sleeve of his gallabiya but they'd pour again. Then all of a sudden he collapsed and sat right in front of her. As for her, the colors in her face kept changing. She couldn't help herself and started slapping her own cheek with her palm in sorrow and self rebuke. She bowed her head and a pool of tears filled her lap. Pity Sayyed Zanati and what happened to him then! He was confused and in pain, as if they had dunked him in a vat of boiling water. All of a sudden the emaciated man got up and sneaked to the microphone, seizing upon the opportunity of the singer finishing one round of dhikr and resting, to give people a chance to catch their breath in preparation for another round. The young man held the microphone and let out of his chest an 'ah' that was divine and moist with the sweat of longing. When he started the traditional opening *Ya lail, ya ain* it attracted the audiences of the nearby pavilions and the passerby. The young man started a *mawwal* in which he told his story from the time the apple of his eye had disappeared to that day and details of what had happened to family and friends. Gannuna's body started shaking violently as she cried just as she was doing now. Sayyed felt that they had become the spectacle for the night. He bent over the woman of Arish's ear and told her to accompany Gannuna and sneak out of the pavilion pretending to be going to the bathroom at the Green Portal and wait there. After a short while he bent over the brat and told her to join them calmly. Then after a few moments he himself sneaked out after them, feeling the gun in his vest pocket and the switchblade hidden in the tight fitting sleeve of his undershirt. As soon as he caught up with them he encircled them with his arms and pushed them into the first taxi they came across, shouting at the driver "Cairo Station, quickly, usta." They took the first train to Damanhour at midmorning. The last thing the woman from Arish imagined was that the young man singer would find out where they were going and catch up with them at the wikala together with some of his friends who had been with him singing and asking for a fair trial with a fair judge and jury.

I found myself jumping up and going out, driven by an overpowering desire to see this young man and listen to his complaint carefully to get every last detail. I was flabbergasted with the sight of the thick crowd gathered throughout the courtyard that nobody had been aware of. It seemed that they had all accidentally found an evening of entertainment, free of charge, and also free of treachery and unpleasant surprises, so they decided to enjoy it all to the fullest. I looked for a spot to sit near the singer who stood almost in the middle, surrounded by some of his companions, who acted like a chorus repeating some pained refrains after him. From time to time he would turn around to face a different part of the crowd as a professional singer trained to deal with audiences would do.

I heard Sayyed Zanati's voice calling me. I looked around and found him sitting on Shawadfi's mastaba gulping glasses of distilled alcohol and smoking hashish cigarettes. I made it through to him wading among bodies sitting or lying in various postures, all eyes glued to the singer. The mastaba was crowded; seated on and around it in addition to Shawadfi were Sayyed Zanati, Zainhum al-Atris, Ramadan Eraiga, Buri, the Undertaker, the supplier of begging children, the maddah, the muwawi, and some of the wikala's neighbors.

The singer had gotten tired of complaining and his wait for a look at the face of his beloved got long. After turning around while singing out of courtesy to the audience, he now started looking around for his beloved's face not only among those sitting but also behind the doors and the windows. When he gave up on the beloved's appearance, he started a new mawwal in which he called her out explicitly and in supplication, asking the saints to intercede for him so that the beloved would show her face, even for a fleeting moment, have mercy on him, appreciate the long distance he had traveled after his bird, to see it and make sure it was still alive, let alone his previous separation and the suffering he had endured on its account.

At that point, Sayyed Zanati said passionately as if talking to himself, "That boy has broken my heart! I can't take it anymore. I am made of flesh and blood so I should have mercy. I swear by God I will treat your heart and heal your wound, may God heal all our wounds! I will do what men you never dream of meeting would do. I will buy you off with an unparalleled act of charity. Do you think I am a nighttime highway-robber tenant of Wikalat Atiya? No, dear sir! I swear by your mother whom I haven't met yet, I am Sayyed Zanati and everyone knows me! I will rule fairly while on solid ground. There are no fair judges so let me try the judge's bench tonight. If ruling fairly will hurt my heart, ruling unfairly will break yours!"

I was certain at that point that I was in the presence of a completely different person. Those sitting exchanged merry glances thinking that excessive drinking had driven Sayyed Zanati to megalomania and hallucination, all except Shawadfi, of course. For he understood Sayyed Zanati's true personality, otherwise he wouldn't have tolerated him and accepted his presence as one of the pillars of the wikala—it wouldn't have been smart to make an enemy of him. Shawadfi had told me several times that Sayyed, despite his viciousness, was exceptionally kind and good at heart. I thought that Shawadfi was saying that to justify his appreciation of Sayyed Zanati to the extent of submitting to his will sometimes. It was now clear that Sayyed had told Shawadfi the story so he could support him if things got out of hand. Sayyed was now giving Shawadfi a signal with his eyes, which Shawfdi understood at once, and made a gesture to Sheikh Zainhum al-Atris. The latter brought his head close to Shawadfi's head and he whispered something which the sheikh received with a nod. Then he went over to the singer, waving his cane in the air, asking for silence. Everybody fell silent; the singer waited, smiling. Zainhum al-Atis leaned on his cane and shouted, "May we all have a wonderful night by praying for the beloved Prophet! This is a night in a lifetime. The singer and his friends have honored us, may God reward them with prosperity. May God reward them all with visiting the Prophet just as they had given us joy. Let me hear your prayers and blessings on the Prophet. One more time! The long and short of it is that the singing gentleman has been singing from the beginning of the night until the beginning of its end and we have been listening and expressing our admiration without living up to our obligations. The singer is flesh and blood like us. He must be starving to death while a stranger in our town, and we are told to be hospitable to strangers, for the sake of the Prophet! Let me hear your prayers and blessings on the Prophet! One more time! That's enough for tonight or have you forgotten that you'd have to get up at first light to set up your displays at the market, which is quite a distance away? As for the singing gentleman, he has an even more important market. Frankly, we have invited him tonight. So nightingale, bring your companions and come!"

A lively commotion started among the crowd under the dim lights as if there were waves in a sea whose bottom was mightily disturbed and there began a tumultuous turbulence in the water. Everyone began to mark his territory by lying down and by stretching, demarcating its borders. There was much pushing and pulling and nudging and slapping and punching and whispering and muffled shouts and threats followed by slaps, kicks, and spitting met with the same as the singer and his group stood in a neutral spot in the middle apprehensively waiting for calm to prevail so they could find their way to where they had been invited. Then there was one growl from Shawadfi sitting on the mastaba, like the roar of that lion that appeared before the beginning of some foreign movies: he opened his mouth and closed it as if a huge gate squeaked harshly as it dragged its weight, and right away the commotion died down totally. It was as if Shawadfi with that roar had cast over them the cover of silence and calm whereupon the courtyard turned into a land dotted with dunes and piles of black rubble.

The singer and his group started moving behind Sheikh Zainhum al-Atris toward the gate through a thin isthmus between the dunes, raising the hem of his gallabiya. Sayyed Zanati, however, got up and waved his arm to Sheikh Zainhum to take them to his room, which he did. Sayyed pulled me by the hand and took me toward the gate without saying a word. He kept walking fast and energetically in balanced, elegant, and sure steps. His cream-colored silk gallabiya with a half collar and sleeves that narrowed at the wrists without cuffs splitting them on the inside swayed robustly with the wind. His chin was level with his chest and he looked far ahead with a strange focus. I was panting hard to keep up with him so there was no opportunity for any questions. But I was apprehensive about his serious demeanor and his frowning, anxious face. I guessed that he was going to call the police to have the singer and his companions arrested on the trumped up charges of pursuing him to his house to attack him with the intent of kidnapping his wife. That was what it looked like to me. I was greatly surprised to see him go through the big, clean, pricey streets, moving away from the police station. Surprisingly, he stopped in front of Khat'an, the kabab restaurant, the most famous and biggest restaurant in the city, frequented only by the upper crust of society, people who appreciated the cuts of meat, their freshness, and delicious taste. He went to the cashier and ordered three pounds of kabab and kufta and six pairs of pigeons, paying an astounding sum without batting an eyelash. He paid a tip discretely in the palm of his hand to the guy who filled the order and kept watching him to make sure he chose the best pieces for him. We carried the large magnificent package and went to the market where he bought several bags of fruits and a bottle of cognac and an assortment of cheeses and pickles. We carried all that and returned as quickly as we went without either of us uttering a word. As we got closer to the gate of the wikala he looked at my surprise, smiling for the first time since his return from the mulid. In the dim light of the distant full moon the smile lit his face, completely changing his features. The side close to me appeared handsome and dignified, becoming thinkers and men of letters preoccupied almost always with thinking and analyzing. He turned his neck looking at my face: "Of course you think I paid too much even though I've just come from an expensive trip? Money in the final analysis is the most trivial aspect of the whole thing. If only it were just a question of money. Being a good guy has a high price, my friend, and not every good guy can afford to pay even though he's a good guy. As for money, it's easy: for just as it comes, it goes and just as it goes, it comes. As for the price of being a good guy, that never changes. This is the most precious advice you can get from your brother Sayyed: if you know what something's worth in blood money, kill it. If you don't know, then get along. A door that lets in the wind, block it and get it over with. If you come across good that costs you evil, forgoing it would be propitious. These are my beliefs in life and yet I cannot practice them most of the time because they need arduous training from childhood. That's why I am telling you about them so you can keep them nailed in your mind. If you know things like these but don't follow them, you'll be tormented in your life whenever you do the opposite. And, by the way, everything I do in my life is the opposite of what I wish and what pleases me. I do not know to this day why I do what I do. If I did, maybe I'd abstain. But I know, deep down that I must know one of these days and my scale will be balanced and I will live like the rest of humanity even if just for one day. Tonight I will make up for all the good behavior I missed!"

He went through the gate sideways. I followed him. Shawadfi saw us off, wishing us good appetite, indicating that he might join us shortly.

The Messenger

There must have been something magical about the room to make it accommodate so many despite seeming so small, as if it were made of rubber. The woman from Arish sat crosslegged to one side of the door opening as Sittat sat facing her on the other side. Sheikh Zainhum al-Atris sat in the center at the other end of the room and next to him the singer and three young men about his age, color, good looks, and good spirits. They each had a well-turned Saidi turban with the edge of the shawl dangling on the side of the neck. They had clean gallabiyas with wide sleeves. They didn't look like thugs or bums; rather, in their dignified silence they looked like shy and modest artists.

We greeted them and set down the packages. The woman from Arish and Sittat took them and went downstairs. All those sitting got up to welcome us. We shook hands very warmly. Sayyed Zanati sat in his usual place and motioned me to sit opposite him next to Sheikh Zainhum, facing the singer and two of his companions with the third sitting on the other side of Sheikh Zainhum. As he turned toward them, Sayyed Zanati said in graceful welcome, "You've honored us! Welcome!"

"The honor is all ours! A prince among men!" they said in unison. The singer had sat crosslegged, relaxed and confident, as if he were now certain that he had finally made it to a safe harbor and that his lost and confused ships had laid anchor after a terribly tumultuous absence in the midst of raging storms. He placed his hand on his chest in a gesture of gratitude and pointing to himself he said, "Yours truly, Badi' Abd al-Mawla." Then he pointed to the one sitting next to him, "And Hadi Abu al-Hasan," and to the one next to him: "Jalal al-Muhammadi," to the one sitting next to me opposite him: "and Haggag Abu Isma'in. We are bosom buddies who were born and raised together. We are inseparable and no one of us is better than the other, present company included."

We all said approvingly, "Welcome to you all! You've honored us! Best people!"

The singer added as if he had forgotten an important piece of information in his birth certificate, "Jirja township."

"Best people!"

The mumbled reply got mixed with the sharp tapping sound of women's slippers on the staircase. The woman from Arish was coming up carrying a tray with glasses, two bottles, the cheese, and the pickles. I bent and pulled the amazing low table that Sayyed had designed which could be folded like a suitcase and placed against the wall to be used as an arm rest. I opened it and with Sheikh Zainhum's help she placed what she had on top of it then crouched and arranged the glasses before those seated. She opened one of the bottles by holding the cork between her beautiful teeth and pulling it. She poured liquor into each glass then went and sat down next to the door. Then Sittat came in with a big tray and we took the glasses in our hands. She started moving platters of kabab, kufta, pigeon, bread, and fruits from the tray to the low table and stood waiting for orders. Sayyed Zanati gave her a signal with his eyes pointing upstairs and downstairs. Sittat turned to the staircase, went up two steps and called out, then down four steps and called out, "So and so." Right away we heard the footsteps coming down the stairs and saw the head of the one coming up the stairs. They both came in and the four women sat on a spot close to the door where the woman from Arish placed a platter of kabab.

Sheikh Zainhum rolled up his sleeve and said, "In the name of God" and began to eat. We all attacked the food and drink, finishing what was placed before us in a few moments. The women's appetite was less healthy for there were left on their platter pieces enough to fill two loaves and a considerable amount of cheese. Suddenly we heard a hubbub at the gate in which the name Hagg Sayyed Zanati was mentioned several times. That made Sayyed Zanati prick up his ears and say optimistically, "That's a good omen! He made me a hagg for free!" In a short while we heard footsteps approaching, then Shawadfi appeared, bowing his head so as not to hit the doorframe. "Peace upon you," and "Upon you peace," then he squatted in front of the leftover food and stuffed a loaf with some choice pieces of meat and folded it like a roll and began speaking to Sayyed Zanati as he gnawed at his sandwich.

"There's a dervish who's asking about you. He says he's a special messenger bringing you a message from Sidi al-Qinawi."

"Bless you, Sidi Abd al-Rahim," said Sheikh Zainhum al-Atris even before the Saidi men.

Sayyed Zanati waved his arm in a gesture of dismissal, then pointed to his head as if to say, "I am not in the mood for these crazies at this time." Shawadfi said in all seriousness, "No, he is not only one of those dervishes you're thinking of. He's not an idiot. He is actually quite rational. He looks no less than a respectable sheikh of a Sufi order. I also thought of brushing him off and I tried. But he insists on meeting you in person because a message is a trust until it is delivered to the person it is intended for. As if Sidi Abd al-Rahim al-Qinawi is still alive and sending messages! But the man is unshakable in his position. I think you should meet him at least to find out who he is and what he wants and do that quickly and get it over with because he is determined to sit by my side until he sees you. I thought he wanted to spend the night for free but it looks as if he has money and is used to being in authority." Sayyed Zananti, still preoccupied, started to give some thought.

Zainhum exclaimed, "And what's wrong with that, master? It's not far-fetched for Sidi Abd al-Rahim to send messages while lying in his tomb. His miracles are undeniable, there's no doubt about it. And who knows? Maybe it's an important message, so there's no need to make fun of the man or else we'd be making fun of Sidi Abd al-Rahim himself. For to honor the messenger is to honor the one who sent him. Are you following, master? I now feel that if we disappoint this man, God will not grant us success in doing what we want to do!"

Shawadfi waved his arm as he tossed the last morsel into his mouth that looked like the opening on an oven and said, "The man said something strange: he said that he had left Sidi Abd al-Rahim's mosque after the night prayer and came all the way from Qena to here on foot. He came so late because he stopped for two prostrations in the Sidi Jalal mosque in Asyut and did the same in al-Sayyeda Zaynab's mosque in Cairo and the same in al-Imam mosque and al-Sayyeda Aisha mosque and al-Sayyeda Nafisa mosque. Then he found himself nearby, so he seized the opportunity and performed two prostrations at Sidi Ahmed al-Badawii and two in Abu al-Aynayn mosque. In Damanhour he performed two prostrations at al-Tawba mosque before coming to the wikala. I thought he was hallucinating but he gave me irrefutable evidence: he said that Sidi Abd al-Rahim al-Qinawi knew that Sayyed Zanati would spend the whole of the big night at the mulid of al-Hussein and that was why he sent his messenger to the tent where he was. When he went there, he saw Sayyed Zanati riding the automobile with his harem coming back here. So he left him knowing that it was Sidi Abd al-Rahim who inspired him to leave because God wanted to protect him and Sidi Abd al-Rahim doesn't do that except for those whom he expects to be among his important disciples the ones to whom he would impart his secret."

At that point Sheikh Zainhum al-Atris exclaimed in genuine passion, "God is great! God is great! May God give his blessings to the Perfect Light! Send him, man! What a hard-hearted man you are. You hear all of this and don't send for him right away? Please forgive him, Sidi Abd al-Rahim. I beseech you in the name of Sidi al-Atris!"

I shuddered and had goose flesh and I heard the hair crackling on my head as I scratched it. The round florescent lamp in the ceiling casts its lights on the faces and they all appeared pale pistachio colored. Getting more perplexed, Sayyed Zanati said, "That's so unexpected! There is no strength and no power save in God! May those staying be spared the harm brought by outsiders."

The woman from Arish said in a voice shaking with a sense of discovery and the intuition of her Bedouin folks, "My heart tells me that the message this messenger is talking about has something to do with our present situation."

"Well, outsiders can bring good. God knows I only meant well. Anyway, bring him, Shawadfi."

Taking two steps, Shawadfi was in the middle of the courtyard, shouting, "Come on in, Chief! It's safe!"

We heard sounds of invocation and indistinct mumblings with steps approaching. Then we saw an imposing, awe-inspiring giant and we all stood up to greet him with respect and veneration. He had a fair complexion with delicate, handsome features with a long, thick, clean beard with a few white hairs that made his appearance even more awe inspiring. His mouth was hidden under thick mustaches connected to his sideburns. He was wearing a fancy gray wool gallabiya, under which peered the silky cotton lines of his qutniya in whose folds the mother-of-pearl buttons of his vest sparkled. His turban was a large silk shawl on top of a red, pointed, pyramid-shaped Moroccan hood. On his shoulders was a black broadcloth cloak. He had boots on and held a thin, finely shaped cane, as if he were the headman of a large village. His kohl-adorned eyes, however, looked distant as if were not conscious of his surroundings. His glances were unfocused as if not looking at anything in particular even for a passing moment. There was a glimmer of mysteriousness but somehow certain craziness in his eyes. He said in a sing-song eloquent voice, melodious as if he were a Qur'an reciter, "Peace on those children of Adam and Eve who follow the rightly guided path!"

"And upon you peace and God's mercy and His blessings!"

One by one, we shook hands with him and he went along arrogantly like someone who wanted to go through a heavy loathsome task. He just touched the tips of our fingers quickly. We made room for him right next to Sayyed who offered him a hefty cushion but he turned it down preferring to sit on the floor, still wearing his boots. As soon as he settled where he was sitting, Gannuna started rearranging the leftover food on the platter and offered it to him. He pushed it aside gently also in silence. He took out of his side pocket a dried date which he split in two and put one half in his mouth and the other half in his side pocket, "Would you like some tea, Chief?"

"Thank you, thank you, my son. But please remove these loathsome bottles from in front of me. You, son of Zanati, don't know your value, but Sidi Qinawi knows it."

The woman from Arish extended her hand and gathered the glasses, but he reached out gently and mumbled something to the effect that he had changed his mind out of confidence in their good intentions and that he had not intended to spoil their fun or good mood. So the woman from Arish returned things as they were, then hesitated a little and poured liquor in all the glasses. At that point the man turned to Sayyed Zanati, "So, you are Hagg Sayyed Zanati, of course. I had your picture with me since I left. Sidi Abd al-Rahim al-Qinawi gave it to me. As for the message, it is simple but important: Sidi Abd al-Rahim al-Qinawi, may God be pleased with him and may He please him, says to you: The trust that you found in the street one day: do not give it up until you have returned it intact to its owners and God will recompense you well."

Then he fell silent and silence enveloped us all. We all looked at Sayyed Zanati who got absorbed in deep thought that made his eyes pop, and he kept thinking, obviously perturbed.

"What trust? I've never found anything in the street, ever! I've often dreamt of a wallet that I'd find in the street or a treasure in a hole but none of that ever happened. God knows I don't remember anything like that. But, if Sidi Abdal-Rahim remembers, I'd be glad if he'd remind me."

The man waved impassively: "This is what my sheikh and master said to me. The duty of the messenger is only to convey the message. I have conveyed it. God be my witness."

We all looked worried. There was a clear look of apprehension in the eyes of the Saidis. The man said as if having pity on us, "In any case, I am staying with you for some time. Maybe you'll remember. Sidi Abd al-Rahim doesn't lie and he doesn't invent things. All there is to it is that life is full of play and fun and ornaments and man by nature is forgetful. Go back to what you were doing. Drink and have fun. Don't be deceived by seeing my body in front of you. I'll run and perform prayers in the Sidi Abu al-Makarim mosque nearby. Let my body be until I come back and take it away back to my sheikh and master to tell him the reply to the message."

Then he fidgeted as he sat there and began to adjust his position in various directions until he determined the direction of the qibla so he turned his face toward it. Now his face was looking at the inner staircase with a slight deviation while his back was facing it with a sharp turn. That made the women move away from the space in front of him as if they feared blocking his way to heaven. He got absorbed into a genuine prayer that cut him totally off those sitting there. Sayyed Zanati sat up, feigning a smile, saying, "Let's go back to our subject. What's your story exactly, Si Badi' ? Don't hide anything; we're brothers. Tell us the whole story from A to Z." Badi' sat up, breathing deeply as if he had been saved from drowning.

Badi‘

“My story, after asking for blessing of the Prophet, is a wonderous tale, if written with points of needles on the eyes, it would provide a lesson for those that listen. I was betrayed by friend and beloved and Time!”

“There was a young man by the name of Badi‘, a fruit grocer by trade. God gave him of His bounty. He had a store in the town market, well stocked, and things were going very well. His heart, however, was smitten with art and the wound of art can only be cured with love.

“He loved God in His creation. In His oranges, His grapes, His peaches, His pomegranates, His dates, His pears, His mangos, His guavas, His apples, and His figs. He was in love with God’s orchard and he thought: “if this is this world’s fruit available even to sinners, what will the garden of the afterlife, promised to the pious and the pure of heart be like?”

“He started singing of the fruit as if he were singing of love itself and singing of love as if he were singing of fruits of various kinds: ‘O fruity, luscious figs! God has sworn by you, O figs! Your country is far away, O grapes, homesickness has taken away your color! O bananas, beloved’s fingers! O apples, beloved’s cheeks! O peach, that some may impeach, but not us!’

“A merry fruit grocer with a pure heart. He sang at weddings for free. For him all the lasses were fruits and each bride was the essence of fruitiness and merriness in one, a fakiha, in short. The fruit grocer’s mawwal never changed, yet was always new. If he forgot it, lovers at weddings would remind him of it.

“His words in song reached Fakiha, sister of his dear friend. He had never seen her nor dreamt of seeing her. But she took his mawwal as a personal message to her. She fell in love with the fruit grocer without his knowing it.

“Love is like perfume; it can never be hidden. Word of longing reached the fruit grocer. It stirred him up, filled his heart with yearning, fantasy, and hope. He started singing to one beloved in particular. The mawwal to fakiha now meant *Fakiha* alone rather than all fruits as it always had.

“The words got hot and they lit the tunes and made the voice ring out of a pained heart burned with the true fire of love. Before, singing was a sweet fantasy, now it was a living experience that captivated the audiences and reached their heart as quick as fire in dry firewood.

“In town there were a hundred girls named Fakiha but the mawwal hit without being aimed and instead of fruit in general it homed in on Fakiha, sister of the singer’s friend. The singing fruit grocer said to himself: ‘No harm done! I am a well-off fruit grocer that any Fakiha in town would desire. The heart’s beloved is my friend’s sister: so what is there to prevent me from asking for her hand in the way enjoined by God, His Prophet and the faithful?’

“The fruit grocer gathered the notables and they went to ask for Fakiha’s hand for the fruit grocer, the singer, and her brother’s bosom buddy. But Time in its very nature has treason, for no reason. The fruit grocer was met with rejection and disapproval. The fruit grocer saw Time’s treachery in his dear friend’s eyes and he was overcome with worry and sorrow.

“The fruit grocer, in pain at his grievous loss cried: ‘What has changed you, Abd al-Mawla, my dearest friend?’ He replied, ‘You are not my friend at all and you cannot ask me for anything.’ ‘Why, Abd al-Mawla, may God keep all evil away?’

"'He who sings publicly about love for his friend's sister and causes scandals at wedding miscrophones is no friend! How dare you come after that and ask for her hand? Do you want to confirm the scandals? Do you want them to say that there has been something between you and her? You think coming as a suitor absolves you of the crime of betrayal and starting shameful behavior, Badi'? How do you know the parts of her body that you describe in your mawwal? You have given a masterful description, Badi', so where did you see her and how did you examine her picture to know the color of her eyes, the length of her eyelashes, her braids, how thin her waist, the pomegranates of her chest, the peaches of her cheeks, and the apples of her heels? Have you seen that with your own eyes, Badi'?'

"The fruit grocer said to his close friend: 'O Abd al-Mawla, it's an old mawwal, as old as fruits and orchard keepers, which others have composed about fruity fruits. I've added to it nothing but my voice which delivers my feelings.'

"Abd al-Mawla said, 'But if we let you marry my sister Fakiha, we would prove to everyone that there was some basis for scandal; for there's no smoke without fire. People will believe that you, being my friend, have been in contact with my sister behind my back—and heads would roll before that can be the case!'

"'Please, I beseech you, Abd al-Mawla!' No use! 'Abd al-Mawla, I am head over heels in love!' No use! 'Abd al-Mawla, the girl loves me and welcomes marrying me!' At that point Abd al-Mawla totally lost it. 'What girl is this one that loves you? Are you saying it to my face, Badi'? Am I not man enough in your eyes? Do we have girls who know this kind of talk? Now is not the time to settle this account, Badi' and from now on you're no longer a friend or even an acquaintance of mine!'

"The fruit grocer left, drenched in tears and pain. He felt that he had done the girl an injustice. He was determined to save her from scandal at any price because young men would not ask for her hand and she would have one of two destinies—either a young man from her family will marry her or Abd al-Mawla will kill her. In both cases she would be killed.

"The fruit grocer started sending messengers every day, to no avail. Abd al-Mawla rejected any attempt to talk about the subject at all. He did not welcome the dignitaries who tried to mediate. The fruit grocer thought, 'The girl has reached legal age and I am a perfectly eligible man so, why don't we get married on our own?' The fruit grocer went and complained to the headman who asked the girl, 'Do you wish to marry Badi', O Fakiha?' And she said, 'Yes, and I'll have no other husband as long as I live!'

When Abd al-Mawla heard that, he was ashamed before the men, so he decided to kill her before the end of the night.

"The girl became certain of her brother's treacherous intention and when the morning came, they didn't find her at home or anywhere else in town. Lamentation began. The fruit grocer was more diligent in looking for her than her brother. He traveled all over in pursuit of her and spent all his wealth on travel. He closed his store and his condition went from bad to worse. He became emaciated. They offered him all kinds of girls but he would accept no other.

"Singing at weddings and mulids became the only consolation that cooled the fire. He began singing the way a wizard would chant his incantations, in the hope that his supplications would reach her wherever she was and her heart would relent and she would go back to him. Meanwhile treacherous Time moved slowly and the post-office brought no mail. People forgot her and she became old news that no one remembered. Only two people in this world waited for Fakiha: Badi' to marry her and begin his paradise on earth and Abd al-Mawla to kill her and wash away his dishonor.

"Yesterday, as the singer was going through the tents of al-Hussein's mulid, some of his friends brought him the good news: the bird you've lost has reappeared tonight in a cage with such a jailer in such and such tent.

"The fruit grocer came back to life. He started running. He was so overjoyed when he saw his bird sitting in front of him, face to face! He almost threw himself into her embrace to cry and complain to her the pangs of separation and express the joy of the unexpected union, but he couldn't because his bird was in the hands of another. He almost fainted out of anguish had God not inspired him to see the microphone the moment the singer had finished. He held the microphone and started unloading his pain to it but, in a blink, he didn't find his bird. Was it a temporary, false dream?

"He ran around in the streets and saw the jailer put his bird in a car and the car moved. Like a mother bereaved of her child he sought people's help to stop a car that had stolen his heart. Luckily someone from the tent who knew the jailer personally saw him and gave him his name and address. The fruit grocer threw himself into a cab and asked the driver to follow the car carrying his bird. He caught up with it and took the same train and came here.

"As for the singing fruit grocer, that would be me! As for Fakiha, she is the one sitting by the door, having changed her appearance and is now a hanim with a bare face and arms. She must have taken another name!"

Fakiha

"Yes, I love him! I loved Badi' the fruit grocer before he put me in the mawwal instead of the fruit. The fact that he was my brother's friend from their childhood has nothing to do with it because if he wasn't my brother Abd al-Mawla's friend, I'd still have loved him."

"He used to come in to our house with Abd al-Mawla a lot but I never really saw the whole of him. I heard his voice when he sang at weddings. No wedding without Badi' the fruit grocer singing! No wedding without me and all the girls sitting on the roof watching Badi' the fruit grocer. His beautiful voice traveled all over the roofs and enchanted us so much we cried for joy and rejoiced in crying. We didn't want him ever to stop singing! All the girls loved him because *he* was the wedding and the joy. Even his name, as soon as it was mentioned before any girl or her mother they would raise their palms toward the sky and exclaim, 'God willing! It's a good omen!'

"Whenever the name of Badi' the fruit grocer was mentioned anywhere, it was a harbinger of the joyous wedding where he would sing and set the imagination of the men and the hearts and chests of the girls and women on fire! Every girl who heard Badi' the fruit grocer singing would hear a secret voice telling her that Badi' meant her in particular.

She would immediately gain confidence in herself and feel prettier and sweeter. When Badi‘ the fruit grocer sang, men were captivated; they'd forget their worries and those who had been fighting would be reconciled so that they could sit and listen in peace without disturbance. Joy would be everywhere and every man would become a bridegroom going back home in a good mood and have a wedding in his own house. The whole town would celebrate and the stores in the alleys would stay up and stay open so that people could buy and sell and there'd be a hustle and bustle in the streets. Crowds of people would come from nearby villages to attend the wedding and everybody would be so happy. There would be ululations of joy and shots in the air, but Badi‘ the fruit grocer's voice would drown out everything else. The loudspeakers would pick up the voice and it would be relayed by the winds, distributing it fairly to every ear in every house, saving its clearest to those working the fields late at night."

"It was a dream come true the night that I felt that I was the Fakiha of the mawwal and that I was the grapes and the peaches and the pomegranates and the apples and the apricots and the mangoes and the pears! In his old mawwal he had likened people to fruits but that night I heard him likening fruits to me: the grapes had the bunches of my chest, the peaches had stolen the redness of my cheeks, the apples fell from my heels."

"A messenger from heart to heart, as the saying goes. My heart has always been more truthful to me than my mind. I heard the knocking on its door and I was shaken. I received the message that alerted my heart to the fact that the mawwal was a letter to me alone sent with my name, address, and description. My picture was in it too: the big eyes with long eyelashes, the long neck with a broad throat. Time after time. Night after night. I felt he was suffering, crying out for some kindness, for a response with one word or one gesture telling him that I'd got the message and that I'd hang in there until the time for a meeting had come.

"Frankly, I responded to him. Should I deny? How can I deny? Can the piper hide his chin while blowing the mizmar? And why should I deny? Did I do anything forbidden? Did I break a taboo? Or commit a heinous crime? Far be it from me, for I was well bred. I didn't commit a crime when I sent greetings to my brother's friend with his sister. Just saying hello! After that my greeting became part of the mawwal which responded to the greeting with a thousand greetings. He asked to come in through the lawful door! Of course I welcomed it and my heart danced with joy. I couldn't find a bridegroom better than Badi'; but how could I say that when our town forbade it to a girl or a boy? Does a girl in our town have any say? Love is a topic for singing only. I was afraid to send him greeting again. I stayed silent even though I was on pins and needles.

"One evening they came into my room and said that Badi' the fruit grocer was in the reception room with Abd al-Mawla, that he had come to ask for my hand but that my brother was fighting him every inch of the way. I don't know what got into Abd al-Mawla's head and why he made such a big deal. The guy came to ask for my hand, and that's something that any girl from the best of families would hope for! And he put himself at Abd al-Mawla's disposal to ask for whatever he wanted so we could have the wedding. Abd al-Mawla flew into a rage and created an incomprehensible feud!

"Abd al-Mawla is hard-headed. And his hard-headedness has brought us trouble more than once. He sentenced me to death! Made me homeless! Deprived me of the love of my heart that I had hoped for.

"I hated Abd al-Mawla because he confined my future to an endless imprisonment. Out of vexation I defied him! I told the headman explicitly and in no uncertain terms that I loved Badi' the fruit grocer and would marry no other. The blood in Abd al-Mawla's veins boiled. He got ready to kill me that very night; to kill me for the second time. I wasn't concerned about being killed by a knife after he had slaughtered my heart and drained its blood for no reason except vanity and selfishness!

"I did not run away from being killed but I ran away to avenge myself upon Abd al-Mawla. I welcomed death but if I had let him kill me, I would have given him satisfaction and caused him to hold his head high in the town at the expense of the wrong he had done me and my anguish. I said to myself: One selfish turn deserves another. I will run away to make Abd al-Mawla live the rest of his life drowning up to his ears in shame.

"I did not bring shame on him! It was he who brought it on himself and on me! Let him drink from the same cup of sorrow from which he made me drink.

"I knew that leaving one's home brings loss of respect; that being away from home is humiliating and degrading. Being away from home is half the death I would have received at Abd al-Mawla's hand. But God is gracious. I left the whole of Said and took the train to Tanta, to the blessed abode of al-Sayyed al-Badawi. It was he who called me. A secret voice told me to ride the train with all those people crowded nearby. I asked the people at the ticket window why all this crowd on this train? And they said they were going to the mulid of al-Sayyed al-Badawi. I said, 'May God bless him,' and I rode with them. I went into his tomb to read the Fatiha and asked him to be with me in my exile and to send good people my way to help me. A short while later I saw this lady from Arish talking to me then inviting me to lunch. One word led to another and I told her all my circumstances. She said not to worry about anything so long as I was with them.

"I slept with them. After the mulid, they brought me here and I started to feel that something was fishy but, the truth be told, Sayyed Zanati surprised me by proposing marriage so I can be reassured and live with him in peace. I said 'And these wives of yours?' And they said, 'The law has made it permissible for him to have four. What matters is your consent.' I figured out, I have no place or relatives and if I live with Sayyed Zanati and his wives I would not be safe from Satan or from people's tongues, so it is better to marry him in the lawful way enjoined by God and His Prophet and get it over with.

"Luckily for me, Sayyed Zanati doesn't like to have children and their headaches. And he who lives among certain people acquires their traits. All the women here bare their arms and hair. But, thank God, I have not taken one step beyond what is permissible."

The Tragedy

The dervish turned around and faced those sitting. He gathered the long misbaha and put it in his pocket then put his folded hands on his lap. Then he said as if ignoring all that went on around him, "Now, what should I tell Sidi Abd al-Rahim? Did you remember the thing that you found in the street and brought over here to use or save?"

Sayyed Zanati chastised him with impatience he couldn't control: "Will you wait until we solve this tough problem?"

Then after a harsh glance of rebuke from Sheikh Zainhum Al-Atris he realized that he had waved in the man's face rudely. Almost apologetically he rephrased his statement calmly, "Beg your pardon! We have a dilemma. Of course you are unaware of what's happening around you. So why don't you stick to your prayers and your worship until we solve this problem that we hadn't expected. Ask God in your prayers to guide us to the right solution!"

The dervish seemed not to understand anything that was said, perhaps he didn't even hear it, saying as if conveying the message for the first time: "Sidi Abd al-Rahim tells you to keep the trust until you return it to its original owners. That's all!"

"Screw the trust and screw the owners! I am telling you we have a tough dilemma. Don't get us off the subject and distract us!"

"And I tell you what Sidi Abd al-Rahim said: keep the trust until you return it to its owners!"

"Okay. Fine. By all means! I understand! When I discover this trust, I will personally take it to Sidi Abd al-Rahim!"

"Well then, hurry up! The train is about to move. You just have enough time to change your clothes!"

Then he bowed his head and began mumbling incomprehensibly. Sayyed stood up and ran to the door overlooking the courtyard calling out to Shawadfi to come right away. Shawadfi coughed and cleared his throat from the effects of sleep and said in a hoarse voice that he was coming. The morning light was now slate colored and had begun to surround the fluorescent light and strangle it. Shawadfi came in rubbing his eyes, expressing surprise that he had slept so soundly that all those sleeping in the courtyard had already left without his being aware of it. He wondered whether last night's exciting celebrations had actually taken place or whether he was just dreaming on the mastaba. Sayyed Zanati said it really happened and as proof, the singer hadn't left yet. Then he added that the truly joyous celebration was what would take place shortly.

Sayyed had become fully alert since going to the door and coming back. Then he added to his alertness by gulping down in quick succession two glasses of distilled alcohol. He passed around cigarettes and fruits and spoke in the tone of a wise man who understood life and its games and who enjoyed living to the hilt: 'Listen, brother. You've broken my heart and my heart doesn't feel right about having your rightful dream all to myself and depriving you of it. It's enough that I've enjoyed it a long time at the expense of your both enjoying it. Everything is a matter of kismet! Here's your beloved Fakiha! I'll divorce her now and you can marry her any time you like. You can have her fully respected and honored. Fakiha is a precious gem and she's a good and chaste girl; this is my testimony before God. You are worthy of her and she is worthy of you. She has some money in a savings account that might come in handy for both of you. Now do your job, Shawadfi!"

Shawadfi sat cross legged and addressed me: "Get a piece of paper and a pen, young man and I'll dictate."

The men looked around, perplexed. Sayyed Zanati explained as he pointed to Shawadfi in all earnestness, "This is the ma'zun of the wikala. It was he who wrote the marriage contracts for me and my wives and for everyone who married in the wikala."

Then he pulled a desk calendar from the bottom of a niche next to his shoulder and tore a page out of it and gave it to me with this calendar to set it on. Shawadfi's eyes sparkled with a sudden intelligent thought. He said, "You've married her under the name of Gannat Abd al-Khaliq Abu Aysh. Are you going to divorce her now under her real name?"

A sparkle lit up in Sayyed Zanati's eyes as if taken aback by the problem, but he said, "You are right, but no. If we divorced her under her new, correct name, we would be divorcing another woman. Divorce her in the name used in the marriage contract: Gannat Abd al-Khaliq. And add to her name the statement: 'Who now turns out to be Fakiha such and such."

Shawadfi said as if advertising his services, "See? This is the advantage of having me do the marriage contract. If you used somebody else, a problem would have arisen and would have delayed the divorce. It would be the same problem that would have delayed the marriage.Okay young man, write what I dictate in two copies so each of the two parties shall keep a copy of her divorce contract."

He began to dictate the divorce formula as the men exchanged glances and suppressed laughter and surprise mixed with this adventure into a novel territory. It was as if we were all children playing a legitimate game. When he was done dictating I made another copy then presented if to Sayyed Zanati who signed it and to Gannuna who marked it with her finger print. I signed as a witness and so did Sheikh Zainhum al-Atris. Shawadfi also signed. I gave each party a copy which they folded and put in their pockets. I chanced to look at the dervish and saw in his eyes the raging fire of a volcano that tremendous force was exerted to put it out.

The men got ready to leave while Sittat started crying in silence and the woman from Arish also shed a few tears. As for the other 'brat' who had been discovered by Sittat, she was in a state of shock and frozen alarm, maybe because she had begun to remember that a similar destiny might befall her some time in the future.

The men actually stood up and the dervish looked suddenly perturbed and extremely tense, with the volcano in his eyes erupting. It was at that moment only that I felt that his eyes were not those of an ascetic possessed with divine love and couldn't be. I was consumed with worrying and apprehension. Gannuna started embracing the women and crying tears of profound joy as if telling them in a secret code that they understood only too well: may your turn be next when you'd be liberated from this pit of humiliating exile and return to the land of the old authentic dream. The men shook hands with Sayyed Zanati and got absorbed in the thanks and welcome and invitations to visit the Said. Then Gannuna sneaked and brought her clothes in a bundle that she had obviously prepared before. When she shook hands with Sayyed she wrapped her hand in her shawl. He said to her, "Consider me a brother to you and to Badi'. I will never forget you, Fakiha, I mean, Gannuna!"

Badi' slipped away, anxiously encircling Gannuna and urging her on protectively. His friends followed, then the dervish then Sayyed Zanati and Zainhum al-Atris then I, our footsteps making quite a racket on the stairs. We were now in the middle of the courtyard. It was here that the volcano in the dervish's eyes erupted. He couldn't control himself. The getup in which he had placed himself unraveled and he started waving with vulgar gestures, almost snorting and using profane language. Perhaps he did that in one way or another before talking. But he soon reverted to the personality he had when he arrived. He shouted, "Stop where you are, all of you!"

The voice was totally different. It was no longer that soft voice, full of naiveté and clarity but rather that of a hardened cruel shady character. And yet he regained his calm addressing Sayyed Zanati while everyone froze in apprehension and shock: "You betrayed the trust, Zanati! You didn't hold the advice of Sidi Abd al-Rahim! You should've returned the trust to its owners!"

"What trust, man. The trust is in jail!"

"This trust that you didn't understand, stupid!" Even though you are a man of experience and understanding!"

He pointed at Gannuna then repeated, "This is the trust! You have to hand her over to her family!"

"Where's her family?"

"I am her family and you have to hand her over to me against your will or anybody's will!"

They looked at him with great apprehension and shock. Gannuna said in obvious confusion, "I don't know you! Where'd you come from?"

With lightening speed he extended his hand removing the fake beard and the turban. Then he said in a malicious and treacherous tone, "I am your brother Abd al-Mawla, whore! Where will you escape from me?"

Gannuna screamed and collapsed. Badi' caught her and propped her up. He carried her like a bundle of sugar cane and started running toward the gate. But Abd al-Mawla's hand was faster than lightening: he pulled a gun from under his arm and in a blink several skillfully aimed shots rang out in quick succession. Badi and his load fell to the ground. He caught up with them and emptied the bullets in their heads and quickly started to replace the clip but Sayyed Zanati, like a leopard, pounced on him from the back and held him with an iron grip. The gun fell from his hand and one of Badi''s friends picked it up, then remembered and let it drop out of his hand after Shawadfi shouted a warning about fingerprints and changing place of evidence. Then he stepped forward and tied Abd al-Mawla with a palm-fiber rope.

Nostalgia

For a long time I was bored, disgusted, and penniless. Then there were the constant disruptions: almost daily interrogations by the police, the prosecutors, and the court. As luck would have it, I had a few expenses lately and work was rare. Sayyed Zanati was in a foul and lousy mood and was no good at devising schemes that produced a high income. The gigs I went on with Sittat were diminished greatly and were of the traditional variety that did not require much experience even though they provided day to day expenses: claiming to be strangers who had been robbed and who asked God—and nothing was too much for God—for the train fare. We would end up with only a little more than the price of the tickets, enough for one or two suppers.

Sittat had listened to my secret advice and developed an aversion for dubious scams that she had never liked to begin with, had it not been for pressure from Sayyed and the need to earn a living. Such scams involved old village headmen, notables, and rich men who pretended to be young, by starting make-believe affairs with them in which she depleted their financial resources without giving in to their amorous advances except by a kiss here or an embrace or a hug there, to lend credibility to the affairs.

Sayyed began to miss writing songs, which this time he started to take seriously by sending them to the broadcasting service and to singers and moviemakers. Every night he would make me listen to a whole new song, steeped in the ethos of life on the streets and alleys, using vulgar words that presented, nevertheless a novel musical approach that had beauty of its own. I would tell him frankly what I thought, but he would brush it aside and tell me that I was fond of elitist, effeminate songs and that the whole future belonged to this new type of songs that snorted, made obscene sounds, and blasphemed just as the people in the street did. He told me that his ideal role model was Mahmoud Shikuku, one of the most famous singers in the whole Arab world. Interestingly enough, he received very admiring responses to the letters he sent to the broadcasting service, the singers and the musical composers at their addresses which he had taken from the magazines *al-Kawakib* and *Akhir Sa'a*. In these responses he was even told that his songs were being in a production phase.

That didn't bother me at all, especially since throughout the time I spent with him I ate and drank and smoked tobacco and hashish without paying anything, whether I went on a gig or not. But he always managed to put me to good use. Thus, without any agreement or discussion he made me his private secretary by dictating to me songs to take down as he was busy playing cards. He would also send me to buy the chicken and food of which, he would keep reminding me, I would eat. I'd also help him with cooking chores and would go and case locations where he planned to operate, then go back and report orally to him. Long months were followed by longer months with even more boring longer miserable months. Sayyed Zanati was, little by little, losing control over his three wives and had grown more tolerant of their censure and disapproval, and sometimes swallowed their cruel innuendoes. He would also swallow his pain if one of them came home late into the night. But when he lost his patience, he lashed out at them so violently it would almost be attempted murder, by beating them with iron rods, whips, and sometimes hitting them with his head, his fists, and kicking them. Several times he swore that one of his wives would not sleep that night in his house since she was late, so the poor woman would spend many hours waiting at the door until I opened my room for her to sleep in while I went back to stay with Sayyed till the morning. His gambling sessions now extended to the morning of the following day.

I got totally fed up and was sure that my life had lost all meaning. I now missed my old haunts, out of a desire to escape Sayyed Zanati's magnetic allure. I began to go back there and spend whole days circling around places where I had friends, colleagues, and memories, only to encounter dejection and boredom as three-fourths of my friends had been arrested, either because they were, truly or falsely, Muslim Brothers, communists, or supporters of the ancien regime. I missed having breakfast with Hamdi al-Zawawi in his store but was surprised to notice that the store was closed for several days. When I had to ask, I learned that he also had been arrested a long time ago and was put in an unknown jail, accused of something mysterious and unknown.

But I became a regular visitor to my cousin's alley for reasons unknown to me. I began to pass by it almost every day at different times and then go through it from the beginning of Sagha Street or its end and find myself forced to turn around and look at my cousin's house as if looking there for something intimate that I had lost and didn't hope to find again.

One day I saw her coming out of the alley, alone, leaving their house in the middle of the alley, turning on the sidewalk to the main street, in the direction of the Administration Building adjacent to the railway station. I looked at her intently, lingering on her distinctive lips. It was Badriya! But she was wearing a black fur coat like a real hanim and black stockings and shoes and wrapping herself with a black shawl. I moved to the other sidewalk to face her. She met me with a smile which encouraged me. I rushed toward her and almost took her in my arms, but I just placed all the warmth of the joy I felt in my hands with which I pressed her soft and tender hand: "How are you, Badriya? Long time no see!"

"Where've you been? What do you do these days?"

"I don't have a regular job yet, but I am managing, thank God!"

"Thank God!"

"Where're you going now?"

"Nowhere in particular! Can I walk with you?"

"That'd be nice!"

I walked next to her in silence, somewhat awkwardly, until we reached Sa'a Square where she stopped and pointed out to me her fourth-floor apartment in a building with distinguished architecture, grayish in color at the end of the side street. She said it was a beautiful and comfortable apartment. The only problem with it was that the Delta train passed parallel to it and when it did, it was as if it went through the building, splitting it in two then compounding the problem with its shrill whistle like the shrieking of a bereaved mother. She also said that she'd rather not go to her house now, because she was in a bad shape and the house was in even worse shape, that she was postponing inviting me to her house until some other time, but now she wouldn't mind if we walked or if she sat with me somewhere for a while. I pointed to the nearby Students' Café with its glass walls and she said, "Fine," and walked next to me. We went in. As I was stirring the sugar in my tea I told her, "My joy at seeing you made me forget to ask you why you were wearing black. What's the story?"

She looked at me in disbelief mixed with surprise and some resentment, "Have you been in a coma? Have you been living in some other world? You haven't read the paper, listened to the radio or the people? That is quite strange indeed!"

"May God protect us! What happened, Badriya?"

She tried to speak; it seemed she was looking for her voice, for her ability to move her lips. Her face turned as red as a flame. Her lower lip contracted and folded under her upper jaw and tears came pouring down from her eyes. Her crying was contagious and my body caught it and I kept resisting a strong tremor that came over me from head to toe. From time to time I was able to control myself and dry my tears, crying at her, "What's wrong, Badriya?" As she started to speak, tears overcame her and her voice rattled and dwindled before she could utter one word. Thus for more than an hour, we sat face to face, our heads almost touching over the table between us, as we tried as much as possible, to avoid attracting attention. The waiter was observing us furtively, his quick glances displaying sympathy and compassion. Finally he came over to the table with a sweet smile as if trying to soothe us: “Have faith in God! What you are doing to yourselves is too much!” He took the tray with the tea and went to the rectangular marble counter reflected many times in the mirrors on the walls. He removed the tea and brought us some fresh hot tea and placed it before us. We began to drink the tea as her voice began to pour into my ears.

The Widow

"They hanged my husband. They said he was one of the founders of the secret organization. They picked the right duty for him: they said he was the one in charge of purchasing and storing weapons, given his military expertise as a former army officer.

"My husband, God knows, was a kind-hearted man. We only had his one pistol for which he had a permit and he used to fear it as much a child feared touching flames. He never took it out of his desk drawer!

"You haven't heard his trial on radio? It was in the newspaper every day!

"They beat him up until they broke his bones! He was going to die on his own without execution, if they had left him one week. The coroner told us he died before they pulled the rope.

"How horrible! I've never seen a government so cruel! They say the occupation ended! I swear by God it hasn't! This government is worse than the occupation!

"They came to me one night and awakened me. They put me, blindfolded like a cow tied to the water wheel in a blue car. When I opened my eyes, I saw my husband in front of me in an office with a solemn looking effendi and officers and soldiers. The effendi talked to a huge man who looked like a pig: 'Take off her clothes and yours and show us what kind of man you are and how she cries asking for more!'

"It was as if he stabbed me with a knife in the heart, that shameless bastard! I thought I was in a lunatic asylum! I stood in shock, trembling all over!

"The other shameless bastard took of his clothes and actually stood there in just his underpants. And he kept coming toward me like a beast with open mouth. I screamed. I yelled. I backed up, holding a heavy crystal ashtray, ready to bash in his skull if he came near me again.

"The shameless bastard effendi raised his arm, motioning him to wait, and turned his face toward my husband and said: 'Will you confess or shall we let him eat her in front of you?' Fearlessly, my husband said, 'First, I have nothing to confess. Second, if this slave of yours is indeed a man, let him show me how he will eat her!'

"I felt that he had given me strength. The effendi looked to the beast and said, 'Do your job, you lucky man! She's beautiful despite her huge lips!' The beast kept advancing slowly toward me, his mouth wide open, showing large yellow teeth.

"I kept screaming and backing off until I had swept the walls of the room in all corners. He paused for one moment then pounced on me in one fell swoop. I slipped from his arms and staggered, then aimed the ashtray at his chest. He caught it in his hand and threw it, then rushed at me with an evil force that meant business this time. He almost managed to encircle me while panting.

"My husband, the former officer, used to work out all the time and had a body as strong as the trunk of an acacia tree. In lightning speed, he grabbed a very heavy chair and with his two hands brought it down on the head of the beast man who fell to the floor dead, with blood pouring from his ears and mouth.

"They all attacked my husband, kicking and punching him until the effendi made them stop, to avoid responsibility for beating him to death.

"They turned the beast man this way and that way, but he didn't say anything. He stayed lying on his face in a pool of blood. The shameless bastard effendi motioned them and they took me away, blindfolded again and put me in the blue car, then dropped me in my house and left.

"For a long time their voices remained in my parlor, warning me not to say a word about what happened; otherwise they'd kill me and my whole family.

"I haven't told you that my oldest brother and the one next to him are still in jail till now, without trial! Sometimes they say they are part of the secret organization and at other times they say they are just suspects because they are related to the big man. May God judge them!

"I loved my dear departed husband a lot!

"He was incapable of having children because of an injury which affected his nerves that he suffered during the siege of Faluja in the Palestine war of 1948. He talked to me often about that war and how they saw death with their eyes twenty-four times a day. He said that Gamal Abdel Nasser was with them. He also told me that Gamal Abdel Nasser was with them in the Muslim Brotherhood, but he never told me the reasons for the feud between the revolution and the Muslim Brothers. And he never told me why they called themselves the Muslim Brothers when we are all Muslims and related to each other. When I asked him he would laugh and take me in his arms and tell me about the women martyrs of Islam until I fell asleep.

"He loved me! He was always sad for me because he was the reason I had no children, even though he never shirked his duty as a man toward me. I asked him to go to the doctor for perhaps it was I who had the problem, but he wouldn't let me, saying he knew it was his fault, that he had been sure of it for a long time.

"To please me and to guarantee my love, he left me all his possessions: the apartment, the feddan of land in his village, and some livestock kept by some of his relatives. And he told his relatives when they visited him in jail. He told them everything so they wouldn't cause any problems for me if he were executed.

"May God have mercy on his soul! He knew that he would be executed and he behaved accordingly. He regretted one thing in his life: when his friends from Saudi Arabia offered him to live there like some of his colleagues, in dignity, in a similar job, and that he could name his own salary. But he declined and told them that his work was in Egypt and not in Saudi Arabia, that it was neither manly nor Islamic to run away from his duty even when he knew that he was facing death.

"I tell you, his having no children and his certainty that he couldn't have any made him renounce worldly pleasures and money. What mattered most to him and what gave him the most pleasure was to see mosques filled with worshipers, as if they were praying for him. All the happiness in the world became his when he managed to get a real Muslim out of difficulty or repaid his debt. And yet he never gave up his rights or what was due him. He had to get that to the last millieme! Even though he may have spent on that same person, under different circumstances, what he was owed several fold.

"His relatives now love me! I haven't seen from any of them anything to make me worry. My father went and got everything recorded and deeded. Today I was in his village to conclude some business with his relatives and they were very hospitable to me. They sent back with me all kinds of fitir and freshly baked hard rolls and cheese and ghee and honey. They insisted I accept their gift.

"By the way, you can help me with the fitir, instead of letting it go to waste. It doesn't agree with me. Come and get it. I will send it down in the basket.

"Please forgive me for not inviting you to the apartment. Everything in good time. I don't like you to see the apartment in a state of mourning for its owner. I also would like to respect his memory for a long time.

"What did you say? Your old project? You mean us getting married? I accept, but it is going to require a lot of work. No one will agree with me. Perhaps his relatives will fight it and it might end up in a big scandal that I can't handle after what happened to me. In any case, this is premature.

Let's postpone it now until the time comes. I promise you, if I think of getting married, I will marry no one else but you, if God wills that we be married!"

The Fragrant End

After ten minutes of standing under the balcony, the basket was lowered down from the fourth floor. It was so heavy, it almost came crashing down to the ground. In the basket there was a canvas bag chock full of rolls of fitir; fancy, delicious-smelling fresh baked hard rolls; a jar of honey; and a tin of cheese. Badriya shouted from the balcony, telling me to untie the rope from the basket and take the whole thing with its contents. Then she printed a kiss on the tips of her fingers and threw it at me. I waved to her, feeling as if the flying kiss had indeed landed on my lips and I felt its taste in my mouth.

I hung the basket in my arm and headed directly for the wikala, filled with joy and enthusiasm, because, finally I'd be able to extend hospitality to Sayyed Zanati and his men.

I took the basket to my room and put it there, then went to Sayyed Zanati's room. Luckily, all the men were there. Sayyed Zanati had not prepared a meal as he usually did, because business was slow and there was no money coming in. When I got there, they were exchanging suggestions about a can of salmon and aged cheese with tomatoes and cucumbers. Feeling a secret pride, I said, "Forget the suggestions. I have dinner for you. I've just come back from the village."

Sniffing, Sayyed said, "I smell fitir."

"Exactly! Swimming in fresh ghee."

"Okay then. Let's go to your room. You invited us, so let the party be in your room. We'll change scenery; maybe God will change our luck to the better."

Then he got up and they all followed suit. We went downstairs in a nice procession to my room, about six men and three women. We carried some cushions and all of us sat on the floor, spreading the fitir, the cheese, and the honey in the middle. It was a huge quantity, so we sent a whole fitira to Shawadfi and half fitiras to those we could find in the wikala at the time. We ate until we were full and a lot was left over. We decided to continue the party in my room, so all the necessary stuff: the goza, pipes, alcohol, hashish, and playing cards were brought there. The card game began in earnest.

The three scantily dressed women sat in our midst, merrily serving us and consoling the losers so they might lose some more. The night continued at a fast pace without any of us paying attention until we heard a noisy commotion at the gate. We heard a resounding slap on someone's face—we all guessed it was Shawadfi's. The arrogant voices, without saying so in so many words, told us that the whole team that knew Shawadfi had all been replaced.

As soon as we began to listen, the door opened and a large government delegation in uniform and civilian attire descended upon us. They made us stand, searched us, and overdid the searching to include the insides of books. They rounded us all up, with the cards, the money, the alcohol bottle, the hashish, the goza and the pipes, in the police wagon to the Administration Building. The cross examination began: "Whose room was it?" "Mine." "Congratulations!" they said. "It's an open-and-shut case about which there's no appeal. Running a gambling house. Using narcotics and drinking alcohol. Facilitating prostitution."

They put me alone in the lockup. The rest were released on bail or on personal cognizance to their known addresses. I alone was left there, resentful and resisting like a mouse caught in a mousetrap from which there was no escape. No one could hear my banging or shouting or anything. Then I got tired, felt defeated and desperate, so I squatted on the floor, curled up, and buried my head between my upright knees. My nostrils were filled with the fragrance of a strong, aristocratic perfume. I raised my head inquisitively as if I were in a dream. I saw no one in the dark except the dark masses in the lockup. There was no sound or movement. I curled again as I squatted there and buried my head. The perfume sneaked again to my nostrils, strong and delightful, but also depressing. I realized that my hands had left on my chest and my face traces of Badriya's perfume which she had left on my hand when we shook hands twice. In the pitch dark, I saw a pale moon, totally surrounded, rebelling against the massive columns of clouds to cast a glance on the earth: Badriya was passing in front of me in a straight line, holding a bouquet of carnations. I could only see the back of her black-clad figure proceeding toward a tombstone that appeared in the twinkle of the moon like a brick of white ashes on a mythical elephant kneeling on the ground.

Translator's Acknowledgments

I would like to thank the following friends and colleagues for help with various aspects of the translation: Eric Chistensen, Jeff Leigh, Dina Rabadi, and Kelly Zaug, and, from the American University in Cairo Press, Neil Hewison and Nadia Naqib.

Glossary

abaya: a loose-fitting outer garment worn by both men and women covering the whole body. In this novel, it is mostly worn by older men.

Abu Nuwwas: an Arab poet (CE 747–813) most famous for writing poems about wine and love.

Ali Abd al-Raziq: (1888–1966) religious judge, writer, and state minister whose controversial book *al-Islam wa Usul al-Hukm* (1925) advocated the separation of state and religion in the Islamic world.

alif: the first letter of the Arabic alphabet.

amud: several interlocking pots on top of one another, each containing a different food item or dish; an elaborate version of a lunch box, each part of which can be heated separately on a stove top.

'anqarib: a sofa/day bed.

ardeb: dry measure equaling 198 litres.

'awalim (singular, 'alma): female leaders of a troupe of female singers, musicians, and dancers.

Ba'una: the tenth month of the Coptic calendar.

barsim: Egyptian clover *(Trifolium alexandrinum).*

basima: a pastry like harisa, but harder and with coconut.

daya: a midwife.

darbukka: a conically shaped hand-drum of pottery or metal.

***al-Da'wa, Minbar al-Islam, al-Risala*, and *al-Thaqafa*:** Egyptian periodicals.

dhikr: Sufi ritual based on the repeated rhythmic mention of the names of God.

effendi: Egyptian man in western clothes; title of, and form of address or reference to, an Egyptian man from the middle class.

Eid: feast or festival marking, for instance, the end of the Ramadan fast or the completion of the essential rites of pilgrimage to Mecca.

fakiha: fruit; a variant of the word, with a slightly different spelling, is a female proper noun.

fasikh: salt-cured fish, especially gray mullet.

ful midammis *or* ful: dried broad beans cooked in a stoppered container over a slow heat.

gallabiya: a long, loose-fitting garment worn, in different styles, by both men and women in Egypt.

gargir: arugula or rocket.

ghagar: (collective noun) gypsies.

ghaziya: a female dancer/singer in rural Egypt.

ghee: clarified butter.

goza: a simple water-pipe, originally made from a coconut shell or a substitute, for example, a jam jar or tin and a reed. Favored by hashish smokers, it works on the same principle as its more elaborate and elegant cousin, the shisha or narghile in which molasses-cured tobacco is lit up and smoked after passing through cooling water in the coconut shell or its substitute.

halab: (collective noun) people from Aleppo, presented in this novel in a negative stereotype as types of gypsies.

hanuti: undertaker; mortician.

harisa: sweet pastry made with flour, clarified butter, and sugar.

"He gets out of the tightest spot like a hair out of dough": an Egyptian saying, describing someone so resourceful and clever that he or she would come out unscathed from difficult, seemingly hopeless situations.

"If you can't find a job, be a judge": a loose translation of an Egyptian saying making fun of those who, instead of finding something useful to do, spend their time judging others.

I'jaz al-Qur'an by Mustafa Sadiq al-Raf'i: "The Inimitability of the Qur'an" written by the above mentioned author (d. 1937).

al-Jalalayn: two exgeses of the Qur'an by the two Jalals, Jalal al-Din al-Siyuti and Jalal al-Din al-Mahalli, traditionally published together with the text of the Qur'an in one volume.

***al-Kawakib*, *al-Sabah*, and *Akhir Sa'a*:** Egyptian weekly magazines.

khatma: an evening ceremony in which the Qur'an is collaboratively recited in its entirety by several reciters, followed by a communal meal.

"A kite never throws chicks": an Egyptian saying to the effect that those who usually take or snatch, in this case, the predatorial kite, never give.

ma'zun: marriage registrar.

maddah: a professional singer specializing in singing the praises of the Prophet Muhammad.

mandal: (magic) a process of divination to locate lost or stolen items and identify the thief.

mashrabiya: a projecting oriel window with a wooden latticework enclosure.

mastaba: a bench of mud, brick, or concrete built against the wall of a building.

mawwal: a genre of songs, mostly improvised.

me'allim: a term of respect for a small businessman.

milaya: a wrap, usually black, which women of the lower classes use to cover their bodies. Worn tightly, however, a milaya tends to reveal rather than conceal the contours of a woman's body.

misbaha: a string of prayer beads.

mish: seasoned milk-based liquid culture in which cheese is fermented and aged.

mizmar: wind instrument made of cane or wood.

mulid: a celebration, often of several days' duration, centered around the birthday of a revered holy figure at or near his or her tomb/mosque/church.

mughat: roots of *Glossostemon brugieri* of which an infusion is made with sugar and ghee and traditionally drunk by new mothers and their visiting well-wishers.

mulukhiya: Jew's mallow *(Corchorus olitarius)*, the green leaves of which are minced and cooked to make a popular Egyptian soup.

"My wife will be divorced, if . . . ": an oath uttered to persuade someone to do something. A host might use it, for instance, to embarrass a guest into eating more food. It is a frowned-upon practice.

nay: end-blown reed flute.

oka: unit of weight equal to 1.248 kg.

qutniya: cotton-based fabric with a silky finish and woven stripe or a garment made of this fabric.

rababa: a musical instrument with one or two strings, used primarily by storytellers.

Ramadan imsakiya: a simple or elaborate brochure listing times for beginning and breaking the fast in the Muslim month of fasting.

sabaris: cigarette butts collected from the street and used by the poor to roll cigarettes.

Sa'idi: someone from the Sa'id, which is southern (Upper) Egypt extending from just south of Cairo to Aswan.

shabka: a precious gift, usually gold or diamond, given by the would-be groom to the bride-to-be at the engagement ceremony.

shadoof: counterpoised implement for raising irrigation water.

shahada: the Muslim creed, "There is no god but God, and Muhammad is His Messenger," spoken by the person tending a deceased person's body just in case the person had forgotten or neglected to utter it just before his/her death.

sheikh al-hara: literally 'head of the neighborhood,' a semi-official acting as a liaison between the government, especially the police and the military, and residents of a small part of town.

Spatis: a brand of soda popular in Egypt in the fifties and sixties of the last century.

Sura of Yasin: Chapter 36 of the Qur'an.

ta‘miya: Egyptian falafel, made with broad beans, vegetables, and spices and deep fried in oil.

Taha Hussein: (1889–1973) writer, educational administrator, and state minister, sometimes called the "dean of Arab letters." *Al-Fitna al-Kubra* is one of his major works on early Islamic history.

tatar: literally 'Tatar' but in this novel it refers to a special type of gypsy.

tharid: a traditional dish of sopped bread, meat, and broth.

Tuba: the fifth month of the Coptic calendar.

usta: a master craftsman; a foreman.

ustaz: literally 'professor,' used loosely as a term of respect for professionals and men in western dress.

Wafd party: Egypt's main nationalist political party from 1923 until the 1952 Revolution.

waqf: a religious endowment.

zakat: almsgiving incumbent upon Muslims and one of the five pillars of Islam.

Modern Arabic Literature
from the American University in Cairo Press

Ibrahim Abdel Meguid *Birds of Amber* • *Distant Train*
No One Sleeps in Alexandria • *The Other Place*
Yahya Taher Abdullah *The Collar and the Bracelet* • *The Mountain of Green Tea*
Leila Abouzeid *The Last Chapter*
Hamdi Abu Golayyel *Thieves in Retirement*
Yusuf Abu Rayya *Wedding Night*
Ahmed Alaidy *Being Abbas el Abd*
Idris Ali *Dongola* • *Poor*
Radwa Ashour *Granada*
Ibrahim Aslan *The Heron* • *Nile Sparrows*
Alaa Al Aswany *Chicago* • *The Yacoubian Building*
Fadhil al-Azzawi *Cell Block Five* • *The Last of the Angels*
Liana Badr *The Eye of the Mirror*
Hala El Badry *A Certain Woman* • *Muntaha*
Salwa Bakr *The Golden Chariot* • *The Man from Bashmour* • *The Wiles of Men*
Halim Barakat *The Crane*
Hoda Barakat *Disciples of Passion* • *The Tiller of Waters*
Mourid Barghouti *I Saw Ramallah*
Mohamed El-Bisatie *Clamor of the Lake* • *Houses Behind the Trees* • *Hunger*
A Last Glass of Tea • *Over the Bridge*
Mansoura Ez Eldin *Maryam's Maze*
Ibrahim Farghali *The Smiles of the Saints*
Hamdy el-Gazzar *Black Magic*
Tawfiq al-Hakim *The Essential Tawfiq al-Hakim*
Abdelilah Hamdouchi *The Final Bet*
Fathy Ghanem *The Man Who Lost His Shadow*
Randa Ghazy *Dreaming of Palestine*
Gamal al-Ghitani *Pyramid Texts* • *The Zafarani Files* • *Zayni Barakat*
Yahya Hakki *The Lamp of Umm Hashim*
Bensalem Himmich *The Polymath* • *The Theocrat*
Taha Hussein *The Days* • *A Man of Letters* • *The Sufferers*
Sonallah Ibrahim *Cairo: From Edge to Edge* • *The Committee* • *Zaat*
Yusuf Idris *City of Love and Ashes*
Denys Johnson-Davies *The AUC Press Book of Modern Arabic Literature*
In a Fertile Desert: Modern Writing from the United Arab Emirates
Under the Naked Sky: Short Stories from the Arab World
Said al-Kafrawi *The Hill of Gypsies*

Sahar Khalifeh *The End of Spring*
The Image, the Icon, and the Covenant • The Inheritance
Edwar al-Kharrat *Rama and the Dragon • Stones of Bobello*
Betool Khedairi *Absent*
Mohammed Khudayyir *Basrayatha*
Ibrahim al-Koni *Anubis • Gold Dust • The Seven Veils of Seth*
Naguib Mahfouz *Adrift on the Nile • Akhenaten: Dweller in Truth*
Arabian Nights and Days • Autumn Quail • The Beggar
The Beginning and the End • Cairo Modern
The Cairo Trilogy: Palace Walk, Palace of Desire, Sugar Street
Children of the Alley • The Day the Leader Was Killed
The Dreams • Dreams of Departure • Echoes of an Autobiography
The Harafish • The Journey of Ibn Fattouma • Karnak Café
Khan al-Khalili • Khufu's Wisdom • Life's Wisdom • Midaq Alley • Miramar
Mirrors • Morning and Evening Talk • Naguib Mahfouz at Sidi Gaber
Respected Sir • Rhadopis of Nubia • The Search
The Seventh Heaven • Thebes at War • The Thief and the Dogs
The Time and the Place • Voices from the Other World • Wedding Song
Mohamed Makhzangi *Memories of a Meltdown*
Alia Mamdouh *The Loved Ones • Naphtalene*
Selim Matar *The Woman of the Flask*
Ibrahim al-Mazini *Ten Again*
Yousef Al-Mohaimeed *Wolves of the Crescent Moon*
Ahlam Mosteghanemi *Chaos of the Senses • Memory in the Flesh*
Mohamed Mustagab *Tales from Dayrut*
Buthaina Al Nasiri *Final Night*
Ibrahim Nasrallah *Inside the Night*
Haggag Hassan Oddoul *Nights of Musk*
Mohamed Mansi Qandil *Moon over Samarqand*
Abd al-Hakim Qasim *Rites of Assent*
Somaya Ramadan *Leaves of Narcissus*
Lenin El-Ramly *In Plain Arabic*
Ghada Samman *The Night of the First Billion*
Rafik Schami *Damascus Nights*
Khairy Shalaby *The Lodging House*
Miral al-Tahawy *Blue Aubergine • Gazelle Tracks • The Tent*
Bahaa Taher *As Doha Said • Love in Exile*
Fuad al-Takarli *The Long Way Back*
M.M. Tawfik *Murder in the Tower of Happiness*
Mahmoud Al-Wardani *Heads Ripe for Plucking*
Latifa al-Zayyat *The Open Door*